BLACK & MIST

Thomas J. Radford

BLACK & MIST

THOMAS J. RADFORD

TYCHE BOOKS LTD.

Published by Tyche Books Ltd.
Calgary, Alberta, Canada
www.TycheBooks.com

Cover Art by James F. Beveridge
Cover Layout by Lucia Starkey
Interior Layout by Ryah Deines
Editorial by M.L.D. Curelas

First Tyche Books Ltd Edition 2018
Print ISBN: 978-1-928025-89-4
Ebook ISBN: 978-1-928025-90-0

Author photograph: Devin Hart

This book was funded in part by a grant from the Alberta Media Fund.

To my parents, Jillian and Dave, for how to navigate impossible, hopeless situations and long term projects. And because mum said I had to.

Prologue

Another pipe had burst, flooding the corridor with mist. The ether-lined hull was driving the spewing miasma into a small whirlwind, pushing pale-faced and sweat-stained crew members past Kaspar, where he stood with his shoulder braced against the bulkhead door. As soon as the last one was clear, the door was forced shut, the wheel spun hard to seal it.

"Everyone all right?" He turned to face the jammed hallway of coughing and wheezing sailors. Most ignored him; a few waved vaguely comprehensible acknowledgements.

"Fine, Ensign, just fine," one coughed, leaning over with his hands on his knees, drawing deep shuddering breaths.

"Take it easy," Kaspar reminded him, crouching down to check the man's eyes. "Don't want to get any in your lungs."

"Aye, sir." The man made a face. Kaspar knew he was stating the obvious. It didn't make any of the crew respect him any better, being that he was half the age of some of them, experienced marines and sailors all. But then none of them had been part of the testing of what drove this ship. Kaspar had, and, unlike most of the others, he'd actually made it back to port.

Kaspar couldn't care less what most of the crew thought of him. He'd endured worse. And neither this man nor any of the rest of the crew showed any signs of having been affected by the mist sickness. The mist was cold enough that breathing hurt. But there were worse things than mist aboard . . .

"Another rupture?"

The crew all snapped to attention in a way they never would have for Kaspar. Backs arrow straight and heels clicking together, salutes all around. Kaspar was the same, saluting the ship's first mate. Not respect that made them stand to when Aristeia Quinn arrived, but something else. Kaspar fought to keep his eyes from unravelling the myriad scars that adorned the bared skin of her arms and could be glimpsed under the collar of her uniform. Where others took to painted skin, the *Fata Morgana's* first mate favoured etched scarring. And it wasn't wise to be caught staring.

"Aye, sir," Kaspar reported. "All hands accounted for."

There was another presence with the first mate. Not her Luscan deputy but Arlin Raines, architect of the fleet's newest vessel. And unofficial captain. The tall Kitsune, wrapped in a loose-fitting coat, acknowledged Kaspar's presence with a flick of the eyes. Not indifferent or dismissive, just uninterested in the presence of his own projects. He peered through the bulkhead porthole. Then, mindless of the cry it raised, spun the wheel and hauled it back open.

"The leak has been closed off," Raines said to Aristeia. "Your people may return to their work."

None of the crew rushed to re-enter the just-vacated area. Shifting glances were exchanged. It was normal to wait much longer before returning to a contaminated area.

"Now," Aristeia raised her voice. There was more of an edge to her tone than what had been used to carve out her markings. The crew moved, Kaspar pulling the door wide for them to pass. Sailors marched in, their faces tense, breathing short, controlled, or held entirely. For all the good it would do them.

"This isn't protocol," Kaspar said, daring to raise eyes to meet those of the first mate. Her brow furrowed in annoyance, a flash of something hotter than anger in her eyes.

"No, it is not," the architect agreed with him. "But time has become something of a concern. We have a destination now. And something to retrieve. Opportunities . . ."

A destination? This ship hasn't even finished her maiden voyage and . . .

"Tell me, Ensign, have your postings ever taken you into the Free Lanes?"

Kaspar glanced at Aristeia. The woman was glowering at how the conversation was being directed towards him but not inclined to interrupt the Kitsune inventor. *No, too important to the brass and braids for you to do that.*

"No, sir," Kaspar replied. "Never sailed outside of the High."

"Makes you something of a minority amongst this crew, I would imagine," Raines mused, almost to himself as was his penchant. "Something we can at least remedy in the near future. Though it will not be sailing, not as such . . ."

"Yes, sir."

There should have been more to the architect's dialogue. More words. But the Kitsune had lost interest in the outside world, retreating into the one inside his head.

"Inform me once the repairs are complete," Aristeia told Kaspar instead. "Mors and I will be in the brig, continuing our interrogation. I do not expect to hear of any more such incidents, Ensign."

Kaspar saluted, edge of his hand held up to his forehead. Safer than replying.

The prisoner, the one they've been interrogating, they brought them in from the Free Lanes. Haven't heard a word as to why.

Don't think I'll be asking either.

He turned back to his work detail, keeping a watchful eye on the piping running the length of all the corridors. He could hear the two sets of footsteps echoing on the metal flooring behind him and allowed himself a moment of sympathy for the prisoner Raines had come aboard with.

The Free Lanes. What the hells are we going to the Free Lanes for?

Chapter 1

A TRIO OF ships had arrived at the docks, coming all the way in and settling at the piers. Violet had watched them enter, uneasy at the Alliance colours they'd been flying. From her perch in the crook of framing above a trading post, she'd seen the whole operation. They clearly weren't warships, with none of the sleek violence that the frigates she'd seen embodied, or even the practical lines of the *Tantamount*. These were void-going tubs, pregnant whales masquerading as merchantmen that steadily disgorged their contents onto the docklands. It was that cargo that had kept Violet perched in her rafters for most of the afternoon, her fingers stiff and sore and her eyes strained from watching the procession.

Draugr, dozens, if not hundreds of the creatures had trooped off the three vessels in slow shambling lines. Violet had counted them at first then given up after the first hour. The Draugr had been loaded into wagons and taken away—she'd counted those, too, until the teams had started returning and made her lose her count.

What are they all doing here?

The *Tantamount* had sailed, limped really, into Port Border a week ago. The stopover was at the end of one of the major High Lanes, named as it was for the gateway and boundary between the High and Free. Still weeks out from the densely populated

Central Band and a last stop of regulated civilisation before one traversed into the more lawless Free Lanes. Alliance presence was minimal, restricted to a few patrols and staging points, or so Violet had been led to believe. She doubted the skipper and the captain would have brought the *Tantamount* in if they'd known about this though. Not after Rim. They were already as close to the High Lanes as both captain and skipper admitted they dared go.

Repairs, refitting, and recruiting. Mend and make sails, as the captain called it. That was what was keeping the *Tantamount* grounded. The repairs were time-consuming and good crew were hard to find. Harder still to afford crew for a ship whose captain had stretched his purse to the limit. The skipper had been scouring the watering holes of Border for days trying to draft another navigator. Much to Quill's, the *Tantamount's* incumbent Kelpie navigator, glee, she had failed.

Violet pushed all that from her mind. She slipped from her perch, feet kicking up clouds of dust as they hit the dirt road. She'd made up her mind about her next course of action. The first time she'd encountered Draugr they'd terrified her to the point of screaming. A reaction that still made the blood rush to her face in embarrassment. Now she had a chance to make up for that, maybe even redeem herself. Because the last time she'd spoken with a Draugr it had been to wish a former midshipman luck, as he and others like him set sail for parts unknown and uncharted, on the run from all and sundry. She needed to know if these Draugr were anything like Stoker and his companions.

She picked a wagon, hitched not to a beast of burden but rather a golem construct. A steam one. She'd seen them before, except this one, like everything in the High Lanes, was better made, all brass and whirring gears, steam flowing in two plumes from shoulder-mounted funnels. Its legs churned up the road, beating a constant rhythm as it pulled the heavy wagon and its silent cargo slowly but steadily. Apart from the golem, the wagon was unmanned, no driver or porter to notice or chase Violet away as she jogged to keep pace with it. Hopefully, that would make things easier.

Violet studied the wagon, keeping one wary eye on the golem as well. She didn't have the best history with golems either and wasn't sure how this one would react if she got too close to its cargo. The cargo, if that was the right word, stood in two neat rows inside the high-walled wagon, swaying with the motion and staring blankly ahead.

"Hello?" Violet called, sounding hoarse and squeaky to her own ears.

Neither golem nor Draugr responded, nor showed any indication they had even heard her.

Violet tried waving, even raising her voice to the point of yelling. Nothing. She grimaced, feeling her breathing start to labour somewhat. The golem was setting a fair pace despite its heavy payload. She decided to take a chance and see how far the construct was prepared, or conditioned, to tolerate her presence.

Breaking into a run, then a hop and an awkward jump, she bounded onto the running board of the wagon, catching hold of the side to steady herself. She tensed, waiting for the golem to come to a heart-shuddering halt and turn on her. But it never broke its relentless rhythm. Violet allowed herself to turn her full, almost, attention to the nearby Draugr.

"Can you hear me?" she heard herself say, positioning herself directly in front of the closest Draugr. Still it stared resolutely ahead, its eyes grey and milky, unseeing. Nothing like the lively animation she'd seen from others.

Taking another chance, Violet reached out and grabbed the Draugr by the arm, pulling until it came around. It moved easily enough and looked down at her arm. Confused, if anything. Under her touch, the Draugr's arm felt like wood, like carved flesh. Unnatural.

The wagon came to a halt then, throwing Violet off. She hit the ground hard, barely managing a roll to shake the worst of the impact. Her heart hammered in her chest, thinking she'd made a critical mistake by actually touching the Draugr cargo. Had that been too far, had she provoked the golem?

But no, it looked as though they'd arrived at their destination. The golem stood motionless at the head of the wagon, secure in its tethered harness. Violet looked quickly but as yet no one had appeared to take charge of the new arrivals. They were outside what could have been a warehouse, a factory, or something else entirely. But Violet took advantage of her run of good luck to make a quick exit, scampering for the corner. She was easily in cover before the Alliance-coloured errand boys came out to receive their goods.

One wasn't wearing a uniform, clad instead in dark-stained leathers. The cut of those leathers left the wearer's arms bare, displaying greyish-yellow skin, sallow and slick looking, a match to the elongated neck that seemed to merge into the narrow head. Violet hadn't seen the like before. It was as though someone had tried to mould a person out of an eel or snake.

The stranger seemed to be in charge, giving orders with flippant, vague gestures, though one hand always stayed close to a belt holding twin wands. Every move they made was languid, lazy, or so it seemed. One of the Draugr missed a step dismounting from the wagon, tumbling face first into the dirt. The creature made not the slightest effort to catch itself, falling like a stone, and would have taken the eel-man down too if they hadn't moved. It was fast—Violet started at how fast it was—but it was minimalist, just a pivot on the heel to shift the torso out of the way. The Draugr hit the ground, and the eel-man laughed, nudging the Draugr with the toe of his boot until they got to their feet. The sight made Violet duck down further. Only duellists carried twinned wands, not something she had good experiences with. And this one had a personality to go with her gut feeling. All bad.

While the lackeys tended to the Draugr, the duellist sauntered back to the warehouse, waving them open. The barn doors opened, slowly and with a groan of timbers, revealing the interior.

More golems. And rows of still more Draugr, standing there like battered toy soldiers in neat little lines. They were still, not motionless, swaying a bit, but unnatural-like. The warehouse minders led the new ones to their own corner of the building. She heard whistling, short little pipes—maybe that was how they got the Draugr to do what they meant. After that, the Draugr minders came back to the wagon. Soon it was off too; she could hear the beat of the golem's brass feet on the cobblestones as it ran back the way it came.

The warehouse was some sort of labour camp, Violet concluded. Between the Draugr and the golems there were plentiful workers to be had. Most of the golems were like the wagon-puller, steam and brass, except one.

It was there, innocuously tucked between two bulkier and

polished fellows, the light from a second storey window just catching it on the shoulder. Dusty and mottled black, not as smooth nor as polished as she remembered it, but familiar.

Familiar enough for her to get closer. Daft an idea as that seemed, curiosity won out. A step through the shadows to the side of the building while everyone and all were busy at the front. She kept her head down, practically crawling on hands and knees until she came to a window, just barely raising her head over the frame.

With her eyes raised above the sill, there was no doubt in her mind. The golem was massive, twice her height and three times as wide. Black with a mottled skein that showed traces of colours beneath, a hoarfrost of white lacquer over rounded curves like it had been flash-frozen, a stain that hadn't quite been removed. And oh so familiar.

Violet turned away, dropping down, and put her back against the wall. Her breath came in short, painful gasps now, and her legs felt to be made of sand. Back to the ship. She had to get back to the ship.

"Skipper!" Violet was bellowing, surprising even herself, before she was even halfway up the gangway to the *Tantamount*. "Skipper! Captain!"

Nobody rushed to answer her hollering. Several deckhands did stop to turn and stare but didn't seem overly put out by her boisterous arrival. As long as nobody was shooting at them, the crew seemed not to worry. That might change once Violet found the captain.

"Quit your yammering," a hoarse and gravelly voice told her. "You're hurting me ears."

"Sorry, Haze." Violet clenched her fists, trying to still herself. She'd run all the way back and her blood was pumping. Haze gave her a brief look of irritation before returning to his work. He was splicing, joining the strands of repurposed ropes together to make lines. Haze was one of the oldest sailors on the *Tantamount*, from a time before Violet had joined. Gabbi said his eyes were going but he didn't need to see well to mend and make ropes—Haze was by far the best splicer on the ship. It was impressive to watch the way his knobby fingers became deft instruments, as nimble as the marlinspike he wielded to taper one of his ropes.

And that was all the attention he gave her. Haze might be older than the captain and more seasoned than the skipper, if his ruddy skin and storied tattoos were anything to go by, but he had none of the warmth. Clearly he wasn't going to point her to them either.

A shadow fell over Violet and she skidded to a stop in front of the caster.

"What?" Quill, the *Tantamount's* navigator, demanded of her, lips pared back from his daggerlike teeth. As a Kelpie, Quill stooped and his legs bent backwards but he still towered over Violet. Since Violet had joined the crew, he had made it his personal mission to make life difficult for her. After Piper's death his behaviour had been . . . odd. He still seemed to resent her but his attitude had lost that malicious razor edge. All bark and no bite.

Well . . . less bite.

"Stop your bleating, girl." Quill waved off the rest of the crew.

"Where's the captain?" Violet said breathlessly, leaning over, hands on her knees. She tilted her head up to Quill. "The skipper? Where's Nel?"

"Not here," Quill said. "Do you have something meaningful to relate or are you merely fawning for attention?"

"I ain't fawning, Kelpie!" Violet snapped. "Just watched three ships drop off the mother-load of all Draugr. Hundreds of them. Alliance ships, colours, and soldiers."

Quill hissed disdainfully but appeared otherwise unmoved. "What of it? None of that concerns us."

"Weren't just Draugr, Quill," Violet said. "Saw golems too."

The faintest edge of suspicion crept into Quill's visage.

"Saw one," Violet added. "Might have been—"

"No!" Quill interrupted her fiercely. "Impossible."

"Looked just like it," Violet insisted. "Just like Scarlett's pet rock."

"The one we left floating in the void," Quill reminded her.

"You think that's gonna bother a golem any?"

"I think it did for the golem's master. The Guildswoman is dead. The golem would not function without her."

"Where's the captain, the skipper, Quill?" Violet asked. "I want her to know."

"Both are ashore. The captain, I imagine, is driving us deeper into debt at the card tables. The skipper is trying to find suitable, acceptable plebs so we may be quit of this tiresome place."

Violet glanced ashore. "I'm going to find her. Where's she at?"

"You," Quill grabbed her by the wrist, "are going nowhere. If there are Alliance ships newly arrived, the last thing we need is someone as unsubtle as you attracting their attention."

"Thought you said them didn't concern us." Violet tried to yank her arm away, but Quill held her tight. His grip tightened at her efforts.

"I have no desire to rescue your furry hide from yet another fracas. You will stay here. I will go ashore and find the skipper."

That didn't sound right, to Violet. Quill was in charge when the captain and Skipper were both away from the ship. Third in command whether anyone liked it or not. And it wasn't like him to waste those opportunities.

"You can't go ashore," she told him. "Who's in charge after your scaly hide?"

Quill opened his mouth to snap a reply at her, then hesitated. He frowned, obviously just as stumped as she was.

"It ain't gonna be me, Kelpie. I'm coming with you and you can't stop me," Violet warned.

"I told you to stay here."

"Can't make me if you don't stick around to watch me."

Quill glared at her, but she could see his wordless concession to her argument. She fought hard not to smile. It wasn't every day she got one up on Quill.

The navigator finally released her, turning his head this way and that over the crew while Violet rubbed at her wrist. She knew his choices were limited. There wasn't much of the original crew left to choose from, certainly no other officers. It would have been Piper but . . . Violet pushed that thought aside before it started to hurt.

The wind seemed to pick up, whistling through the timbers, until Violet realised it was Quill, breathing out through his teeth. The Kelpie turned on his heel and strode towards the stern of the ship, where the galley was. Violet grinned now that his back was turned and hurried after him. She didn't want to miss this.

"Cook!" Quill snapped, stopping in the doorway to the smoky galley. He blocked the entrance, obstructing Violet's view.

"What do you want, Kelpie?" She heard Jack, the galley assistant, bellow back.

"Where is the fat one?" Quill said. Clearly Gabbi, the *Tantamount's* cook, wasn't inside then.

"Not here," Jack confirmed. "Why? You sick of cooking your own meals now?"

Quill declined to answer Jack, ignoring him and turning back towards the hold. Violet scurried after him, determined not to miss the encounter. Quill didn't slow as he descended into the dark of the cargo deck. Violet strained her eyes trying to see, just managing to keep the dim outline of Quill in her sight and cursing as her feet bashed into badly stowed items littering the floor. Ahead of her, Quill was repeatedly yelling out "cook" at the top of his lungs, covering any noise she herself was making.

"What in all the Lanes do you want, Kelpie?" a woman called from up ahead. Peering around Quill, Violet could vaguely make out Gabbi's plump and squat outline. The cook dropped the sack she was hauling and put her hands on her hips, matching glares with Quill.

There was a moment's indecision before Quill spoke. His words came out quickly and rushed. "I am going ashore to bring back the skipper. Ensure nothing happens to the ship until I return."

Without any further explanation, Quill turned his back on Gabbi and started making for the stairs. Violet had time to register the shock and surprise on Gabbi's face before something sailed through the dark and struck Quill on the back of the head. The Kelpie stumbled, covering his head protectively, and spun to face the cook.

"Don't you turn your back on me, Loveland Quill," Gabbi admonished him sternly, hefting another missile. "I was gonna mash these tubers anyway and I can use your head to do it. Now why are you dragging your scaly behind ashore?"

"To find the skipper," Quill growled, scraping something from his head with one clawed hand.

"Why's she need you to walk her home, Quill? She's a big girl, can handle herself."

"Not so big as some aboard this ship," Quill muttered contemptuously. Gabbi hurled the potato at him for that. Blue sparks flashed around Quill's hand as he batted the projectile aside with a wave. The tuber burst in mid-air as Gabbi used her own thaumatic abilities to send it back again, covering Quill in a shower of white fleshy vegetable matter. The navigator shrieked his fury, and Violet clapped her hands over her mouth to stifle herself.

"Keep flapping that mouth, Kelpie," Gabbi told him. "Got me a whole sack of these things here. I can do this all day."

With very deliberate, barely restrained caution, Quill wiped the mash off his hide. He glared at Violet as if this were all her fault.

"This one," he said grimly, "has seen Alliance ships arrive. With Draugr and golems both. She is concerned."

Gabbi looked suspicious. "Since when do you care what Vi thinks?"

Quill turned his head and spat, refusing to answer.

"Fine," Gabbi relented. "Go find the skipper."

"She," Quill pointed with one finger, "is not to follow me. Make sure of it."

"Violet, don't follow Quill."

"But . . . !"

"I said don't be following Quill." Gabbi held up her weapon of choice in warning. "Kelpie says don't be following, you don't be following!"

It was doubtful either Gabbi or Quill could see the face Violet made. She made it anyhow.

"Good." Quill wiped the last of the potato mash off his face but appeared deeply satisfied with the outcome. "I will return with the skipper once I locate her."

"Be quick about it," Gabbi said.

"Yes, yes." Quill waved his hand in dismissal, still crowing about his victory that he didn't bother responding to her pestering.

"Since when do you side with Quill?" Violet demanded once the navigator was out of earshot.

Gabbi shrugged. "Quill's in charge. End of discussion, Vi."

"That's not fair!"

"Who ever said it was?"

"Well, it ought to be."

"You know better, Vi. Skipper's at the Pavilion. Pike's."

Violet stared. "But you . . . Quill said."

"Said don't follow him. You ain't. Skipper said anyone needs to find her she'd be at the Pavilion. Quill didn't ask that neither. Kelpie needs to learn to talk better. Still won't take him long to find the skipper but if you run you should make it there before him."

Violet grinned. And took off at a run.

QUILL AND VIOLET reached the watering hole within moments of each other. It hadn't taken Quill long at all. Maybe he had stopped to ask another of the crew on the way or maybe the Kelpie had some innate tracking abilities that let him keep tabs of their erstwhile Skipper. However he managed, any satisfaction he had derived vanished upon sighting her. Even then he didn't appear surprised, or Violet just couldn't recognise Kelpie surprise. He muttered a string of incoherent nothings, either nonsense or foreign, impossible to tell, before ignoring her and pushing his way inside.

The tavern was a dive. Violet had seen dozens like it on as many worlds. Built on the cheap and close to the docks, meant to attract the dregs of society and scrape the last few coins from their purses. It was a favourite haunt of sailors and labourers, the general riffraff of public life, and those more privileged who were looking to slum it. Then there were those who were looking for easy marks and some who just didn't know any better. And finally them who were bruising for a fight.

The skipper had been in a fight. Bruises mottled her bare arms, her neck, her face. One eye was dark, the flesh around the socket angry, and her lip was swollen, blood still trickling down her chin, though mostly dried. Not all of Nel Vaughn's injuries were recent. They'd started blooming the day the *Tantamount* had reached Port.

Everybody dealt with grief in their own way, Violet thought, her feet frozen to the floor as she stared at her skipper from across the taproom floor. Violet's own shoulder was still red and raw in remembrance. The skipper's way involved finding a different kind of pain.

Quill was likewise frozen in shock beside her. The skipper had never looked this bad that Violet could recall, not even after Rim. Violet glanced at Quill just after he started forward, so she missed his expression. There was little doubt about his resolve though as he shouldered and barged his way across the room. Even the normally hardened and raucous sailors got out of the way when they glimpsed his face. Violet stepped along in his wake.

The Kelpie stopped at the skipper's table. She wasn't alone but her drinking companions were mostly in a state of unconsciousness. Whether from partaking of the empty vessels adorning the table or from being beaten into submission it was hard to say, but a half-empty tankard was clutched in the skipper's hand. She didn't acknowledge either of their presences.

Quill didn't speak. The bench opposite the skipper rose in the air at a gesture from him, tilting until its insensate occupants slid to the floor in a heap. He took his seat after that, placing his clawed hands on the table in front of him. Violet hovered awkwardly at his shoulder.

Quill reached across and took hold of the skipper's arm, the right one, festooned with inked artwork. His touch looked almost gentle, nothing like the callous handling he subjected Violet to, turning the skipper's forearm over for inspection.

"This is new," he said quietly, tracing a clawed finger over the design. The skin was still raw and inflamed, spotted with blood, the design sharp against a red background. The skipper pulled her arm back, holding it tight against her chest. Quill waited until her eyes rose to meet his.

"Quill," Nel muttered, "why am I looking at your ugly maw?"

"You seem to have exhausted all other options. Perhaps your behaviour has something to do with this."

"You giving me advice on playing nice now?"

"No." Quill glanced at Violet, letting out an exasperated sigh. "The girl has seen something."

"Is it my next drink? The servers have gotten slow."

Quill made a show of looking round. "I believe you have had enough to drink. No, the girl has seen Draugr, golems, Alliance colours. Perhaps more."

"More?"

"A certain . . ."

"It was Onyx," Violet broke in. The skipper and her navigator both stared. Under their combined gazes, Violet felt her throat go dry. "Least . . . I think it was."

"You think?" the skipper repeated.

"It was dark, but I know what I saw," Violet insisted.

"And what exactly was that?" Quill rasped.

"A golem. Made of rock. Dark."

"You said it was dark. How could you tell?"

"Because it was dark!"

"Then how could you see?"

"The golem was dark, Quill." Violet glared at him. "Dark rock. Black. Black, like wet rocks. How many golems you know go around looking like that?"

"One was enough," the skipper muttered. She pushed her drinking vessel away, watching it teeter on the edge of the table before falling to the floor with a clatter. Nobody seemed to pay it any mind.

"Did it give you any trouble, lass?" she asked.

"No, Skipper. Don't think it saw me."

"But you saw it."

"Aye, Skipper. But I got out real fast."

"It is likely nothing." Quill looked across at her. "But it is time you returned to the ship."

"If it were nothing why'd you haul your scaly backside down here to come bend my ear about it?" the skipper growled.

"A discussion we can continue later." Quill stood up. "Back at the ship."

"Don't need your hells damned nursemaid routine, Quill," the skipper muttered.

Quill ignored her. "Help her up, girl," he ordered Violet. "We are leaving."

Chapter 2

THERE WERE HALF a dozen souls clustered near where the *Tantamount* was docked. Violet didn't recognise any of them, but one stood out: a Mantid, multi-legged and covered in chitinous plating.

"Violet, go see what they want," the skipper ordered. She twisted her shoulder with a grimace, throwing off Quill's hand. Violet shrugged and walked out briskly ahead of the pair. The group didn't notice her approach at first.

"You all waiting for something?" Violet called out loudly.

"Looking for the *Tantamount* and her captain," one of them said—a woman, dusky skinned and covered in sailor's ink. One side of her face was significantly darker than the other, already swelling under the noon day sun. Sweat glistened on bare and heavily muscled arms. She seemed to be the leader of the group from the way the others deferred to her.

"That's the *Tantamount* right there," Violet pointed. "Says so on the side."

The woman shrugged. "Ma always said reading might come in handy, never did believe her. All right you lot, guess this is the one after all."

"Told you so, Hounds," one of the others replied.

"Told me about the last two ships as well, so find a new parrot to stick your hand up, Denzel." The woman, Hounds, heaved a burlap sack atop her shoulder, grimacing up at the deck of the *Tantamount*. "This is the one then, boys and girls. All aboard." Then to Violet, "You're aboard for the ride then too, little lass?"

Violet opened her mouth to reply, then hesitated. There hadn't been any new crew since she'd come aboard. She wasn't sure she cared for the idea of strangers on the *Tantamount*. Didn't feel right.

"Who hired you?" she asked instead. "Was it the captain?"

"Ain't met no captain yet," Hounds admitted. "Was some redhead who pointed us this way. Said she needed the crew and gods know there's precious other work going of late."

"She hire us before or after you two tore up the tap room?" Denzel cat-called.

Hounds touched the side of her face gingerly. "After," she admitted. "Woman's got a mean right hook. I respect that in an employer. Speaks of a good negotiator."

"Never cared much for negotiating," the skipper called out, coming up behind Violet. "See you found the ship easy enough."

"Aye, eventually." Hounds touched a hand to her hairline in an odd salute Violet hadn't seen before.

The skipper gestured to Quill. "Mister Quill here will show you to your berths. Quill, after that you can take Mantid to the chart room and show him the lay of the ship."

"And why would I do that?" Quill muttered darkly.

"Because he's our new navigator, and as such he'll be sharing duties with you, taking the load off so to speak."

"Which he doesn't," Hounds volunteered. "Speak, that is. Makes some clicks and such, but don't speak none."

"I can live with a crewman who don't talk back." The skipper grimaced. "All aboard then, and after you, Quill."

It would have been impossible to miss the murderous look Quill directed at the other navigator, but the Mantid didn't seem to notice. Or maybe he did and Violet still couldn't tell. And she'd thought the Kelpie navigator a hard one to read.

"Ain't never had another navigator aboard before, Skipper," Violet said after the new crew followed Quill aboard.

"About time we did then. Hells, my head is pounding."

"Quill don't like the Mantid none."

"That's his problem."

"The Mantid got a name, Skipper? Or we just gonna stick to

tradition?"

"You want I should start calling you Kitty, Vi? Mantid is his name, or at least they don't got individual names. We call Quill Kelpie oft enough so there's your tradition, if you must. We were lucky to find him. This close to the High, navigators are scarce on the ground and we need them up in the sky."

"If you hired them all, why'd you send me out as if they were strangers?" Violet asked, suspecting she'd been played.

"Forgot, mostly," the skipper shrugged. "Woman's got a fist like Jack's head and a head like I wish I didn't know. Rattled me some. Lass, do me a favour and stop with the questions. Go find Gabbi, and get me something. She'll know what."

"Kelpies and Korrigans and Kitsunes. And now Mantids," Gabbi muttered, searching through her cupboards. "Sometimes I think the captain's just out to found some collection. Got one of everything aboard these days and no two alike."

"Thought the captain liked to do the hiring." Violet sat with her legs dangling off the galley bench. "He got the skipper doing that now too?"

"Captain knows if he puts this and that off long enough the skipper will do it for him." Gabbi shrugged. "You know he knows that too, Vi. You got something against our new hands?"

"No," Violet shook her head quickly. "Just strange, is all. Last time we had new hands . . ."

"Ain't had no new hands since you," Korrigan Jack grunted, heaving a crate of dried goods up next to Violet. "Still waiting for you to start earning your keep, at that."

"Hard work, making up for your lazy self, Jack," Violet told him. The Korrigan barked a laugh and left the galley for another trip to the hold.

"Look at you, all tough and vinegar," Gabbi approved. "Act like that with the new hands and you'll have nothing to worry about."

"Be less worried if the captain would find us a paying job," Violet mused. "Feels like it's been a while."

"Been a long while," Gabbi agreed. "But no sense us worrying about that. What'd the skipper say she needed?"

"Didn't. Said you'd know what."

"That's no help. She after more of the hairy dog she's been biting or something for the beatings it gets her into?"

Violet stared.

"She hungover or just beat up?" Gabbi elaborated.

"Both. One of the new hands took a few swings at her."

"Ah, negotiating," Gabbi nodded.

"And she's been drinking since we hit Port. Ever since Piper," Violet added, staring down at the floor.

Gabbi put her hand out and tilted Violet's chin up. "How's your back, lass?"

"Still stings some," Violet admitted. "Not as bad as the first one. Bigger though."

"Let's have a look. Quick, before Jack comes back."

Violet twisted on the bench, pulling the back of her shirt up, exposing her newly decorated shoulder blade.

"You and Nel got the same," Gabbi observed. Violet twisted her head when she felt something brush the sensitive skin, Gabbi dabbing at her with an oil-soaked rag.

"Not the same, Skipper's got more detail."

"Seen it," Gabbi sighed. "For all Cyrus and Beaks and the rest. Skipper won't let herself forget. Hard woman."

"Hard woman," Violet agreed.

Gabbi pulled Violet's shirt back down, patting her on the other shoulder. "Healing just fine, lass. Piper would be crowing to know you had this. Just keep it moist. No letting your skin dry out or you'll scar and the ink will run."

"Aye, I will."

"Anyways," Gabbi continued, "there's a bottle on that hook over there. Get it down and take it to Nel. If that don't cure what ails her, she'll not be in place to complain about it to either of us."

Violet hopped down and retrieved the bottle in question, a clay jug in twine netting. She pulled the cork and took a cautious sniff, familiar enough with Gabbi's concoctions to be wary. Even so she had to push the jug away, hacking and coughing.

"Hells, Gabbi, that's nasty," she complained to the cook.

"Aye, it is, so don't be sampling any on your way, and hopefully it helps knock some sense into Nel. Don't get none on your clothes neither, stains something awful and don't ever come out. You'll look like you got dipped in berry juice."

"QUILL, STOP TALKING, your voice is hurting my ears." The skipper waved the clay jug in the Kelpie's direction. Violet watched closely, curious to see what would happen when the skipper finally partook of the vile beverage. She'd raised it twice and both times Quill had unleashed another tirade about their new many-legged crew member.

"We do not need another navigator," Quill insisted yet again. "I am more than . . ."

"More than loud enough, for sure," the skipper grumbled. "Captain?"

"It's just a precaution, Quill," the captain tried to placate his navigator. The captain looked scrawny next to the simmering Kelpie, like a stick-insect with his frail-looking limbs, appropriate given the new crewman they were arguing about. "A spare in case something were to happen to you. Someone to spell you between watches."

"We have managed fine before now. I do not see . . ."

"Because we ain't fine now," the skipper said grimly. "And we all know it, so let it go, Loveland."

Finally, the skipper raised the jug to her lips, tilting it. She swallowed heavily before wiping her mouth with the back of her hand.

"What?" she asked, catching Violet's stare.

"Nothing," Violet replied, not letting her disappointment show. She caught the jug when the skipper tossed it to her. It was empty.

Quill made a noise that might have been offensive if it weren't so unintelligible. "If we are taking on extra mouths, do we at least have the means to carry them? We will be heading out soon? Away from these High Lanes and their Alliance peacocks?"

"No, Quill," the captain sighed, sinking down into his chair. "Not soon."

The captain and the skipper exchanged a glance. A grim one. Violet kept very still, expecting to be asked to leave any moment now.

"We have work, Quill," the skipper said, flicking her eyes towards Violet, acknowledging that she hadn't forgotten the girl was there. "But not here."

"Where then?"

"Vice," the captain said. "Back in the Free Lanes."

Vice, Violet thought, *is a long journey without a paying run.*

"The problem for now is we can't afford to make the run," the captain explained. "We need to finish our repairs here, pay down enough debts to leave Port Border, and make our way to Vice. But we need paying work to tide us over for that run."

"The run from Vice is well paid," the skipper explained. "Very well paid, bonuses all round if we can only get there. But until we find a way to do that we're going to be living on the edge. That's why we took on crew now. If runs come up we're taking them, no questions asked and no bells wasted. We take them whenever and wherever they go because frankly we don't have a choice anymore."

While Violet took all that in, Quill wasn't silenced for long. "And why are you saying all this in front of her?" he pointed.

The captain shrugged. "Because trying to keep secrets from a cabin girl is a waste of time. The crew will figure it out soon enough, whether Violet tells them or not. But she's always underfoot and around the three of us anyway, so I trust her to be discreet for a bit longer."

"Aye, Captain." Violet saluted the old man proudly, touched. "You can count on me."

"Of course I can, Violet. Never thought I couldn't. In any case, wasn't there another reason you were here? Apart from Nel's morning coffee."

"Ain't morning, Captain," the skipper said.

"I'm aware of that, Nel."

"Draugr and golems," Quill was succinct. "The girl saw them and got frightened."

"The girl has a name, Kelpie," Violet bristled. Every time she thought Quill was mellowing towards her . . .

"The girl has fleas," Quill snapped back. "Courtesy of that mangy rodent she associates with."

"Say that around Jack, I dares you."

"Of him my opinion is even lower, impossible as that seems."

"Port Border is a nexus between the Lanes, Vi," the skipper said, ignoring their bickering. "Plenty of Alliance ships pass through here, nothing to do with us."

"Ain't seen so many Draugr together since Rim, Skipper," Violet said.

"I've heard talk about that," the captain said. "Labour shortage and the like. Supposedly they're scraping Draugr in from gangs in the Free Lanes to run the High."

"Hadn't heard that." The skipper turned to him.

The captain shrugged. "It's not just us short of work, Nel. Seems there's a cascade of trouble, one after the other. All the folks who ought not to be falling."

"Perhaps there is work to be found in moving these Draugr to where they are needed," Quill suggested.

"Perhaps there is, Mister Quill. But that is not the sort of work we can accept. The associations are wrong for this ship and this crew."

"Then we are not desperate?"

"There is desperate times and there is desperate, Mister Quill."

"And then there's just stupid," the skipper muttered.

"And that is our situation," the captain concluded. "We need work and we need it soon. So one of us needs to find it, wherever it can be found."

THE CAPTAIN FUSSED around the great cabin after Nel and Quill left. It was just him and Violet. Horatio was clearly searching for something. Just as clearly, he had not found it. Eventually he turned to Violet, beaming, a sense of accomplishment.

"Very good then. Now that we've hidden the silverware, I do believe we have some new souls aboard?"

"Aye, Captain. Hounds' lot." She wasn't sure if the captain meant what he'd said about the silverware or if he was just making excuses for his patchy memory. She didn't remember any silverware. "Tall woman, almost knocked the skipper out."

"So I hear, but I've yet to acquaint myself with her. If you would be so good as to find her and send her here so as I can assign her a watch. Who's on watch now, in any case?"

"Dead Man's Watch, Captain, would be Quill's turn and . . ." Violet bit off the rest of her words, looking up at the captain. You weren't supposed to name the watches in front of the officers, captain included.

Dead Man's Watch, the name of the shift, so called because of Quill's reputation for working those sailors on his until they dropped like dead men into their hammocks. There'd be more complaints if Quill didn't work himself just as hard. He'd been covering most of Piper's old shifts as well. An act he might not have done had he known what the crew had nicknamed both watches. Watchstanders rarely knew what the crew came up with and the names changed over time. The skipper's watch had been the Salty Swab a while back, on account of her language. Far as Violet could tell, the skipper had never known.

From the barely restrained grin, the captain already knew the names.

"I'll be putting Hounds on Piper's old watch."

"Crew call it the Loompa's Long Night, sir," Violet said. Might as well go all in. The captain nodded knowingly.

"A good name, though odds are it'll be the Dog's Watch before long, or some such. Very traditional name that one, smart person would put money on it. Not very original though, best to keep it from the woman herself. Oh, and you'll be standing watch with Quill."

"Sir?" Violet stared. "Why?"

"Because he asked for you to, Violet," the captain said, as if it were obvious. "Has been for a while now. Now run along and fetch Miss Hounds for me. We've words to discuss between us."

"WHY THE DARK and stormy, Vi?" The skipper was with Hounds down in the hold. Both were bent over a pile of hammocks and rope.

"Captain sent me," Violet said by way of answer. "Wants a word with Miss Hounds."

"Just Hounds is fine," the woman said, looking her up and down while her hands made quick work of a knot Violet didn't recognise. Hounds dangled the ring and hammock in front of herself critically before shaking her head and loosening the knot.

"Can't sleep in anything but a hammock these nights," she said. "Don't feel right if the bed don't move."

"Sleep with one eye open most nights," the skipper said. "Ever since someone threw knives at me through the wall."

Hounds turned her head quizzically at that but made no comment. "Should I be worried about this mythical captain of yours? Seems to have worried this one."

"Vi, tie me a hitch, maybe an anchor bend." The skipper passed her a metal ring and the end of a hammock. "And tell the woman if she should be worried."

"No." Violet brought the rope behind and through the metal ring then looped it around once.

"Simple as that, Hounds. No," the skipper nodded.

"I am relieved."

Bring the loose end through the stand, through the double loops, set and dressed.

"Bit traditional there, Skipper." Hounds pointed at the knot Violet had made. "Think we'd be safer going with something quick to release. Maybe a highwayman?"

"You know a highwayman's hitch, Vi?" the skipper asked.

Violet shook her head.

"Here." Hounds held out a loose bit of rope and one of the hammock's spreader bars. "Start with the bight under the load. Then do with the same with the standing." Violet watched closely. It was the same knot Hounds had first tied. She said as much.

"Sharp eyes, this one," Hounds complimented the skipper. "It's a good knot, just tug on the unsupported end and it comes away, just like you'd want."

"What do you want it for?"

"Need a perch to rock our new navigator," the skipper said. "These slings weren't made for Mantids or the like, got to rig something different for him."

"What'd he sleep in before now then?" Violet asked. "Can't be his first time sleeping aboard?"

Hounds shrugged. "Caught him napping on the side of the ship once, just hung there with those feet of his. Can't do that here."

"Because the ship runs cold, Vi, 'fore you ask," the skipper said. "Didn't go to all the trouble of finding us a new navigator just to have him freeze himself after his first watch."

"Your ink is running," Hounds pointed. The skipper grimaced, straightening her arm out for inspection. The skin around her new tattoo was slick in an unhealthy way.

"Pass me that rag, Vi."

"It ain't clean, Skipper," Violet objected.

"Didn't ask if it were." The skipper snatched it away, wadding it up and dabbing at her forearm. "Damned back alley scratchers," she muttered to herself.

"Got a few of those," Hounds said. "Spent a whole crossing's purse once getting them covered over."

Violet took her first real look at the woman's tattoos, trying to remember everything the skipper and Piper had taught her about ink since she'd come aboard. First, she considered the twin swallows under the collarbone, either side of the chest. Piper had been fond of swallows; he'd had seven in total. Violet had been present when he'd gotten the seventh—she'd received her first tattoo from the same artist. Piper had paid. She glanced down at the braided rope circling her wrist and palm, smiling a little.

"You have a lot of tattoos," she said, then flushed when Hounds caught her looking.

"You can't see half of them, lass. The best ones take up a lot more skin. You wanna see?"

"Um . . ." Violet looked at the skipper, who just shrugged.

"Look all you like," she said. "Just don't go believing everything she tells you."

"The best part of belief is the lie," Hounds winked, standing up. She turned around, pulling her shift up.

Over half her back was taken up by a single, intricate design. A fully rigged clipper under sail. All it was missing was the accompanying waves or mist. On her lower back was an anchor on the rocks, a blue skinned octopus wrapped around it in place of a rope. It might have once been attached to the clipper, except the space between was obscured by scar tissue.

"You were in a fire," Violet said. "But you had these before."

"Aye." Hounds let her shirt drop, turning around. She pulled her sleeve up, exposing an eight-pointed windrose, a compass. It was wreathed in fire, the flames colouring over more scar tissue.

"Got this one after, to remember folks by."

Violet found herself nodding. She reached up to adjust her shirt. It rode uncomfortably on her shoulders over her own memories. "You've been to the Fata Morgana, haven't you? That's what the ship means."

"There and back," Hounds nodded. "Close as you can, I suppose. Went as far as you can go before the mist becomes too thick to push through. Longest, longest trip of all my years. We took the long way . . ."

The eye of the mist, heart of the black. The Fata Morgana . . .

"Skipper," Violet asked, "you ever been?"

"You see a clipper on me?" The skipper looked amused.

"No."

"Then what do you think?"

Violet frowned. "That ain't an answer."

The skipper chuckled. "Forget about the Morgana, back end of nowhere and no reason to visit except for bragging rights. First thing folk who get there want to do is drink and that's only until they try the beer. Now what else can you tell me about our new shipmate here from all the pretty pictures?"

"Captain's making her a watch-stander," Violet said.

"Damn," Hounds said.

"Not half as fun when she already knows the answers," the skipper agreed. "Knowing's cheating, Vi."

"Meant damn as in now I might have to do some actual work." Hounds sounded glum. "Suppose I should be going to see our captain then. Get it over with."

"Might be we've kept him waiting long enough, though the captain does love to wait on a lady," the skipper told her.

"I can show you the way," Violet offered.

"Think I'll manage, lass," Hounds said. "Captains always like the big cabins and there's only the few places you can put those. I'll see you both later."

"You still owe me for drinks," the skipper reminded her. "Last ones ended up going to waste."

Hounds laughed, causing the skipper to scowl and shake her head as the other woman left. She leaned her head on one hand, turning to Violet.

"It was the anchor," she said. "Means she ranked as an officer, as a mate or higher."

"Thought it meant something different," Violet protested. "Like home or attachment or what."

"Octopus means she cut all those ties to the past. Nothing pulling her back. Attached to the ship like that means she was someone you salute."

"She salutes funny."

"Just different."

"Thought you didn't like her, Skipper."

"Why'd you think that?"

"On account of you both being all black and blue."

"Fastest way to get to know someone, Vi. Only people worth drinking with is those who stick around after a fight. Speaking of which, you still look like you're aching to hurt someone. Is it Quill or Jack this time around?"

"Quill," Violet muttered, sinking down onto a crate opposite.

"Figured it might be. What's our blessed navigator done now?"

"Captain wants me to stand watch with him. Says Quill asked."

The skipper actually dropped the ropes she was working on, staring wide-eyed stupid at Violet. "Oh, Loveland is asking for something," she said finally. "You're on my detail, Violet. Ain't nothing changed about that."

"Captain says otherwise," Violet pointed out. She was cheered by the skipper's reaction. Anything was better than being on Quill's watch, and being on the skipper's was much better.

"Then I'll be saying some such to the captain, don't you doubt that," the skipper said. "Now, in fact." She looked down at the mess of ropes and hammocks. "I've a task for you, Violet. Figure out some rig our new navigator can nap in. I'm at a loss."

Violet looked at the tangle of half-finished knots helplessly. If it had already gotten the better of the skipper, what hope did she have?

"Good lass," the skipper tapped her on the shoulder. "I'm off to see the captain. Tidy up when you're done and then go see Gabbi. She'll have something else for you to do, I'm sure."

<h1 style="text-align:center">CHAPTER 3</h1>

"Need a word with you, Captain," Nel said.

"Nel," he looked up from his table. "I didn't hear you knock."

"Didn't knock." The captain's eyes were clear. There was even a flicker of annoyance filling them at her abrupt entry. He shut the book he'd been making entries in, his own personal ledger.

Good, maybe we'll be able to get this settled quick then.

"I want Violet put back on my watch," she said.

"Whose watch is she on now?"

"Quill's."

"I see. How did that happen?" the captain asked her.

"You put her there."

"Ah, then I must have had a good reason for doing so." Horatio leaned back in his chair, watching Nel.

Nel scowled. "Captain . . ."

"I believe Mister Quill raised some concerns about the girl."

"And since when has Quill ever cared a damn about Violet?" Nel objected.

"Have a seat, Nel," Horatio motioned to her. "And you do our good navigator a disservice. But in point of fact, I can give you a very clear point at which Quill decided to give a damn about our beloved cabin girl."

His eyes were hard and steely as Nel sank down into the chair opposite him. "When he made a promise to a friend in the man's final moments."

"Quill and Piper weren't . . ."

"Nel, please," Horatio forestalled her. "Quill came to me with his concerns about you. Your conduct has been unbecoming since . . . since . . ."

"Since we got half the crew killed in a job that weren't nothing to do with us?"

"That," the captain said, "is quite enough. Violet will stay on Quill's watch. That is all I have to say on the matter."

"And the other matter, Captain?" Nel pushed him, feeling her stomach twist at the necessity. "When we get to Vice, are we flying in wide-eyed stupid again? Getting caught up in things that aren't ours to get caught up in?"

The captain's fingers drummed irritably on the leather-bound cover of his journal. "Seems we should speak plainly, Nel. Out with it, what do you really wish to accuse me of?"

Fine, you want it plain, Captain, I'll speak plain.

"Sharpe, whoever he was, knew we were originally bound for Vice. So did damn near everybody else, from Stoker to that damned rock fiend we floated into the black. So tell me true, is any of that mess waiting for us when we make port?"

"No, Chanel," Horatio said calmly. "As far as I know we are clear of that, as clear as we will be staying of the High Lanes, in fact."

"It'll come back to us," Nel warned him. "One day."

"All good deeds do, my dear."

"And have you thought anymore about what you're going to say to Sand when we're standing in front of her?" Nel asked pointedly, changing the subject before he could.

"No," the captain winced, successfully distracted. "But I imagine it will be profuse. Genuine, even. And there will be concessions on our part."

"Can't afford to slide any further into debt, Captain." Nel knew she was being unfair but didn't care too much at this point. "Woman's going to want her cargo, cargo we left sitting on Cauldron that has since gone walking."

"Can't be helped."

"You didn't mention it before."

"Quill knows," the captain said. "We've discussed it."

"Seems you and he have been discussing all sorts lately."

"Yes. We have."

"You think Sand will still be holding that run for us, Captain? Hand on your heart, you think we still have work waiting for us at Vice?"

"The fact of it is, Nel, I have no choice but to believe so. The alternatives are . . ." He shrugged.

Unpleasant alternatives. Unthinkable. How very typical.

Nel glared at her captain. "Fine," she said. "One less thing for me to worry about then. I'll just focus on finding us our next job."

She rose to her feet, angrily shoving her chair back.

"One more thing, Nel," the captain said to her.

Minutes later Nel emerged onto the deck. The crew, those who were present, were unusually committed to their tasks. A deliberate focus to the apparent exclusion of anything else that might be occurring within earshot. Not one of them looked her way.

"Cretins," Nel muttered.

There was one constant, though. A one-sided argument emanating from the bridge. Maybe it wasn't her the crew were avoiding eye contact with, though she wouldn't put coin on the matter. She followed the clamour, taking the steps to the raised quarterdeck.

Give me an excuse, Kelpie, that's all I want from you right now.

Quill and Mantid, poised on opposite sides of the collapsible chart table. Several charts lay scattered on the table; a handful were clutched protectively to Quill's chest. And his fist was repeatedly pounding the table, making the flimsy structure shake. Their new navigator fretted opposite him, spiky arms raised and all twitchy.

New navigator, now there's the problem. Never seen Quill get so careless around his precious maps. Must be proper riled.

"The hells are you two doing?" Nel barked. Mantid jumped, actually lifted an inch or two off the ground on all four legs, then his head twisted all the way about to face . . . her. Nel almost did some flinching on her own. Unnatural it was and made her own neck hurt just to witness. Quill took the opportunity to scoop up the rest of his maps. By the time Mantid's head rotated back to him, Quill was pushing them into their tube-shaped container.

"This . . . thing . . . is going to damage my charts. I will not allow it." Quill crossed his arms in defiance.

"He's our new navigator, Quill," Nel reminded him. "He needs to see them. Let him be."

"No!" Mantid tried to edge around the table. Quill darted to keep it between them, pushing the shoulder-mounted map case protectively behind him. "Those hands, he will rip them."

Mantid turned his head towards Nel, tilted at an uncomfortable angle. A shrug, maybe?

"Godsdamnit, Quill," Nel sighed. "I've no patience for this."

"Nor have I."

"Quill, put the damned maps on the table."

"I refuse. This thing is unqualified. I will not have it."

"You don't got a say."

"They are my maps."

"They're the ship's maps."

"Not all of them."

"Even if that were true, which it ain't and you know it, Mantid needs them to do what I hired his prickly self for. And besides that, he's probably got maps of his own you ain't ever seen before."

Quill hesitated.

Oh, got your attention did that, Loveland? Didn't think this tantrum all the way through now, did you? Wait until someone drops that this lot has been to the Fata Morgana. All the way through the Dark Flow in corridors I know you haven't sailed.

She could see Quill's inner turmoil, his arms wrapped protectively around the map case, weighing up the contents of a potential treasure trove of unfamiliar lanes and worlds. The paranoia that twisted the Kelpie's face at the gamble he might be taking. Maps? What maps? What if he had already seen them?

"To hells with the both of you," Nel turned her back on them. "Figure it out amongst yourselves."

Halfway down the stairs before the panicked Kelpie called out to her. "Where are you going? You cannot leave me here with this! What are you doing?"

"Figure it out!" she yelled back.

"But where are you going?" Nel heard Quill try to follow her, then cursing. She imagined Mantid confronting him at the top of the stairs and grinned at the image that came to mind.

"To find a bar. With beer, lots of beer. And I'm signing every tar-fingered navigator I can find, black help me, Loveland."

The cursing that followed her off the ship; that she didn't have to imagine.

IN HER DEFENCE, they had left her alone. And now she was at the bitter end. The bitter end being the very end of the very last rope she'd been able to find. The others had all been . . . incorporated.

It had occurred to Violet that a Mantid was rather like a spider, because spiders were insects, or close enough, and Mantid were essentially very large insects. Therefore it followed that if a cocoon-like hammock wouldn't serve then perhaps more of a webbed design would.

And somehow that web had grown to involve a dozen ropes of varying sizes, all knotted together and hung from five separate posts' hooks. She'd dismantled two other hammocks, scavenging the ropes and discarding the spreader bars. Her construct had taken on a life of its own and she'd had to take down several other slings just to make room. That wouldn't do as the other sailors needed to sleep and most were particular about where they hung. There was a seniority involved and they wouldn't be tolerant of her moving things about. But she needed them out of the way so she could see how things looked when hung and raised.

Terrible.

Bandit at least found it amusing, walking the ropes on all fours, cautiously moving his weight from one strand to another. To him it was a new obstacle course to explore and play, no different than the rigging. But she didn't need anyone to tell her it would never do. Even if this was the right approach, the economy of size was all wrong. Her creation covered more space than the captain's cabin.

She sighed and pulled on a knot, loosening one of the major strands. It fell slack, the tension gone, and half the web collapsed. Bandit squawked at her in protest. He managed to cling on, barely suspending himself above the deck in a most undignified manner. Another vote of disapproval.

She'd need another notion. Of those at least she had plenty.

Violet's head was packed in such a way she imagined stray thoughts might be coming out her ears. Full of tattoos and twisted nights and a touch of dread at future watches she might have to stand with Quill. She'd stood watches with both the skipper and Piper—not many and hardly full watches. Everyone was always finding jobs for her to do and errands that needed running. And always with the lessons. Lines and knots and signalling and other stuff that jostled for space in her crowded skull. And now she had to figure a hammock for a sailor she'd only glimpsed once.

Gabbi's shrill fishwife calls were still able to drown them out. Violet followed the noise to the open-cut galley. Inside, Gabbi was rifling through the nooks and crannies. Jack stood behind the bench, ducking and occasionally grabbing a pot lid as it whizzed around the room. Gabbi was being indiscriminate in her search, floating utensils out of the way and seemingly forgetting about them just as well. A sack of potatoes threatened to spill its contents. Violet grabbed it by the neck, hauling it down and pushing it into a corner before what had happened to Quill repeated itself on a larger scale.

"Where did all our stocks go, Jack?" Gabbi called from behind the range.

"Got ate," Jack grunted back.

"Why didn't you tell me?" Gabbi's head came up in annoyance.

"We got money?"

"No."

"That's why."

"Crew's gotta eat, Jack."

"Crew would rather drink. Should let them fend for their food."

"Ha!" Gabbi's laugh was caustic. "Crew can't fend off what needs fending. Fend for themselves—we must got grog left if you're talking such."

"Captain's always got some," Jack admitted.

"And you know where it is, right Jack?" Violet spoke up.

Jack gave her a knowing wink.

"You two are funny today," Gabbi observed.

"Need some advice." Violet hopped up onto a shelf she'd perched on countless times. It creaked at her. Either she was getting big, which didn't seem likely from the empty cupboards, or the ship was getting old.

"What do you need, lass?" Gabbi asked. She held up a wooden box, shaking it. "Is this all the salt we got left?"

"Must be," Jack said.

"How do I hang a hammock for a Mantid, Gabbi?" Violet asked.

"We need more. Town has whole warehouses of it, why don't we have more?" Gabbi frowned at Violet. "You want to what now, lass?"

"Skipper gave me a job. Got to figure out how the bug sleeps and make him something cosy."

"Don't call him a bug," Gabbi disapproved. "Sounds hateful."

"Sorry." Violet ducked her head. "Still need help."

"Asked the bug?" Jack grunted.

"No, ain't had the time yet."

"Find time."

"Gotta find him first, Jack!" Violet said. "Gabbi's here and the bug ain't—"

"Violet!" Gabbi snapped.

"Sorry," Violet said.

"You don't sound sorry."

"Well . . . maybe I ain't. Don't mean it to be hateful."

"Don't mean it isn't."

Jack laughed.

"And you ain't no better, Jack," Gabbi admonished him. "And since you're both so eager, you can go round up my list."

"But . . ."

"Don't want to hear it, lass."

"Don't wanna go," Jack complained.

"Then don't run your mouth."

"Was being helpful."

"Mouth's still going, Jack, wrong kind of running."

"Where's the list?" Violet asked, recognising a lost cause.

"By the door," Gabbi said.

"You order all ready?"

"Aye, but just a barrow's worth. Won't go far, and won't go down well. And I need you to find salt, too."

"How much?"

Gabbi pursed her lips. "Much as you can get for what we got, got lots of cabbage and beans that need curing."

Jack made a disapproving sound.

"Don't be giving me none of that, Jack," Gabbi said. "You'll eat what I give you. Violet, don't let him do the ordering, just what's on the list. Now get going."

Chapter 4

Rain had turned Port Border's streets into a river of not so swiftly flowing mud, something not lost on Nel as she discovered the woeful state her boots had fallen to. Feeling the viscous liquid between her toes did nothing for her mood, neither did the droplets running down her back that her hood failed to keep out. In stubborn defiance, she pulled the hood down further over her face.

The Pavilion waterhole was more crowded than usual, locals and Laners both seeking shelter from the weather and a different kind of way to drown. Most were deep in their cups but Nel still managed to shoulder her way to the bar, the other patrons too far gone to notice any bruises she left in her wake.

She grabbed a pint from a server's tray at first chance, flicking a coin in payment, and settled in to scan the crowd. The *Tantamount's* roster was mostly full now, though they were lacking in experience. The captain choosing to fill the position of mate left vacant by Piper came with its own headaches. Nel liked what she'd seen of Hounds, despite a still-throbbing face. But it was not the best course, as the woman came with her own crew, and making her an officer could create factions aboard the ship, not something desirable. Still, if her search came up dry, it might be for the best.

Either that or put Violet forward. Bit early but she might take to it. Could be worth it just for the apoplexy it would give Quill.

She and the captain had been putting more responsibility on the girl, giving her more rope, so to speak, and so far the girl had avoided hanging herself. There hadn't been much choice with their roster as thin as their purses of late.

"Hey, Vaughn."

Nel looked up from her musings. One of the servers. She'd been spending too much time here if they knew her by name.

"What?"

The server inclined his head towards a corner, back of the room where the bar met the wall. "Had a fellow in here earlier asking after you, by name and by ship."

"Aye, thanks, appreciated," she muttered, dropping another coin on the man's tray. The coin vanished just as quickly. She remembered now—she'd asked the servers at some of the bars to point her towards people looking for ships to crew out on.

Except, she mused, she hadn't advertised her ship's name. Learnt more than once to keep names out of it where she could.

So who's been asking about us? Too many damned sailors looking for a berth off this crass piece of rock. Doesn't have to be on my ship though.

Nel stretched out her legs, making no effort to draw attention to herself, keeping an eye on the door where the server had pointed, studying from under the brim of her hood. There was a lot of foot traffic coming and going from the bar, foul weather, sailors at the end of their runs with coin in their pocket. Or sailors without work drinking to forget, the result was the same. Nobody she recognised and nobody who looked like they were looking.

There was one fellow. A drink in one hand went untouched, empty or just for show, the man was watching, waiting, eyeing all those who passed him by warily.

He didn't look like a Free Lanes sailor. The hair was too short and the clothes not rough enough, good quality if not expensive. Recently purchased. A bit older, seasoned then. Not someone who ought to be scrounging for work.

Aye, you stick out like the proverbial. Not someone I'd be looking to hire. Is it me you're looking for or am I just going to turn myself grey worrying over naught?

"Move over, Nel."

"Move over, Skipper," Nel responded with a raised eyebrow

but still pulled her legs in. Gabbi plopped down, shaking herself and spraying water everywhere. Nel turned her head so that her hood took the brunt of the deluge.

"I said what I meant," Gabbi grumbled. "Damned rain, gonna delay my deliveries. Had to send Jack and Vi out after them. Only way I know how to give Jack a bath but now the whole galley is gonna smell like wet fox fur. Can't win."

Nel snorted. "You sent them out? How long did you wait before making for this bar?"

"Longer than you and you might as well live here. Are we drinking?" Gabbi made a face. "I feel like we should be drinking."

Nel reached out and pilfered another drink, earning a scowl from the waylaid server. That was their problem though. She delivered the drink to her cook.

"To husbands and sweethearts," Nel said.

"May they never meet," Gabbi agreed.

"Never," Nel toasted.

Gabbi sipped hers conservatively. "Been hitting the sauce hard lately, Skipper."

Nel shrugged. *Woman's not wrong. No sense denying it, it's how I deal. Or don't.*

"Piper?" the cook guessed.

Another shrug. "Piper, the rest. And being this close to the High. Brings back things. Things I'd rather stay lost."

Gabbi nodded. "You and the captain both. Easier for him. He can forget."

"Doesn't have much choice," Nel said glumly. "Been going that way since he took me on."

"He took us all on."

"He does that. Bleeding heart of a man."

"Aye, good man, our captain."

"To the captain." Nel raised her drink, not bothering to toast. This one was almost gone—she started looking around for another. The sailor she'd eyeballed earlier was still there. Not the sharpest one if he were looking for them. Big and dumb. Gabbi's type.

Gabbi, now there's an idea . . .

"Care for an admirer?" Nel asked the other woman.

"Not even a little." Gabbi drank deep. "The men can go sod themselves. My drowned kitchen wench state is not my finest hour."

Nel coughed, suppressing a laugh and almost choking on her beer.

"And sod you too, Skipper."

Nel grinned. "Never leave me, Gabbi, never ever leave me."

"Would if I could," Gabbi muttered. "Which one is it, anyways? Not that I care."

"The one in the corner, dark and brooding, Gabbi, just the way you like them." Nel gestured freely with her vessel.

Gabbi turned her head, resting her chin on one hand. Her snort of disdain was loud enough that several people turned to stare. "What do you take me for, woman? That fellow might be the man of my dreams after a dozen more of these but unless you're buying I've no ken to wake up next to him."

"You could have just said no, you'll hurt the poor lad's feelings."

"Poor I can live with," Gabbi said. "Known nothing but poor men in my whole life. But lad . . . you're being generous, Skipper, and whatever comes after generous. That lad is out to pasture, not fit for . . ."

"All right, you've made your point," Nel kicked at her friend. "Save me from filthy-minded galley wenches."

"You're a wench, Skipper," Gabbi sulked. "Just because you're miserable Castor Sharpe is long since gone is no reason to drag me down into your wallowing."

Nel rolled her eyes. "Sharpe? Hells, you don't all still feed that rumour, do you?"

"Aye, we do, Skipper, believe me we do," Gabbi grinned evilly.

"Last drink I buy you," Nel warned her.

"Didn't buy me this one, believe you still owe for it."

"Find your own then."

"Aye, I will," Gabbi agreed, casting her eye around the room.

"I was referring to the drink, wench."

"And that's why you'll be an old maid of a wench, Skipper," Gabbi ignored her. "Oh, now there's a lad I could rest my head against. Goodness, but he's a pretty one, Skipper. What do you think?"

Nel almost laughed but followed Gabbi's pointing finger. The woman wasn't subtle.

"Aw, hells . . ."

"What?"

"Hells, Gabbi," Nel whispered, knowing her face must have turned chalk-white.

"What?" Gabbi looked at her, sudden concern writ over her face.

What to say, what to tell her? Hells. Hells, hells, hells!

"We need to go." Nel bit down on her lip.

"Why?" The woman's eyes widened, the man she'd pointed out momentarily swallowed up in the crowd. Nel kept her head down, letting her hood cover her face.

"Nel, you didn't," Gabbi's voice was mixed between reproach and admiration. "Never saw you as the type. Is that boy even old enough to shave?"

"He's not . . ." Nel caught herself just in time. "No, not that. Was in here before asking about me."

Gabbi leaned back, eyebrows rising. "Nel, have you been . . ."

"Damnit, woman, get your mind out of the gutter. He's Alliance, use your damned eyes. Asking after us, the ship. You know what that means!"

"Oh, hells . . ." Gabbi's eyes went as wide as dinner plates now.

Nel's hand shot out and grabbed her friend's shoulder, hard, hard enough to make her wince.

"You're sure? Nel, are you absolutely sure?" Gabbi's voice quivered now, her lower lip trembled.

"Sure, aye, I'm sure. It's him. He's Alliance. Look under the coat, can see the whites of his uniform. Damned fool," she shook her head angrily, "wasn't even smart enough to change out of it. Thought I . . ."

But no, couldn't think about that now. Just had to get out of here, before he saw them. Before he recognised her.

Because that would be all kinds of trouble.

Nel hadn't moved her hand yet. She kept it there, feeling Gabbi squirm and shift under her grip. The woman wanted to run, to bolt right out of the tavern and head for safety. So did Nel. But they had to be smart. For all their sakes.

"Give me your vessel, Gabbi," she said through gritted teeth, leaning close. "Raise it up, here next to mine."

Gabbi did as she was told, the liquid frothing and swirling at the rim. Her hand was shaking.

With a grin as forced as it must have looked, Nel knocked their drinks together and brought hers to parched lips.

"Drink up, damnit," she said over the rim. Gabbi didn't need encouragement there, gulping the contents and slamming the empty vessel down on the bar. The bang she made shouldn't have stood out any more than the racket everyone else was making.

Only the racket and clangour had died down to a murmur. The silence that caused all of Nel's joints to seize up and her blood take a chill. She expected to find all eyes on her.

But no one was looking at her. It was like some dreadful puppet pantomime: two stooped and struggling figures labouring under the weight of a hardwood cask. The height of a small man and wrapped in metal hoops, the barrel would have been rolled along the floor by anyone right in the head. The two Draugr were carrying it, backs bent in a way that would have been torture if they'd been able to feel it. Yet they carried their burden in a crab-like manner, oblivious to the attention they were receiving. A nervous server opened up the bar to give them access to the backroom behind the bar.

"Skipper," Gabbi spoke in no more than a whisper.

"Hush, Gabbi," Nel said, watching the room. There were dark grumblings making themselves heard. She could make out the more aggressive ones, those far gone in drink, those who did their thinking with their fists.

Damn, won't take much. When did it get this bad?

There was the one she wanted to avoid, all grave and serious, watching like everyone else.

So serious in your neatly pressed uniform. They teach you that in the High Lanes along with how to salute an admiral just so? Least you're watching the show and not me. Just keep watching the show now.

Someone stepped between the Draugr and the dubious safety of the bar. Knuckles cracking and a rosy tint to their cheeks, flush from a day's drinking. The Draugr stopped their slow delivery, two grey and sagging heads turning to look at the belligerent obstacle.

"Come on," Nel said, shoving her empty drink away. "We're leaving. Get up, lean against me, but don't you dare run, Gabbi, don't you dare."

She threw an arm around her friend's shoulders, just two drunken friends headed home. That was all they were. All anyone should see. Voices were rising, high pitched. The staff were protesting. For all the good it would do against the ugly mood of the crowd. She risked a quick look around, couldn't find the man who'd spooked Gabbi, and her, she had to admit.

Alliance, here and asking about us. That tears it. Captain's not going to like this. Hells. Hells, hells, hells!

Because like it or not, it was time to leave Port Border, paying run or no. A cold hand was twisting its fingers through her insides now.

We're going to struggle. Just have to stretch to the next stop and start praying.

But that was a problem for tomorrow. For now she had to leave without drawing attention to herself.

Splinters and splashing behind them. The sound of a ruptured beer barrel hitting the floor behind them. There was a collective groan from the patrons that escalated into a roar.

"Now you can run!" Nel pushed Gabbi in front of her, driving for the door. She ducked low as a plate went over her head to shatter against the wall. She threw a shoulder into a woman that got too close, sending her reeling into the man behind her. The man swung and missed, hitting a troll with a glancing blow. The troll responded as all trolls would have. They had just cleared the door before the brawl enveloped the whole tavern.

GABBI'S SHOPPING LIST was short. Not only short, but bland, boring, unappetising. Jack was unimpressed. Not only was Jack unimpressed, Bandit had picked up on the mood. The loompa still hadn't settled on a new partner, alternating between Violet and Jack most of the time but occasionally venturing further afield, sounding out the skipper and Quill. The skipper shooed him off most days but for some reason Quill tolerated the small, furry presence in a way he never had previously. For short periods at least. Bandit had attached himself to the captain once but a disagreement over the man's hat had seen the end of that.

"Need meat," was Jack's summary, echoed by the loompa.

"Ain't got no meat on the list," Violet repeated.

"Still need it."

"Ain't got no money for meat, Jack."

Jack grunted. Then, loudly, "Shopkeep, how much for Kitsune tails?"

"Jack!" Violet snapped at him, twisting to keep her tails well away from her Korrigan shipmate.

"How much?" Jack repeated.

"Trading in such . . . items is restricted in the High Lanes," the merchant told him, clearly not wanting to be drawn into the discussion.

"Black market then? That means a lot more."

"I wouldn't know."

"Who would then? Who do I ask?"

"Jack!" Violet kicked the Korrigan, who was half a head shorter than her, hard in the shin. He didn't feel it.

"What?" He sounded annoyed.

"Eyes off my tails."

"You got two of 'em. Why all the fuss? They grow back anyways."

"They don't grow nothing so you shut your mouth or I'll shut it for you." She handed over the list to the vendor, glaring at Jack the whole time.

"This all?" the merchant asked.

"It's what I got," Violet said.

"No credit. Show me you got the coin so I don't waste my time."

Violet upended the purse Gabbi had given her onto the counter. The small collection of coins spilled out. Gabbi had counted them out exactly before sending them on their errand. Bandit made the jump to her shoulder, peering down at all the shiny coins. She slapped his hand when he made to reach for one.

"You don't have enough."

"What do you mean? We counted it up!" Violet objected indignantly.

"For the jams and syrups. Maybe the salted vegetables. But not the pickled ones, the grain, or the cheeses. Not at today's price."

Violet glared. "We made this order yesterday! This is just the pickup."

The merchant shrugged. "Price is what it is."

Jack whispered something about the black market again.

"Price don't change between order and delivery," Violet said indignantly. "You're trying to short me."

"If you don't like it, you can go somewhere else."

"Ain't going nowhere else, ain't got nowhere else to go." Violet could hear her own voice rising and found she didn't care. The merchant looked at her in annoyance, perhaps surprise. "I go anywhere, I'm coming back with some fancy folks on account of you trying to swindle me."

"Swindle?" Jack growled, taking an interest for the first time.

"Nobody is trying to swindle anyone, girl!" The merchant was getting agitated now.

"I says you are!" Violet slapped her hand down on Gabbi's list. "That your signature? That your price? And now you're saying it's not?"

"The market has . . ."

"A bargain is a bargain," Violet said stubbornly. "And we struck a bargain."

Jack pushed at the list with one thick finger, glaring up from under his gnarled brows. "That right, merchant? You trying to hustle her?"

"I am doing no such thing."

"On account of her being a girl and not knowing no better?" Jack grabbed the list, waving it in front of the man's face.

"Oi!" Violet protested. Bandit added his shriek of protest, making the jump from Jack to the bench top.

The merchant recoiled from the flailing loompa in alarm. "What's it doing? Get that thing away!"

"Thinks you're trying to hustle us," Jack said. "He don't like that."

"There is no hustling taking place!" the man insisted. He looked up nervously. They were beginning to draw a crowd. Bandit began to jump about on the bench, stamping his feet angrily.

"Can't lie to a loompa," Jack told him. "Can smell a lie. Everyone knows that."

"Want what's on my list." Violet snatched the paper off of Jack and thrust it at the shopkeeper. "For what we agreed on."

"Fine, fine," the man capitulated. "Just get that thing away from my store."

"STILL NEED SALT," Violet said, looking up from the list at the barrow of goods they'd left with.

"Then you go get some." The muscles on Jack's low-swinging

arms bunched as he lifted the barrow up, almost to eye height for him. The irony of being short and squat.

"Don't get lost on your way back, Jack," Violet stuck out her tongue.

"Don't lose your tails," he replied. "Still wanna sell them one day."

"Sell you if I could."

"You can't." Jack cocked his head at Bandit. "Me or her?"

Bandit bobbed up and down, peering intently at the barrel of goods. Then jumped to Violet's shoulder.

"Ha!" Violet grinned at Jack.

"Not smart, Bandit." Jack sounded disappointed. "Always go where the food is."

He set off towards the docks with his delivery. Bandit watched him, making forlorn chirping sounds.

"Too late now," Violet told him, feeling him tense on her shoulder. "You're stuck with me now."

Bandit twisted to face her and patted her awkwardly on the head.

"Come on, you big lug."

Gabbi hadn't give her specific instructions about where to find the salt traders but it didn't take her much asking to find. Turned out there was just the one in Port Border. That wasn't so good. A lone trader meant a monopoly and she needed to negotiate. Nor did she have much to negotiate with, doubling her woes.

The trader was to be found in one of the warehouse districts, inland from the waterfront ports. It meant trekking past some familiar streets, those where she'd seen all the Draugr and golems. She paused at the turnoff she knew led that way.

More than paused, stood there so long Bandit dismounted and stared up at her from street level.

"I'm thinking, I'm thinking," Violet told him, tucking her thumbs into her belt and chewing on her own lip. She was of more than half a mind to head back to the warehouse. The longer she thought the less certain she was of what she'd seen. Quill's words were playing in her head.

She turned away with a sigh, towards the salt trader, knowing she'd be back this way. Wasn't smart, she knew, pushing her luck and snooping around Alliance folk, but the doubt was gnawing at her something fierce. First things first, though.

Salt trader weren't what she thought it would be. She'd been to one before, with Gabbi. Local market one, stall and pots, where they sold salt by the handful. This one was different. Big fence, tall buildings. She could see mounds of what looked like white sand crystals rising over the fencing and between the canopy. Canopy itself was huge, big tarred canvas pulled over the salt to keep the wind and rain off. Wouldn't do to get the merchandise wet, though Violet was at a loss as to why it wasn't kept indoors. The nearby buildings were obviously owned by the same folk. Unless they were full of it and this was the overflow.

Truth be told, Violet felt a bit weak at the knees at it all. Rich folk, haughty traders and all. She'd been hoping for someone like the last vendor, someone for whom getting yelled at and by was just part of the finer points of negotiating. These folks were more likely to kick her onto the street and slam the door if she got too uppity.

Best get it over with then.

There were steps to climb, a half dozen or so, to an imposing brick-faced building. It was domed, not square cut like most buildings in Port Border. Not thatched with straw nor tiled, but pressed stone, holding itself up like a bridge would. It was an oddity that stood out in the urban landscape.

And she'd not gone two steps up when Violet realised something even odder.

Her feet were wet.

There was a steady stream of water running down the steps. Cold, even icy to the touch. In fact, there were small chunks of ice in the flow, being carried out onto the street only to melt in the midday sun.

What the hells is going on here?

The sound of commotion began to wash over her as well. As Violet reached the top of the steps, she saw people running around like so many headless chickens. And there was the source of the water, the domed structure was only the top. Stairs led down, deep underground and carved into the earth. The straw saved from thatching the dome had been press-ganged into service, stuffed into all nooks and crannies and cavities, all to provide a protective layer around the . . . ice?

The dome was full of ice, a massive underground room full of half-melted ice. A handful of workers were shin-deep in the sleet, hauling buckets and pouring them out into the street.

The bucket brigade were all Draugr, Violet noted through narrowing eyes. The only other person present, a Chrol.

Ugly, big bruiser. Looks like the back end of a grandpa pig. So grey he's almost blue. And those tusks . . . are those his teeth, how does he eat? Violet realised she was staring, also that the Chrol was staring back.

"What's you looking at?"

The tusks moved. Lower jaw. Violet found her head moved up and down in time with them, bobbing as the Chrol talked.

"That's amazing," she said, turning quickly to stand at the top of the stairs. A Draugr promptly emptied a bucket of glacially cold water over her feet. She squealed and jumped. The Draugr stared, puzzled.

"What happened?" she asked, darting between the Chrol and the ice cellar. It looked immense, several times the size of the dome. The melted water inside was maybe as deep as waist high, wet stalks pulled free from the walls floating on top. Maybe half the space was still taken up by cut ice blocks, each half the size of Violet herself.

"It's melting. Why is it melting? Should it be melting? Is that what you want?"

The Chrol stared. He looked confused. Maybe he wasn't so smart. Ah, the doors, that was the problem.

Violet crouched down in front of them, shivering as her tail dipped into the water. They were double doors, one wrenched off at the hinges. That was why the ice was melting, must have happened a while ago. The metal twisted and blackened. No . . . not wrenched. Blown, exploded. Someone had used black powder or maybe even . . . yes, there were shards of broken glass scattered around the base. Only not glass, crystal, thaumatically charged crystal.

Violet twisted to face the Chrol. "Someone doesn't like you." It came out like a song. That was bad.

Hadn't meant to sing. Still need to buy salt. Should probably mention that.

"I need to buy salt. Do I talk to you? Are you the one I talk to? Because if you're not I should go talk to the salt man. Is it you?"

"Go away."

"That's rude." Violet made a face. "Who broke your door?"

"People who not like them," the Chrol said, waving a hand at the bucket brigade behind her.

"People don't like Draugr?" Violet said.

"Why are you still here?" the Chrol asked.

"Need to buy salt, said so. Weren't you listening?"

"You see that?" the Chrol growled around his formidable tusks. Violet still couldn't stop staring at them. "Warehouse is flooded. Bad. Boss be very angry. Very. Ice melt. Melting. Melting fast."

Violet shrugged. "You still have salt. Can I buy some?"

The Chrol gave a huge sigh, the jowls around his magnificent tusks shuddering. "How much salt?"

"A bag, maybe two. No, two, Gabbi said two. Two should be enough."

"Two?"

"Is that too much?"

The Chrol bristled, stabbing a finger at the mounds of salt in the fenced area. "Sell by wagon! Not by bag. Not! You waste time, no time for you. None!"

The Chrol pushed one of the Draugr by the shoulder, causing it to stagger and nearly spill the bucket it was holding. The water sloshed around as the Draugr regained its footing. "Faster, water must go. Bucket faster."

Water must make it melt faster, Violet thought. *Sod him though, all I wanted was some salt to take back to Gabbi.*

"Don't see what the big deal is," she said aloud. "Spend half a run scraping ice off the hull anyway. Can't get rid of the stuff."

"Huh?" The Chrol stared. "You what?"

"Nothing. We'll just be going then."

"Wait, you wait." The Chrol reached for her only to snatch his hand back when Bandit bared his teeth.

"You have ship? You ship girl?"

"Yeah, I got ship," Violet said cautiously.

"Got mascot too. That good, lucky. Mascot lucky."

Lucky. Better you than me, Bandit, for once.

"Cold ship," the Chrol went on. It was like watching him pull on a string. Clearly he'd had an idea, he just hadn't got there yet. "You have ship, run cold."

"Yes . . ." Violet waited for him to finish.

"You want salt, good, fine, give you salt. Lots of salt. And ice."

"Don't want ice."

"Everybody want ice. Ice hard to get. Good Draugr work. Good price. You take."

"It's all melted," Violet pointed out.

"Not this. This ruined. You get new ice. Good ice. Take to buyer. I win, you win, everybody happy. And salt. You get salt too."

Violet looked at Bandit. Was the Chrol saying what she thought he was? Bandit didn't offer any answers.

"What buyer?"

The Chrol told her.

Chapter 5

Here we are again, Violet thought. *All done for the day, been a good day, a real good day.* She couldn't wait to get back and tell the captain. And the skipper. Especially the skipper. Just the thought made her grin. Skipper was going to spray her drink when she heard. So long as she didn't do nothing stupid between now and then.

Like walk down a certain dark alley. Not really an alley. More like a street. Maybe a promenade. Whatever a promenade was. Fancy word for street, isn't it?

Could just walk on by again, just head on back to the ship. Ought to do that, nought down that way but trouble and asking for it. Asking for it. Questions. Questions were for answering. Weren't they?

Violet sucked in a deep breath, tasted all dust and gritty. Thumbs hitched into her belt, loompa on her shoulder. *All indecisive. What was that word for when you felt like you'd been in a moment before?*

Should go back to the captain. Tell him about the job. Make sure he don't forget about the job. Only . . .

Hells.

Violet chose the path that went towards the warehouse, where the Draugr and golems were kept. Her feet carried her faster the further she went, like they were afraid she might change her mind. Bandit didn't like the pace and dove for the ground, scampering along beside her. The streets here were mostly empty so she didn't worry he might get stepped on.

And there it was: her destination, her target, her goal. The building she'd spied on the other day, full of golems and Draugr and Alliance uniforms.

"Now how do we get in?" she said aloud. The barnlike doors at the front were shut, probably barred too. She didn't see anyone on watch like she had last time but there was certain to be some inside. Hard not to notice doors like that being opened.

She found Bandit had left her. A moment of cursing before she found him again, in the shadow of the warehouse, the mouth of an alleyway. Running on all fours, he looked back towards Violet, for approval perhaps or maybe to see if she was just watching, before running full tilt into the unlit passage.

There was still no one watching but Violet made the dash across the street as fast as she could, feeling guilty and watched, heart pounding in her chest. She expected a shout of discovery but none came.

Bandit was looking down at her from refuse piled in the alley. Discarded barrels and pallets, mostly scrap lumber, probably awaiting collection. And conveniently providing an aid to reach the open second storey doorway set into the side of the building. Bandit made the jump look easy, pulling himself up onto the doorway platform. It took Violet longer, once she was confident the pile of wood scrap wouldn't collapse under her.

The second storey doorway was some sort of loading point. One that doubled as a refuse dumping site. There were more barrels stacked up by the opening, all she could see as her eyes adjusted to the inside lighting. Some looked to be empty, waiting to be rolled out. Others were still full and sealed. Bits and pieces of Alliance paraphernalia, flags and the like. A couple of boxes of neatly pressed uniforms, some blank sea journals, even a signaller. It was half the size of what the *Tantamount* had, all polished and shiny but the colours were wrong.

"You hear that?" she asked Bandit. The loompa gave her wide eyes but no answer.

There was almost no sound coming from the warehouse, no voices or footsteps, no sounds of business or any kind of life. Just a heavy stillness. Violet could hear her own and Bandit's breathing.

But from outside there was a commotion building. It was an angry hum, getting louder by the second. Like bees.

Violet held a finger to her lips, which Bandit imitated with careful precision. Until the finger went up his nose.

"Come on," Violet sighed. She set out, keeping low and hunched over, looking for a gap between the upper level packing through which she could see the ground floor.

What she saw only confirmed her suspicions. The warehouse was empty. Empty of people, at least. There were still rows and rows of Draugr, standing silently around the edge of the lower floor. Some were seated—on the ground, on crates, a few on actual benches. There was a handful of sleeping mats too, though not nearly enough for all of them. Violet tried to recall whether Draugr slept. She didn't remember Stoker or any of those from Thatch ever doing it. But then they were different.

Weren't they?

The golems were at the back, where it was darkest. Violet started to work her way towards them cautiously, staying high and out of sight from below. No sense being careless.

At the far end of the building, opposite the barn doors, there was an overhang with a ladder. The golems were all lined up underneath, meaning she'd have to descend to inspect them any closer. And if it turned out she was right . . . that was no good thing.

"Want to go look for me?" Violet whispered to Bandit. He gave her more wide eyes but no suggestion he had any such desire.

"Me neither."

Crawling to the edge of the platform seemed the safest compromise. Flat to the floor, hands holding onto the skirting, she ducked her head over and under, peering at the golems from upside down.

And there it was, just as she'd first seen. An obsidian golem, solid and foreboding. Nestled between two mechanical contraptions.

Bandit's head appear beside her, hand raised, rock in hand. He must have picked it up from outside and carried it in. Before she could stop him, Bandit threw. He hit the brass golem to the right, the clanging sound of rock on metal echoing around the warehouse. Bandit shrieked at the noise, only adding to the cacophony.

"Hells, Bandit!" Violet grabbed him by the scruff of the neck, standing up and twisting around in alarm. Surely someone would have heard that.

The whole warehouse did. In a silent mass shuffle, the Draugr, those not already standing, came to their feet and began to congregate towards the doors. The silence didn't last long as the golems themselves began to join the movement. Brass cogs and gears began whirring to life, steam and smoke started to fill the building. The automatons moved with more precision than the Draugr but with less regard, pushing the labourers aside indifferently as they moved towards the doors. Doors that were barred shut. Soon the sound of straining timber could be heard over the gears. The door held for a moment, but only until two of the golems backed up and rammed it together.

The whole building shook, including the upper level. Violet stumbled and lost her footing, tumbling towards the ground. She grabbed at the edge and managed to slow herself, swinging awkwardly from one hand before falling on the dirt amidst a crowd of Draugr streaming towards the outside. She started to curl up and cover her face to protect herself from being trampled. Then she saw the obsidian golem coming towards her. And it wasn't moving mindlessly like all the others in the warehouse. It was reaching for her.

She couldn't get up, not with the crowding Draugr. Where were they all coming from? All she could do was scoot away, trying to get her feet under her. Onyx, for it had to be the same golem, reached out for her with one hand, only a few feet away now. Violet flailed, desperate for anything she could grab. She found an arm, a solid, wood-like arm. Draugr. She held on for dear life, and the Draugr dragged her along with it, barely slowing. It pulled her out of Onyx's immediate reach so the golem quickened its pace and made to lunge at her.

Until Bandit launched himself at the golem, shrieking all the while, landing firmly on its head. It could have been an accident, it most probably was, but as the loompa clung to the golem's face his hands perfectly covered those red eyes. His small clawed limbs found the eye sockets perfect handholds and refused to let go. Onyx stopped coming for her, halting while Draugr pushed past, reaching up to rip off the annoying creature. Only the design of its arms seemed to limit their range of motion. Onyx couldn't quite reach Bandit, not with the loompa ducking and weaving atop, still covering the eyes.

Violet used the Draugr she had latched onto to haul herself to her feet. When she let go of them it was like a spring. They barrelled into several other bodies, taking them all down in a heap. Violet jumped over them, hoping they'd slow Onyx. Hoping they wouldn't get hurt in the slowing of it down.

"Bandit, let's go!" she yelled over her shoulder. For once the loompa was in full agreement, vaulting from the head of the golem to safety. Only he didn't make it to safety. Violet's heart lurched, her feet skidding to a stop. Bandit had slipped, his feet sliding off the smooth purchase on the golem's head. He didn't make the distance before the golem's hand snapped out and plucked him from the air.

"No!" Violet ran at the golem, throwing herself onto its arm. She gasped as the swinging arm knocked the breath from her lungs. The impact stunned her. Wherever she had touched the black-rock golem her skin felt numb, thousands of tiny prickling needles stabbing into her. Like touching Quill or Gabbi when they used their power, only ten times worse. There was no give, no sag in the arm even once she latched. Onyx was able to swing both her and Bandit around as if they weighed nothing. But the golem tried to let go of Bandit to grab onto her, with the same hand. The second she saw Onyx's fingers uncurl, Violet let go too—she couldn't have held on anyway—but she grabbed for the loompa instead, snaring him in the crook of her elbow. The golem's motion sent them flying straight at the wall; Violet curled up around Bandit and squeezed her eyes shut.

Everything hurt. Violet opened her eyes, not realising they'd been shut. Everything was grey, kind of hazy. No focus and no colour. Bandit struggled in her arms, kicking and scratching to get free. She relaxed her grip but he drew blood before she sat up. The pain made her gasp, blinking rapidly. Bright and vivid red against her skin. Not just the one cut, half a dozen, shards of broken glass covered them both.

Glass?

She was outside. The golem had thrown her right through the window; glass, panes, and timber. Violet was lying in what remained. No wonder she hurt all over. Through the shattered window she could see Onyx, pressed up against the wall, staring at her. There were no tiny hands to cover those eyes now. Violet tried to stand, unable to look away from those blood red eyes. She had the sensation of falling, cold, then her legs gave out under her and she dropped back to earth, eyes to the dirt.

When she looked back up, there were people all around, yelling and screaming, waving torches and makeshift weapons. There was smoke. The warehouse was on fire. And barely a second look for a beaten Kitsune girl.

Violet staggered to her feet, one step falling into the next. Pushing her way into the crowd, letting the masses swallow her up.

CROWDS WERE BAD. It was a rule that Nel held hard and fast to. The proverb was between the devil and the deep, and personally, Nel would rather be caulking the devil seam than find herself with a crowd between her and the *Tantamount*. To say nothing of the riot still raging behind her and Gabbi. The brawl had spread from the tavern almost as fast as they could put distance between them. Felt like half the city was involved now so maybe it hadn't started at the tavern. And there were fires. Fires were very bad. One more reason to start laying sail. It had all gone to the black and if Nel got her way so would the *Tantamount*. Metaphors aside, the city was one big tinderbox.

"Gods . . . blast it . . . and damnation . . . woman," Gabbi wheezed next to her, leaning one arm against a shack wall. Her face was red and her cheeks were pillowing out, gasping for air. "Slow down. I don't have your thrice-damned unnatural stalk-legs! Gods!"

"Sorry, Gabbi," Nel apologised, not really paying her much mind. She checked behind but it seemed they were safe from the ongoing turmoil further inland.

"No you ain't," Gabbi sulked. "The hells got into you? You just enjoy making me miserable. Jack, where you been?"

"Godsdamnit, Jack," Nel started, looking back over her shoulder. The Korrigan sailor was there all right, carting a barrow full of sundries. The barrow lacked a wheel, as evidenced by the gouged trail in the muddy street from Jack pushing it like a sled.

"What . . ." Gabbi paused to gather her wits, "what took you so long? You shoulda been back an age ago."

"Got held up." Jack flicked his head, tossing a matted braid over his shoulder.

"You hurt anyone?" Gabbi asked him pointedly.

"Dunno. Might have been they were somebody."

"Don't think anyone is like to know the difference right now," Nel told them both.

"Where's Vi? She was with you," Gabbi said, making Nel wince. Violet was out there?

"Went to get the salt. Didn't have none at the shop."

"Alone, Jack? You let her go alone?"

"Course not. Bandit went with her." Jack's tone was sulky.

"That don't count!" Gabbi cried.

"Not now, Gabbi. Maybe she's back on the ship already," Nel said. "I'm more worried about all those people in front of her."

Jack squinted. "Looks like a delivery, got cargo with 'em."

"Yeah, except we ain't expecting no cargo," Nel said.

"Maybe the captain fixed us up with something."

"Maybe." Nel kept the rest of her thoughts to herself. "Let's go find out."

There was a growing pile of shipping on the loading dock next to the *Tantamount*. Crates, sacks, and, oddly enough, bales of hay. A few trade actuaries made up the better-dressed part of the crowd, followed by the captain, Quill, and a few other crew members. The rest were dockside labour with a handful of Draugr thrown in. The Draugr caught her attention. A number of them were covered in burns, reddened and blistered flesh, particularly their hands and forearms. Some of the labourers had the same injuries but to a much lesser degree. Had they come through the fires? Didn't seem to make sense.

The captain called out to them as they approached. "Nel, good to see you, good to see all of you, Gabbi, Jack. Capital. And just in time."

"Which one of you started the riot?" Quill inquired. Nel glared. It was a stupid thing to say in front of clients. Which from the animated way the captain was behaving was what she concluded the crowd was.

Beside her, Jack grinned widely. There was blood staining his teeth. She hadn't noticed before, but he had fresh bruises too. For all she knew, maybe he had started the riot. She wouldn't put it past him. Quill made a sound of disgust but he and Jack moved a few feet away to discuss something. Gabbi went with them, perhaps to keep the peace. No, that was wishful thinking. More likely she was getting her barbs into Quill as well. Bizarrely, she saw Bandit riding Quill's shoulder. Stranger and stranger.

"Captain?" Nel saluted, every appearance the obedient officer.

"Ah, Nel, yes. Yes, this good man, well one of them at least, has come to finalise the agreements for our next run. All very official, payment of half up front, we like that. Bill of lading just needing a scratch and then we can begin." The captain beamed at her.

A run? Hells, Horatio found something?

"Aye, sir. A moment, if you will?" She nodded respectfully to the traders before turning her back on them and leaning closer to the captain. "What have we got here, Captain? What's the run?"

"Salt, my dear. Glorious salt." Horatio rubbed his hands together gleefully. "And half up front! Marvellous!"

"The salt?" In some parts, salt was as good as coin; some planets used it as currency. Wars had been fought over salt mines and flats.

Didn't Jack say Violet had gone for salt?

"No, the coin. Even better, don't you think?"

Nel considered the cargo. "So . . . that's all of it? Captain, it's not much."

"No, not all, not all at all, Nel. The salt is only the first stage. We load up on the salt, very important. And the straw, one cannot forget the straw, my dear. Then we ship out towards the Glassy Run."

"What's that? The Glassy Run?"

"A river, more accurately, a tributary running down mountains to a lakeside village. Not more than day or so, by Quill's guess."

"Need a lot of salt, do they?" Nel was sceptical.

"Indeed, that is to say, some. In fact, not a lot. Most of that salt will be leaving with us."

"I'm confused, Captain," Nel said politely. *Captain's got a run, which means we're getting paid. Can afford to be polite.*

"Naturally, my dear. I was too when our good friends the salt merchants first arrived. But you see there is the beauty of this run."

"The Glassy Run?"

"And you know what that is, Nel?"

"I'm rather hoping we'll get to that soon, Captain," Nel sighed.

"The village of Glassy Run does a very special run, Nel, but only for a short part of the year. Indeed, some years they may not trade at all. But when they do, they export a magnificent quantity of ice. Ice cut from the river and lake, cut into blocks to be shipped off to where all the gallant and rich reside."

Ice. Well, if that don't beat all. And we do run cold, after all. Going to be a damned miserable trip but if the coin is worth it . . .

"You know where the gallant and rich reside, Nel? Do you know?"

Nel studied the captain. He was happy. Bouncing on the balls of his feet happy. So he knew something. Where did the gallant and rich reside? The answer was, of course, wherever their comforts or pleasures took them.

Pleasures . . .

"Vice? You got us a run to Vice?" She couldn't help but start to grin herself. After what she'd seen in the tavern, she'd been prepared to push the captain on leaving, hard as that would be without paying work. And here was the answer to all her problems, served up on loaded dice.

"Vice indeed, my dear, we have our run. But it wasn't me, I had nothing to do with this job."

"Who then?"

The captain scratched at his head. "I do believe it was Violet. I'm quite taken with our stowaway, Nel, quite taken. I do believe we'll keep her on after all."

Nel stared, both relieved and bewildered. *Violet? How'd that happen?*

"Where is she?" Nel asked.

"Oh," the captain said. "Then she's not with you?"

"Buy you a drink?"

The voice startled Violet. She hadn't expected anyone to actually talk to her. The streets were filled with rioters, angry mobs smashing and looting. She wasn't sure what had set them off or why it was still going on. What was interesting to her was that while she'd seen a lot of opportunistic looting on the street, all the taverns and watering holes seemed off limits. At least this one was. She'd snuck in rather than go straight back to the

Tantamount. Too dangerous until she knew if she was being followed—didn't want to lead Onyx straight back there. Who knows what would happen. The golem didn't have its master around anymore. Maybe it would just stay in the warehouse. Or maybe it would never stop. Maybe it would chase her for the rest of her life.

What am I thinking? Building collapsed on it. Caught fire and collapsed. A whole damned building dropped on it. Take it days to dig itself out, if that were even possible. My head . . .

Her head was pounding. Everything else had settled into a dull ache but her head felt like it had an angry badger trying to claw its way out.

That was what happened, right? Or maybe Onyx just hadn't found her because it was still chasing Bandit. She'd lost sight of him back in the crowds.

"Look," the stranger said, slumping down on the bench opposite her, "it's a mess out there. It's cold, I'm lonely, and if you don't share this with me, I'll drink it all me self."

"Lots to drink." Violet nudged the foaming pitcher with one finger. "Would get awful drunk on yourself." She noticed her hands were still tingling. Splinters and sawdust clung to her fingertips from where she'd been scratching at the table. Her random skein of lines and curves that made her look away.

"Aye," he said, pouring the first of two tankards he'd brought. "So you'll help me then?"

Violet made a face. "Don't drink."

"Then this promises to be an unhappy ending for me," he sighed. "At least promise you'll put me back on me barstool when I fall off."

Violet uncurled from where she sat, back against the wall in the darkest corner with the best view. She didn't feel cornered. Her new drinking companion wasn't much older than her, or bigger. Thin, wiry, with mousy hair and crooked teeth. He didn't look like a bad sort. If she were any judge.

"All right," she conceded.

"That's something," he said. He reached across the table, offering his hand. "I'm Gravel."

"Really?" Violet was amused.

He shrugged. "Grew up in a mining camp. Got another name, just don't recall what."

"Fall off your barstool?"

He grinned at her. It was a nice smile, despite the crooked teeth.

"I'm Vi," she allowed.

"Just Vi? Sounds short."

"You calling me short, sailor?"

"Guilty, Miss Vi." He held up his hand, showing the braided rope tattoo on his right palm. "Saw yours too. Figured you weren't a local."

"Don't care for the locals?"

"Not for what they're doing out there. You been in town long, Miss Vi?"

"Too long," Violet nodded.

"I hear work is scarce for folks," Gravel nodded.

"Not for you though?" Violet asked.

"Naw, steady employer, is mine. Hard captain but never had to worry about the next job."

Gravel leaned forward, hands on the table in front of him. "I hear it's cause of them Draugr."

"What about them?"

"Taking all the jobs, all the work."

Violet rolled her eyes. "That's stupid."

"Is it?"

"Yeah," Violet insisted. "Draugr can't sail or trade. Can't bake bread or lay bricks. You ever seen one farm or fish or do a hundred other things?"

Gravel leaned further in, conspiratorially. "But there is stuff they can do. And then regular folk get used to not doing that, only now there aren't enough Draugr to do all those jobs people don't do no more and folk won't do them. So there's no jobs. And people say it's all cause of the Draugr."

Violet stared. "You talk too much."

And she was regretting not taking that drink now.

"Ah, well, you could share the burden with me perhaps. Tell me what a nice girl like you is doing in a mud hole like this?" Gravel asked.

"Really?" Violet asked. "That's the best you can do?"

"Alas, it is. Never had no schooling to learn the fancy ways of talking."

Violet sighed. "And what makes you think I'm a nice girl?"

"Always been a believer in the inherent niceness of girls, love."

"My da wouldn't have agreed with you," Violet told him, putting her elbows on the table and leaning forward. "Sold me off, he did, soon as I was old enough to walk and talk back to him. Couldn't have none of that, so I had to go."

Gravel blinked at her. "Go where?"

Violet traced a circle with her finger in front of him. "Where all bad little girls whose families don't want them end up. A High Lanes workhouse. Spent my childhood sweeping floors and collecting cinders for the rag-and-bone man. At night they'd send us down to the river to look for drowned bodies and search their pockets for coins.

"When I got older, I started hiding some of those coins, keeping them for myself. Snuck out early one morning and paid my way onto a trader bound for I didn't know where. Didn't care, neither. Had some trouble with another passenger. Didn't go well."

Gravel stared at her over the rim of his tankard. "Man trouble?"

"What?" Violet frowned. "No, woman trouble. Primrose thought I stole her purse, slit the bottom, and emptied it all out."

"And did you?"

"Of course I did, but she didn't know that. Just being spiteful. Captain wanted to throw me off at the next port. If not there, into the black, except one of the other passengers spoke up for me. Never knew him before then but probably wouldn't have known anyone else after if he hadn't."

"Why he'd do that?"

"He was a Guildsman," Violet said, warming to her story. "And you know the thing about them, what everyone says?"

"No," her audience shrugged. "Never heard nothing about them, have to say."

"No?" Violet sat back down. "What do you mean, no?"

"Little fish like me don't swim in your big ponds, Miss Vi. Just keep to ourselves and keep our heads down. Can't say I heard much if any about this Guild of yours."

"Well . . . life was hard. Ain't no nice girl." It sounded petulant even to her.

Sod him though, who doesn't know about the Guild?

"Aye, I hear you. Grew up in a mine family. Had an uncle who was a miner, anyways. Then one day everyone went on strike. Next day there weren't no mine. Just a big hole in the ground."

"Sounds like they should have gotten some of those Draugr to do the mining," Violet suggested, not caring that she was being petty. "Might still have a mine."

"Maybe so," Gravel raised his drink, "but that's why them out there are painting this town pitchfork red.

"And speaking of red," he leaned back on the bench, waving his drink expansively, "Kaspar, my friend, come have a drink with us."

Violet couldn't help but flinch at Gravel's "friend." They were dressed in an Alliance uniform. Starched white and trims, if a little stained by smoke and sweat. The reference to red was clear, a shock of neatly clipped red hair, vivid like blood against the pale uniform. The uniform made him look older than his young years.

"Think you scared her," Gravel nodded his head. Violet glared, realising she'd pulled her feet up onto the bench in fright. She'd literally backed herself into the corner.

"It's the uniform, isn't it?" Gravel bobbed his head knowingly. "Told you, you ought not to wear it if you want to impress the womenfolk."

Kaspar gave the other such a long-suffering look of contempt Violet actually felt reassured. He sat down next to Gravel.

"You're supposed to be on duty," he said, looking uncomfortably at Violet. "Not . . . impressing the womenfolk."

"Ah, but I am on duty, on watch. Cleverly disguised, I am. Blending in," Gravel confided. "Sadly there's not much impressing going on. Allow me to introduce my sober drinking companion. This lovely young lass is Miss Vi, sir."

"Sir?" Violet gave the new arrival a questioning look. He coughed, embarrassed.

"And, Miss Vi, this esteemed gentleman is the eminent Ensign Niko Kaspar of our good ship. Or sir, as I have to call him."

"That's enough, landsman," Kaspar said firmly.

"Aye, sir."

"Are you drunk, sailor?"

"No, sir, just stupid. But I can fix that if you like, the not being drunk. Don't know no cure for stupid though, sir."

"Landsman?" Violet chuckled. Not yet a seaman, he'd spent less time on the decks than she had. Less than a year.

"Aye, that would be me, Miss."

"Sounds like you should be calling her sir, too, landsman," Kaspar suggested.

"Aye, sir," Gravel bobbed his head. "Landsman Gravel reporting for duty, Miss. Sir. Miss Sir."

"Landsman Brandon Gravel," Kaspar added, folding his arms smugly.

"Brandon?" Violet chortled.

"Aye," Gravel hiccupped, wiping his mouth with the back of one hand. "Well, we all must start somewhere."

"And finish in a tavern?" Kaspar said pointedly.

Gravel shrugged. "This is where you left me, sir, and in my defence I was left alone. Seemed as good a place as any to wait out these riots. Speaking of such, you've mussed your uniform, Niko."

Kaspar looked down at himself. Gravel reached out and ruffled his red hair, messing it up.

"Almost makes you look like a real sailor. All we need is some tar to finish off the look." He looked at his hand and started patting down the ensign's hair. Kaspar grimaced but for some reason tolerated it.

"You must feel this, Miss Vi," Gravel encouraged her. "It's all soft and fluffy, like a puppy."

"Brandon," Kaspar growled at him. Violet noticed when he got mad his face turned red like the skipper's did. It made her laugh.

"What, did I say something stupid? Is that offensive, Miss?" Gravel asked.

"I'm not offended," Violet said.

"See," Gravel said quickly. "She's not offended, why would she be offended, sir. There now, hair's all done, pretty as a picture, sir."

Violet bit her lip to keep from laughing at the picture. Kaspar's hair was far from down. Loose strands of it were waving around and standing straight up, giving him the look of a freshly awoken scarecrow. She suspected he knew this.

"We should go," Kaspar said. "Captain wants us back before dark."

"Us? He said that? He mentioned us by name?"

"All hands, Brandon," Kaspar sighed.

"One drink, Niko," Gravel insisted, reaching out to snag an

empty tankard off a passing server. With that and the two he already had, he finished pouring the last of the beer from his pitcher. "One drink, one toast, then we can go."

Kaspar sighed heavily. "Fine," he conceded defeat. "One toast."

"That's the spirit, and so is this," Gravel grinned broadly, pushing a tankard in Violet's direction. "One drink, Miss Vi. You can do that."

Violet shook her head. "Fine," she agreed. It seemed easier than arguing. Kaspar it seemed, despite being the superior officer, had long since given up.

"What's today's toast, sir?" Gravel raised his tankard halfway.

"Today's Thursday. That would be ourselves. Ourselves alone."

"Because no one else is like to care about us," Violet finished. The two boys turned to stare at her. Violet shrugged. It was an Alliance naval toast. She'd heard the skipper make it plenty of times.

"And that's why you call her sir, landsman," Kaspar said.

"Aye, but I call you that, sir, and you make boring toasts. I've a better one if you both please."

He waited until both Violet and Kaspar waved him on.

"Here's to lying, cheating, stealing, and drinking." He winked at Violet. Beside him, Kaspar winced as Gravel raised his tankard high. But he wasn't done.

"If you're going to lie, lie to save a friend." He nudged Kaspar until the other reluctantly raised his vessel too.

"If you're going to cheat, cheat death." He tapped his tankard against Kaspar's.

"If you're going to steal, steal the heart of the one you love."

He did the same to Violet's. Before he could finish, she leaned over and clinked with Kaspar.

"And if you're going to drink, drink with friends both old and new," she finished Piper's favourite toast with a wide grin. "And see you at the bottom, landsman."

The three of them raised there tankards until the bottoms showed. Tradition demanded they could only be put down empty.

Gravel finished first and turned to Kaspar. "Permission to desert ship and abscond with this woman, sir. I believe I'm in love."

"Denied, landsman," Kaspar paused his own efforts long enough to respond.

"Sorry, Miss Vi," Gravel apologised. "I fear ours is a doomed love."

Violet couldn't help the grin that threatened to split her face apart. She was at a risk of choking she was smiling so damned hard. Even the maudlin Kaspar was holding back a smirk. She was starting to feel better about the whole day. Until she saw who was standing behind the boys.

Oh, hells.

It was Quill.

The Kelpie's scowling face had been hidden until she finished drinking, gradually revealed as she lowered the tankard. Violet cringed, wishing she could blot his face out by lifting it again. That was how the skipper would have handled it.

It was almost comical, watching Kaspar and Gravel realise there was something going on behind them. Then the slow turn as something was revealed to be someone. Except that they didn't know Quill. Not yet.

"Something we can help you with there, mate?" Gravel wiped at his mouth with the back of his hand.

Quill ignored him, gesturing at Violet. "Come with me."

"She's with us," Gravel said, starting to rise.

"Perhaps she was. Now she is with me."

"Easy, Brandon." Kaspar reached out with one arm. Gravel brushed it aside, still standing between Quill and the table.

"Gravel, it's fine, I know him," Violet said quickly, coming around to stand between them before the tension could escalate any further.

"This one is drunk," Quill noted, looming over Violet. "And stupid."

"Yes, he is." Kaspar pushed Gravel firmly back down to the bench. "But in the morning he'll just be stupid."

"Stupid is and stupid does," Gravel said mulishly from the bench.

"You said you know him, Miss Vi." Kaspar didn't take his hand off Gravel's shoulder. "You're happy to leave here with him then?"

"Yes, of course, he's . . ." Violet hesitated, "he's a friend."

Quill snorted. "I am not her friend."

Violet rounded on him. "Not helping. Not helping at all!"

"We are done here, yes?" Quill grabbed her by the arm, steering her towards the door. "Let us go. There are questions at the ship you must face."

"What's with the facing, Kelpie?" Violet shook her arm free but kept up so he didn't try and manhandle her some more.

"Explain your association with those Alliance monkeys, girl."

"Least them two used my name."

"Yes, how clever of them. And of you to divulge such information. Were you at least circumspect about the name of the ship on which you so brilliantly serve? Or have you forgotten those who wear such uniforms have done us no favours of late?"

"No," Violet said, refusing to look at Quill.

"No what?" He sounded irritated. Good.

"No I ain't told them nothing. See, don't have to use so many words to say something, Quill. No."

Quill's walking gait became stiffer and faster. He bared his teeth but refused to say anything further. When he reached the crossroad beyond the tavern he stopped, looking up. Violet followed his gaze and found Bandit watching them from atop a cobbler's sign.

"Get down here, you," she called out, pointing at the ground. Bandit did so in a flying leap, his tail billowing out behind him and landing with a splash of muddy water. He looked up at Quill with his head cocked to the side. The Kelpie bared his teeth in a silent growl at the loompa, enough to deter him towards Violet.

You went to Quill? Violet thought incredulously. *Quill?*

"What's happened at the ship, Quill?" she asked as Bandit tracked mud up her clothing climbing to her shoulder.

"A discussion you can enjoy with the captain and the skipper. Though I expect you will not."

"What?" Violet winced as her hair was pulled.

"Enjoy it. It beggars the mind that it need be said at all, but do not mention our history and recent difficulties to any of the new hands either."

"History?" Violet felt a migraine coming on.

"Yes, girl."

"Don't know what you mean." A sharp pain behind the back of her eyes, gnawing at her brain.

"Grange, Rim. That Guildswoman."

"Scarlett," Violet said. "Her name is Scarlett."

"Her name *was* Scarlett," Quill snorted. "She has no use for a name now."

"No," Violet said, recalling Quill striking the woman off the deck with the ship's anchor. "No."

"And nothing of Draugr," Quill droned on. "Or that infernal man you brought back."

"Sharpe."

"A man we are well rid of."

"Thought you liked him."

"I did not."

The migraine was spreading. Quill's words weren't helping, making her think about things she didn't want to think about. Things he didn't want her to think about, but wouldn't shut up about it. So she kept thinking about them. It made no sense.

"Where's the skipper?" Violet asked.

"She did not wish to come for you," Quill said.

"And you did?" Violet was sceptical.

"I," Quill told her, "will always come for you."

Bandit jerked on her hair, pulling her face around. She found herself staring into angry little animal eyes. Right then she wanted to throttle the creature.

Kaspar manhandled his friend back into his own seat, keeping his own body planted squarely between the disappearing girl and his friend.

"Miners," he shook his head. "Can't trust a one of you with a drink in your hand."

"Ain't a miner no more, Niko." Gravel was slurring his words and sulking to boot. He thumped his chest. "Proud sailor of the Allied worlds, just like you. Like my ma would have wanted me to be."

"Thought you never knew your mother."

"It's what she would have wanted," Gravel insisted.

"She want you to go about picking fights with folk twice your size and three times as mean? Did you even see the teeth on that Kelpie, Gravel?"

"Seen bigger."

Kaspar was getting exasperated. "And I'm looking at dumber. What was all that about?"

Gravel shrugged, reaching for his drink.

"No, you've had enough." Kaspar pulled it out of reach. "All that over a girl? You just met her. She's not even your . . . your . . ."

"My what, Niko? My kind, my lot?" Gravel gave him the eye. "You gonna lecture me, Ensign? Really?"

"Guess not," Kaspar relented, realising the corner he'd talked himself into. Gravel wasn't the only one running his mouth off tonight. He gave up the argument, sinking down to the bench next to his shipmate. He ran his hand idly across the table, something scratched into the surface. He frowned. Had the girl done that?

Then Gravel muttered something he couldn't make out.

"What did you just say?"

"Wondering where yourself was while I was here on my lonesome."

"Captain ordered all the Draugr removed from the ship," Kaspar told him, frowning as he thought back to it. "We were marching them over to the warehouse, next thing I know a riot is breaking out."

"Think the captain was worried about that?"

"Think it's none of our business, sailor."

"You're a good sailor, Niko. Know just how to salute right."

"What's wrong with your hand?" Kaspar noticed the other was twitching. All restless.

"Thaumatic," Gravel grumbled. "Kelpie was a thaumatic."

Kaspar scowled at him. "How could you even tell?"

"How could I not? Was bleeding all out him, made the hair on my nethers stand all up."

Kaspar sighed. Of course, Gravel would know. Fellow was worse than a bloodhound when it came to the thaumatically inclined. "Just being that way don't mean anything, Brandon."

Gravel snorted. "Yeah, I know. Don't think good drunk, ok?"

"So don't drink."

"Think too much when I'm sober."

"I know, I know. I just don't want to have to explain anything to Aristeia."

"Aye, now that we can agree on. Woman scares me more than Mors does and I didn't know anyone so scary as Mors Coldstream before signing on with you lot."

"Be grateful you've never been alone with her, landsman.

Come on, let's go."

"Back to the ship, aye, sir? Orders and such." Gravel rose to his feet, and Kaspar clapped him on the shoulder. "Wouldn't want to have to explain nothing."

They hadn't noticed it but the whole tavern had gone quiet. The noise of the riots outside had long passed but the room had all the festivities of a wake.

Almost the same time as they left the table was when the golem stepped through the door. Ducking and turning sideways, a brutal grace it did not look to be capable of. And there it stood, blocking the exit, surveying the room with red eyes, firelight bouncing off the glassy hide. The golem had no neck to speak of but gave the impression it was searching the room.

"Niko," Gravel whispered hoarsely, visibly shaken.

"What?" Kaspar didn't take his eyes of the golem, him and everyone else in the tavern.

"That thing is looking at us!"

Kaspar shook his head fiercely. "It's not looking at us."

"The hells it isn't!"

"How could you even tell what it's looking at?" he demanded.

"Because . . ." Gravel broke off, the next words coming out mangled and blue.

The golem was moving. Through the room. People got out of its way fast enough but tables and benches had legs that didn't move. And soon a trail of both lay broken and splintered on the floor. The golem didn't even acknowledge the obstacles, either stepping through them until they caught and cracked; or onto them to snap the timber in half. It had already crossed half the room.

And there was next to no doubt now it was coming for them.

Hells, was all Kaspar could think as the golem raised its hand towards them.

Chapter 6

"THIS ONE HAS been drinking," Quill said, stopping in front of Nel. She looked up from the bill of lading she'd been going over. It held a rundown of everything delivered to the dock as well as an estimate of haulage awaiting them at the Glassy Run, given recent stocks and the rough capacity of the *Tantamount*.

"And fraternising with Alliance sailors."

That did get Nel's attention. *Fraternising? Violet? Alliance?*

Quill had been towing a very demure looking cabin girl behind him. That demure Kitsune suddenly transformed the air around them blue as she laid into Quill with every foul-mouthed obscenity the crew had ever let slip around her and a few she must have picked up ashore. Bandit chimed in with a few opportune squawks, doubling the racket.

"You done there? Got it all out?" Nel asked when Violet finally paused for air.

"One would hope," Quill muttered.

"Weren't fraternising." Violet kicked at him angrily. "Was one drink."

"Go help with the loading, Quill." Nel passed him the bill. "Seems you're always vanishing when there's cargo to be shifted."

"Seems I am always running to rescue this one," Quill said.

"And we're all grateful, Loveland, now move your hide. I'll deal with our little fraterniser."

Quill was not so easily mollified. "And this will prove helpful how? I can smell the dockside swill upon you as well. And the girl needs no lessons in fraternisation from you, I think."

Nel glared. "Nobody asked what you think, Quill, and you don't get paid extra for it. Get."

"Bah," was all the Kelpie had to say to that, storming back the way he had come and down the boarding ramp.

"Now, what's the truth about what he was saying, Vi?" Nel asked, trying to talk calm and slow. Quill had touched more of a nerve than she wanted to admit, damn Kelpie, but she wasn't going to let it show. "You been getting in trouble? Be straight with me."

Violet made a face. "Weren't getting, Skipper, was staying out. Tavern was the only quiet place with that commotion that went on."

"And that bit about fraternisation?"

"Dunno," Violet shrugged. "What's fraternisation anyhow? What'd I do? What'd the Kelpie say I done?"

"Ah," Nel smiled. "So you're not so grown up as all that after all. Was worried you'd grown another tail on me."

"If I had I'd be . . ." Violet's mouth shut hard and fast, enough that Nel heard the girl's teeth snap.

"Yes?" she asked.

"Nothing."

"Didn't sound like nothing."

"Didn't say nothing. Ain't saying nothing. It ain't nothing."

"Then it is something?"

"Skipper!" Violet groaned.

Nel changed tack. "Tell me how'd you end up drinking with Alliance sailors if you were staying out of trouble. And when'd you start drinking, more's the point."

"Don't." Violet screwed up her face. "Didn't. Just ran out of ways to say no."

"So they were buying you drinks?" Nel pressed. "These Alliance sailors?"

Violet shrugged. "Guess so. Least Gravel was. Until Quill showed up and made a ruckus about it."

Nel chuckled but decided to let up on the girl. On this front. They still had serious matters to discuss. "All right, Vi, we'll let it go. Let's talk about your meteoric rise in rank. Since when is it your job to find us jobs?"

"Since . . ." Violet hesitated.

"The captain ask you to do this, Violet?" Nel asked sternly.

Hells, would he remember if he did?

"He said we were desperate."

"We were, we are."

Violet looked crestfallen, her lower lip was trembling. "You mad at me, Skipper?"

No, just wanted to skip port before . . . anyone comes calling. Hells, and you drinking it up with boys in white and blue. No chance of running out early now, not with a run on the books.

"No," Nel sighed. "I ain't mad, lass. Just that committing us to something is no small thing. We need work, aye, but we need to know who we're working for and what strings they're trying to pin on us."

"I'm sorry, Skipper," Violet mumbled, hanging her head. "Was just trying to help."

"Yeah, I know, lass, I know. Just next time before you think about doing something like this come get me or the captain. Pass it up the chain, like. Last thing we need is more of what happened on that run to Thatch."

"Aye, Skipper," Violet nodded, her whole manner stiffer now.

Aw, hells, shouldn't have mentioned Thatch. Not with Piper and . . . hells.

"And no more drinking with boy folk, neither."

"Aye, Skipper." Still glum, a sniffling nod.

"Nothing else you need to tell me then? No more surprises you signed us up for? No more midnight trysts or fell adventures?"

"No, ma'am." Violet's response was short and clipped. Not even a *skipper* to sign off with.

"Go help with the loading, lass. Make sure Quill ain't slacking off."

Hells, Nel thought, watching the shaking girl go. *Handled that something awful. Violet ain't the only one who needs to shape up and watch what she does. Damned if I don't need a drink now.*

MANTID WALKED WITH an odd four-legged shuffle, crabbing sideways around the growing pile of salt. It had been transported in a mix of barrels and sacks, containers of dubious quality, and at least one of the containers was failing since being hoisted into the ship. A small but noticeable mound of the coarse grains was starting to gather at the base of the pile. A tell-tale trail littered the floor of the hold, a loose scattering of white rock crystals being ground into dust as the crew went about their duties. Just being around this much salt was causing Violet's throat to become dry and parched, but Mantid seemed outright anxious.

"What is it?" she asked her strange new crewmate, anxious for anything to take her mind off her own troubles. At least the pain in her skull was gone, head didn't feel so cotton-swabbed anymore. Hopefully, the drink was all worn off.

Mantid's feet skittered on the wooden boards of the hull, and she wondered how he managed to avoid getting the angular limbs tangled and ending up in a twisted heap. She watched him do another half circle around the cargo and then cautiously back away. His head turned to face Violet. She felt herself flinch at that—she was almost directly behind Mantid and yet he could rotate his flattened head almost all the way around to look at her.

How is that possible? Damn creepy bug man.

"You don't like salt?" she asked.

The head twitched, tilting to one side. Strange, multi-faceted bug eyes staring at her. There was a hiss from beside her. Bandit, the loompa's fur almost standing at attention, paws tucked under him and teeth bared. Indecisively poised between fight and flight.

"Bandit, stop that!" Violet snapped, his obvious display of aggression sparking a pang of guilt from her.

"He's confused," a voice said. Hounds. The woman was damned near as sneaky as the skipper for creeping up on a person. "Loompas eat insects. One big enough to turn the favour ain't right with the little fellow's world."

Violet turned and pointed an accusing finger at Mantid. "Back! Don't you be eating Bandit. He's not for eating!"

Mantid pulled back a spiked, almost grasping foreleg. The jointed appendage folded into an almost prayerlike position. To Violet it looked like something just waiting to attack.

"Not for eating," she repeated, shuffling Bandit back with her foot. The loompa continued to snarl silently at the much bigger Mantid, though from safely entwined between Violet's legs and tail.

"He's just shaky from the cargo," Hounds told her. "Salt dries his kind out something horrid, leaves them all brittle like dead leaves. Bodies ain't meant to deal with so much of it. Speaking of that, you weren't here when all this was delivered."

"No," Violet said quickly. "Couldn't get back."

Hounds nodded. "Saw the commotion, laying low was smart. But you missed your moment of glory, lass."

Violet hung her head glumly. "Don't need no glory and don't care for folks looking."

"Aye," Hounds grinned. "As you say, but aside from missing your own triumphant return you'd have seen those that carted it to us. You think Mantid is skittish, you should've glimpsed these ones, lass. Salt burns, the lot of them. Salt and ice, take the skin right off your bones."

"Makes me thirsty too, salt," Violet admitted. That was all she could think to say.

"Be sure and drink your ration, lass," Hounds said. "Your skipper said we were taking on extra casks on account of this job. Between the yelling."

"Not happy about the job," Violet said quietly.

"Then she's the only one. Me and mine, lass, we were a long time here. Not so many paying jobs as we can afford to turn down ones that ain't quite right."

"Yeah."

"It was you who found us this run, lass," Hounds said. "Maybe Vaughn's just dark on being shown up."

"Skipper ain't like that," Violet said quickly. "She's just thinking about what's best for the ship, is all. Always is."

"What's best for the ship is that we make some coin," Hounds said. "I'm not wrong here, lass."

"No," Violet said, thinking back to all she'd heard in the captain's cabin. "I guess not."

"Keep thinking that way," Hounds said. "Most folk want to be paid, don't much care how or what they get paid for, long as there's coin at the end of it. Better if there's some at the start too but at the end is what matters. You got a knack for finding paying work then most of us won't think too much more about it. You're right with me and mine, lass. Don't doubt it."

Violet felt herself grinning. It was nice to be appreciated on the ship for once.

"Your pet's got some fight in him." Hounds eyed Bandit. As

was often the case, the loompa seemed to realise he was being talked about. He clambered up Violet's body to perch on her shoulder, one small black hand gripping her hair for balance.

"More than is good for him, I'd say." Violet rolled her shoulder, trying to dislodge Bandit. For some reason he sat odd on her just now, didn't feel right. He squawked at her in protest and pulled on her hair. Not going anywhere.

Little rat sold me out to Quill, who sold me out to the skipper. Can't trust nobody no more.

"Captain says we're headed to Vice at the end of this run. Be some laytime with a hold full of ice to unpack once we get there," Hounds said. "Lots of opportunities in Vice."

"How do you mean?"

Hounds winked at her. "Means you and I should take a walk there when we get the chance. I know some people who know some folk. Could be some coin in it for all of us."

"Sure, I mean, maybe." Violet shrugged.

"Time for that later," Hounds said. "In the bye, we should be setting up the pumps down here and getting our hands on some sawdust for packing. We'll want this place caulked nice and tight or else you and the plucky pack rat there might freeze your tails off. And that'd be a crying shame."

"What is a shame is that none of you seem capable of hearing the bells that are ringing right now," Quill's voice interrupted. Violet saw him halfway down the stairs leading to the orlop deck where the bulk of the ship's cables were stored.

"You," Quill peered into the mostly unlit cargo hold, seemingly untroubled by the dark. For once he wasn't looking at Violet. "You are needed, or so the captain would have me believe. We are launching the ship."

Mantid scuttled on multiple legs towards Quill, forelimbs held in that odd prayer position. Quill regarded the other navigator with distaste as he moved to allow him passage.

"Cargo's secured, Mister Quill," Hounds told him. "Been making a start on the packing. Have my watch finish attending to that once we're under way. Less loading time when we arrive that way, and it's a dog of a job to do once we start filling this space with ice cut."

"Very good," Quill nodded approvingly. "I am gratified to see the skipper has hired someone who knows their job. For a change." He ran his hand over one of the seams in the hull, already loosely packed with straw caulking. "Very thorough. Most likely this also dampens the sound of the ship's bells. Understandable."

Violet shook her head. Quill was being nice. Never good.

His eyes moved to Violet. "You should be up in the nest, girl. Keep a lookout for the first bell after we launch and then join me for the remainder of our watch."

Violet bristled but nodded her compliance. She'd almost forgotten she was going to be standing watch with Quill from now on. Though maybe that was better than being around the skipper for a while. She'd rather not face the woman again so soon.

Maybe I can get the captain to let me go on Hounds' watch. He might agree—she's got everyone coming around to her side. Even Quill.

These thoughts kept her occupied until she was almost halfway up the ratlines to the nest. She swallowed hard as the familiar vertigo of being up high threatened to overwhelm her. A lot of sailors were afraid of water, so it went, on account of most couldn't swim. A lot less were afraid of heights like Violet was, which seemed unfair.

Stupid, got a lot further to fall in the black. Falling and freezing takes longer than drowning, and slower is worse.

She hauled herself into the nest, hanging her arms over the sides but keeping her eyes shut until her stomach settled. When she opened them she was looking up at the sky, a trick she'd learned, and gradually brought them down until she was focused on the docks. Fixating on single points further away helped her keep her mind off the drop to the deck right below her. Made it less real.

Until the ship rolled under her. Breaking free of the water's suction and lurching skyward, ungainly and powered by the brute force of the *Tantamount's* navigators. They would have been assisted by the port's own navigators as it was extremely draining for a solo navigator to break the claim gravity made on a ship. Once they were a hundred or so feet in the air, Violet felt the shift in momentum as Quill and Mantid took over, the port's influence dropping away. It felt different than usual, when Quill did it alone. Violet hadn't been aboard the only time Quill hadn't launched the ship.

That Guildswoman, Scarlett.

Scarlett and her pet rock. Violet's thoughts turned dark. Her eyes scanned the dock below, nausea and vertigo forgotten for the moment. Was the golem still out there somewhere?

No, it's gone. Gone. Like we're about to be. Doesn't matter either way. No sense wasting sweat worrying at it. Don't you go wasting thought on it.

She could see other ships, mostly free traders and merchantmen. There was a pair of Alliance ships as well, medium-sized frigates. Maybe one of them held the two young sailors she'd drunk with. She smiled as she remembered the way Gravel had fronted Quill. It was a good thought.

The crew were a hive of activity below her. Most were manning their ropes, either up in the rigging or working on those below. Quill was at the helm alongside the captain. Further up the ship, Violet spotted Mantid by the foremast. Quill always did his job from the bridge at the stern of the ship, though it made sense that with two navigators they would be positioned differently.

Also, Quill probably can't stand the competition.

Violet couldn't see the skipper anywhere, but there was Hounds, the new mate, running point from the forecastle. She was working one of the signallers, probably talking to the port authorities. There was a second signaller up in the nest with Violet. On most ships there would be a third mounted at the stern. That one had been lost overboard long before Violet joined, which meant they were forever shuffling the survivor from one end to the other.

The landscape below was rapidly dissolving into a patchwork bird's-eye view. Far away from the reaches of any golem. She imagined the lumbering, rocky behemoth stepping out onto the dock, only to glimpse sight of her and the *Tantamount* disappearing. Could a golem get angry? She didn't know much about them, she had to admit, other than she was surprised Onyx was still functioning in any way without Scarlett around. He'd stopped doing much of anything that time Violet had hit Scarlett with a rock. Another good memory.

Her thoughts strayed to the last time she had seen the golem, tumbling away from her, from the ship. Fallen through the weakened timbers of the *Tantamount*. Too late to save Piper. She relived that memory for a moment, watching the golem fall away into the black with a dark glee she didn't recognise. Becoming smaller and smaller. It brought the vertigo back in a rush.

Violet rolled into the middle of the nest, one hand grabbing at her mouth to keep the contents of her stomach in. She saw black, black filled with pinpricks of light. Stars. It was the opposite of falling.

They'd crossed into the black. Must have. There, the air shimmering as the envelope formed around the *Tantamount*, pushing against the black. Soon the mist would form up around them, ether drawn to ether. She should get back up and watch, for stars, for rays, for other ships. But she took a moment, just to settle her stomach, she told herself. A moment to look up at the holes pierced in the black. Falling away from her.

It was like falling.

SHIP UNDERWAY AND cargo stowed. Should have been a good feeling. It wasn't. The empty bottle in her hand was more how she felt. Empty, unfulfilled. Thirsty. Sober.

That was wrong: she wasn't sober. The cotton-wadded feeling in her head wasn't just from the pressure change passing into the black, though her ears did feel blocked and stuffy. Nel watched the last drop of sweet, sugary rum trickle down the edge of the bottle. She did resist the urge to catch it on her tongue. She wasn't a drunk, just had things she'd rather not think about.

It was quiet in this part of the hold, feet up on a barrel, back against the grog cage, just a sliver of light from the stone she'd brought. Silver and cold. All alone in the bottom of the ship. It felt good to be away from the hustles and commotion of the crew, if only for a few minutes. Privacy was a rare thing on the ship. The quiet was comforting. It also meant she could hear the captain coming long before he arrived.

Nel could often tell who it was from their footsteps. Quill clicked because his feet scraped the deck, Violet always ran everywhere. Jack stomped and Gabbi had a lopsided shuffle. Piper, funnily enough, had been light on his feet, but had sometimes waddled too if Bandit was riding his shoulder.

The captain wore boots. Hard-heeled and steel-capped boots. He was one of the only ones aboard who did so constantly; most of the crew went barefoot to help their footing in the rigging. Horatio preferred his boots and almost never went up into the rigging.

"Captain." Nel tilted the empty bottle his way, holding it between her fingertips. The glowstone light splintered into rays if she held it just so, casting little diamonds among the shadows.

"I hope that bottle wasn't full, Nel." The captain took a stand opposite to her. He swung the door to the cage shut with one boot, the clang reverberating around the hold.

"What if it was?"

"I'd be disappointed."

Nel shrugged. "Life is full of disappointment."

"Yes, yes it is."

"Hate being this close to the High Lanes." Nel leaned back, looking up. If she squinted right, she could imagine the splashes of light were stars against the black.

"I know."

"Allied worlds." Nel shook her head. "Pretty colours and pretty worlds. None of it means a damn."

"It does to some."

"How can you say that?"

The captain didn't answer.

Pretty worlds, pretty sailors all in a row. Lined up and saluting just so. Too many reminders. Didn't expect to see them here.

Didn't expect to see him.

And I don't want to talk about it. Anything but that. Even . . .

"We're a week's sail from Misery. You know that?"

"I was born there, Nel," the captain said with an edge to his voice. "Long before it was called that."

"Before me."

"Don't be ridiculous, Nel. What happened there had nothing to do with you."

"Didn't it?"

"Were you the captain of the ship? No, you were just another sailor, a soldier following orders."

"Another helpless soul."

"It was a horrible situation. People made difficult decisions."

"Difficult!" Nel threw the bottle away in a fit of rage. It shattered against the inner hull, the pieces vanishing into the gloom. "Difficult? Heathen made a decision and an entire planet died because of it. And there's me, saluting, watching it happen."

"Not everybody died. Some got out. Because of you."

"My defection," Nel chuckled bitterly. "Too little, too late. And look at us, five years later and it all happened again. You know what that was like? Watching her smash Rim to pieces like that?"

"Sometimes."

Nel flinched. *Damnit.* "Captain, I'm sorry, I . . ."

"Sometimes I remember, Nel," the captain said. "On days like today, I remember. The me of today envies the man who doesn't recall. The man who is blissfully ignorant. Who can't remember. Only that man isn't happy, he worries. He frets, he agonises about something on the tip of his tongue, hidden in the back of his mind. Something he knows is important and deathly afraid to recall."

Guilt twisted her up now. The captain was the way he was because of what happened. His . . . ailment . . . the reason Heathen had done what she had, when Nel had served under the woman. Cast across an entire planet, spreading, and no one knew why. Scaring those outside, sitting above, safe in their ships. If the captain hadn't gone back, he would have been fine, would never have been afflicted.

But it had been his home. And he'd wanted to help.

"I miss my wife," the captain smiled, a little wistful. "When I remember her. And our children, on the days I think I ever had any."

"You did. Two daughters. Pretty wee things."

"Of course they were," the captain beamed. The proud smile of a father. That was the saddest part. "I remember a man as well. Sandy hair, blue eyes. Very blue eyes. Who was he?"

"Markus."

"Ah, yes. That one. Good lad, if I recall. Miserable sod. Drank worse than you."

"Yeah. With a saviour complex."

"Did he?"

"Got him killed. I think. I don't remember him making it out."

"Your family did though. They made it out."

"Weren't there, Captain. Still back in the High. Don't see them. Better that way."

"As you say, Nel, as you say." The captain ran his hand up the inside of the hull, following the curved line of the hull's ribs. "She's a good ship, the old girl. Proud of her."

"Aye, Captain," Nel said. "That she is."

"Did you always drink so much, Nel?"

"No." Eyes on the bottle, easier that way. Could hear the disappointment, didn't need to see it too. Couldn't close her eyes either. Saw faces if she did.

Piper . . . Thyme . . . Sharpe . . .

Faces she needed to forget.

"Since Misery."

"You mean Vintage."

"Close enough, Nel, close enough."

"The old names are the best."

"Only if you're in on the joke."

The two of them shared a laugh. And it was silent again.

"I'm going to ask you for your key, Nel."

And now the silence became uncomfortable.

Chapter 7

Violet was tired, wasn't sure why. Spent enough time in her sling but woke up worse than when she got in. Too tired to be on watch with Quill. He hadn't done anything yet but he would. Was just waiting. To look at him one would think Quill was preoccupied. Head down, hands splayed over the map table. His tail lolled back and forth along the deck, a few inches above the woodwork, an elegant curve to it. Violet watched that tail. It was the key to it all. The Kelpie couldn't keep his temperament from affecting the dance of his tail any more than she herself could. Which was why she sat behind him, perched on the railing, tails out to the back end of the ship. It could spin a hurricane in the mist surrounding them and Quill would never see it. Though it wasn't mist so much as cloud that surrounded them. Thicker, denser, wetter. The whole of the ship was covered in a fine drizzle of spray. She'd long since given up on brushing off her oilskin and was resigned to it. If she could avoid the smell of wet fur following her below decks she'd be happy.

The tail is the key, Violet pulled her distracted mind back on track as she tightened the knotted scarf she'd tied over her hair. Quill's was going to give him away. He had some plan for her, some nefarious plan she wasn't going to like. There was no other reason he would have had her assigned to his watch.

Possibly he might have done it just to spite the skipper, Violet thought. But Quill and the skipper had always maintained a surly respect, content to let it go at barbed comments. And if there was one person Quill wouldn't goad it was the skipper.

Not that he wouldn't, just never has.

"Stop doing that," Quill said, not even bothering to look up.

"I'm not doing nothing," Violet told him.

"Then do something."

"I am. I'm watching."

"It is irritating."

"We're on watch."

Quill straightened up with a sigh, finally deigning to look at her. "You have lessons when you share a watch with the skipper, yes?"

"Yeah," Violet said, not hiding her suspicion.

"And before then you had them from . . ." Quill actually hesitated, "from Piper."

Violet nodded stiffly.

"One assumes they covered the basics of navigation with you. One would hope you were paying attention."

"Won't have you badmouthing Piper or the skipper!" Violet jumped to her feet. "You don't get to talk like that. Not ever!"

To her surprise, Quill laughed. "Good. If nothing else, the two of them managed to instil some semblance of respect for one's tutor into you."

He took a step toward her, looking down at her. Violet stared back defiantly.

"But my criticism was not directed at your tutors. Merely their student."

"You mean me."

"Yes."

Violet glared.

"Tell me, girl," Quill turned away, "what are the principle challenges we face when navigating through the black?"

"Kelpie navigators?"

"Do not test me."

Violet bit off her next comment. "Everything is always moving."

"Is it?"

"Well, yeah, where we're going isn't going to be where it was when we get there."

"So we need to account for where an object's transit would carry it before we set our course. And suppose we do not know the route our own destination travels, how then might we compensate?"

Violet stared. She had no idea. At length Quill seemed to realise this.

"Perhaps another question," he allowed. "Given that we are still within the grasp of this planet's winds, how often must I refill our sails?"

"Thought you didn't have to," Violet said. "Why would you when we've got crew and canvas out there catching real breezes?"

"Good," said Quill, with something that might almost have been approval. "But this planet is still trying to pull us down."

Violet glanced over the side. She could see the world below them, a world whose name escaped her for the moment. The sea coast of Port Border had given way to a rockier, more mountainous region. There were touches of snow now, which was a good sign given their intended cargo.

"We are, in fact, falling."

Falling . . .

"Don't feel like we're falling," Violet said, even though she knew it was true.

"Perhaps because our new . . . friend . . . and I spent the better part of the morning carrying the *Tantamount* against this planet's gravity. Sailing, flying rather, through the air is a much more challenging endeavour than through the black."

"Could have just sailed upriver," Violet said.

"The river would have frozen before we reached our destination. And launching the ship from the bed of a frozen river is much more challenging still."

Violet nodded.

Sneaky Kelpie, trying to lull me.

Her eyes caught the snap of a billowing foresail. A sailor called out, a line was tweaked, and the canvas settled.

"How does it work, Quill?"

"How does what work? What is *it*?"

"How do you use magic to make a ship sail the black?"

Quill's eyes narrowed to mere slits.

Violet beamed at him. *Two can play at this game.* "How do you use thaumatics to fill a ship's sails, I mean?"

"I push them."

"Doesn't seem like it would work."

"No?"

"No, cause you can't be around to push them the whole time, so how do they stay filled like there's actual wind when you're napping? Why don't they go still?"

Quill snorted. "An actual nuanced question. I am almost impressed."

"So? How does it work then?"

Quill looked down the length of the ship. Everything was tied down, a good thing on account of the wind and the rain lashing them.

Violet instinctively ducked when one of the coarsely woven sacks of salt they'd taken on came flying towards her. It came to a sliding halt at Quill's feet.

"Watch," he said.

The sack of salt rose between them, drifting lazily around the deck, tumbling end over end.

"Not everything in the black is in motion," Quill said, gesturing idly with his hand. "Most, but not all. Objects that possess an envelope . . ."

"Like us."

Quill stopped. "Do not interrupt."

"Sorry." Violet bit down on her lower lip.

"Like the *Tantamount* will . . . slow down. The miasma we sail on and through will drag the ship to a halt, clap us in irons and hold fast," Quill's voice became more distant as he mused, perhaps concentrating on his prop. "A natural current or wind is rare in the black, thus we rely on ether and thaumatics. Ether to keep the black at bay, to forge our way through the mist. Do you know what happens to a ship when it ventures too far into the black, to a place where the miasma is thin?"

"No," Violet blinked. She'd started to get caught up in the telling, surprising herself.

"It falls," Quill said, dropping his own hand. The salt fell too, hitting the wood hard, a handful of coarse white grains spilling out onto the deck. "It falls, as if one had sailed a ship off the edge of the world. Sometimes," he looked at her, "it falls forever. Others will fall until it finds the miasma again. Only perhaps the mist is not thin but thick, places like the Morgana. The effect is no different than if one sailed into a cliff, the outcome the same. This is why we keep to the Lanes, the ways of the black."

Quill raised his hand, causing the salt to rise, still leaking small white rock crystals over the woodwork. "A navigator's thaumatics obey the same rules. Left alone, a vessel set in motion, under sail, will wither and stop, as it would were a sea breeze to die. Unless it were to be . . . structured in such a way as to sustain itself."

Violet watched as Quill tossed the sack in one direction then another, weaving a convoluted design in front of her. She narrowed her eyes as she watched the container being buffeted in mid-air. "I don't understand."

"You, like our gluttonous cook, prefer to goad and prod," Quill said, "to provoke until you elicit a reaction you can see and gloat over. Some of us . . . are more subtle."

The sack was starting to fray under the abuse Quill was dealing to it. Violet took a step back, expecting it to rupture and for salt to fly everywhere at any moment.

"Some of us are more subtle. Some work with currents and forces you are blind to, that you cannot see because you do not look. But the results . . ."

Quill stopped talking, now drawn to the display between them as Violet was. He smiled, visibly, teeth and all. The sack burst apart, spilling its contents. Violet flinched, raising her hands reflexively to cover her face.

Only she wasn't covered in the gritty substance as she expected. Peering cautiously through her fingers, she saw that Quill's display was not yet done. The complex pattern he'd traced with the unwieldy sack was now fully realised, a twisting design drawn in salt that flowed continuously. Violet could no longer see where it began or ended, like a mythical snake chasing its tail.

"What is that?" she stared. It was strangely beautiful, Quill's self-sustaining pattern. For he wasn't feeding it anymore, if that was the right term. To look at him she couldn't see the tell-tale glimmers of thaumatics, the tension in his limbs, or the visible flicker of his own energies.

"That," Quill said, reaching out to pluck away the still entrapped and now useless sackcloth, "is what you do not see when the sails fill."

"How long will it stay like that?" Violet walked around the

pattern. It was changing as she watched, taking on a more spiral shape, ever twisting.

"Until it exhausts itself." Quill shrugged. "This is a mere cantrip, a simple training exercise. I perhaps misspoke before. What it takes to fill the sails of a ship this size would be more complex. It would require anchoring, or one might experience . . . unpleasantness."

Or you just don't want to admit your job might not be as easy as you make out, Violet smirked.

"Can I touch it? What happens if I touch it?"

"Nothing," Quill snorted. "What has ever happened when you try and touch a breeze?"

Slowly, carefully, Violet extended one hand towards Quill's model. There was a prickling, the hairs on the back of her hand standing up as she edged closer, tracing one of the outer tributaries of the pattern. She could feel her eyes widen as the pattern started to change, that one flow stretching out as if reaching for her touch.

And then it bit her. Violet snatched her hand back, crying out and cradling it to her chest. The pattern shuddered and collapsed in on itself, the whole pile of salt falling to the deck, any trace of elegance or design gone.

"Damnit, Quill!" Violet yelled. "You meant for that to happen!"

"I meant no such thing." Quill blinked at her. "I touched it before and this did not happen. The fault clearly lies with you, girl."

"You said it was safe."

"I did not. I said nothing would happen. In any case, you are not injured so it was safe."

"Yeah?" Violet held up her hand. The tips of her fingers were red and blistered. Burned.

"Curious." Quill grabbed her wrist, turning it so he could see.

"You're hurting me." Violet yanked her hand away angrily.

"You will live," Quill was dismissive. "Tell me, are thaumatics common amongst your kind? I admit to little familiarity with the adults of your kind. You are an uncommon race."

"I don't know. What does that got to do with anything?"

"Nothing," Quill said. "Be sure you clean up that mess."

Violet glared at the kelpie's back as he turned back to his

charts. She shouldn't have been surprised.

"EASY THERE, LASS, you look fit to murder."

Violet stopped up short at the sound of Hounds' voice. It carried over the carousing of her watch on the gun deck. As the *Tantamount* only had a handful of guns, none of which resided here, it was more of a secondary cargo deck. It was also where the crew hung their hammocks; the swinging canvas reminded Violet that she still had to attend to Mantid's special circumstances.

Why can't he fix his own hammock though? Where's he sleeping now?

Violet heaved the sack of salt off her shoulder. There was a gritty white residue on her shoulder where it had sat. She'd fixed the bag up as best she could, knotting the end, but it was a patch job and she knew it. She needed to find somewhere to stow, or another container to store it in. Problem was, having just left port, most nooks and crannies were well stuffed and every spare box had been pressed into service. Gabbi had gone on a shopping spree with the advance, and sundries had done for the rest.

"This one burst," she said to Hounds, who was surrounded by a half circle of card players. "Need to sort it somehow."

"You break it?" Denzel asked, then immediately held up his hands defensively. "Didn't mean nothing by that, Miss Violet. Here take this, weren't using it anyhow."

"Thanks." Violet took the offered apple crate the sailor had been using as a stool. She wedged the ruptured sack as best she could into it, looking around for where she could leave it. She settled on weighting the crate between a trunk and somebody's seabag.

There. Not my problem no more.

"Play a hand with us, Violet," Hounds said, dealing cards as she spoke. The woman flicked cards to all the players in the circle, making it look deft and easy.

"Not much of a player," Violet said.

"Tell that to Denzel," Hounds smirked. "Not even a round and you've hustled him out of the best seat in the house."

Denzel rolled his eyes; his crewmates laughed and pushed him. With Denzel's apple crate gone, only two of the circle, one of them being Hounds, had seats. The other was Haze. The old sailor had a folding stool of some sort. The others crouched or knelt on the floor.

"All right," Violet said. "What's the game?"

"Tricks and trumps, lass," Hounds said. "Bid with your partner and no skipping rounds."

"Who's my partner?"

"Volunteers?" Hounds peered over her cards, pushing Violet's five towards her.

There was a round of coughing from the players and eyes were averted.

"How about you, Shellfish?" Hounds said to Haze. The old sailor looked at her ugly.

"Shellfish?" Violet repeated, causing the look to be turned upon her. Didn't care much, she was well used to it.

"Aye, Shellfish," Hounds grinned. "Man here's a certified shellfish, been to the Edge and everything."

"Ain't a shellfish, woman," Haze complained. "It's a damned turtle."

"Aye, which is a fish in a shell, ain't it, Shellfish. So you partnering up with little Miss Murdersome here or not?"

"Not."

"It's like that, is it? Shameful. Bringing bad luck on yourself. Who will it be then?"

Mantid tapped the deck impatiently.

"Thank you kindly, Mantid," Hounds grinned, tilting her head towards the secondary navigator. "The Kitsune and the Mantid, fearsome as they come, lads. Least we know there'll be no table talking."

No table talking, Violet thought, looking at the new navigator, *no bloody talking at all*.

"You know all the lads, Violet?" Hounds asked. "You've met Denzel, surely, and Mantid. Evil card player that one. Darkest bluffer I ever set eyes upon. The ugly one calls himself Haze and the one with the face is Mugs. The two of them against me and Denzel and you and our peerless navigator as the wild cards. First call for trumps is spades. How do you all plead?"

Mantid had his cards splayed out before him, facedown. His head swivelled to face Hounds and he tapped his cards.

"Mantid passes," Hounds said. "Just to be different. Haze?"

The man shook his head. He also cleared his throat with a hacking cough that made the two either side of him lean away.

"Pass," Denzel said in disgust. "How about you, Miss Violet?"

Violet looked at the cards she held. Scarcely a spade to be seen. Nor an off suit bower. She followed those who came before her and passed.

"Same here," Mugs grunted.

"Useless layabouts," Hounds muttered, picking up the kitty and tossing away a few of her own cards. "Not a shred of courage amongst the lot of you."

"Rules are if no one calls trumps we stick with the dealer," Denzel winked. "Faster game that way."

"Stick it *to* the dealer would be more apt," Hounds scowled. "Who dealt these miserable hands?"

"A miserable dealer."

"The boss lady would have shot you out of the black if she heard talk like that," Hounds said. "Right, ante up."

All the players pushed in a coin.

"I don't have any money," Violet said, alarmed.

"Want to stake your partner?" Hounds elbowed Mantid, to no response. "Fine, cheap sod. Here, lass." She grabbed a handful of coins from her own pile and trickled them in front of Violet. "You do well, those come back out of your winnings; you lose and we've got a problem. So don't lose."

Violet swallowed, not sure if the woman was joking. She took another look at her cards. Not good. Only a single trump and a few face cards. Not good at all.

"What was that about the boss lady?" she asked as betting continued. She wanted to fold but didn't have the nerve to in front of them all, not after Hounds had sponsored her in. "Did you mean the skipper?"

"The skipper, a skipper, not your skipper," Denzel said.

"Our old skipper," Hounds said. "Back in the days when we sailed proper colours, Denzel and I. Crow too, come to think, except he wanted to stay back in Border. Good eyes that man, shame about the nose."

"The good old days," Mugs grunted. "I fold."

His partner Haze made a sound of disgust.

Damnit, should have folded too. Hells.

"Alliance?" she guessed. "You sailed the High Lanes?"

"Sailed everywhere, in the good old days," Hounds said, opening the round with an off suit. "The High and the Free, the

Dark and the Far. Didn't stay long enough to make citizen before we had to get out."

"If you call being sent out in a bubble to be used as target practice for the gunners the good old days, sure," Denzel shrugged, throwing a discard.

"Hence why we got out," Hounds said.

"One of the reasons we got out," Denzel muttered. "Oh, let me count the reasons."

"I don't understand," Violet said. She looked down at her cards again. No way to win this hand, best just to discard something.

"Folk called her the Gunner's Daughter. Went through crews like weevils through biscuits. Got things done though. Braids loved her, the way everyone loves a villain, us . . . not so much," Hounds said grimly.

"Meanest skipper in the High and the Free," Denzel said. "Crews changed. She never did."

Hounds nodded. "Crew got out of line, she'd send her least favourite person out in a bubble."

"And shoot it out of the black," Denzel continued.

"And how's that for sticking it to the dealer!" Hounds grinned, taking the round. She played a high trump the next round but her face dropped when Mantid awkwardly pushed a card forward facedown.

"Is that what I think it is?" She glared at him before Denzel turned it over, revealing the left bower.

"Sneaky shark always plays high." Denzel shook his head, playing his ace trump. Probably all he had. Haze off-suited and Violet had to throw in her solitary trump. So much for being a good partner.

"Don't get angry, sailor," Hounds told hers. "You're a lousy player to start and when you're mad you play stupid."

"Not angry, just tired," Denzel said. "Woke up last night to find someone watching me sleep. All big and shadowy. Had glowing eyes too. Thought it was the old man's pet Luscan. Damned horrible, it was."

"You sure you woke up?" Violet asked him. To her it sounded like Bandit. The loompa's eyes would glow like that if there was a light to reflect. It was the only way to find him sometimes.

"Damned sure," Denzel shuddered. "For a moment I thought

I was back on the—"

"Play your damned card," Haze interrupted. "We're all waiting."

"Where in the Far Lanes did you learn to play, you damned cockroach?" Denzel stared at the card Mantid had played. He'd gone off suit again but played low, a poor choice on the face of it. Denzel played a high suit, but it was one of the only suits Violet had a face card for. She threw it down with a grin.

"I swear he cheats." Denzel leaned over the cards. "Not even using a third of the deck and somehow he's counting."

"He ain't counting," Hounds told him. "Not proper anyway. Sorry, Violet." She played another trump to win the round, scooping the cards up.

"But that was my move," Violet protested as Hounds dealt her next card.

"And it was a good move," Hounds said. "Mine was just better. One card at a time, navigator."

Mantid waved a forearm over the cards. He'd pushed his last two cards out, facedown again. Denzel threw his own cards down in dismay.

"Gods damnit," he muttered. "Are those going to be trumps, Mantid?"

Hounds leaned over her navigator. "When I turn those cards over am I gonna be seeing spades staring back at me?"

"He counts," Mugs nodded his head. "Every time."

"Least the shark plays," Haze grumbled. "Not folding like some pissant fish dribbling coin."

"That folding chair you're so fond of, old man? Got a new place for you to stow it," Mugs warned him.

Mantid tapped the deck insistently.

"The black take you, crawler." Hounds flipped the cards. There were two spades, both lower than what Hounds had won the last round with. Violet put her cards down as well, though facedown. With no trumps between her and Denzel it didn't matter what she played. It was all down to what Hounds still had left.

The woman stared at Mantid so long her frown lines started to etch. Then dropped two off-suit aces on the table.

"Thought we had him that time," Denzel sighed.

Haze snorted. "Not likely. Your table talk is awful. Even the girl could tell you were holding."

"She could?" All eyes turned towards Violet.

"Whose turn is it to deal?" Violet pushed her facedown cards across the table. All the eyes followed them. Except Mantid's.

Does he blink? Can he even?

"The cockroach." Denzel pushed the pile of loose cards across the floor. "And ain't that a sight to see."

"Good, give you time to grow a pair," Haze said to Mugs.

"Almost long enough for you to shuffle off this mortal plane," Mugs shot back.

"Neither of us are that lucky," Haze said.

Hounds and Denzel waded into the conversation while Mantid shuffled, moving the cards awkwardly around on the floor before trying to gather them up into a deck. He looked up at Violet and flicked his chest twice with one forelimb.

Wait . . . hearts?

CHAPTER 8

"You shouldn't be down here."

Gravel didn't turn around; he wouldn't be able to see anything in the dark. He could just barely make out the silhouette in front of him. Squat, bulky. Massive. And pure black.

"Apologies, Ensign, won't be happening again."

"You said that the last time."

Didn't have to see Kaspar to hear the annoyance.

"Don't trust this thing, Niko. You saw the way it came at us."

"It's not moving now."

"Aye, and that don't bother you? Like it's just sleeping. Or waiting, maybe. Waiting for what though?"

"Need you at your post, landsman, before someone marks you as absent."

Gravel climbed to his feet, still warily watching the thing hidden in the darkness. It hadn't moved. Didn't mean it wouldn't. "That's your *officer* voice, Niko," he said. "Something the matter?"

"Got another signal from the . . . from that ship."

"*That ship* bothers you, don't it? Feel like telling me why?"

"No. It's nothing."

"Bad liar, Niko."

"It's . . . not something you need to know, Brandon."

Gravel nodded, wondering if Kaspar could even see that much. "Aye, sir. Leave the worrying to you. It's what you're best at. Be at my post when you need me, then, sir."

Gravel stopped, his back to the Ensign. "Be best if you didn't break the ship afore asking for help though. This time."

He actually got a weak laugh in response.

Damn, things must be worse than I thought . . .

BARELY A DAY since the lower decks had been packed with salt and sawdust and the crew were hauling it back onto the docks. They weren't complaining though—a short run and a double one at that which was going to take them all the way to Vice. Better than Nel had hoped for. Might be she even owed Violet an apology.

All right, more than might. That can wait though.

Quill paced the length of the ship beside her, all bundled up in a blanket. The *Tantamount* might run cold but it had been a long time since they'd made an ice run, and few of them had the clothes for it. Ice could form at the lowest point of the ship during long runs, but with the entire hold packed, the whole ship was going to chill. And Quill was already wrapped up in the warmest blanket he could find.

"Too cold for you, Kelpie?" Gabbi prodded mercilessly. She was watching his discomfort with undisguised glee.

"I envy you your many layers of blubber, cook," Quill admitted. To Nel he sounded almost sincere.

"Yes, Quill," Gabbi narrowed her eyes at him. "Must be hard for you, all snake skin and bile for blood. You going to be all right with weeks, maybe months of this until we get to Vice?"

Quill stopped long enough to glare at her. Just looking at him made Nel pull her own coat tighter around her shoulders. When had it gotten so threadbare?

"Where's Mantid?" Violet asked. Of all of them, she was the only one who didn't seem to feel the effect of the cold.

Hells, girl has ice forming in her hair!

Nel had to resist the urge to reach out and brush it off Violet's head.

"He and the captain are huddling in the galley," Gabbi said. "Last I looked, they were fighting over who gets to hug the stove."

"Pathetic," Quill shivered, stamping his feet.

"You want to go wait in the galley too, Loveland?" Gabbi asked him sweetly. "Maybe thaw the frost off? Take the chill out of your bones?"

Quill looked at her suspiciously, before shaking his head and clutching his blanket. "No, I do not."

Nel sidled up to Gabbi. "That was cruel," she said.

"So?"

"Just an observation."

"Might want to check the lockers, Skipper. Just an observation."

"What for?"

Gabbi held out a crystal, round and covered in grit. "Found a couple of bed warmers in my sandpit. Someone's been borrowing from the ammo locker. Could do without my kitchen being set alight. Got Jack for that."

Clever sods. Wish I'd thought of it—except for the part where they overcook the crystals and set their hammock on fire. Have to remember to check the cage. And the guns, come to think of it . . .

"Cargo's coming, Skipper," Violet pointed.

Young eyes, Nel thought, following Violet's direction. *I miss being young. That part anyway.*

She could make out the incoming train, little more than a grey smudge coming down the hills now, but she trusted what Violet said.

"Quick delivery," Gabbi commented.

"Always is with ice runs," Nel said. "Less time spent sitting around and shifting ballast is more coin at the end."

"How we getting paid for this, Skipper?" Violet asked, her head twisting back and forth between Nel and the docks.

"You didn't figure to ask that when you were setting all this up?"

"Skipper," Violet sounded reproachful.

This time Nel did ruffle her hair. Violet ducked her head, looking annoyed.

"Leave off, Nel," Gabbi told her. "It's a fair question."

"Get paid by the pound, lass," Nel said. "They'll weigh the run at beginning and end, and we get paid for what we deliver. Minus the advance."

"Why would it change?" Violet asked.

"Because it's ice."

"So?"

"Ice melts, Vi."

"But we run cold," Violet objected. "That was the whole reason we got the job."

"Still gonna be some loss of product. Normal run could lose maybe half the cargo by the end."

"Half?!"

Nel nodded. "We should be able to do better than that."

Quill leaned out over the ship's railing, lizard eyes peering through the sleet-misted distance. His profile was remarkably akin to that of an old woman, stooped and bundled.

"What?" Nel asked him, suddenly suspicious.

"Draugr," he pronounced. The blanket started to slip unnoticed down his shoulders as he straightened up.

Hells.

"Violet, stop, come back . . ."

Too late though. The girl either couldn't or wouldn't hear her, already belting down the gangway and weaving through the slow-moving crew on the dock. Some reacted in annoyance at her passage but most were too slow to react much at all, numbed by the cold as they were.

"Gabbi, go find the captain," Nel said grimly. "Quill . . ."

"I know." The Kelpie made for the gangway, blanket now hitched up.

Draugr at both pickups, Nel thought as she followed him down. *So much for a labour shortage then. No wonder they caused a riot. And just what does Vi find so damnably fascinating about them?*

There were a dozen sleds, each with half that number of Draugr harnessed up the way one might harness dogs or horses. The sleds all carried a payload of ice, cut into blocks of roughly the same size and lashed down with rope and hides. As Nel got closer, she could see how much of a toll the frozen environment took on the Draugr. Their skin was frostbitten and haggard, like tanned hide or—a more stomach churning thought—cured jerky. In places, the skin was worn through, exposing muscles and tendons as they moved with an unnatural stiffness.

That ain't right. Not by a long shot.

Violet was amongst the Draugr now, poking and prodding them, far too curious for Nel's liking. The girl tugged on hands and what tattered remains of clothing there was, speaking animatedly at the Draugr and peering up into their eyes. Eyes that were glassy and framed by frosted lashes. Almost the only hair visible on any of the Draugr present, Nel observed. They'd been shorn at the head. It had the effect of making them less distinct, almost faceless. Violet was studying them, she realised, looking for telltale clues as to any past or identity. Tattoos like Stoker and his crew had. Something that would tell her these Draugr used to be real people.

Maybe.

Where do all the damned Draugr come from them? Too many of them for someone not to notice if it were all like Grange and such. People would notice.

Wouldn't they?

"You are the captain, I presume?"

"First officer," Nel said to the man in charge. He had to be the man in charge because he was the only one who didn't look dead. A Korrigan, bundled up in furs. Fair taller than usual, he almost came up to Nel's shoulder. Or maybe it was she. Nel wasn't about to ask. She already liked them more than Jack though, as this one had the good sense not to extend a hand, meaning Nel could keep hers tucked away where they were less cold. "Captain pulled rank on account of it being colder than a miser's heart here."

"So long as you're here for the pickup, it don't matter to me. If you got the papers, we can do our business and be done with it. Weather can turn foul here so best we move things along."

"This is not foul?" Quill asked, teeth chattering beside her.

"This is spring," the foreman said gruffly. His breath gushed out in great steaming plumes.

"Papers are aboard," Nel said. "So is the ink and so is the brandy. We can talk aboard if you've a mind."

That at least cracked a smile, out of the foreman if not Quill. The Kelpie scowled, looking on disapprovingly. Nel didn't care. Let the Kelpie judge her.

The foreman glanced back over his shoulder. "That girl never seen Draugr before?"

"Used to have one as a pet," Quill muttered. "It died. An unfortunate fascination ever since."

Clever, Quill.

The foreman grunted. "Folk are strange. Draugr as pets. Strange."

Quill shrugged in agreement.

"Your workers look battered," Nel said.

"Yeah," the foreman nodded. "They do. Harsh living up here. Safer with them kind. Cheaper in the long too."

"What do you do with them during the summer?"

"Sell 'em on. Those that make it through the season anyway."

"You lose workers?" Nel asked, frowning. She was watching Violet involved in a silent staring contest with one.

"Plenty. Some fall through the ice when we cut, avalanches take some. Lost a whole hut once to a moving drift one year. And every season some of them just stop."

"They stop?"

"Dead, frozen maybe, or run out of whatever makes 'em go. Everything breaks eventually. Better than things used to be though."

"How so?"

"Used to be real folk. Good folk, mostly. Those that ain't afraid of a hard job. Didn't like to see them when they came back with frostbitten bits. Better like this."

"I guess so," Nel nodded. She didn't know how that should make her feel. A few months ago she wouldn't have given the Draugr much thought. Because there hadn't been anything to think about. Even Stoker had said he didn't believe there were others out there like him.

Still . . .

"Your girl's about to get a fright," the foreman said while he fished a bone-carved whistle out from under his furs. He blew a series of short notes on it. To Nel it sounded like louder and not-so-loud noise but there was a substantive reaction from the Draugr. All the teams stepped forward together, hauling their cargo to the makeshift docks Quill had brought the *Tantamount* into. The sleds came to a stop by the ramps, essentially slides that would assist in loading the cargo hold. Their initial pickup had included a number of tools; grapples and tongs, for shifting the ice itself. Even so, it was going to be fiddly work.

It occurred to Nel she hadn't seen Draugr work that much. There'd been few, if any, under colours when she served. More in the Central Band but she hadn't been stationed there. There were more to be found on ships now but she'd never had a chance to really watch the creatures at work before.

In rough unison, each of the Draugr reached up and

unbuckled their harnesses. They must have been snap releases as Nel couldn't imagine those frozen limbs had the dexterity to manage complicated knots or latches. What was more impressive was seeing the Draugr fall into work crews. The ice was untethered and the sleds tilted, dumping the blocks by the ramps. Half of the Draugr workers stepped back into their harnesses and began towing the sleds back the way they had come. They passed Violet on the way. The girl hadn't taken fright at all, and she just stood there, turning to watch them go.

"Gonna be a couple of days to load your ship at least," the foreman explained. "Lot of hauling trips to make. Lads by the ramps will shift what comes in. Your crew need to handle the loading itself. No problems, right?"

"No," Nel said. "No problems at all. Follow me and we'll see to those papers."

She leaned in to Quill as she passed him. "Get Violet back here and set the rest to work. The sooner we quit this frozen wasteland the better."

Quill nodded, still muffled shamelessly in the folds of his blanket. "I agree, Skipper."

Well, that was something.

IT WAS THE second day of receiving deliveries of frozen water when things went spectacularly wrong. Quill and Mantid had been cajoled into assisting with the unloading. Mantid had acquiesced willingly enough and even Quill had gone along with the idea. Violet thought both were united for the first time in wanting to be quit of the frozen wasteland, as Quill described it.

She had thought Quill looked odd shivering in a blanket but Mantid looked outright bizarre draped in an ill-fitting rug. His kind did not have the frame suited to any kind of wrap and the new navigator was already moving stiffly, seemingly in danger of freezing solid along with their cargo.

Violet was watching along with the rest of the crew. There was little else to do as the ice Draugr were handling most of the operation with an eerie efficiency. Efficient if you didn't count the time one group had run over another with their sled because the first hadn't moved out of the line fast enough. It was the way the rundown ones picked themselves up and went back to work that made it eerie—completely silent.

Quill was not silent when half a sledful of ice exploded into sleet and rain directly over his head. Either he or Mantid had been in the process of shifting them thaumatically from the levered platform the foreman had set up to the hold. There were crew working down in the hold who were on the receiving end of the unexpected show. Their curses mingled with Quill's, mostly directed at his rival navigator. The other thaumatic did not take it lying down though, aggressively waving his forelimbs at Quill and half-charging him with both raised. Both appeared to blame the other and neither was willing to back down.

"What happened?" Violet asked. "How'd they get it wrong?"

"Didn't do it wrong," Gabbi clucked her tongue from inside the relative warmth of the galley. "Problem was that both of them were doing it in the first place."

Violet recalled the exploded tubers from a week ago when Gabbi and Quill had clashed. How the opposing forces had ripped their impromptu missile apart. She asked as much.

"No," Gabbi said. "Not that. Even worse. Things get hot when you try and push and pull them around like they were. Do that to something cold, it shatters. Every other time."

"Really?" It seemed astounding to Violet, not so much the concept but rather that neither Quill nor Mantid had anticipated this.

"Really," Gabbi confirmed. "Lost more than a couple of saucepans because of it. Good thing though. You'd be eating biscuits and cold porridge most nights if I had to rely on tinder and coal to keep the fires going. Didn't you ever wonder that?"

"No," Violet admitted.

"Aye, which is why I'm the cook and you're the cook's help," Gabbi winked.

"Ain't the help," Violet complained. "Jack's the help."

Gabbi laughed. "Jack ain't no help, lass."

"How come the sails don't explode, nor catch fire?" Violet asked. Seemed like they should if Gabbi was right and thaumatics did what she said.

"Too big, aren't they, spreads it all out. And folks like Quill who push ships ought not to be throwing their weight around on little things."

"Skipper won't be happy," Violet predicted. "Going to need more ice now."

"Or more sawdust," Gabbi predicted. The skipper had been down in the hold, helping pack the empty spaces around their cargo with salt and sawdust. Salt so it wouldn't melt so fast, though Violet didn't understand that part so much, seemed to her salt ought to do the opposite, and sawdust so that it wouldn't shift around during their run. Several hundred tons of frozen water being thrown loose deep in the black was something nobody wanted to see happen.

And there she was, emerging from the hold like a drenched cat, sodden red hair clinging to her scalp and twice as mad. Her sharp voice cut through the others and made everyone stop and stare as she started laying into both navigators.

"Time to look scarce, lass," Gabbi advised. "Skipper's not looking to make friends right now. Just be back later, we got work to do."

"Be out on the ice," Violet told her promptly.

"Gods only know how you don't freeze to death out there, lass," Gabbi wondered aloud.

"Because it's not that cold," Violet said.

Gabbi pointed at the skipper, still admonishing a pair of non-repentant navigators. The woman had ice already forming in her hair,

"Be fine, Gabbi," Violet grinned at her. She grabbed a rope, casting one last look at the drama on deck, before swinging herself out over the edge the ship. The *Tantamount* had dropped itself into a thin tributary river, full of slush and floating ice but not yet solid. It was banked by snowdrifts along the edge. Snowdrifts which Violet had since discovered made excellent cushions.

Her landing left a girl-shaped imprint, and Violet soon added a shallow trail of footprints as she made her way towards the Draugr picket line. There were still a few unloading their deliveries before making the return trip. Violet wondered if the foreman would let her ride back with one of the sleds. There was little to do and she was curious to see how they cut the ice from the source.

The snowball caught her right on the jaw, so unexpected it took her clear off her feet and dumped her onto her side. She'd barely recovered from the shock and sat up when the second one got her, again in the face.

Violet shook her head, rubbing snow off of her face. She saw a small furry head atop a snowbank only a few feet away and felt a flash of unfamiliar anger at the sight. Bandit watched her cautiously, poised in that fight or flight instinct. Violet waited, and sure enough a face just as wizened as the loompa's popped up next.

"It was Bandit!" the captain called out earnestly. "I tried to stop him. It was a valiant effort, Violet, it was, but he got the better of me."

Violet hesitated, her hand curled around a fistful of snow. Would it still be insubordinate to strike your captain? Did she care?

There didn't seem to be anymore fire incoming so Violet discard her own ammunition.

Too undignified. I'm no child to be throwing snowballs. It was a strange thought, maybe prompted by the constant disappointment she was always drawing from the crew. Or perhaps she was just growing up.

Violet decided she didn't much care for the notion.

"Respectfully, Captain, I surrender," she called out.

"Ah," Horatio doffed his hat, using it to brush snow off his coat. "I suppose that means I win? All well and good then but rather unsatisfying. Very bright out here, isn't it?"

He wasn't wrong. When they'd first arrived, it had been overcast, but now the sun had emerged and the glare forced all to squint their eyes. The captain was only making it worse for himself, shading his face with hat but peering up towards the sun.

But as it happened he had a reason. "It seems we're not the only ones to pass this way, my girl. Can you tell me what manner of ship that is?" He pointed to a faint shape passing overhead.

Violet peered up, having to shade her own eyes to do so. There wasn't much to make out from below. All her lessons had focused on being able to identify other ships by the silhouettes: how many masts there were and whether they rigged as square or fore-and-aft. With some, they had wings to the side to make it easier, but this ship had none of those. And it was passing at such an angle that she couldn't make out any masts at all. Without that she couldn't even hazard a guess at the size.

"I can't tell," she said.

"Nor can I," Horatio admitted. "Bothers me that. Feel I'm

failing as a sailor if I can't tell from looking. Old eyes, Violet. Never get old, not if you can help it."

"No, sir. Never get old."

"One does require less sleep though. I suppose we have that in common. Thank you for the tea, by the way."

"Captain?" Violet frowned.

"The tea we shared the other night, during the Loompa's Last Watch." The captain reached down to scratch Bandit and the loompa pushed up into his hand. "Far too much tea in fact, very dark, stained my teeth. And I was up the rest of the night visiting the privy. And thinking about what you said."

Violet clenched her teeth, not wanting her feelings to escape to her face. *That wasn't me. That didn't happen. Captain . . . oh Captain.*

"Think you're confused, some, Captain," Violet said, trying to find the words. "Can't make tea, never learned how."

The captain frowned. "Strange. I was so sure. I wrote it down." He tapped his jacket, striking something solid inside. His journal, probably.

Violet shrugged. What could she say?

"Very industrious workers, Draugr, aren't they?"

The captain's change of tack took her by surprise. From snowballs to ships to Draugr in as many breaths.

"How do you feel about them these days, Violet?" The captain watched her as he spoke. He didn't do that often, look you right in the eye.

"Wonder about them," she said. "If they think, if they feel. If they know."

"Stoker said they did not."

"People say a lot of things, Captain." There was ice under them, Violet realised. The frozen river that the Draugr sleds had been using as a makeshift highway. Covered by only a thin layer of snow where they were standing. She began kicking at the loose snow, moving it aside with her foot, tracing a pattern of lines and abstract curves with her foot.

"Yes, yes, I suppose they do at that. Though not often about Draugr, which is surprising if one were to consider what might happen if they weren't there anymore."

She could see the ice now, thick and dark, enough to cast her reflection as good as any mirror she'd ever seen. She could even see the distant ship overhead, not much more than a dark smudge on the ice but still there. Everything looked darker on the ice, more so as the ship passed in front of the sun, momentarily blotting it out and casting a shadow over the landscape.

Violet's own reflection became blurred and indistinct, and the captain's beside her was one hulking shadow, huge and distorted by the ice. Except for the eyes, deep set and luminous, almost glowing.

My mind playing tricks, she thought. *I know what you want me to think. You want me to whimper and moan, to jump at my own shadow. Captain's shadow anyway. Those eyes, that's just Bandit sitting on his shoulder. Not gonna work, you're gone, at worst back in Port Border. You'll never see me again, and I don't have to think about you no more neither. So get out of my head, you big rock. No one needs to know about you. No one.*

"All right there, Violet?" The captain's voice cut through the daydream and it was just the three of them standing there on the ice.

"Fine, Captain," she said. "Nothing to worry about."

"Wouldn't be much of a captain if I didn't worry, lass. Gabbi is waving at us. She never waves at me like that so it must be for you. Best we not keep her waiting."

SALT PORK. IT made a change from the hard-as-nails biscuits the crew had been surviving on. Except that there was still a pile of the slablike bread on the bench next to the galley oven. The cast iron monstrosity that was the most solid and complicated thing on the wooden ship. It had sheet-iron stoves mounted on fireboxes, with large holes within which sat large round pots. Below that was a cavity for baking covered by black iron doors. Copper pipes, a considerable expense, were wrapped around the oversized hearth and connected to a water tank the crew couldn't have moved if they tried. Violet had measured it once, and it would never have fit through the doorway so she was unsure how it had arrived in the galley.

It was designed to be efficient. Violet had long ago decided efficient meant complicated. The only simple thing about it was the open tray of bricks and sand the galley oven rested on to prevent excessive heat being transferred to the ship. And burning them all alive.

The ship was in the process of turning into an icebox itself. Violet thought the crew might appreciate some additional heat being transferred.

"How long does this need to cook for?" Violet asked, peering over the rim of one of the bubbling pots.

"Until the worst of the salt boils away," Gabbi said. The woman was upending her own cupboards in a search. Hadn't said what for. Had the face that suggested it were best not to ask.

"How long is that?"

"I'll tell you."

"But how will I know?"

"Because I'll tell you. Don't make that face at me. I'll tell you and then you'll know."

"But . . ."

"Biscuits, Violet. Take that sulk out on them. Need them to fill out the chowder. Crew need something hot or I won't be able to keep them out of here." Gabbi was sweating from the heat in the kitchen. Everywhere else on the ship was freezing, icicles forming on the brightwork, and those crew with beards or fur were all brushing out ice.

Violet glared at the hardtack, a meat hammer held between both her hands. "We got to boil the pork and pound the bread before we can eat it. Jack is right. We do need better food."

"Shush. Less talking and more pounding." Gabbi stepped back, hands on hips, looking glum. "Damn."

"What?"

"Lost my favourite jug. Pretty thing, all glass and perfect for tea. With flowers cut into it. Think Jack broke it and won't tell me about it."

"Why do you think that?"

"Think that because I cut my foot on broken glass this morning, and I didn't break no glass." She gave Violet a suspicious look. "You break my jug, Vi? Was it you?"

"No!"

"Good. Biscuits, now!"

Violet sighed and began to grind up the biscuits, hitting them until they broke into smaller portions. Then those until she was left with more malleable crumbs.

"Twice baked and now we're cooking them again," she complained.

Gabbi reached over and flicked her ear. "Stop your whining, lass. If this was an Alliance galley it would be thrice baked, at least. They don't stop at port as often as we do. And you'd be lucky to see half so much meat."

"Jack says they serve fresh kill on Alliance," Violet recalled. "Only good thing I ever heard him say about them."

"Ha," Gabbi laughed. "That's what I say. Stiff collar starchies are too soft for fresh kills. Have to swap out the butcher every tour. Heard one kept a pig so long it died of old age, all fat and gristly. Heard the crew were so touched in the head with grief they buried the hog at sea. And if we was Alliance, I'd have a peg and you'd have a hook. That's how they do things there."

"What? Why? I don't want no hook! Why would I have a hook?"

"Because you gotta do something with sailors who can't man the ropes, so the thinking goes. And cooking for a crew of ungrateful louts, why that's easy, ain't it?" Gabbi shook her head in disgust. "Stop worrying so much, Violet. Nobody's looking to trade your hand for a hook."

"Jack might," Violet said, louder than she'd meant.

"You ought not to listen to Jack so much. We don't keep him on for what comes out of his mouth."

"It's cause of his pretty face, ain't it, Gabbi?" Violet nudged the woman.

"If you must know, it's what's in his breeches that's real pretty," Gabbi winked.

"Ew, no, enough, enough!" Violet covered her face with one arm and tried to wave it off with the other. "I don't want to be thinking that. Why would you make me think that?"

"Because you're a brat, Violet," Gabbi smirked.

"You're evil."

"And don't you dare forget it."

Not likely, Violet thought. *Damned well be trying though.*

HOUNDS EXHALED, LONG and slow, breath misting in a billowing plume. Nel found it an impressive display. The woman had big lungs on her. Bosuns often did. Bellowing came with the job.

"Remember the first time I saw snow," Hounds said, rubbing her arms against the chill. "Was a little kid still riding my da's shoulders. Took a snowball to the face from my brother. Squealed my head off. Spent the rest of the day thinking I was a dragon. Spent the whole of the next day trying to get warm."

"Never done an ice run before?" Nel asked.

"Swore I'd never do one again." Hounds shook her head ruefully. "Save I like eating and drinking and having a bed to rest my head in more than I care to mean what I said. And now I feel as I've earned that drink, it must be time for grog, yes? Where's the blasted grog, woman?"

"Half a bell yet," Nel said, tapping the hourglass by the ship's bell. "I'm early. It happens."

"Something to help me sleep then, when it does happen," Hounds said. "Night watches are the worst."

Nel snorted. *Night watch.* The woman wasn't wrong, but there wasn't a true night or day on the ship. Just the three watches. Hounds would have two watches, Nel's and Quill's, before she had to stand watch again. If the woman had sense she'd use that to sleep but there were always jobs to be done and distractions to be had. It had happened before that Nel had stood three watches or more without pausing to sleep. It was easy to lose track when the sun didn't set. And on the occasion that it did, it was the wrong sun, the wrong colour or size. Or there were too many suns. That one was the worst. In some ports the suns never set. Made one long for the black.

That and sleeping on an ice run was proving as difficult as she remembered.

"Where's your man?"

"Which one?" Hounds tilted the sandglass slightly on its axis with one finger. Nel recognised the temptation to flip the timepiece, thus ending her watch and making it grog time. It was a temptation most sailors succumbed to at some point, though rarely in front of other officers and usually broken before long. A navigator's logs and dead reckoning would usually be thrown out by the flip and that would send the more fastidious ones into a frothing frenzy. On occasion it could even throw them off course if the navigator misunderstood the error.

"The one with his mitts tied to your apron strings," Nel said, not commenting on the timepiece.

Hounds looked at her. "Which one?" she repeated. "They're all momma's boys. Which one?"

"Denzel."

"Ah, that boy. Sent him off a bell ago. Hasn't been sleeping well, on account of your captain. Kept forgetting to turn the piece."

"The captain?"

"Poor lad woke to find the man watching him sleep. Said he had glowing eyes. Think he were just walking that pet ferret your girl Violet keeps, but it was right unnatural to wake to. Gave the boy mares and been giving me a headache all watch because."

Nel winced. Captain was sleepwalking again. Perfect.

"Captain does that," she muttered. "He's . . . eccentric."

"More than that, Vaughn," Hounds said. "Seen it before. Not hard to recognise when you have."

"What do you mean?" Nel asked. "Seen what?"

"Been in the fog, ain't he?"

"What do you know about it, Hounds?"

"Vintage. I was there. Whole place was struck down by the fog."

"Whole place was struck down," Nel said. "But not by the fog."

Hounds nodded. "So you do know it."

"I was there. Ain't called Vintage no more. Not after."

"Aye, it ain't, and so was I. There, I mean."

"Really," Nel growled.

"Did my service, that was part of it. Must be, what, five years now? Since."

Nel shrugged, not wanting to speak. Not trusting.

"Captain's a good man." So much for not speaking.

"Don't doubt it," Hounds said. "What happened out there was wrong, Vaughn. I saw what happened."

"I was on her," Nel muttered darkly, hating the words. "Second mate. Women who did for Vintage . . . she were my captain."

Was. Was my captain.

"Ah," Hounds said. "Thought that might be. And the captain? Our captain, I mean."

"Born and raised on Vintage."

"Now that's a sorrow, truly."

"You can't catch what he's got, Hounds," Nel warned her sharply. "And I hear any talk otherwise—"

"I know you can't," Hounds interrupted her. "Said I was there, didn't I? Fog and mist, same thing ain't they? All around us out here but not meant to be down in the dirt. Does weird things to a person. Hells, brass and braids figuring that much out was the only good thing to come of that day."

"Come too late."

"Always does, don't it. Braids don't keep time."

Nel stared at her, suspicious. Couldn't forget what happened at Vintage, not with the captain around to remind her. A living reminder to her.

"Fog ain't like mist," she said to Hounds. "It's something else."

"What then? And from where?"

"Don't know. But mist, been out in it. Myself. Mist didn't do nothing to my captain."

"Wasn't always your captain though, was he? When'd you sign on with him?" Hounds asked.

"After," Nel said.

"Was he already starting to show? Back then?"

"Got a rule on the *Tantamount*, Hounds," Nel said. "Past don't matter. Don't care about who you were before you stepped on here. So don't ask."

"Captain is the captain," Hounds nodded agreeably. "I get that, I do, Vaughn. Got no problem on my end. Only Denzel and I have had our run of bad captains. Just wanting you to know I ain't pulling with my eyes shut."

"I like you, Hounds," Nel said. "So far. Much as I like anyone. Don't make me regret hiring you."

"So long as the captain is the captain and you're the skipper we're square rigged, you and I, Vaughn," Hounds said. "And to be fair, if I'm getting paid I don't care much beyond that."

Nel reached over and flipped the sand timer. "Call the bells, Hounds. Your watch is over. Go get your drink."

"Aye, aye, Skipper." Hounds saluted as she took her leave.

It was an Alliance salute, one the marines favoured. Odd how it hadn't bothered her until now.

ONE OF THE more innocuous changes to the *Tantamount* since they'd passed through Port Border had been to her armament. Gone were the cast iron and smooth bore cannons, pitiful though they had seemed the last time they'd been pressed into action. The weapons had been pawned at their previous stop, most likely due to be melted down for scrap and slag according to Jack, replaced instead by the even less intimidating wand batteries.

Violet did not care for them. They were made from bronze and mounted on a pedestal that twisted and swivelled, though the bracket locked at just under a half circle to ensure it couldn't be pointed directly back at the ship. Both "cannon" and mounting required a great deal of polish and grease, the cannon so it wouldn't corrode and the mounting so it wouldn't lock up. Polish and grease were two mutually exclusive conditions, or so Violet had become convinced since it was her job to maintain the armament. And in the cold and ice creeping aboard the ship they required double the maintenance.

For now, she sat perched on the ship's railing, legs hooked under her for balance, wiping in vain at grease-stained hands with an already grease-stained rag while the captain talked. He was trying to justify the transition. In part, just to himself. In part, so he didn't have to be out on the ice.

"Compressed thaumatics, my dear, way of the future. Nothing like archaic powder. Alchemical contraptions, confounded things. Never liked them, far too noisy. Outdated.

"See this here?" The captain pointed to a series of ridges and a metal circle at the firing end. "Three point sighting system. Marvellous. Could put a broadside through a porthole with this. So I was told. Must test it. Fires faster too, like all thaumatics. Oversized wands really. Wand weaponry. Must be a name for it, can't recall it for the life of me. Smaller, faster, less likely to send a cannonball through the galley. Gabbi never did forget that. Terrible tragedy. Waste of good soup. But there's always a cost. A price. A downside. No more cannonballs now."

He tossed a smooth, rounded crystal in Violet's direction. The condensed thaumatic crystal that powered the new cannon. Like an upscaled version of what was locked in the armoury or what the skipper kept in her cabin. Violet caught it, despite her greased hands.

"They get hot," the captain explained, gesturing with his hands. "Volatile, explosive. Boom!" He jerked his hands apart sharply.

Violet looked at the shard of crystal in her hand. It was barely warm. "Boom?" she expressed her dubiousness.

"Boom," the captain nodded. "A very big boom, my dear girl. Very big indeed. One must be careful, very much so."

"So isn't this dangerous to have aboard? Couldn't it go . . . boom?"

"It could, it might, it has, it will. But no more so than black powder. There are always risks, always, nature of the job, part of the fun. But thaumatic crystals take up less space than powder kegs and shot. A barrel here is a coin there, another successful trip, another hot meal. A girl needs to eat, Violet. We all need to eat."

"And one barrel makes a difference . . ." Violet shook her head, biting off her next words. Yes, it did. She knew it did. She'd seen the ledgers with all their squiggly lines and numbers. The skipper had explained it. They were running close to the red, as it were. Red was bad. They were broke. It all mattered. It all counted, or would count if there were anything to count at the end of it. There needed to be counting, as the captain would say.

Violet shook her head. The inside of it was starting to sound like the captain. The thought made her smile ruefully. It could be worse. They had work now.

"Violet," the captain called to her. Violet's eyes came up to find him looking at her. "What are you doing in my cabin?"

"This isn't your cabin, Captain," she said.

"It isn't?" The captain did a slow spin, taking in the open deck of the *Tantamount*. The confusion in his bearing made Violet drop her head, unable to watch.

Captain gets confused.

"Ah, well, I must have come to see you then." Horatio focused back on her. He smiled inexplicably, as if pleased with this outcome. "Violet, yes?"

"Captain?" Violet frowned, confused.

"Careful with that, my dear, volatile, you know."

"Aye, sir. Steady as she goes."

"Capital. I've been thinking, Violet." The captain twirled his finger towards the sky for emphasis.

"Sir?"

"About you, Violet. And your place aboard this ship."

"Captain?" Violet felt the first trace of alarm.

The captain began to pace in front of her. "We've lost people in my time as Captain. Not just recently, it's been a long run. A lot of people, Violet. A lot of good people. Some not so good and some who I wish had gone sooner. But none I wished ill."

Violet's hand went to her shoulder. The new tattoo felt hot and itchy under its wrapping.

"It bothers me, Violet." The captain stopped his pacing, hands clasped behind his back, facing her. His head came up, eyes distant and glassy. "It bothers me greatly to lose people. The idea that people, my people, people under my protection would be hurt. Have been hurt, lost . . . gone.

"I like," the captain started his pacing again, "to tell myself that I am not a captain who would . . . leave people behind. Not one who would give up on his someone. That is the kind of captain I want to be. That is the kind of man I want to be remembered as. But then . . . have you met the crew? Inordinately unrestrained bunch. Despicable even, some of them. Miserable, miserly." The captain plucked his hat off, letting his hair waft freely in the faint breeze while he held it to his chest. He smiled as he spoke. "Loyal, generous even. Perhaps to a fault? Is generosity a fault? Nel would say so. Says so all the time in fact."

"Captain?" Violet chanced an interruption, swallowing the lump in her throat. It felt intrusive to listen. Like she ought to leave.

"I adore my crew, Violet," Horatio's voice was quiet. "Like the family I left behind. My daughter . . . daughters. The idea of . . . losing them, there are no words, Violet. Sometimes I forget. And then . . . I remember. It is like losing them all over again. I would not wish it upon anyone. I would do anything, *anything*, to prevent it from happening again."

Horatio smiled. That sad smile, when all of him was there. Memories.

"I walked into the fire for them, so Nel tells me. Yet . . . . it wasn't enough, was it? Fire on the *Tantamount*, now that truly does scare me. Hopefully it never comes to that. Not again . . . because I like to think . . . I tell myself . . . would I truly?"

"I think you would, Captain," Violet told him, whisper quiet.

"That's very kind of you to say, Violet, but the truth of it is I have Nel to do those sorts of things. The heroics. They don't go so well if I have to do them. Not the heroic type, myself. Nel is, was born to it. A parent would be proud."

"She gets it from you," Violet told him.

"Well," the captain puffed out his chest at the praise, settling his hat back on his head, "one would like to think so. I hired the woman, surely I can take some credit for that."

"Never did hear that story, Captain," Violet said. "About how the skipper came to be the skipper. Nor how Quill got to be here. Don't neither of them like to tell it."

The captain looked amused. "And what do we tell people about how you came to be here, my dear?"

"Mostly lies, Captain. Truth don't make for the best story."

"Except when it does, of course. I see you side-tracking me here."

"Just don't wanna spit and polish no more, Captain." Violet held up her grimy hands as proof.

"You do seem to have worn them down." The captain leaned in to inspect. "Rather filthy, in fact, what a shame. I had a present for you."

"A present?" Violet perked up.

"Yes, but you have grease on your hands. It wouldn't go well," the captain fussed.

"They're clean!" Violet insisted, holding one hand up as evidence.

"Which is more than one can say for your breeches, young lady," the captain said.

"It's good for them." Violet slapped her thigh, surreptitiously wiping another smear off her good hand. "Stops them tearing, keeps the ice off."

"Who told you that?"

"Everybody knows that, Captain."

"I didn't know that."

"You making fun of me, Captain?"

"Never!" The captain reached into his coat, buffing the present on his sleeve before holding it out. Held careful in such a way that Violet couldn't make out what it was. No matter which way she twisted and turned.

"When you first came aboard, my dear, I believe you had little more to your name than the clothes on your back." He looked at her critically. "And since then you have added a good layer of tar. And a tail."

Violet grinned, swatting the air behind her with the twin appendages.

"Yes, one cannot forget the tail. Very awkward if one does. But it seems to me that a girl should have more possessions than the bare necessities. Not much, mind you—frugality and minimalism are traits to be admired aboard a ship. But it occurs to me that I have too many possessions, whereas you have none. This seems a great imbalance to me. I believe I should do something about it."

"What is that?" Violet leaned from side to side, still trying to see.

"It," the captain said through a wide grin, "is timeless. It is magical, a masterful contraption of exquisiteness. An encapsulation of our lives. This, my dearest Violet, is what we are."

The captain opened his hands, holding his prize out on flat palms.

It was a water globe, a miniature scene encased within a glass sphere. A tiny model ship, complete with sails and rigging. And it wasn't water that the ship floated on, Violet realised. The medium was mist, black and wispy. There was no base to the sphere, it rolled on the palms of the captain's hands but the ship stayed upright, barely listing. It must have ether set into the tiny hull, just like the *Tantamount*.

"Hold it," the captain winked, passing over the sphere.

Violet held it, not like the captain had but between the fingers of both hands, staring at the ship intently. No matter which way she turned the globe, the vessel stayed upright. In addition to the ether in the ship and the mist contained inside, she realised there were tiny flakes, mere shavings of ether floating in the mist. And what she'd first taken to be dust or impurities in the glass was still more of the substance in the sphere itself. The ship inside was suspended between all the swirling currents this created.

"This," Horatio touched his finger to the globe, tracing a line up from the bow of the model ship, "now this once belonged to my daughter. A precocious girl, much like yourself. She'd stare at it for hours, trying to get the ship out, I believe. Whenever she held it, the mist would turn into a storm, tossing the ship to and fro. I never did know why that happened, but it was only when she held it. Never worked for me, no matter how much I shook it."

The captain smiled, lost in the memory for a moment. He sighed. "She . . . well, she outgrew it, I suppose. Left it behind one day, as children do. But I still carry it around. Helps me remember . . . things. Who I am, who I used to be. And it's pretty to look at and better that than sitting on some dusty shelf somewhere or buried at the bottom of a chest."

"So," Violet considered what the captain was saying, "can I keep it?"

"You," he said, "may borrow it." The captain twirled his finger theatrically. "And one day you may give it back to me. Or you may give it to someone else. Perhaps that will be the way of it. But for now, Violet, yes, you may keep it. As a token gesture of what you mean to me, my dear. And how very much we all hope you stay with us."

Violet threw her arms around the captain, hugging him tight.

"Ah, yes, well then," the captain grinned sheepishly. He seemed a bit embarrassed by her affection. "Perhaps you can remind me where my cabin is now. Damnably cold out here, isn't it?"

NIGHT WASN'T PROPER night when you had snow. Damned stuff caught the sun and stored it, then went on to add the moon and stars at night until it practically glowed when it ought to be dark. Made sleeping impossible. At least that was the theory the foreman of the Glassy Run had concocted. With a lot of time to himself and only Draugr for company, he had more time than he liked for thinking.

Thinking wasn't an honest working man's pastime. It was for scholars and bearded types, philosophers who went around battling each other from across town squares in booming proclamations about the whats and whys of the worlds.

That he'd come to consider what was and what wasn't an acceptable definition of night said he'd been out on the ice for far too long. Night was meant to be when the sun went down and things got dark, only when the sun went down on the Glassy Run it didn't get dark. Maddening.

This would be his last winter on the Run, the foreman resolved. Some other fool could take over for the next cutting season. The cutting was the worst part. Much of it was done at night, particularly on still nights like tonight, when the ice was thickest. His team of Draugr, brilliant conversationalists one and all, had been scraping the snow off the surface of the run. Several were waiting nearby, harnessed to the plough, a pair of parallel blades fixed to a harness for more uniform blocks. All the harnessed Draugr were wearing cork shoes, a necessity for when they would soon have to drag the heavy cutter across the ice.

Lonely, miserable work, the foreman thought again. But that last ship had cleared out the storehouses and they needed refilling. It didn't feel like it at present but a cold winter was a good thing. A warm winter could waste an entire year of trade.

"Enough slacking," the foreman called. "Start the cutting."

Nothing happened. The Draugr who'd been doing the scraping stood motionless on the other side of the river, clutching their brooms. The foreman cursed and reached for the whistle around his neck with numb fingers. Of course nothing was happening. Draugr wouldn't do squat without being told to squat the right way.

He blew on the whistle, harder than he ought with lips so chapped from the frost they felt like to bleed. His last season for sure, one way or the next. Yet still there was no response from the cutters.

"What's wrong with you miserable layabouts?"

The foreman turned around, still treading carefully despite his spiked shoes.

There was a golem on the ice, if that was what it was. The foreman couldn't think of what else it might be, couldn't think of anything else that hulking, animated rock creature could be. All the golems he'd ever laid eyes on had been steam powered, noisy and billowing contraptions full of gears and cogs. This thing was sleek, silent, menacing. And he backed away from it as fast as he could, terrified the ice might crack under its weight at any moment. There were good reasons they used Draugr instead of golems or anything near as heavy on the ice.

For now the golem didn't seem interested in him, as oblivious to his presence as the Draugr were to it. Those that remained, that was, the scrapers on the other side of the river.

The cutters, those who had been harnessed behind him, they lay motionless on the ice. Decapitated, heads severed from their bodies, limbs ripped off. Dismembered in a silent surgery, neither golem nor Draugr making a sound. Dark stains were spreading from the mutilated bodies, if not blood then something very much like it. The foreman felt his own guts begin to heave as his mind struggled to accept what he was looking at.

The golem took a step towards him, footsteps loud, frighteningly loud on the brushed ice. One step then another, but not towards him, he realised with something that was both panic and relief. Its attention was solely fixed on the remaining Draugr across the river, its intentions as obvious when it raised one clenched fist. The arm attached to that fist extended out like a fin, tapering to what looked like a razor-sharp edge, and gleamed wetly in the night. *Redundant*, the foreman thought madly, the thing was clearly capable of tearing whatever it chose apart with its bare hands.

It must have heard his thoughts, or else he was babbling out loud. It was the only explanation for why those infernal red eyes suddenly fixed on him. The golem slowed, seemed torn in indecision for a moment, before it changed direction towards him.

The foreman squealed and began to run, feet slipping along the ice despite the spikes. Then came the sound he'd been dreading.

The sound of ice cracking. The sight of a crack racing out from between his feet ahead of him. He risked a look behind him. The golem had paused, looking down at its foot where the crack had started. It raised that foot again and brought it down hard.

The ice under the foreman gave and all he knew was cold.

THE NOON BELLS were tolling, four sets of pairs. Violet didn't have to turn around to know that sailors were already lining up in front of the galley for their daily ration of grog. She wrinkled her nose. The smell of the undiluted rum was enough to make her gag. Not that she was permitted a share, on account of her age.

Her age didn't excuse her from the daily ritual though. The shout of "up spirits" was making the rounds; as if anyone needed to be made aware.

Stepping out onto the deck, Violet watched as Jack came down from the mainmast and made the trip across the quarterdeck and towards the stern of the ship where the skipper was on watch. What happened next was unusual. The skipper waved Jack off, angrily and to the Korrigan's considerable confusion. After a moment, Jack turned about and made his way back towards the galley.

"What's going on, Jack?" Gabbi asked, emerging from the

galley with her measuring jugs.

"Captain's got the key," Jack told her.

"But it's the skipper's watch," Violet said. The watch officer always held the key to the rum jug. Always.

Jack shrugged, headed now for the captain's cabin at the very back of the ship.

"Hells," Gabbi muttered.

"Why's the captain got the key, Gabbi?"

"No good reason, Vi. For pity's sake don't be asking the skipper why either. Just let this one go."

"But . . ."

"Please, lass, just hush this once."

Violet chewed on her lower lip until Jack came back holding the key to the spirit locker. He waved to one of the sailors loitering near the galley and disappeared below decks. He emerged a few minutes later with the ornately decorated rum jug carried between him and the other sailor.

The officers all lined up in front of it, calling out the numbers of sailors present from their watches. Gabbi measured out each sailor's allowance, their daily tot, before mixing it all in a separate tub with water from another cask. One-part rum to four-parts water, if Violet remembered correctly. The crew all filed through with their drinking vessels in hand, and Gabbi doled out their ration. Most drank it then and there in one long gulp.

The officers went last, Hounds being first in line.

"Thought I was done being back of the line," the woman said with a crooked grin.

"Captain's orders," Gabbi told her. "Crew comes first."

"Aye, keeps them from jumping every other port. Still, always thought cutting the line was the best part about making officer."

"Cook," was all Quill said, holding out a tin cup when he stepped up.

"You started drinking all of a sudden, Loveland?" Gabbi asked in surprise. "Never thought I'd see the day."

"I require it straight, cook."

Gabbi chuckled. "Now that'd be a sight." She measured out Quill's share of rum from the jug without mixing it with water. Only the officers were allowed to request their ration be served neat. The Kelpie turned stiffly and strode away, showing no signs of actually intending to drink his. Violet didn't think she'd ever seen Quill drink. Already she could see the crew take note of this development.

Gabbi winked at Violet. "Wonder who he owes."

"Maybe he's looking to trade," she suggested. Rum was as good as coin during a run. Most crew were happy to trade favours and goods for extra rations.

"Kelpie don't do favours or ask them," Gabbi said confidently. "He owes someone."

Jack shuffled up, looking unhappy. "Tastes different," he complained. "What'd you do?"

"Added limes, Jack. They're good for you. Stop your teeth rotting and your gums bleeding."

"Tastes different."

"Limes make it better. Oi, who's Quill gone and got himself indebted to? You know?"

Jack shrugged. "Denzel maybe. They've been playing cards."

"Kelpie plays cards?"

"Kelpie loses at cards."

"Ha, now that makes my day. Skipper, you collecting or no?"

Violet saw the skipper leaning against the sterncastle stairs. She looked both angry and miserable at the same time. But she did push herself up and made the walk over.

"Straight or cut, Skipper?" Gabbi asked.

The skipper made a face. "Six water," she said.

Gabbi hesitated, ladle halfway up. "I hear that right?"

The skipper sighed. "Six water grog, Gabbi," she repeated. "And just say no more about it."

"Six water it is," Gabbi said quietly, pouring Nel's ration and adding an extra third of water to it. The skipper took it and turned around, making her way back to her post. It struck Violet as a long, lonely walk.

She heard a door close, turned her head fast enough to see the back of the captain through the window. No wonder the skipper had looked miserable. Not only had the captain cut her rum ration, but he hadn't trusted her with the key to the spirit room.

"Not a word, Violet," Gabbi looked at her hard. "Not one word."

Violet nodded mutely.

"Jack, take the jug back below. I've got work that needs doing."

Chapter 9

JACK HAD MANAGED to retrieve the jug without her but had insisted Violet accompany him and Mugs as they manhandled the rum jug back down below. She led the way with a glowstone in one hand, the fist sized orb putting out a silvery light on the *Tantamount's* innards.

Funny things, glowstones. Only glow when it's dark and only aboard ships and only down in the hold. That's a lot of only. Probably more etheric mishaps, Violet mused. She could see mostly fine without the stone's help so she held it behind her back, lighting the way for the two grunting seamen. Grunting was good though. Meant the jug was heavy and it wouldn't run dry too soon. Bad things happened when the rum was gone.

"Jack," Violet called, stopping halfway into the cargo hold.

"What?" It sounded like what. It was mostly an unintelligible grunt as he hauled away. There was a thump as he and Mugs rested the rum jug. Violet thought they would have been more respectful of it, or at least careful.

"This ain't where she goes," Jack said more clearly. "Gotta be tucked away or the layabouts will be tapping the admiral. Don't want that."

"Don't use rum for an admiral," Mugs disputed his claim. "Gotta be brandy."

"Don't got brandy. Rum's just as good."

"Ain't proper. Admirals go in brandy. Officers go in whiskey."

"Then what's rum for?" Jack challenged.

"For drinking. Can't waste good rum on an officer."

Jack actually burst out laughing, clapping Mugs on the shoulder. The sailor staggered and winced under the approval.

"Jack," Violet called again, holding back a long suffering sigh.

"What?" he yelled, annoyed again.

"Got wet feet."

Unlike a lot of the other sailors, Violet hadn't yet switched to wearing boots aboard for this run. She got sent to the nest too often and found she couldn't grip the ropes so well. The cold had seeped into the ship but so far she had been all right. Tails were going a bit stiff but the extra fur helped. Better than Quill anyway.

But now her feet were both cold and wet. She was standing in a very thin layer of water, like what you'd find on a cottage window on a misty morning. The kind that filtered through from the other side.

Jack ambled up beside her, kneeling and reaching out with one big paw to touch the deck. He stared at his hand unhappily. He turned around and made a signal to Mugs. The two both grabbed an ear of the rum jug and started back the way they'd come.

"Jack!" Violet called after him. "Where you going?"

"Up top," Jack told her between grunts. "Ice is melting. Not leaving the rum down here. Wouldn't be safe."

"Can't waste good rum," Mugs agreed.

Bad things happened when the rum ran out. But right now the rum was running away.

THE FIRST ATTEMPT to investigate their melting cargo was doomed before it began. The hold had been packed to the gunwales, or as far as the blocks of ice could be packed and kept cold. Packed in such a way that it was impossible to investigate deep into the hold. There was nowhere to shift the ice that needed to be cleared away.

"Condensation," the captain had announced upon inspection. "Most likely a split seam on the underside. Leaking ether, shifting the envelope around."

An unstable envelope, as Violet came to understand, meant trouble. It was like a small tide, rising and falling, the worst kind of shifting ballast. If it was a bad leak, it could start to affect the entire ship, putting them all at risk. But right now it was creating friction, the folds and bulges of a shifting envelope creating heat. Not much, but certainly enough to begin the thawing of the *Tantamount's* cargo.

Which was what needed to be confirmed now. Violet had offered to go over the side to investigate just that.

"Absolutely not," the skipper had told her. Swaying. Shaking. The skipper didn't look at her. She had the trembles, both in her hands and feet. Withdrawal, Gabbi had whispered when the woman's back was turned. All the grog leaving her body the same way the ether was being leeched from the ship. And it didn't look an enjoyable experience.

"Can't go walking down the hull." The skipper shook her head, hugging her arms to herself. "Not with a shifting envelope. One wrong bank and you might not have enough pull to keep your feet stuck. Ain't jumping out after you."

"Indeed not," the captain said. "Far too dangerous a job. We'll use the bosun's chair. Lower a man down."

"I'll go," the skipper said immediately, stepping up to the edge and casting a speculative glance over.

"I think not," the captain said, looking his first officer up and down.

The skipper started to object. "Captain, I am more than capable of . . ."

"Chanel," the captain said, quietly. The skipper stared at him, open mouthed. She turned away, walking stiffly to the far end of the ship, joining Quill on the bridge. The navigator gave her an odd look but didn't make any obvious comments to her.

Names are powerful, Violet thought, unhappily. You didn't call the skipper by her proper name. Violet could count on one hand the number of times she'd heard folk do it, and none of those had been good times.

"Miss Hounds," the captain raised his voice to be heard.

"Aye, Captain?" The woman appeared at his side quickly. If she'd heard any of the exchange she gave no sign of it.

"Bring the bosun's chair around and take a view of our underbelly," he told her.

"Aye aye, sir." Hounds saluted. She still saluted different to all the other crew Violet noted. Even her people followed the usual form when salutes were required. Odd, that.

Hounds worked quickly, Violet was forced to admit. The crane was unlashed and the bosun's chair detached from the mainmast's rigging and brought over. Hounds gave Violet a wink as she disappeared over the side.

With nothing to do but wait, something she had never been good at, Violet made her way to the bridge. Quill gave her ugly looks. Nothing new there, but the skipper ignored her as well, holding tight to a rope and staring down the back trail of the *Tantamount*.

"Skipper?" Violet called to her.

No answer. The woman kept her back stiffly turned about. The hand that held onto the rope was white knuckled and trembling.

Violet took a step closer. Something struck at her feet, fast and whiplike. She could only gape at Quill in surprise as his tail retracted behind him. His head turned down towards her, teeth bared.

A shout from behind her. They were pulling Hounds back up. Quill jerked his head back the way Violet had come. There was little to misinterpret about any of it.

"You all right, Vi?" Gabbi asked. The cook leaned against the galley door under the bridge, watching Jack and the other hands as they worked the crane.

"Fine," Violet snapped, meaner than she'd intended. She dashed at her eyes with the back of one hand, blinking furiously. She faced away from Gabbi too, like the skipper had done.

"Skipper's a real bear hung-over," Gabbi offered. "Kelpie's more of a dog, don't know when to back down."

"It's fine," Violet repeated loudly. "Don't care, anyways."

"Course you don't," Gabbi nodded. "Best go, Captain's waving for you."

"Right," Violet said, sucking in a deep breath.

"It's bad, Captain," Hounds was saying. "And by bad, I mean whoever patched your woodwork did so something awful. Can see where you had a chunk bitten out of you."

That had been Violet's handiwork. Her idea. Not the repairs but dropping the golem through the bowels of the ship.

"Timbers are warped outwards," Hounds went on. "Wasn't caulked properly so we're going to need oakum and pitch to fix it."

"We laid in both last stop," the captain confirmed.

"Going to need lots," Hound said. "It's the devil that cracked."

A pall of silence hung over the gathered crew.

The devil seam. It would have to be that, the garboard seam, the devil.

Means the leak is directly underneath us, right along the bottom of the hull.

Means it is my fault.

"Who's our best caulker, Captain?" Hounds asked.

"Piper, naturally," the captain frowned at her. "Where is he? Ah, Violet, where's Piper? Haven't seen him. Not like him, not like him at all."

"Don't know no Piper, Captain," Hounds said, looking confused. Violet stepped up beside her.

"Piper's not here no more, Captain," she said, speaking directly to him. "Not since before we stopped in Port Border. Remember?"

"Ah," the captain sighed, putting a hand to his temple. "Yes, yes I do remember, Violet. I miss him, that's all that is. That's all it is, you get used to people being around after a while. That's all it is."

"You any good with a caulking iron or hammer, lass?" Hounds said to Violet.

She shrugged. "Used them once or twice."

"Don't be false modest here," Hounds said. "What I'm gonna ask you . . . it ain't safe, won't lie about that. Need to caulk that seam, and it is that seam, the one and only. It's a two-man job and the chair don't like to hold two. You though, you're little and light, won't notice so much."

"I can do it," Violet told her. "Who you sending with me?"

Hounds appeared to consider but Violet suspected she already had a plan in mind. Woman was just talking her way through it.

"Mantid. Lighter than he looks. Sent him out on plenty of walks before too. Spikes and pincers are good for making sure you don't come loose. We'll tie a rope to you though, just take it slow and do it right."

Mantid was making his way down from the crow's nest. There was something unnatural about the way he walked, face first, legs all out and splayed. Like some great big spider rather than . . . whatever else he was meant to be. Bug's head was doing that odd twist again, all the way to the side with one eye up and the other down, looking at everything askew. Looking at her, Violet concluded.

Didn't look any more thrilled about their job than she was.

THERE WAS A step involved in caulking the devil that Violet hadn't thought of. Hadn't even been aware of up until now. In all her time aboard it had never occurred, close but never actually, though she had seen it happen to other ships. Throwing the *Tantamount* off her axis.

Quill hadn't been happy about it. Quill was never happy about anything but this he had objected to vehemently. Even yelling at the captain. Violet hadn't seen who had shouted him down, too busy boiling pitch, but she would have paid good coin to have witnessed it.

Crew had to be sent to disrupt the etheric ballast. There was a more complicated term for it that Violet had missed. Something about realignment. They were going to shift the plane the *Tantamount* sailed on.

She hadn't liked that part. It had been sudden and violent. There had been cussing up and down the ship, a crash from the galley. It was like someone had taken the world and all its orientations and twisted it hard.

All so the ship's crane could swing out over the side and lower the two of them to the spine of the ship.

The chair was crowded. Crowded and cold. Mantid's chitinous body was rigid, and Violet found herself edging to the limit of the seat, hips half off the edge of the plank as she skived away from Mantid's spiky forearms. It couldn't have been much more comfortable for Mantid. His irregular body had him almost squatting over the plank, legs wrapped around it. Too bad they couldn't have been lowered down in the bubble but then they wouldn't have been able to get at the seam.

The air got colder as the crew lowered them. Thinner too. Violet's breath became more laboured, emerging in small puffs. Mantid seemed to move more slowly too but he might have just been holding still, trying not to jostle the tin of molten pitch hung between them. Violet hadn't been keen on riding down with a bucket of boiling black goo. But it was preferable to being underneath it when it was lowered down from a pitching ship.

Hounds had explained that in graphic detail to her.

"There," Violet pointed, leaning forward. She could see the patch job, crude like Hounds had said. Right where she'd taken an axe to the bottom of the ship. Piper had died on the other side of that.

No, that wasn't right. She hadn't seen that happen. When she closed her eyes she could still see his face, solemn and wise. Not gone. The burly arms and shoulders, the perfect place for Bandit to ride about. All covered in ink, tattoos like the one on her shoulder. Not dead, just gone, just for a little while. That was what she told herself, over and over.

Just gone, just gone.

Her eyes were hot and her face was cold. Stupid tears. She shook her head angrily, dashing them away to form tiny puffs of sleet. Now wasn't the time to think about this.

She remembered splinters flying, the sounds of fighting above her, then the gleaming black golem falling past her into the black.

Forever into the black, nothing but stars and mist.

Violet shook her head again, making the chair sway a bit, and reached for her scraping tool, pushing all that aside. She could see the faint clouds of ether now, where they were seeping out of the hull. They left a trail like water through snow, cutting through the nearby miasma in a river before it became difficult to see where one ended and the other began.

Mantid reached out with his front two legs, latching onto the garboard seam and transferring his weight from the bosun's chair to the hull. Violet was envious. He was managing to hold on even with the unstable pull from the ballast. The rope around her waist was already chafing.

Before they could caulk the seam, they had to remove the old fibrous wadding filling the seam. Mantid was doing so with his forearms, walking backwards along the seam and scraping it away. Violet had to do the same with a raking iron, digging out the caulk and tar without damaging the seam. Despite the chill air, it wasn't long before she was sweating profusely, her arms and back starting to moan in protest. The hardest part was not being able to brace her feet against anything, and taking care not to knock over the hot pitch beside her.

A sidelong glance told her Mantid had already finished his share of the work, clinging at an angle to the hull and watching her.

"You can start working on the patch," Violet told him. "I'll manage the devil."

Again the odd, quizzical tilt of the head. Maybe it was his way of nodding. He did set to work, reaching out and plucking a strand of oakum delicately from the bag slung over the bosun's chair. Despite not having fingers, Mantid managed well enough.

More than well enough. Seemed his forelimbs were perfect for driving the oakum into the cracked seams, especially where the timbers had warped, like Hounds had said. Probably from all the ice melt inside.

The rope caught at her waist again when she leaned forward. Violet cursed and reached for the knot. She hadn't fallen since her first few weeks on the *Tantamount.* You learnt to hold on or you got what you deserved. With the rope gone she could reach the edges of what needed clearing. Once Violet had finished clearing the devil seam, Mantid started filling in that as well, forelimbs hammering away at the tarred ropes. Violet still had to go over them all again with a caulking mallet to make sure they were proper wedged. Hounds had explained that it would have to be her as Mantid couldn't manage a tool like a hammer.

A likely story, she thought as she took up hammer and iron, leaning out to start tapping away at the tightly packed seams. It was a slow process, but not half so hard as Hounds had made it out to be.

Between the devil and the black, she'd called it. Violet looked down between her knees; wispy miasma, brightly coloured stars. Off in the distance the grey turned to purple and shades of blue. A nebula, maybe. Quill had mentioned there was one near Vice. Something to aim for if she fell.

She could see the other side of the hull, due to the unnatural tilt of the ship. It was covered in hoarfrost, a thin layer of fresh ice moulting.

Ether must be gathering there. Least it won't melt the cargo on that side.

It was too bad they couldn't just shave the ice off the side of a ship. When it formed on the inside of the hull it was fine, good enough for chilling drinks at least. Mostly. But on the outside it formed and froze with bits and pieces of miasma littered throughout. Ether or the opposite of what ether was. Seemed a waste, but the captain and skipper both said never to use that ice.

"Be out of a job though," Violet said aloud, causing Mantid to stare at her funny. Or maybe he wasn't staring at her. Big bug seemed worked up over something. He was turning in place, all four legs doing a sort of jig. Head kept watching her though, through a complete turn. Violet shrugged her shoulders and got to tapping again.

"Violet, Mantid!"

Someone calling from above. Sounded like Hounds, or maybe the skipper. Both sounded alike when they bellowed.

"Gonna pull you up." It was Hounds, leaning far out over the edge too.

"We ain't done yet!" Violet called back, leaning out so as she could see Hounds. "Still got to pay these ropes over."

"No time," Hounds yelled. "Into the chair, both of you. Kelpie says there's a broken corridor ahead. Can't risk hitting it with the ship on a lean like this."

The words had an immediate effect on Mantid. His head swivelled back and forth rapidly, clearly agitated. Then he took a flying leap from the hull to the chair. Violet had to grab for the support rope as Mantid's arrival sent the chair swinging, scalding hot pitch splattering everywhere.

Violet planted one foot, in almost the only place that wasn't tarred. She reached for her discarded safety rope with her free hand as Mantid called out above them, a sound Violet had never heard him make before that was somewhere between a chirp and a hiss. She had the absurd thought that it was Bandit and Quill singing together.

Whatever it sounded like to her, to Hounds and the crew above it clearly meant haul on the ropes, as the chair started ascending jerkily. Violet cursed again and wrapped the safety rope around her wrist. Opposite her, Mantid had all four feet out and splayed, one hooked over a rope. His arms with their sharp spines were tucked tight against his chest, maybe so he wouldn't cut the ropes himself. That would be bad.

"Brace!"

The word rang out from above, moments before the whole ship shuddered. Violet thought she could hear the *Tantamount* scream in protest as if it was buffeted by an unexpected envelope, causing timbers to strain against themselves and ropes to heave.

The chair swung toward the hull. Violet brought her feet up instinctively, hoisting herself off the wood and taking the impact through her legs. Out of the corner of her eye, she saw Mantid do another one of his flying leaps, back to the hull this time and sticking there. All six limbs were out now, sunk into whatever purchase he'd managed to find. Meant she had the chair all to herself, though Violet felt better off trusting to the ropes she was holding.

The *Tantamount* shook again and there was an explosive crack. One of the ropes holding the chair gave. Violet snatched for the safety rope with her suddenly free hand as the other arm now took all her weight. She dropped maybe a foot in height as well, swinging wildly. The wooden plank that had been the chair battered against her, hanging now by a single rope.

The *Tantamount* was flying level again, which left Violet hanging almost a dozen feet from the hull. Above her, she could see Mantid still clinging to the underside of the hull, as stuck as she was. He was able to rotate his head and watch her, but little else.

Holding tight with both arms, all she could do was wait for the crew to pull her up. Her arms were already burning. She doubted she had the energy to haul herself up, arm over arm. Too far to swing to the hull and no way to grab onto the curve, not without insect arms.

The breach was directly opposite her now, the poorly patched breach. The thought came to her; it hadn't stood up to the weight of an obsidian golem, how had it held this long against tons of ice pushing at it? She imagined how fitting it would be if it gave right now, at this moment. How fitting it would be if she went the same way as Onyx had gone.

Serves you right.

Violet was watching the outline of the patch when the first trickle of water began. First a trickle, then a geyser, as the wooden plug was ejected violently from the body of the ship. It struck her in the shins but any pain was forgotten as the deluge of icy water rushed over her. Violet's scream was swallowed up in the wash as she was swept away from the hull.

All she could do was cough. Water had entered her mouth, filling her lungs. One hand came away and again she found herself hanging by a single arm, the rope burning as it slid through her clenched fist. Then the torrent took her outside the envelope, the swing of the rope carrying her into the black. The water turned to ice. Already freezing, it became a winter cloak, draping her body in a rigid second skin. Violet had to shut her eyes against the cold before they froze over themselves. She could barely move and felt herself sliding further down the rope. She must be almost at the end now. But even the reality of falling into the black couldn't force her to lift the other hand to grab hold.

Then there were hands on her; hot, burning hands. Hands that grabbed at her arms and the folds of her clothing, dragging her over rough obstacles before laying her down on an unyielding surface.

Solid ground. It felt strange to her numb mind.

"Open your eyes, Violet," someone told her.

It took time but she managed that much. She was on the deck, swaddled in blankets. Half the crew were arrayed in front of her, wide eyed. Skipper, Captain, Gabbi, and Jack. Even Quill was there, dark and angry as always. Probably wishing she'd been swept all the way out into the black, never to be a nuisance to him again.

Violet found she couldn't stop shivering, despite all the blankets. And her hand hurt something fierce. She turned her head to the side and found Gabbi cradling the injured appendage.

"Don't be looking, Vi," the woman advised her. Violet realised the woman's hands were shaking as she wrapped Violet's in castoff rags. "You got some nasty rope burn."

"You held fast there, lass." Hounds clasped her shoulder proudly, white teeth showing a wide grin. "Not a soul here could have done it better."

"Shouldn't have had to hold fast," the skipper growled at her. "What the hells went wrong down there?" The woman sounded as angry as Violet had ever heard her.

"Our past come back to haunt us," the captain could be heard to say. "Nel, Hounds, a word with you both."

"Don't mind them," Gabbi told Violet, tying off a knot between her thumb and forefinger. "Scared us, that's all. Always where the trouble's deepest, you are. Worse than the skipper, Vi. Least when she jumps she keeps the rope tied off and don't do it soaking wet."

"Wasn't my idea," Violet protested weakly.

A shadow fell over her. Quill.

"What?" she said, glaring at up at him.

The Kelpie studied her through slitted eyes but said nothing, leaving without a word.

"Ignore him," Gabbi said. "Best thing for it."

"Like you do?"

"Best thing for you, then."

"Mantid!" Violet sat upright, remembering. "Where is he?"

"He's fine, lass," Gabbi assured her quickly. "Came up with the chair right after we pulled you up. In a state but none the worse for it."

"Good." Violet nodded her head. It was a struggle to keep it upright. "That's good."

Gabbi held Violet's mummified hand between hers. "Putting you to bed, lass. Stop by the galley when you come to, I'll oil your burns and we'll wrap it proper. Any luck and you won't scar. Can even get your tattoo touched up next port if you've a mind."

"My tattoo?" Violet's stomach dropped. Her injured hand was the same one she'd received her first tattoo on. The rope snaking around her wrist and palm.

"Don't fret, lass," Gabbi said. "You held fast, just you were ought to. Piper would be proud of you, right proud."

Violet managed a small smile at that. Piper and the skipper had taken her for that first tattoo, half a lifetime ago now.

"Someone else to see you," Gabbi pointed.

It was Mantid, skittering towards them cautiously. A steaming mug clasped precariously between his two folded forelimbs. Very, very carefully, he held it out to her.

"Better take it," Gabbi advised. "That's a right unnatural way to hold coffee."

<h1 style="text-align:center">CHAPTER 10</h1>

GRAVEL WAS COUGHING up blood. His nose was broken, gushing red, and he was drowning in the stuff.

Mors Coldstream gave him a disgusted look, placing his foot on the landsman's shoulder and kicking him over onto his front. Blood splattered on the deck but at least Gravel could breathe again.

Mors walked back up the gangway, turning to face the crew from atop the tender. Crates and barrels had been placed around the ship to give the scene some window dressing. The objective was simple: board the ship, claim the prize. The marines just had to go through Mors to do it.

Gravel hadn't been the first to go down, just the bloodiest.

"Again!" Mors called out.

Three marines rushed up the planking, seeking to close. They knew better than to engage the ship's premiere duellist at range.

They didn't fare much better up close.

"You all right, sailor?" Kaspar knelt by his friend, holding a swab of bandages out.

"Fine, sir," Gravel pressed the cloth to his face. It turned damp and sodden and crimson. "Just dandy. Hoping to hold out long enough to see those two go at it."

Kaspar looked over at his shoulder where the rest of the marines were gathered around Aristeia. The woman wore leathers and vest, sleeveless, staff slung over one shoulder. A group of shellbacks surrounded her, waiting their turn.

"Be grateful it's not both of them," Kaspar told him. "Get up, you've laid down long enough."

The landsman groaned, whether from pain or the idea of facing down both Mors and Aristeia, Kaspar didn't know. Together they made it over to the makeshift triage set-up for Mors' earlier victims.

Boarding drills. Everyone got a turn.

"What are we doing this for, Ensign?" Gravel eased himself down onto one of the cots.

"Captain's orders, sailor," Kaspar said.

Gravel coughed. More blood. Not much of an answer.

"Ensign!" the first mate called out. "Line up with the next wave."

Kaspar flinched, though not from Aristeia's words. He looked down at Gravel. The landsman was clutching his own hand arm tight but it was the half-chewed nails that made him flinch. There was a charge coming off the lad.

"Push it down." Kaspar clapped his friend on the shoulder. He forced himself to ignore the shocks running through his bones from the joint. He had to, else Brandon would be sent back to the Allied worlds. They were part of the Alliance. And that was what was required from all thaumatics.

"Fine, fine. Sir." Gravel broke the contact, drawing a deep breath. "Go do your duty, Niko. Before Mistress Quinn misses yourself."

The first mate's eyes were on Kaspar as he took up his position at the back of the line. Wand in hand, a marine on his left and able seaman on his right. Everybody drilled. Captain had yet to say why.

Aristeia's smile was mocking as he passed her, the shellback scars on her shoulder a reminder of what he wasn't.

At least it was over quickly.

"Damned stupid, Sir," Gravel said to him later, lying slumped in an out-of-the-way corridor. Backs against the wall and legs stretched out. Everything on the ship was metal—for once the cold embrace felt good against bruised skin. "Spent enough weeks drifting on that dinghy. Never thought we'd be trying to board her back."

Kaspar would have made a face at the landsman but his own hurt too much. Mors had cracked him along the jaw. Been lucky though. Aristeia had decided to take a turn alongside Mors after. Beating on marines and sailors was more fun than facing a fair fight.

"Might still be out there if it wasn't for you," Kaspar said.

"Best not be telling anyone that," Gravel winked.

"Need to keep your temper," Kaspar told him pointedly. "You want to be found out? To be sent to some training camp?"

"Temper's just fine, sir," Gravel assured him. "Maybe you could come with me though, back to the inner band. Before Mikel starts to think you've wandered off into some tavern of disrepute."

Kaspar scowled at his friend. "Mind your business."

"Am. Quite liked your bearded love, Ensign. Made you smile once. Saw it myself. Wondrous thing. Just have to keep you out of the watering holes til we can get you safely home to him."

"I was looking for you," Kaspar reminded him pointedly.

"Aye, but you and I don't look for the same, sir. And I was looking in the all wrong places. Was so sure I'd found that someone special. Biggest eyes I ever did see on that lass."

"Eyes," Kaspar repeated.

"Aye, sir. Eyes, everybody has them. Not all eyes are the same."

Kaspar shook his head. "You talk a lot of nonsense, Brandon."

"I tell it to the marines, sir," Gravel winked. "Sometimes yours even believes me. Why did you think the fellow was so smitten with you?"

VIOLET DIDN'T SLEEP well anymore. Not since Port Border, maybe even before. Her sleep, when it came, was filled with nightmares, visions of falling, of being cold, lost, and alone. Adrift in the black. She'd wake up, biting back screams, to find that the cold was real now, her breath steaming in front of her. For a moment, she'd think she was adrift in the miasma.

One time, not long after they'd left the periphery of the High Lanes, she had screamed. The only thing louder had been the bollocking Jack had given her afterwards. Gabbi said it was just because she'd scared him. Violet hadn't believed it then. Still didn't. Jack didn't get scared, Skipper didn't get scared, Quill didn't get scared. Even the captain, a frail stick-figure of a man, never seemed to get scared. It was just her.

The hardest part had been the way the crew looked at her the day after. Sidelong, out of the corners, behind whispers. She saw it. And what she didn't see she could imagine. No place for a scared little girl on the *Tantamount*, you had to be hard like the skipper.

A hard woman, that one.

All the women on the *Tantamount* were hard. Gabbi had Jack licked good and proper and gave back whatever she got from Quill. Hounds was tough—the woman had got fire scarred and then painted over it. And then there had been Scarlett. The Guildswoman. Mysterious, that Guild. No one would tell Violet anything about it. Just some group everyone was afraid of.

But Scarlett had been tough, hard, went up against the skipper even. Probably would have killed her if Violet hadn't hit her with a brick. From behind. Knocked her out.

That wasn't brave. And then she'd done it again, pulling the rug out from under Onyx, sending the golem drifting out into the black to be swallowed up by the miasma.

Falling like she dreamed of every night. Onyx should still be out there, falling, forever. Onyx and Scarlett, the two of them frozen, covered in ice. And Piper, Cyrus, the rest of the crew that hadn't survived the battle. All of them. Falling.

It should have been her, Violet knew.

She heard the clack of claws on woodwork, muttered cursing. A shuffle as Quill settled into his hammock. It wasn't long before a rasping snore added to the choir of slumbering souls. Sleep came easy for Quill.

Violet curled up into a ball in her hammock, wrapped up in tails, trying to get warm. It was futile, but she had to try. Something rubbed at her head, a lump inside the rolled-up shirt she used for a pillow. Round, hard, she dug into the wadded clothes with her good hand. Fingers closed around glass, smooth to the touch.

Violet pulled out the captain's water globe. An area the size of her thumb was cracked, a dense spider's web, like fractured ice. She must have had it on her during the caulking. The surface of the sphere still felt smooth to the touch, or else her fingers were too coarse and callused to tell the difference.

The mist inside was no longer still. It boiled, crashing against the curved glass, trying to escape. Violet held the sphere close to her face, watching the tiny ship twist, thrown about by the storm inside. Like the *Tantamount* must have in the unexpected corridor. There were even miniature bolts, the same that would dance around Quill when he drove the ship, arcing between the model and the cloud. Some unseen interaction from the mist and the ether. One arced out from the storm, same as lightning striking the earth, only it reached out in an incandescent fork to strike the glass. There was no sensation of heat but Violet pulled her head back sharply and dropped the sphere onto her lap. It lay there, until she hesitantly picked it up again.

The crack was gone, melted away by the lightning. And the mist had settled again. She waited but it did not return. Turning the sphere over in both hands, she could make out where the crack had been, a slightly smokier, fogged section of the glass. A closer look in the bad lighting showed several other such patches. Was that meant to happen?

Clever little toy.

Violet watched and waited, studying the globe with heavy-lidded eyes. But the show was over. Only the snoring of the crew to keep her entertained.

She dreamed of drifting golems and falling stars. And Kelpies. A whole ship full of Kelpies.

TOO DAMNED COLD.

That was all Nel could think, turning restlessly in her hammock. The worst part was her feet. They stuck out the end of the blankets and wouldn't stay warm no matter what she did. She was contemplating pulling on her boots and seeing if that helped.

It wouldn't—she never could sleep with boots on. At least not in a hammock. Legs wouldn't sit right. Head hurt, legs were too long. She wasn't right.

"Hells," Nel muttered, quiet though no one would hear her. She swung her legs over, wincing at the cold touch of the floorboards under her feet. The wood seemed to soak up the chill even though her room was next to the galley, the warmest part of the ship. At least she wasn't down in the crew deck. Gods only knew what it was like trying to sleep swinging above an ice locker.

She pulled on her boot. Stamping her feet to try and get the blood flowing back through them. Her jacket was too cold to pull on. She considered taking the blanket too but her pride balked at it.

Stupid pride.

The deck was mostly deserted, and why wouldn't it be? Any sane member of the crew would be rolled in blankets by now, nursing whatever spirits they'd managed to secret away.

"Evening, Skipper."

Nel turned to face the caller, Denzel, top of the bridge, standing his watch with Hounds. Both were bundled up in blankets and nursing steaming drinking vessels.

Stupid, stupid pride.

"You're a harder one than me, Vaughn." Hounds twisted the knife as Nel climbed the steps.

"Couldn't sleep," Nel said, "thought I'd make my rounds."

"Not much to see," Hounds said. "Never is on this dog's watch. Coffee?" She held out an empty mug.

"Thanks." Nel sat and held the mug while Hounds poured. It was hot, precious warmth in her hands. That was all she cared about.

"Lass did well today," Hounds said, eyeing Nel cautiously. Nel felt a warm flush go through her that didn't come from the hot beverage she was holding. She'd gone off at Hounds after Violet's scare. Captain had pulled her in.

Rightly so, one had to admit.

"She did," Nel allowed. It was enough, and Hounds let the subject drop.

"Care for a game, Skipper?" Denzel held up a wooden cup. From the rattling inside Nel deduced it held dice. "Helps keep your mind off the cold."

"What are we playing for?" Nel noticed the scraps of paper and tokens scattered between the two.

"Sips, favours, and watches, Vaughn," Hounds told her. "You can bid your grandmother's secret biscuit recipe if you care but it better live up to any boasting."

"Rather play for coin," Nel grumbled. "Need some to buy me some fleece-lined boots when we make port."

"Stand in line, Skipper." Hounds raised her vessel. "I'm buying me the boots, the pants, might even take the whole sheep in case you sign us on another run like this."

"The pay would have to be exceptional." Nel took a drink and shuddered. "Hells, woman, who brewed this and how much did you fleece them for?"

"Try some of this," Hounds offered, producing a flask and tipping a dollop into Nel's coffee.

"Smells nutty," Nel said, inhaling the steam. "Like almonds."

"Should do because it is. Go ahead."

"That is better," Nel said approvingly. "Hells, I didn't think anything could make sludge like this taste good."

"First taste is free, from here on you live off your winnings," Hounds warned. She shook the dice cup, upending it onto the deck. She looked over at Denzel. "What are you bidding, sailor?"

Denzel made a face. "Got nought but the clothes on my back, woman."

"Won't have you freezing on my watch, Denzel. Don't want to have to carry your workload too. What about your next grog ration? What do you think, three wets or a sip?"

"Bite your tongue. I'll owe you out of my pay when we finish this run."

"Have it your way, sailor. How about you, Vaughn. Care to put in?"

"Bad form beating your superior officer, Hounds," Nel told her.

"Says the woman drinking my liquor. How about you stand the last hour of my watch?"

"Done." Nel took a long draught from her cup. It tasted better again.

"What if I win?" Denzel asked.

"Sailor, you're so deep in the hole you'd need another watch just to win your way out." Hounds pulled the cup away. "Two pair," she announced happily. "With a roll still to come."

"Don't get overconfident, woman," Nel cautioned. "We haven't even . . ." She turned at the sound of someone coming up the stairs. For a moment, a part of her worried it might be the captain, but it was Violet. Girl looked like a shuffling Draugr, pasty faced and hand bandaged up tight.

Shouldn't be up but I'm not the one to say it.

"Evening, lass," Hounds called. "You look right tired."

"Couldn't sleep," Violet complained. "Crew snores."

"Which crew?"

"All of them."

"Get this down you, lass," Hounds offered the girl a drink. "How you're not freezing your tail off is beyond me."

"Fleece-lined tail," Nel commented.

"Fleece-lined tail," Hounds repeated, chuckling. "Lucky for some."

"Not lucky," Violet muttered, pulling a face. The girl swayed on her feet, holding her drink awkwardly in her good hand. "Where's Quill? Supposed to be on watch with him."

"Not for a few bells yet, lass," Hounds told her, causing Violet's face to drop in dismay. "Quite a few, fellow barely walked off. And don't be so cruel as to tease me with thinking my watch is over already."

"Hells."

"Violet," Nel chided.

"Lost cause there, Vaughn," Hounds said, soft enough so that Violet might not hear. The girl did look to be out of it. The girl wasn't even wearing boots but didn't seem to suffer for it.

Fur-lined skin, Nel shook her head. *Even after all of yesterday.*

"Where's your navigator?" Nel looked around, realising either Quill or Mantid should indeed be here. Finally had two navigators aboard and neither to be found. And gods save her from the gloating if Quill should chance on the rumour that his newfound rival was slacking.

"Made himself a bit of a nest up top." Hounds pointed to the top of the mast. "Didn't find any crows so he just moved in. Something about not having a working hammock of his own."

"Wasn't that your job, Violet?" Nel said, then winced at a knowing look from Hounds.

Violet hung her head, almost dropping her nose in her coffee. "Sorry, Skipper."

"You can still climb, right, Vi?"

"Course." Violet had the sense to look affronted.

Affronted ... almost woke her up too.

"Go check on the poor thing," Nel told her. "Take him some coffee. Does Mantid like coffee, Hounds?"

"Like?" Hounds considered it. "Won't say, least he never has. Drinks it though. Polite. So you take him some, he'll drink it."

"You heard her, lass," Nel said to Violet. "Coffee, top of the mast, off you go."

"Aye, Skipper." Violet sounded as tired as she looked, slugging the rest of her own brew back with a shudder. Hounds refilled it to halfway for her and Violet dutifully set of towards the main mast.

"Any reason we didn't send her back to bed?" Hounds asked.

"Wouldn't have listened," Nel said. "Be stroking her fur the wrong way to suggest it."

Hounds leaned over. "Double or nothing the coffee doesn't make it."

Nel squinted at Violet, shuffling on an almost icy deck. The girl made it to the ratlines and stopped there, resting her head on the cords before starting her climb. One handed, coffee cradled to her chest.

"How much did you give her?" Nel asked, feeling a touch of concern at Violet's unsteady ascent. "She looks drunk."

"Nothing," Hounds said, holding up her own mug. "Unless . . ."

"Unless?"

"I gave her mine by mistake."

"Hells, woman." Nel climbed to her feet, wincing at cold-numbed joints. "Better go catch her before she breaks her neck."

"GET OUT OF it, Bandit." Violet waved her hand at the creature stalking her on the ratlines. The loompa bit down on the edge of her hand, the one wrapped in bandages. His eyes were wide, deranged. The sharp teeth didn't break the wrap, let alone her skin, but Bandit refused to let go, hanging onto the ropes by a hand and a foot and leaning precariously out to keep his jaw clamped down. Staring up at her with those mad eyes. Growling.

"Hells."

Violet made her fiercest face at the loompa. His was fiercer. More feral. More teeth. She bared hers back at him; he bit down harder.

"I need that hand," she said. "That's my climbing hand. Let go."

More growling.

"Fine, you hang on then, see what happens." She lifted her climbing hand, loompa and all, for the next handhold. Bandit squawked at her in protest as she pulled beyond his reach. He fell, tumbling headfirst through the gap in the ratline netting. He grabbed on, with one foot, hanging upside, protesting loudly.

"You look ridiculous," Violet said as she climbed, coffee cradled to her chest, taking extra care where she placed her feet as the ratlines shifted under her weight.

The mast seemed to be swaying more than usual but it didn't give Violet the sense of nausea it had in the past. Maybe it was the sleep fog hanging over her. She should try getting by on less sleep like some of the crew did. She'd see them stumbling around in an almost dreamlike state, going about their duties like automatons.

Like Draugr.

Maybe the crew of the *Tantamount* could be replaced by Draugr entirely. She wouldn't cry any tears. Not after . . .

A wedge-shaped head darted over the rim of the crow's nest, tilting so multi-faceted eyes could stare down at her. Violet looked up, not even startled, blinking slowly.

"Hey, Mantid, brought you some coffee."

She held out the coffee she'd carried up from the deck. It was still mostly there. A good thing.

Mantid reached down with both forelimbs, pinching the cup between the two spiky appendages and raising it to his mouth. Mandibles worked furiously as the beverage was tipped back.

"Thirsty, right," Violet said, swaying on the ropes.

Should climb into the nest. But it's his nest. Might be rude.

Violet climbed another few rungs higher, high enough to be able to sling her arm over the edge of the nest and hold on. She rested her head on that arm.

Why so sleepy?

"How do you sleep?" she asked Mantid. "I never see you sleep. Do you do it when I'm not watching because I haven't made you a hammock yet? Is that why I'm so tired?"

Mantid tilted his wedge head on its side, watching her curiously. He held out the empty mug.

"I don't have any more coffee. That was it, no more coffee. No more coffee for you."

Her eyes were heavy. Would anyone notice if she just closed them? The nest was comfortable, even just halfway into it. No wonder Mantid stayed up here.

The clattering sound of something metal striking wood roused her, then the bristling fur of Bandit perched on the rim of the nest, growling at her. The skittering sound was Mantid backing away from the loompa, one forelimb raised and making defensive stabbing motions. Bandit advanced on both of them, snarling.

"Damnit, rodent, I will drop you out into the black if you . . ." Violet stopped, stunned at her own outburst, staring at her hand outstretched; fingers tense and curled.

And something beyond. Starlight reflecting off metal, running silent as a ray. Violet stood up, the others forgotten, needing a better look. Her foot slipped, missing the run in the line, finding only empty air beneath. She grabbed for the nest and missed, saw a blur from Mantid, a spiked limb lashing out at her, a shriek from Bandit. And then the nest tilted away and all she saw was the black and stars. Falling.

"VIOLET."

Falling.

"Violet."

Black. Stars. Falling. Pain.

Violet opened her eyes, seeing the skipper above her. It felt like she was holding her. Her face hurt. She reached up to feel the stinging sensation, realised her arm was burning as well. There was a shallow gash along her forearm, like she'd run through a thorn bush.

Not having much luck with that one.

"What happened? Why was . . . did you hit me, Skipper?" she asked reproachfully.

"Woke you up," the skipper shrugged. "You almost fell off the top of the mast. Mantid caught you."

Violet held up her arm. That explained the blood work.

"Twice in as many days, Vi," the skipper grimaced. "Hells, I never should have let you above deck. You're in no state for it."

"I fell?" Violet said, focusing on that one fact. Seemed she was always falling now. Asleep or awake, always falling.

"You did." The skipper examined her critically. "Haven't seen you take a tumble off the ropes in a long time. You get dizzy up there again? Thought you were past it."

"I . . . know, I . . ." Violet winced; her arm really did hurt. Blood was dripping onto the deck.

"Have Jack take a look at that," the skipper said. "Guess we know you can't hold your liquor though, not on an empty stomach. Sorry, Vi, should have been paying more attention to you."

People were starting to gather behind the skipper. Captain included. Violet sat up straighter; her head didn't swim so much now.

"Captain," she called.

"You had us all worried, my dear," Horatio said as he came over. The skipper looked down, her face clouded as she fussed over Violet's arm.

"I saw something, Captain," Violet said. "Up in the nest, before I fell."

"Yes? Well, go on, Violet, tell us."

"It was a ship, least I think it was a ship, but it had no lights on it. And it were different to every other ship I've ever seen."

"No lights, you say? Different?" Horatio mused.

"No good reason a ship would run without lights, Captain," the skipper said. "Whatever else Violet thinks she saw that ought to strike us as odd."

"Thinks I saw!" Violet objected.

"Easy, lass," the skipper hushed her. "You weren't right up there."

"Just tired, is all. Bad sleep."

"Bad sleep and worse grog."

"Don't drink," Violet muttered.

"Not intentionally," the skipper sighed.

"No," the captain agreed firmly. "Tell me about the ship, Violet."

"Shiny," Violet said.

"Shiny?" The captain repeated the word several more times, like it was some exotic animal he'd only just encountered.

"Aye, sir, like metal. Caught the light."

"New brightwork, maybe," the skipper shrugged. "Or a crew with too much polishing time on their hands."

Violet shook her head. "More than just that. Didn't have no sails neither."

"No sails?" The skipper leaned back on her heels, looking concerned. "No lights and no sails means trouble, but not for us."

"Yes," the captain agreed. "Perhaps we should turn and investigate if they require aid."

"You're not forgetting the fiasco that landed us in last time," the skipper said.

"No, Nel, I am not. Nor should you—"

"She weren't adrift, Captain," Violet interrupted. Both turned to stare at her. "I mean she was moving, on a course like. But she had no sails. No sails and no masts to hang them from."

A pause, then a long look between Skipper and Captain.

"We have a delivery to make," the skipper said. "Best course is a fast course."

"Yes. Yes, of course, Nel," the captain said. "Have the crew make full sail. And set proper watch in the nest. Just to be safe."

"Aye, Captain," the skipper nodded.

"We'll talk more later, Nel. Violet, do get that arm looked at it. The last thing you need is an infection."

"No," Violet said firmly, pulling her arm out of the reach of Korrigan Jack.

"It'll fester," Jack warned her.

"Will not. Just a scratch. Don't need you pawing at it."

"Ought to shave it. Can't even see what's wrong. You always been that hairy?"

"Ain't hair, it's—"

"Shove off, Jack, you ain't one to talk." Gabbi pushed him aside, none too gently. The woman's eyes were sunken and red veined, pulled out of bed before her usual bell on account of Violet. It wasn't a good thought. "Here, show us."

Violet held out her arm, making sure Jack kept his distance.

Gabbi clucked her lips together. "Looks nasty but it's not too deep. Got some boiled rags we can wrap it in to stop you making it worse, and that'll be that."

"See?" Violet said to Jack. "Ain't bad at all."

Jack just grunted in her general direction. "Where's Bandit?"

"Why?"

"Cause you got his bite marks on your arm."

"Yeah." Violet acknowledged the red indentations on her forearm, just below where Mantid had gouged her.

"Never seen him bite you. What'd you do?"

"Nothing."

"Must have done something."

"Yeah, well, I didn't!"

"Calm down, Vi." Gabbi looked worried. "You ain't acting

right."

"Women's stuff," Jack pronounced.

A flick of Gabbi's wrist and a flying saucepan almost took Jack's head off from behind. He ducked, at the last second, but Violet didn't think Gabbi had been trying that hard.

"You asked for that," the cook said to him, starting to wrap Violet's arm tight in still-hot, boiled bandages.

"Be looking for Bandit," Jack said, as close to an apology as anything he ever said.

Gabbi sighed and pulled a knot tight. "How's that?" she asked.

"Sore."

"Good, means your hand is still there and working. Try and leave it some before you overdo it. Give those cuts a chance to close up. For goodness' sake, girl, can you not go a day, just one day, without getting into some sort of trouble? Be nothing left of you by the time we make Vice."

"Yeah, ok, Gabbi. Sorry." Violet looked from her hand and its wriggling fingers to the pot Gabbi was floating back to its hook.

"Gabbi, how can you tell if someone is . . ." Violet broke off, unsure how to ask what was on her mind.

"Is what?"

"All wizard-like."

"It's kitchen pots and pans, very wizard-like, Violet."

"You know what I mean."

"Thaumatic-like."

"Yeah. That."

"Then why not say that?"

"Annoys Quill when I say wizard," Violet shrugged. "Reminds me of Piper too."

"Ah," Gabbi smiled wistfully. "Two good reasons then."

"So can you tell? Could you tell, Gabbi, if someone was like that?"

"Why you asking?"

"Want to hit Jack with a fry pan from across the way next time he runs his mouth at me."

"Aha." Gabbi floated her frying pan back into hand and pointed it at Violet. "Too early in the day for you to be making me think, girl. Why you really asking?"

"Quill," Violet admitted. "Said some things, showed me some. Said what happened when he showed me meant I might be. In a

Quill way."

"In a Quill way meaning he didn't say much of anything," Gabbi summarised. "Violet, sweets, if you was going all wizard on us folk would notice."

"How?"

"How? Gods, lass, you've been around myself and Loveland long enough to know the signs." Gabbi held up her hand, faint blue sparks running around the outline of her fingers. The jolts were much smaller and finer than what Quill normally conjured. "Crew would be getting shocked from mast to mainsail around you, not to mention the toys you'd be throwing. You've seen Quill in a temper. Me too. Can't hide a wizard who don't know their up from their down."

"So . . . I'm not then."

Gabbi stepped back, hands on her hips, looking Violet up and down. "I don't think so, lass, and I think I'd know. Think we'd all know. Afraid to say I think Loveland is just messing with you, tan his scaly hide."

"Yeah," Violet nodded, "that's what I thought."

"Thinking will get you trouble, lass," Gabbi said. "Look at the skipper. Woman's too clever by half, always over-thinking everything."

"Ain't that her job?" Violet felt obliged to say.

"Of course, it is, but it's what makes her such a harridan too."

"Harri-what?"

"Bitch," Gabbi said. "She's the one you want at your back in the bar fight, not the one you want to wake up next to. Woman snores. Why you think she gets her own cabin? It ain't her false sense of modesty, that much is plain."

"Thought you'd be wanting Jack in a fight," Violet said. "You being so sweet on him."

"Oh, there is nothing sweet about Jack, Vi," Gabbi laughed. "And he's sweet on me because I feed his sorry behind. Not the other way around. And what are we talking about Jack for? Boy ain't even here and we're mincing words about him. Make his head fat if he hears. Don't need that, don't need it at all."

"You been together a long while, since before signing on even?"

"Now what gave you that idea? You see those scars on Jack's wrists? When he was done doing his time, the captain was the only one who'd take him on. Skipper didn't like it, but then she don't like anything. Got used to him eventually. Didn't talk when he first came aboard. She liked that about him."

"Why didn't he talk? What was his time for? Why did the captain—"

"Black and mist, Vi," Gabbi stopped her. "You don't want for questions, do you? You want to know, ask him yourself. All I recall is the first words that did come out of his sauce box was him moaning about turnips and leeks. And that ain't stopped since."

"But . . ."

Gabbi hefted her saucepan. "Don't make me."

"Ease off the lass," Hounds called from the doorway, announcing herself with boisterous good humour. "Girl's filling up the infirmary all on her own, don't need any help from us, and if you dent that pan the skipper will take it out of your share."

Gabbi snorted. "Fine, the girl is all patched up anyhow. Take her away before she starts talking."

"Aye." Hounds sauntered over, clapping Violet on the shoulder. "That's why I'm here. Skipper and the captain have locked themselves away, and I'm for bed. Soon as I make sure the girl is too."

"The girl can still hear you both," Violet complained.

"Good," Hounds said. "Then the girl is coming with me."

"Don't let her ask questions," Gabbi advised. "Not if you've a mind to sleep any."

Hounds waved her off, draping an arm around Violet's shoulders and steering her out the door.

"Could have had a lucrative career in the Alliance navy, little miss tails," Hounds told her as they walked. "Pay by the stitch and the scar they do. Lose an eye or a hand and it's worth half a year's wages. Lose the whole limb and they double it."

Violet didn't answer, tucking her hands under her arms. The tips of her fingers were tingling. She squeezed her arm tight against her chest, trying to get the blood flowing proper.

"Don't know what the payoff for a tail is but you've at least one to spare."

Again with the tails. Violet pulled away from Hounds angrily, sick of it all, stopping halfway across the deck. The older woman stopped too.

"Didn't mean nothing by it, lass," she said quietly.

Violet refused to look at her. "No one ever does."

A sigh. "Aye, true, don't make us right. Ain't done much right by you of late, it seems. Always falling on account of me, you are. And for that I'm sorry."

Violet shuffled. "Not your fault," she said at last, grudgingly.

"Generous of you, lass."

"Why do you go on?" The question burst out of Violet. "If the Alliance was so grand, why aren't you sailing her colours?"

"Wasn't grand at all, lass," Hounds said quietly. "If I've given you that notion, then I ain't been speaking right."

"No?"

"Lass, come below, we'll sit and talk. Too cold to be standing about deck like this." The woman turned, huddled up in her wrap, and descended the stairs to below decks where the rest of the crew swung in their hammocks. After a moment, Violet followed her. It was that or stay above deck playing at being a statue. Hounds settled in the hammock opposite hers and motioned for Violet to take hers.

"That one ain't yours," Violet said, keeping her feet planted while Hounds pulled hers off the cold floor.

"Didn't plan on sleeping, just going to talk for a spell. Or maybe I will spend the night or what's left of it and then whoever's it is can surprise me when I wake."

Violet opened her mouth to inform Hounds whose hammock it was, then decided not to. The woman watched her suspiciously, likely guessing the way of her thoughts.

"Face for cards, you have, lass." She shook her head. "Any of my motley crew made the small talk about how we came to be in the Free?"

Violet shook her head. "Just that time was you were Alliance and now you ain't."

"Aye, except we spent a lot more of that time not being starchies than we ever did in those colours. All sorts of folk in the High, lass, same as in the Free. And the Central Band is one big mess, six dozen worlds and most of them with folk on. Most of them folks are squatting on rocks the size of your average moon but they all think the High Lanes revolves around that very same rock."

"Aye, but that's what you got the Alliance for," Violet said. "To make sense of it all."

Hounds shook her head. "Only one way to make sense of folk like that, Violet. You got to have a bigger rock. In the High Lanes that rock is the fleet. The navy, air corps, whatever folks call them in whatever parts they live. Wooden ships and iron men. There's a thousand ships in that fleet, Vi. A thousand ships flying Alliance colours, all to stop folk tearing themselves apart with their petty wants and needs."

Hounds leaned in towards her. "Thing of it is though, never enough iron men to go around." She winked.

"What do you mean?"

"A thousand ships, lass. That's a lot of ships and that means a whole lot more crew, and that's just the fleet. Don't count folk like us, the merchants and the traders, folk just trying to get by. Never enough warm bodies to go around, not by half. And in the High Lanes, the fleet comes first. First and foremost. They can't find enough bodies to sign on, then they'll take them where they can find them."

"Find them where?"

Hounds sighed. "Not everyone can sail, lass. Truth is, most folk aren't cut from the right cloth for it. So the Alliance gangs, they press you. Take you out of the waterfront dives when you're sleeping. Board your ship when you come into port. Denzel and I were lucky, lucky in that we got took together. Were on a trader making a run from Red Waters into the Queen's Shilling. A milk-run, easy as you please. Some ships keep secret crawl holes to hide their best from the gangs if they run the High a lot, but we didn't have that. Denz and I and a score more, all good hands, we got took. Got ourselves a brand-new ship we never did ask for. See, they tie you to the ship when they press you, you and her until she don't sail no more. And they scratch her name on you, so if you run, they'll know. You don't want them to know."

"You ran though," Violet said. "To the Free Lanes."

Hounds held out her arm, the one with the burning windrose. "Didn't have no more ties, lass. They got cut, made sure of it. Denzel and I, we got out. Not everyone else did. Most of those from before, who got pressed with us . . ."

The woman sighed. "Think we've talked enough for one night, lass. You should sleep. We both should."

"You should find your own hammock," Violet said. "You don't

want Quill to find you in his."

Hounds stared at her, then broke out laughing. There were groans from nearby sleepers at the sudden outburst.

"Worse things than fire and ice and press gangs, lass." Hounds grinned at her, returning to her normal humour. "And you having to listen to that Kelpie snore, now that do beat all."

CHAPTER 11

THE MIST WAS thicker here than what Nel was used to. Like fog on a cold river against a cloudy sky, hard to see where one ended and the other two began. Their cargo was starting to sweat. Looking down the deck from atop the bridge gave the impression the *Tantamount* herself was breathing. Or maybe smoking. Not a pleasant thought; the old girl didn't have the best history with smoke and fire. The vapour was so much coin running through their fingers, being paid by the pound as they were. Normally the miasma wouldn't come within spitting distance of the main deck but it was billowing up from below like it was some wanton geyser. Made navigating both above and below arduous. Nel had gotten herself so turned around she'd mistaken the foremast for the main until she bashed her shins into the forecastle deck.

Could have sworn I saw lights atop though. That's what being sober does to you.

If she felt miserable then most of the crew looked it. Two-thirds were above deck when half ought to be sleeping, except they were all coughing and hacking from breathing in the ice fumes. Have hoarfrost on the inside of their lungs if they hadn't been about to make port.

On that note . . .

"You ever been to Vice, Vi?" Nel asked.

"I dunno, have I?" The girl was listless of late, a state that concerned Nel. Slow to rise, quiet, subdued. Hadn't taken to being on light duties well. Even worse she was being kept out of the rigging, forbidden to climb until her injuries healed. For all that she could be an annoyance, Nel found she missed the girl's usual exuberance.

"That was the question, lass."

"You know everywhere I've been, Skipper. You're the one who takes me there." The girl sat with her legs dangling over the forecastle, head resting against the brightwork. Personally Nel chose to stand. The decking had taken a chill that wouldn't go away, often sweating icy condensation. Exposed skin would stick to metal if one weren't careful. She'd be glad when they were done with this run.

They were on approach to Vice now, just waiting to sight their destination through the roiling mists. Violet had come off watch with Quill a bell ago and the Kelpie navigator was fuming about it. It hadn't been deliberate but with the shift falling under Mantid's watch, it would be him and not Quill who brought the *Tantamount* into dock at the trading hub.

Quill's complaints had fallen on deaf ears. It amused Nel that Quill's reaction had been to sulk in the nest. True, he would likely be the first to sight Vice and have the best vantage point to observe if things went wrong but as far as protests went it was a pleasant out of sight and out of mind reaction. It was also the first time Nel could ever recall seeing Quill take a turn in the nest. She suspected it would be the last.

"That's not true," Nel said. "Wasn't me that dropped you on Warren. Someone hadn't done that then you'd never have stowed away, meaning we wouldn't be having this deep and meaningful here."

Violet turned so that her cheek was resting on her arm, still bandaged, the barest hint of a smile on her lips. She was playing with something, Nel saw. Glass ball. Little ship inside. Captain had one just like it—when had Violet inherited that?

"Unless you want to admit that you crawled out from some sinkhole on Warren, hmm?" Nel asked.

"No," a shake of the head. Not much of a response.

"One day we are going to talk about where you're from, Vi." Nel poked her in the ribs with the toe of her boot. Violet swatted the boot away.

"One day," she agreed. "When I'm older."

"How many tails older?" Nel asked.

Violet held up one hand. "This many."

"So a while then."

Violet shrugged. "Maybe."

"How do those tails of your work anyway, lass? Seems to me we never discussed that either."

"They're tails, Skipper. For swatting flies and keeping warm. How else are they supposed to work?"

"Most folk don't have more than one tail. Look at Quill. Just the one tail, sensible-like."

Violet looked upward to where Quill was hiding out. "Sensible- like."

"Don't be sassy, Vi," Nel said.

"What can I tell you, Skipper? We get older, we get more tails."

"Figured some of you were just born with more."

"That makes no sense, Skipper."

"Makes sense to me. How many tails does a girl need?"

"It's not about need." Violet frowned, the kind of expression that said like it was a stupid question. "Just like folk don't need to grow beards or go grey or have their milk teeth fall out."

"Not sure that's quite right there, lass."

"I dunno then, Skipper. Happens as we get older, that's all."

"So how many years before you get your next duster?"

"Duster?" Violet sounded offended.

"Be good for it," Nel said. "Clear the cobwebs out of the hold."

"Ain't no cobwebs in the hold, Skipper. Spiders all froze to death."

"How many years, Vi?"

Violet gave a long-suffering groan. "It ain't like that, Skipper. Some get 'em fast, some not so fast."

"So there might be some little Kitsune your age wandering out here with nine tails?"

"No."

"Why not?"

"Because if someone had nine tails they wouldn't be my age, would they? They'd be back home being all elderly and imparting wisdom."

Nel considered this. *More tails means you're older, all elder-like, but being older didn't mean you had more tails. Made sense. Some.*

"Way I see it," she said. "Tails are like tree rings to your lot. Fox-folk, I mean."

Violet looked pained. "You making fun of me, Skipper?"

"Would I do that?"

"Yeah, I think you would. Tree rings? Fox-folk?"

"I'll tell when I'm messing with you, lass," Nel winked. "Wouldn't want you to suffer needlessly. Wouldn't be right."

Violet was about to reply when the girl caught her first sight of Vice.

"Oh, now that ain't right!" she said, standing up and peering through the mists that were starting to shred away. "That's not . . . how is that even possible?"

"Hey!" Nel called and reached out futilely. She missed her grasp by a wide margin as Violet hopped the railing, darting out to the very point of the bowsprit, holding on only lightly with her one good hand to a stay. If the girl fell there was nothing below her. She was well out to the edge of the envelope, no chance of sticking to the hull.

"Skipper," Violet turned back, still pointing at Vice. "How? Just how?"

"Violet, get back here now," Nel snapped. "If you go fall off the ship, I am not gonna be the one to jump off and get you."

"You jumped off for Sharpe," Violet called, her head still on a swivel between Nel and Vice. "Twice."

"Second time was for Stoker," Nel said.

"You thought it was Sharpe."

"Thought no such thing. Back. Now."

"Fine." Violet rolled her eyes, walking the wooden tightrope bar back to the forecastle, arms held out and swaying for balance. Nel didn't settle until the girl was back on the right side of the railing.

"You're gonna turn me grey, girl," Nel chastised her.

"Skipper!" Violet was doing her agitated dance again. The way she got with something new. Something remarkable.

And Nel had to concede that Vice was remarkable. In many ways it was the closest thing to the mythical and primordial flat world, though a better way to describe it would be a floating mountain.

A continental-sized mountain, certainly, but it was no

spherical world. Even Cauldron was more of a regular shape than Vice. Water tumbled off much of the circumference, the edge of the world, in great shimmering curtains, probably the largest natural waterfall in the Lanes. Rivers, lakes, and seas; all led to the edge, creating a curtain of falling water around half the world. Ships had been lost trying to ride that curtain down, a death-defying pastime that had been going on since before ships sailed the ether's foam.

Some of that water travelled inward, sucked under the curve of the flat world to travel back through subterranean rivers until it emerged topside from geysers or springs. But much of it evaporated, diffused inside Vice's massive envelope, creating the mist, real waterborne mist that then mingled with the more etheric miasma, which shrouded the underside of Vice. A mist that would climb and drift back across the over-world in dense rain showers, beginning the whole self-contained cycle again. It was through that haze that the underside itself could be seen, vast inverted mountains, in effect gargantuan stalagmites. The under-mountains were said to be home to shoals of lusca and rays. Nel had heard rumours of spiders that nested underneath Vice which spun webs large enough to trap entire ships, but she'd never seen anything to make her believe such.

Most people came to Vice not for its secrets but rather for its openness. Law wasn't so much non-existent on Vice as selectively and loosely enforced. Short of theft and murder, there were few things that were considered crime on Vice. Sins and virtues were intermarried, often mistaken and traded for one another. Everything was available on Vice, and not always for a price. Sometimes it just required knowing who to ask.

Even the architecture was something to behold. Impossibly high towers that reached skyward. Buildings that were more patterned curves than straight lines. Structures that would be impossible on most worlds, unable to support themselves let alone be inhabited. The core of Vice, the centre of the world, was said to be one of almost pure ether. Such a concentration prevented the world from being shaped as others were. The people of Vice had grown rich off of mining and exporting the element. Wealth and the fantastical nature of Vice itself made it a den of curiosity. The rest had evolved from there, creating the impossible spectacle that had enthralled Violet.

And leaving Nel with the challenge of trying to explain it all to her.

"A wizard did it."

Sometimes the simplest explanations were the best.

"Skipper," a sailor called from behind them. "Captain's cabin, says it's urgent."

And sometimes she'd rather not have one.

"WHAT'S THIS ALL about?" Nel asked again. Urgent, he'd said. Been waiting half a bell already. And not a word as to why. "Should be out making ready for landfall, Captain."

"Quill requested the three of us meet. The crew will manage without us this once," Horatio said, barely looking up as he jotted notes in his ledger. Horatio's book was different to the ones Nel and Quill kept. Quill kept the official records of their course and heading, ports of call and destination. No erasures were permitted in the navigator's logs because if the ship were to be charged with criminal activity they might be seized as evidence. In practice, most navigators became lax about keeping their books updated. Quill, of course, was fastidious.

Nel's record keeping was more important to the crew, since at the end of a run if affected their pay. She kept the records of cargo as it was loaded and delivered. A right pain but the captain had long since delegated it to her. There were other records that were meant to be kept, supplies and records of payment. Bills of lading. The all-important rum diary. Gabbi managed the galley with a minimum of paperwork, something Nel envied. The crew did care about when and where they were paid but thought little about the bureaucracy behind it. That came with its own set of headaches.

It was entirely possible, Nel realised, that all the minutes and details she thought the *Tantamount* had managed to ignore were in fact recorded in the captain's log. Not that it would do anyone any good. Having chanced to look over the captain's shoulder once or twice she knew it was written in a cipher. While she might be able to guess what the code word to that cipher was—in fact she was fairly certain she did know—the laborious process of unravelling Horatio's scrawling script did not appeal to her at all.

"You were drinking again."

Snapped out of her reverie. *Damnit.*

"Been on the six water. Captain." It was hard not to feel bitter when she spoke. The crew looked to her at muster. You didn't get put on six water for no good reason. It was reserved as a punishment for sailors. That and giving up her key sent a message to the crew. The wrong one as far as she was concerned.

"I could smell it on your breath, Nel. The night Violet fell."

The captain didn't say anything else. But then he didn't have to.

For once Quill saved her. The Kelpie barged in unceremoniously, a signaller bundled under one arm, himself wrapped up just as tight. He dropped the device atop the captain's desk.

"This," Quill said.

"Aw, hells," Nel rolled her eyes. "Did we break another of the damned things?"

"No," Quill said while the captain reached out to examine the device. "Though I have resisted the urge to smash this one since I found it."

"You picking a fight with the ship now too, Loveland?" Nel shook her head. "Run out of real folk to annoy?"

"This isn't ours." Horatio turned something over in his hand. "These colours are wrong."

"Filters," Quill told him. "Crudely made, but sufficient."

"Sufficient?" Nel took it from the captain. A glass lens, crude as black iron and even more fragile. The edges were rough, fractured and sharp to the touch. She handled it gingerly, not trusting her near-frostbitten fingers to know they were cut. "For what?"

And then she saw. *Damn, but I'm slow today.*

"Alliance. These are Alliance signalling colours. Quill, where in the hells did you find this?"

"In the crow's nest," Quill said. "I cannot say how long it has been like this, other than it was not so before we returned to the Free Lanes."

"Damnit!" Nel threw herself into a chair, biting down on her fist. The signaller lay on Horatio's desk. Taunting her with its implications.

"Who aboard the ship would know Alliance signals?" Horatio asked.

"Not sure if it matters who would know," Nel sighed.

"Everyone aboard knows how to work a trader's flash, not hard to learn a few more codes. Some of them are almost the same once you swap out the colours."

"You found it like this?" Horatio asked.

Quill nodded in confirmation.

"Careless," Nel muttered. "We should smash it so they can't send anymore messages. The filters at least."

"Indeed," Horatio agreed. "We should, but we won't. It would be more useful to find out who is sending messages."

Nel scowled, as did Quill. She was surprised the signaller had made it to the meeting intact in the Kelpie's arms.

"You want me to put it back," he concluded.

"Precisely as you found it," Horatio said. He leaned back, folding his hands in his lap. "Do either of you have any suggestions as to who the operator might be?"

"I do not suspect the two of you," Quill allowed grudgingly.

"Your faith moves me," Nel told him.

"I am not as generous where the rest of the crew stands," Quill continued as if she hadn't spoken. "It could be any one of them."

"What if it's all of them, Loveland?" Nel drawled.

"Unlikely."

Unlikely. So he's not unreasonable, just cynically paranoid.

"What were you really doing in the nest anyway, Loveland?"

Quill opened his mouth, a barbed comment about to fly off his forked tongue. Yet he said nothing.

"Quill?" Nel folded her arms stubbornly. She wasn't about to let him get off this one.

"It occurs to me that the girl's fall may not be entirely due to her own ineptitude."

"Meaning what?"

"Meaning she has had two near accidents since we left Port Border. It cannot have escaped your notice who was present both times."

"Meaning what? Mantid is out to get her? I was watching her on the ropes, Quill. She fell, he caught her."

"Perhaps."

"Perhaps nothing, Kelpie."

"And yet it is in our new friend's hideaway spot that I found this." He pointed at his evidence.

"Because that's where the signaller is, damnit. Stupid, careless of whoever left it there, but at least the nest signaller makes sense."

"I am sure we can eliminate many of our long-standing friends from suspicion," Horatio suggested. "That much at least we know."

Quill pointed at the signaller again, with its Alliance colours. "Our recent . . . troubles with their kind may have swayed the loyalty of some. Coin and fear would do the rest."

"You suspect Gabbi?" Nel asked him pointedly, offering up his favourite gripe. "How about Vi? Maybe she signed up to earn her citizenship. It could be her."

"Indeed it could." Quill rolled his shoulders in a shrug, either not detecting or ignoring her sarcasm. "The girl is on frequent watch in the nest and has considerable access to the signaller. The cook I do not suspect because the ratlines would break under her bulk if she tried to climb them. A more likely suspect amongst our old hands is the Korrigan. He would sell out the entire ship if offered enough coin."

Would he? Maybe, well, Quill's got a point, it's Jack we're talking about. But would he?

"You're not wrong, Quill," Nel conceded. "About Jack. Maybe."

"So you would suspect the Korrigan over the Mantid? How interesting."

"Ain't interested in what you find interesting, Quill."

"It seems to me we are missing something," Horatio said. "If we have a signaller, to who are they signalling?"

"Alliance, obviously," Nel said.

"Ah, yes, but where are they? We've seen no other ships for days. Certainly it would be difficult for our errant sailor to signal one without us also catching sight of the receiver."

"Violet did mention she saw something, from when she fell."

"A metal ship, without lights or sails," Quill reminded them both.

Horatio smiled, a dreamy look coming over him. "A metal ship. How remarkable. How simply marvellous."

"The product of a deluded mind," Quill dismissed it.

"Then tell me why you went up to the nest, Quill?" Nel jabbed.

Quill snapped his jaw, again biting off his own words.

"It seems it would be best if we kept this matter between the three of us," Horatio decided. "Nel, is there anyone who comes to mind? Anyone you suspect?"

"No," Nel said truthfully, giving Quill one last glower. The Kelpie was . . . being himself. And it grated more than usual. "No one we've taken on has given me cause to think they might be on another payroll. There's Hounds and her crew, the obvious suspects, but I haven't seen anything that stands out, despite what Quill might wish."

"You are too trusting," Quill told her.

"I trust you, Loveland," Nel replied. "Far as I can throw you."

Quill snorted. "That . . . is never happening again."

"It does seem to come back to that," Horatio said, almost to himself. "Grange and Rim. Our finest hour, the . . . *Tantamount's* . . . finest hour."

Nel and Quill exchanged a look. Their squabble was set aside for the moment. Quill reached for the signaller, pulling it to his chest with one arm and draping his ever-present blanket over. "I will return this device before our turncoat becomes concerned at its absence. You will find me on the bridge for the next bell if words are required."

"You do that. See if you can do something about that damned breach while you're at it. We're bleeding coin as it is." Nel waved a hand, Quill already forgotten as he shut the door quietly behind him. "Captain?"

Horatio turned to her, distant. "Yes, Nel?"

"Tell me about the *Tantamount*," she said. "Tell me again, why you chose that name."

Horatio smiled. "A good name, *Tantamount*. As good as what came before. As good as anything else. A good name."

"Tell me the story, Captain."

"Looking for something, Vaughn?"

There it was, that churn in her stomach whenever she heard her last name mentioned. Vaughn was her mother, her father, the family name. It was what marines saluted and sailors in colours called you. *A name, where it stops and I begin, Chanel, my father's angry little girl.*

Hells, am I making up for Piper not being here? Where'd all the damned poetry come from? Black take me.

"The competition," Nel said to Hounds, still surveying the

other ships making port at Vice. "Seeing if anyone I know is making runs."

"You know a lot of people?" The woman put her back to the docks, leaning over the railings with one hand on a line. "How often do you run into folks you do know in this life?"

"Less than I could and more often than I'd like," Nel said.

"There are a lot of lanes out there," Hounds said. "You sail the High and Free enough you're bound to make some friends. Useful that, having friends. I know that much, if not a lot else."

"That's what this life is, Hounds. Never about what you know but who you know. And who their friends are."

"And who do you know in Vice, Skipper?" Hounds asked.

"I know someone owes us for what's left of this hoarfrost." Nel cast a glance over the ramps running from the cargo hold to the docks. Had to admire Vice's efficiency. When they'd signalled that they were on an ice run, they'd immediately been directed to a berth with a lowered pier to accommodate their unloading. A running team was already waiting with a counterweighted platform and ice wagons. Once it was loaded onto the wagons it was weighed and no longer their problem, but it was that final weight that determined their payment.

"How much do you think we brought in?" Hounds interrupted her thoughts, watching as the crew worked to hoist the cargo out of the hold. There was nothing like a shifting amount of coin to motivate them all. Any bonuses on the run would come directly from a profitable run and their profits were literally melting away before their eyes.

"Several hundred tons, maybe two thirds of what we left with." Nel made a face. "Lost more than I'd like but it could have been worse."

"Long tons or short tons?"

Nel gave her newest mate a withering look.

"Fine, fine, forget I asked," Hounds grinned. "Gave up my second favourite shirt to rag-stop the leak, literally gave up the clothes on my back. Just hoping to see some coin I can bite sometime soon."

"You will."

"All I need to hear, Skipper."

"What about you, Hounds?" Nel fired back. "Anyone you're going to look up while we're in town?"

"Thought I'd swing by the bazaar, check out the local skin painters. Used to know a few good ones here, and you can't leave Vice without some new work. What about you, Skipper, going to collect your piece?"

Nel rubbed at her sleeved right arm self-consciously. Her latest piece still itched, just barely healed over. Her old bosun's tattoo, an anchor crossed, but crossed now with a dagger stained red. A memento to an old friend.

"No."

"You've already got the one," Hounds shrugged. "If you've a mind, there's a tea shop I plan to visit. Beats the black out of the six water."

Nel scowled. Another reminder she didn't need.

"Never figured you for a tea sipper, Hounds. Haven't seen you touch a cup all run."

"Brewed a pot my first watch," Hounds said. "Was struggling to settle in. Borrowed this pretty little kettle off Gabbi. Did wonders for the brew, but just the once. Could never find the thing after that. Second time I went to make some I couldn't find the thing. Can't be the only one who likes tea though. The only other kettle was stained blood red from some fool steeping black too long. Had glass splinters all through it too, cut my mouth something awful."

Nel stared at her. "Never knew tea to be so dangerous. I'll pass on your tea house and stick with tradition."

"Not dangerous if you remember to warm the kettle," Hounds said. "That damned ice run, like being halfway up a mountain. I've suffered because of it, Vaughn, believe me."

"If I wasn't hearing it from you I never would have, Hounds, not in a year of runs. And how the hells does black teas turn red?"

"Black teas are red, Vaughn."

"Hells."

"Won the reddest black tea you ever did see off your Kelpie mate, too. Haven't dared try it this run, for reasons what I said. Ice and all."

"Quill lost a bet to you?" Nel asked. She knew the Kelpie drank tea. It was as close to a vice as ever he got.

"Lost a handful," Hounds winked. "Kept trying to win a peek at Mantid's private stash of charts and squiggly maps. Never seemed to occur to him to just ask so kindly. Couldn't bring himself to do it, I suppose. Ha, fellow was such a lousy card player and worse with dice that I weren't going to suggest it either. Took him for rations for a week before we settled on the tea. Didn't sleep so well but waking up didn't hurt so much."

"Starting to worry about you, Hounds," Nel said.

"Why's that?" the woman grinned at her.

"You found something in common with Quill, that's why. You just made my blood run colder than all that ice we're unloading."

Hounds laughed. "Getting wet down there." She pointed to where Jack, Mantid, and a handful of sailors were focused on pulling ice up from down below. They were using the crane and close woven nets to hoist it up in uneven loads. Jack and another sailor were using tongs to move the blocks onto the ramp that led down onto the dock, where the ice wagons were backed up. As fast as they worked there was still water collecting on the deck, mostly from shavings chipped off the blocks as they were grabbed.

Jack leaned forward on his tongs, saying something to Mantid. Nel was too far away to it make out. Mantid shuffled his feet until he was facing Jack, forelimbs tucked in against his chest and head tilted. The last block floated up from the net hung in the air between them.

"Looks like trouble," Hounds commented.

"Too early for trouble." Nel turned away. "Go sort it out, tell Jack to get his backside up into the rigging if he can't stay civil on the line."

"Smart coin is on Mantid if your fellow starts anything."

"Jack ain't my fellow," Nel dismissed the idea. "Ain't anyone's fellow, not even the captain's. Hells, maybe Gabbi's, but only because she feeds him."

"Done time, hasn't he?"

"Done that and more, I imagine. I don't ask, for the most part."

"So you're not asking me to go settle it then?"

"No, that I'm telling. So move."

"Throw me under the keel, sure, why not," Hounds grimaced. "And where will you be while I'm risking life and limb collaring your rogue Korrigan?"

"Getting coffee. Fingers are fair frozen and you've put me off tea."

Chapter 12

There was screaming from the docks.

Much of the screaming came from Bandit as he pursued a birdlike creature, trying to corner it near the slip. A mouthful of feathers suggested Bandit was having the better of the ordeal but his prey was proving a difficult quarry. The rest of the noise was provided by Violet as she tried to rein in their errant mascot.

"What is that thing?" Nel leaned on the railing, coffee clasped between both hands. She still craved warmth. Felt like her skin was sweating coffee of late but at least she could move her fingers. The Vice dock was a far warmer environment than the *Tantamount's* self-contained envelope. The sooner they transferred their cargo the better, particularly since they were paid by the pound. But until she could hand over at least she had this show.

"I think it's a bat," Gabbi suggested, squinting as Bandit and prey scaled a mooring pole, climbing it in a spiral motion.

"Got feathers," Nel argued. "Makes it a bird."

"Some lizards got feathers, don't make them birds," Gabbi said. "Look at how it flies. Bat-like."

Nel grunted as the bird-bat jumped from the top of the pole, gliding down on outstretched leathery wings and leaving Bandit seething with rage atop. *Maybe it isn't a bird*, she thought as Bandit made the awkward reverse climb. He couldn't go straight down headfirst so the loompa was forced into a jerky drop and grab sequence.

The bird creature wasn't any more elegant, squawking back at Bandit from below. It was of a size with him, wings, feathers, and a beak. A long, tapered tail that dragged behind it as it waddled on the ground. It had all the ingredients of a bird but it didn't take flight like one.

It could make short hops though, powerful feet launching it off the ground before gliding back. Actually not even gliding, Nel conceded, just an awful lot of wing beating to try and shift its weight out of the way. It seemed to need height and currents to move through the air.

It easily avoided Violet as the girl lunged for it, leaving her spitting dust and clutching a stray feather on the ground. There was a round of laughter from the rigging. Half the crew was watching. Free entertainment—Nel wasn't about to call them on it.

It was Violet's third attempt to restrain one of the combatants. She'd stopped trying to catch Bandit after the first two. Bandit hadn't given up though, diving from halfway down the pole onto the bird.

"Jack," she called out to the Korrigan up on the yards. "What is that thing?"

"Dinner!" he yelled back to the roar of approval from his shipmates.

"Jack!" Gabbi hollered at him. "Name!"

"Yiqi," Jack grinned down at them.

"Want to bet that's just Korrigan for dinner?" Nel muttered.

"Don't know about that but I'll bet half my ration it's not going to be dinner." Hounds joined them at the railing. Even the off watchers were coming to join the show. Fur and feathers were both flying now as the two scrapped in a ball, rolling back and forth. Violet stood by helplessly, hands half outstretched but the girl knew better. At least Nel hoped she did. Any more injuries and she'd start docking the girl's pay.

Of course, then I'd have to start paying her more than room and board . . .

"Not for me," Nel shook her head.

"You're mad," Gabbi said. "Best ratter the ship's had. It's all over."

"That ain't no rat," Hounds told her.

"You're on," Gabbi held out her hand. "Half the next ration says I don't have to feed Bandit for a week."

"You're wasting food on that ratter?" Nel muttered. "The ship's best ratter?"

"Done," Hounds said loudly as they shook on it. She started to cheer, her cries taken up by the rest of the crew. Half of them probably had stakes wagered as well. Grog if not coin. Nel saw Gabbi look up to where Jack stood aloft. Both quietly confident.

"Bandit!" Violet was yelling and stamping her feet. "Leave it alone!"

Nothing the Kitsune girl did had any effect on the loompa or yiqi scrap. The two animals rolled atop one another, batting and flailing to the best of their ability. Bandit bit with his feral teeth and the yiqi stabbed back violently with sharp talons. There were specks of blood flying but nothing that looked too serious.

Something occurred to Nel at nearly the same time the answer presented itself. The yiqi must have an owner. It clearly wasn't wild and was making a minimal effort to escape now. It had figured out Bandit wasn't big enough to pose a serious threat, and now it looked more of a dispute over territory. The question on Nel's mind became; where were its owners?

Kelpies. It had to be Kelpies.

A whole clutch of them. Clutch? Is that right? What else would it be—a pack, a swarm? There's three, maybe not a whole clutch. Half a clutch?

Three Kelpies. Two were the stock green and stoop shoulder variety, not so different from Quill. The third was more unusual, something Nel hadn't seen before.

It was bearded. Not bearded the way most of the crew were a week after leaving port, but bearded in a more alarming way, face and upper body covered in rows and clusters of spiny scales. It made for an intimidating display, probably the purpose, and it was this one that stepped forward, barking out commands that Nel couldn't make out.

His words had no more effect than Violet's had. The platter of salted fish dropped on the two did cause them to break apart in alarm. There were no more flying fish to arrive but Nel could hear something behind her. She sighed, closing her eyes for a moment.

"Hells," she muttered.

"Skipper," Gabbi whispered hoarsely. "What's the damned Kelpie doing now?"

There Quill went, striding past the crew. He didn't have to push his way through; they moved to let him pass.

"What is he doing?" Hounds asked angrily. "I've got coin on this."

"We bet grog, not coin," Gabbi said quickly.

"Same damned difference." Hounds leaned out over the railing to see past her. "What is he doing?"

Quill marched down the gangway, onto the docks, and right into the middle of the fracas. For a moment, Nel thought he was going to start something. The three other Kelpies watched him cautiously. It was hard not to recall that Quill's religious beliefs put him at odds even with his own kind. But for once the Kelpie didn't poke that particular bear. He barely even slowed, plucking Bandit up by the scruff of his neck and turning around immediately. The loompa hung limp in his grip, feet swaying just above the docks, oddly not fighting the retrieval. Violet stared after them both for a few seconds before following meekly. Behind her, the Kelpies merely watched. They seemed to consider the *Tantamount* for a while before conferring briefly amongst themselves. One of them retrieved the yiqi, and the group left.

"Damndest thing I ever saw," Gabbi voiced their collective confusion.

"More importantly," Hounds said, "I won the bet, right?"

Gabbi sucked in a breath, then immediately launched into a full denial. Nel moved away to meet Quill at the top of the gangway, before she was asked to adjudicate.

"Spoiling the crew's fun there, Quill," she told him. Quill held Bandit up between them. Bandit stared back with big eyes, still not struggling.

"Let him down, Quill." Violet arrived. Her eyes were wide, she was breathing fast but not hard. Exerted but not worn out in the least, just dirty from her missed catches.

Quill looked over his shoulder back at the docks. The other Kelpies had departed, taking their pet with them. Across the ship, the finer points of how this affected the stakes was being discussed. Loudly.

Quill handed Bandit over to Violet. She clasped him in her

arms, holding him tight, waiting. Bandit, settled until now, started to squirm.

"What?" Quill growled at her. "Have you nothing better to do with your time?"

Violet left without another word, running for the ratlines. Bandit dislodged himself from her grasp and climbed with her. He could easily have outdistanced her but kept a similar pace.

Strange, not like her to head for the ropes without being told.

Quill was watching her too. "How old is she now?" he asked suddenly, turning to face Nel.

A subject she'd only just discussed with Violet and Nel had to admit she didn't know either. How long was a Kitsune's lifespan anyway? Hells, she'd long since given up trying to track her own age relative to all the different Lanes and worlds they traversed.

"Adolescent," Nel folded her arms. "Since when do you care?"

"When will she be done with this adolescence?"

"Not soon, Kelpie," Gabbi said. She and Hounds had come up unnoticed, both looking like they wanted a piece of the navigator. "And just as well. She keeps us all young."

"Good to have a bit of fun around here," Hounds agreed.

"Did we mention fun, Quill?" Gabbi added. "Of the kind you like to spoil?"

Quill snorted. Only the lash of his tail betrayed his annoyance at being ganged up on by the three.

"How old is Violet?" Nel said in an aside to Gabbi, completely ignoring Quill for now.

"The kind of old that's not," Gabbi floundered, pushed off course by the question. "I don't know, Skipper. The months go by and I'd just as soon not think how they're piling up. Got no seasons to track them with and I'd sooner not count the grey hairs neither."

"I figured her for a dozen winters," Hounds shrugged. "All short and easy ones."

Nel gave her a pained look. "She's older than that. I don't let children on the ship."

"Can't be much more, Skipper," Gabbi said. "My sister was married at fifteen and dropped a sprog not long after."

"Often the way, isn't it?" Hounds laughed.

"What is a sprog?" Quill frowned.

"Something I'm praying you never do, Loveland," Gabbi told

him.

Quill only looked confused. "A baby, Mister Kelpie," Hounds told him mercifully. "A wee one. A spawn, a hatchling, if you will. I don't need to explain the mechanics of this, do I?"

"I do not believe it necessary," Quill said, oblivious to the barb. He reconsidered then, looking curiously at Gabbi. "Unless . . ."

"What?" Gabbi growled at him, looking murderous.

"When will you be dropping your sprog, cook?"

"Out of my sight, Loveland."

Quill shrugged, but Nel mentally notched one for the Kelpie. It was a low blow, to be sure, but a point nonetheless.

"Am I to understand none of you have bothered to ascertain the girl's age? Despite all of the attention you lavish upon her?"

"So ask her, if you're so damned curious," Nel told him.

"I will," Quill said, looking up at the mast. "I grow tired of rescuing her and that diseased vermin."

Rescuing? That what this is all about? Quill . . .

"I say a dozen," Hounds said.

"Fifteen," Gabbi said grumpily. "Fifteen."

"Done," Hounds fished a coin from a pocket, flipping it with her thumb. "Vaughn, care to wager with us?"

Nel listened as Quill yelled his inquiry up to the top of the mast. Violet's tangled mess of hair poked itself out of the nest, Bandit riding her shoulders.

Nel gave her answer before the girl gave hers. The other two stared at her, then realisation slowly dawned. Heads snapped skyward, jaws hanging low.

Just like tree rings. Violet gave Quill her answer in a two-fingered shorthand salute. Facing the wrong way, of course.

The look on Quill's face was the best part. But the coin Hounds and Gabbi silently handed over wasn't to be laughed at.

Obvious, when you think about it.

"I AM NOT looking forward to this, Nel," the captain said. "Not looking forward to it at all."

Horatio fussed with his coat, brushing dust of the road off and fiddling with the front buttons. Nel sighed, the sigh of long suffering patience even she was sick of making. But she empathized with the captain. This was going to be an unpleasant discussion.

"Perhaps you should go in without me," Horatio suggested brightly, as if the idea had just occurred to him. "Delegation, a representative of the ship. Trusted representative, our most capable member in fact, a sign of the high esteem in which we hold them."

It was the third time he'd suggested this since they'd left the *Tantamount*. For herself, Nel was glad to get away from the *Tantamount*. She was missing Piper again, not least because they still had a warped timber hole in the hull, the sort of problem she would have left to him. It was something she was avoiding, but that didn't mean the captain got a free pass on this trip.

"Sand is going to want an explanation as to why we arrived with a hold full of ice cuts instead of her cargo," Nel said. "Better if we front ourselves before they come calling with ledgers and debt collectors."

Horatio's sigh echoed how Nel felt. Losing their Vice-bound cargo on Cauldron had hurt, both their reputation and their finances.

No idea how we're going to explain this one. Alliance blockades, Guild agents, smuggled cargo, at best we'd be blacklisted. At worst they might sell us out.

Regardless, they were shown into the factor's office. An air of calculated officialdom, predictable and almost cliché, a tired theatre they were forced to play the roles of. And sit patiently while the clerk finished filing whatever meaningless paperwork was at hand.

"Now," the man said at length. "Who might you be?"

And there it was. The moment of confession. Nel let her captain take the lead. It was only fair.

"Captain Horatio Phelps of the *Tantamount*," he recited. Then a sidelong glance at her.

He wouldn't . . .

"And my first officer, Chanel Dominica Vaughn."

She gave him the most withering look she could muster. They'd be coming back to that later.

"Yes, yes, the *Tantamount*, inbound cargo of opiates. We expected you some time ago." The man looked up and reached for a small brass bell at his side. Nel tensed as it rang but all that happened was the appearance of a Draugr. Neatly dressed for one, almost in liveries.

"Bring me the green, wrapped package, Roam. Second shelf next to the outbound expenses."

"We were delayed," Horatio said, the words tumbling out. "Unavoidably so, repairs were needed. Significant repairs, multiple repairs."

"Indeed?" the man said. "My, that does sound serious. I do hope your ship is able to pass muster again. I imagine you might struggle to make your living if not."

Nel resisted the urge to look to the captain. Had they just been threatened? "Same as any other crew. The ship is seaworthy though, more than. Fully crewed and awaiting her next contract. What we came here to discuss."

The Draugr manservant returned, cradling a wax-sealed parchment in two cupped hands. The factor took possession of the letter and waved the Draugr off. It went to stand awkwardly in the corner.

"Captain Phelps, you are expected, it seems. This was delivered at the same time as your cargo with instructions it be handed over to you. Mistress Sand will see you now. Roam, be a dear and show them in."

Horatio looked as stunned as Nel felt. Had she heard that right? The cargo had been delivered? The same cargo they'd returned to Cauldron to find vanished without a trail?

She kept her mouth shut on the subject. So did the captain, or else he was too shocked to speak. Either way.

They followed the Draugr Roam into Sand's office, a spartan affair as far as furnishings went, only a single chair in front of the desk that Horatio quickly occupied, forcing Nel to stand at his shoulder. She tucked her hands under her arms to keep from fidgeting while they waited for Sand to arrive. Aside from the mounds of papers covering every flat surface, there wasn't much to see. It seemed the clerk's fastidiousness didn't extend to his employer's office.

The side door opened and Sand came through it. Not walked so much as invaded the room, the woman was all business, heavyset and a face carved out of granite. This wasn't Nel's first encounter with the woman. Sand ran a significant part of the shipping interests through Vice. Anyone who did more than the occasional stopover through the port was likely to be aware of her even if they hadn't outright done business with her.

"Horatio, Nel, good to see you both," she said curtly, dropping into the seat behind the desk. She looked down at the piled papers on the desk, as if she was perplexed as to how they got there. A sweep of one arm sent most of them fluttering to the floor. Nel imagined a despairing wail from the other side of the door. Not an unpleasant thought.

"To the point," Sand looked up, as brusque as ever. "Your cargo turned up late but not nearly so late as you. Some of my partners don't care for sub-contracting runs like that. Myself, I'm just happy the goods turned up at all with what I've been hearing."

"Yes, well, happy to oblige, my dear Sand," Horatio said. "More so, guaranteed delivery, that was our bond and our word is our bond. A given contract, nothing more sacred, a captain's word is a sacred oath, one which I take seriously."

"You were as surprised as I was the cargo arrived at all." Sand leaned back in her chair.

"Cards on the table?" Nel put her hand on the captain's shoulder as he slumped with a theatrical sigh. "Yes."

"Cards on the table," Sand repeated. She flicked a card down between them. A black queen. "Recognise that?"

"Should we?" Nel frowned at the card. Then at the captain. Cards were much more his problem than hers. And yes . . . he was smiling.

"My last card," he chortled. "Won me the round. Near cleaned him out with that card. Luck turned after that, like the man could see my hand, every time. Kept calling my bluffs. Terrible luck. Great play though, the black queen. One of my best."

Nel sighed, rubbing at her face. "Cauldron," she muttered. Now it was starting to make sense.

"That came pinned to the bill," Sand told her. "Along with that letter you're holding, Horatio. Don't open it here. Whatever Guild fracas you're involved in, I don't want any of it. Keep it to yourself."

Guild, Nel thought, as Horatio turned over the letter, exposing the seal, a complicated conglomerate of lines and angles Nel couldn't have drawn if she tried. She ought to be grateful to Ebon for following through on their original contract to Vice. Only . . .

"Regarding payment for the run," Nel said.

"Tendered to the ship delivering the cargo," Sand said.

"Standard sub-contractual arrangement."

"Of course." *Damn him, that was a good run. Mind you, we're better off than when we walked in the door, thought Sand was going to have us up against the wall for this one. No coin and no rep. Now it's just no coin but thanks to Violet's ice run . . .*

Where to from here though?

Sand was watching her. Not smiling, the woman never smiled, didn't know how. Congenial enough if you did what she asked, which worked just fine for Nel. She could respect that. But if she doesn't know she must be guessing.

"You had another run lined up for us," Horatio said what Nel was thinking. *Brave question, give the man his due.*

"Had," Sand nodded.

"Had, past tense, in the present, yes, yes," Horatio actually sounded irritated, tapping his private Guild message on the arm of his chair. "Do you have a job for us or not? Or are we done here?"

Sand regarded them both with those cold slate eyes. "I have a job for you."

The tapping stopped.

"Just not the job we had talked of. That run had to be filled. You understand."

Not much choice here. Beggars can't be choosers.

"Let's hear what you have for us. Start with a direction."

"The High Lanes."

Hells.

"We just came from there. Wouldn't be my first choice of ports," Nel said.

"Nor mine," Horatio said firmly, immediately aligned with her. "And there are few shipments we could undertake from Vice that would be welcomed there."

"With open arms," Nel added. "Running to Vice is one thing, folk here are relaxed as a drunken troll. Folk in the High are that same troll but the morning after."

"Normally you would be right," Sand agreed. "But in this case the cargo will be something both in demand and perfectly legal. Believe me when I tell you they won't clear you through customs fast enough."

"And just what is this invaluable trade good?" Nel said. "Last I knew there's little out in the Free that those in the High care about."

"Have you been to the Allied worlds of late? To the Central Band?"

"I try and avoid it."

"Things are difficult there," Sand said. "An outbreak of disease, some call it a plague, left the work force on several major worlds devastated."

"The fog," Nel said.

Sands eyes drifted over to Horatio, for the barest moment.

"There's no known cure for it."

"It's not something you cure, Sands. And it's not a plague, either."

"The Alliance would disagree with you on both counts."

"I lived through it. The so-called cure was worse than the disease."

"Nel . . ." The captain started to turn towards her.

"It's fine, Captain," she said firmly. "What does this have to do with anything? The plague was years ago."

"As I said, with much of the labour classes decimated by disease, the good citizens," of which Sand didn't even try and hide her derision, "had to find other solutions. The most successful of which were the Draugr."

"Hells," Nel said it out loud this time. "Captain . . ."

"I quite agree, Nel," Horatio pushed himself to his feet. "I believe we'll be taking our search elsewhere, Mistress Sand. A pleasure, as always."

Sand could have waited until they'd gotten to the door. It would have been more dramatic, more traditional. Hells, Nel didn't expect to get out of the room without some last word. She'd barely turned around when it came.

"The run pays half again what your original job would have."

Hells.

THE NEST USED to make Violet queasy. The black below didn't bother her, but being up high with a visibly long fall did. It made her think about falling but even that wasn't the problem. It was the idea of hitting. And the all sorts of wrong that would be.

Only now it didn't bother her, not so much. Leaning forward and arms slung over the cradle, she watched the crew lounge about on deck, flexing the fingers on her injured arm, scraping the outside of the nest with her nails, making patterns. They were going stiff from all the scrapes she'd picked up, didn't even feel like hers sometimes. Ropework was out, couldn't manage the knots. Meant more watches, more idle hands. And they were all at idle hands now, mend and make clothes the captain had said before he and the skipper had trooped off into town to see about business. Most had took clothes to mean dice or cards. The sailors were huddled in small groups atop the deck, the weather being of the inclination to make it much preferable to below. There was still a chill to the timbers and the *Tantamount's* insides hadn't dried out as yet.

Someone looked up at her, shading their eyes from the sun. Mugs. Violet raised a hand to wave when a shoving match broke out. It wasn't much of a scuffle but when the players returned to their seated circle they all looked firmly down.

What's that about?

A creak and a chirp told her. Bandit, perched awkwardly on the signaller, getting grubby paw prints all over the stained glass. Sunlight was bouncing off both frame and lenses, half blinding her.

"Off of there, furball," Violet shooed him. "They think we're shoulder spotting up here."

Maybe if I had the captain's spyglass I could. See someone's hand, work out a system. Jack would be up for it. Hounds too, I bet. Naw, can't see it working. Mugs just got a stomping and we weren't even being underhanded.

Violet lay her head back in the bottom of the nest, feet to the sky.

Much more comfortable, though blue sky is a strange sight. Got used to black. Black and mist . . .

Something was digging into her back, something hard that crunched as she shifted around. Violet reached under and scraped it out. Whatever it was caught on her clothes. In disgust she saw it was a piece of dry, moulted skin. It could have been Quill or Mantid, she didn't care to look close enough, and both had been looking mottled and scabby since the ice run. She threw it away, over the edge to wherever it would go. There was enough castoff littering the nest as it was; blankets, mugs, a few bedraggled playing cards, scraps of uneaten food that even Bandit wouldn't touch. She pitched that as well, not really caring where it landed. With any luck the previous owner would be walking by and take the hit. Probably Mantid on both counts, more she thought about it. Fellow had been spending much of his off-duty time up in the nest, like a second home. Or an actual nest.

Violet's eyes narrowed with a dreadful suspicion as she looked more carefully at her surroundings. It had more than a touch of lived-in to it, like someone had indeed been sleeping there. The more she thought about it, the more it seemed a natural fit for Mantid. Whose body was a most unnatural fit for any kind of hammock, at least any hammock or hammock-like arrangement she'd been able to hang.

He had been sleeping here. He'd never wanted or needed an actual hammock at all. Even though both Hounds and the skipper had . . .

Damn them . . .

And now the light was in her eyes.

"Hells, Bandit!" Violet snapped at the loompa, reaching for something to throw at him. He was still balanced on the signaller, staring down at her with bared teeth. In a right mood these days, the miserable rodent.

She squinted at him, trying to convey the levels of her contempt for him at this very moment through a puckered face.

Bandit was holding something, turning it over in his paws. He took a testing bite of it before she could stop him, to the sound of cracking. It was enough to startle the loompa into dropping it. Whatever it was hit the floor of the nest to the sound of breaking glass.

"What'd you do?" Violet sat up, speaking more to herself than to Bandit. He went back to ignoring her. Maybe he was in heat or some such. Seemed he didn't much care for her lately.

It was a scrap of twisted metal with a very thin glass pane fitted to it. The glass was curved, broken tableware or a window maybe, not something designed as a lens for the instrument. It was held in place with a few spots of tar, and the makeshift lens had been crudely coloured; a deep red.

"The hells are you for?" Violet wondered aloud.

Whatever it was, it was broken now. Or as good as. A fine web of cracks covered a third of the face, spreading out from where Bandit had tried to bite it. Violet felt a hot flush, an immediate sense of guilt that something important had just been broken.

Best to front up and get it over with, she thought glumly, tucking the broken trinket into a pocket. Maybe she'd catch the skipper in a good mood.

Chapter 13

"My vote says we don't take the job," Hounds said.

"We do not vote, this is not a vote," Quill snapped at her, though his attention was mostly focused on Mantid, who stood silent and still behind her. It made for a crowded meeting in the captain's quarters.

"Wasn't so long ago you were suggesting this very idea, Quill," Nel reminded him, then wondered why she had. She didn't want the run, not a bar of it. But the captain had tabled it in front of the officers and now it was up for discussion.

"Things change," Quill said, twisting this way and that awkwardly. Nel could see he wanted to pace but the cramped confines didn't allow it. It had the amusing effect of transferring all that nervous energy to his tail.

"What doesn't change is a ship needs runs and a crew needs paying," Hounds told him. "I've been to the High, more of late than all of you. Work is scarce and it's these Draugr that are to blame, by the large."

"You just said we ought not to take the job."

"Stand by it, too, Vaughn." Hounds shook her head. "You take a run into the High Lanes, you'll make a pretty penny, but you won't have time to spend it. Soon as we make port the gangs will be on us. The fleet needs bodies, both warm and cold."

"Just how bad are things?" Nel asked. Hounds was right—she hadn't been in the Free Lanes in a long time. Nel hadn't been closer than Border to the High since she last wore white.

"Bad." Hounds fixed her with a stern look. "There's a lot of jobs Draugr can do, lots more than most people think. And each job they take means one more soul to push and shove for those jobs that they can't do. It all flows downhill, Skipper, and folk like us are at the bottom."

"Not quite at the bottom," the captain interjected. "At least not yet."

"Closer than you think, Captain," Hounds said. "Respectfully. You know what Draugr can't do? It's crew. Can't sail and splice. Can stand fast with the best of them but can't trim a sail to keep from capsizing in a pond. You take a run into the High Lanes you'd best be running a cache that looks prettier than you do, because we're all just warm bodies to the gangs."

"Colours already run with Draugr," Nel said. "Have for a year or so."

"Running ain't crewing, Skipper," Hounds pointed out. "But it's the turn of the tide."

"A run such as this would be accompanied by official writs," Quill argued. "Protection enough, I think, from these gangs you are so fearful of."

"Writs expire the moment you step ashore," Hounds said.

"Didn't think you'd be so keen to head back to the High," Nel said. "Seems like tempting fate."

Quill just shrugged.

"The offer remains," the captain said, not giving away his own feelings on the subject. He regarded each of his officers in turn, waiting for them to finish thrashing out their opinions.

Nel rubbed at her face. "I don't like this," she admitted. "Not one bit."

"How long must we consider for?" Quill asked. "How long do we even have to consider?"

"We're in good standing," the captain said. "Sands knows us and she's a woman who prefers what she knows."

"Only because that last run turned up," Nel said. "The other crews won't have missed that, knowing the reason or not. Sands said as much, already got other people queuing up for this job if we don't want it. Name is what we got going, because Sands heard we made port. But she won't wait forever."

"She must have other jobs," Hounds said. "Reputation is coin, we just want a different direction."

"There is more to life than earning coin, Miss Hounds," the captain told her.

"Maybe so," Hounds said. "But for me that's where it is. I'm the new hand here, I don't forget that, but you all know where my thoughts are at so there's no point saying no more. I'm for town. If there's other jobs to be had then great, but if not . . ."

"We'll talk it some more," Nel said. "Let you know."

"Just don't talk for too long, Skipper. Shifting tides and all that," Hounds said on her way out. "I'll keep my ear to the ground while I'm out, but this run . . . don't care for the hooks on it."

There was a knocking on the door, followed by the door being opened and Violet rushing through it with little more than a breath between all. The girl pulled up to an abrupt stop, narrowly avoiding running into Hounds.

"Oh, Miss Hounds, was looking for the captain," Violet's voice came as she twisted trying to see around Hounds, who made no particular effort to get out of the way. "Captain . . . hi Skipper . . . oh, everyone's here, you're all here."

"Now's not so good, lass," Nel told her, pulling a series of maps out and placing them on the table. "Is it urgent? Can it wait?"

"Urgent . . . uh, well, no, that is. Didn't think you'd all . . ." The girl trailed off.

"Tell me all about it, little one." Hounds turned Violet around and steered her towards the exit. "These folk have talk to make and that don't include us. Come on, now."

Hounds shut the door behind her, leaving the three of them alone. No one spoke for a while.

"I vote we do not take the job," Quill broke the silence.

"You're a piece of work, you know that, Loveland?" Nel said.

Quill just snorted in response.

"What other options do we have?" The captain reached down to the chart table, unrolling one of the maps Nel had placed there. It showed a sparsely detailed view of the Free Lanes, at least those within a month's sail. Significant though were the trade routes marked on it, two dozen names and contacts, some crossed out or covered in wine and ink stains. A collection of barely legible scrawled notes and incomprehensible pictograms. Even to those who could decipher the clues it did not make for easy reading.

"From Vice we don't have many options," Nel said, tracing a

ring around the planet. "Vice imports. Everything here is for sale."

"There's always something." Horatio leaned over the map. "Always. We brought ice into port, that wasn't such a bad job."

"Because ice is in demand here. There's almost nowhere on this floating mountain it will form naturally. It's not a two-way route, Captain."

"I understand that, Nel," the captain waved her off. "If not ice then silk. Incense. Salt and pork rinds for goodness' sake."

"None of which Vice exports," Quill growled. "This is a waste of time."

Horatio sat down in his chair, spreading his hands over the map. He looked as though he might sulk.

"Vice is a staging point, if anything," Nel reminded them both. "A place to transfer where people don't ask too many questions but won't stick a knife in your back. We should be looking to pick up a second stage run here, take it on to wherever some other ship isn't headed."

"Such as a shipment of Draugr headed for the High Lanes," Quill muttered. "Or has this hive suddenly become the home and birthplace of those wretched things?"

"No," Nel said, frowning. "No, it hasn't." *Quill makes a good point. Where the hells did all the damned Draugr come from? If they were all being shipped into the High Lanes . . .*

"What is in that?" Quill stabbed at the Guild letter with one clawed finger. Horatio still hadn't opened it; the seal unbroken.

"That is the mystery of how our cargo made it to Vice all by its lonesome self," Nel said.

"If it is more Guild business, we should burn it and forget we ever saw it," Quill declared.

"I agree, for once," Nel said. "*Are* you going to open it, Captain?"

For a moment it looked as though he would, the captain tracing the intricate seal with his thumb.

"No," Horatio said firmly. "I am not."

Nel and Quill exchanged a look.

"Do either of you have something to say?"

They shook their heads.

"Excellent, then we are all agreed then. Perhaps a round of drinks to celebrate? No, perhaps not." Horatio took one last look at the sealed letter, placing it between the pages of his journal. He shut the heavy book and pushed it aside.

"We still have the issue of whether or not to take the job," Quill broke the silence.

"Port Border was bad, Captain," Nel found herself saying. "Battered ship, fragile crew. If there'd been work to run to I think most of them might have jumped then. If we hadn't been seeing old hands sleeping rough in the streets they might have anyway. As it was," she shrugged, "we ended up being the ones people ran to. We need to keep working. Crew's only as good as the next run."

"You have a suggestion then?" Horatio asked.

"Need a few days in port anyway, Captain. Restock, take the black chill out of the timbers. Fix the damned hull again."

"Was not the last repair guaranteed?" Quill mentioned.

"It was, except that breach didn't come from no fault in the repairs. Came from someone taking an axe and a really big rock to her. A fine point but one I'd expect Troshka to argue."

"Perhaps worth a try," Horatio said.

"Perhaps," Nel said. "If we're careful about how we explain it."

"I would inspect this potential cargo," Quill said, to Nel's surprise.

"You? You would? As in yourself?"

"Yes."

"By cargo you're meaning Draugr. Shifting ballast of the kind we've had a world of pain on account of."

Quill shrugged.

"Fine, but not alone," Nel said.

"You do not trust me?"

"Hells, Quill, you really have to keep asking?"

Another shrug. "Then let us stop wasting words and be about it."

"YOU ARE AWARE of what the crew says about you?"

The thing about you, Quill, can't tell if you're making a point or asking a question. Is that a thaumatic thing? Folk can't tell which way the wind is blowing because you're the one making it blow?

"So long as the crew do what I say I don't much care what they have to say about my saying it."

"You obfuscate when you are unwilling to address a subject," Quill said.

"And you use big words to try and look smarter," Nel shot back. "You might have more luck with a hat. Make you look better too."

"Perhaps." He didn't seem offended. "But what the crew says, what they have always said, is that you are a hard woman. I have never believed this. I find it more implausible the longer I know you."

"Still got a hard boot, Kelpie. Heel and toe."

"And if your temperament were as hard as your footwear I would not be seeing this."

"And what are you seeing?"

"A heart. Breaking."

"I will maroon you here, Quill, black take us both, if you continue to test me."

Quill shrugged. Inscrutable. It was something Nel believed he worked at for times like this.

Breaking. Is he right?

The two of them stood on a raised walkway overlooking the pens. Nobody had outright called them pens but it was what Nel likened them to. Corrals made of timber and iron separated the standing merchandise into files, neatly lined up like toy soldiers. The corrals led back to wooden buildings that resembled dormitories, expansive enough to hold several thousand billets.

More, maybe. We packed them in like silver spoons to get them off of Thatch. They could be doing the same here.

Only these Draugr weren't like the ones they'd shipped with. There was no awareness in the glassy eyes, no spark of intelligence or life. Barely so much as a reaction as they stood rigid as soldiers on parade. Potential buyers walked up and down the fence. Every now and then a gate would be opened, a dozen or so Draugr would be led away. Their fellows never reacted.

"This isn't right," Nel heard herself say.

"How is it not right?"

"These aren't like the ones . . . the ones . . ." She found she couldn't finish.

"No, they are not."

"But remember those from the Glassy Run? All torn up and frostbit? I wouldn't treat a dog that way, and never something that looked and moved like a person."

"But are they?" Quill asked her intently. "Are those down there people? Would you point to anyone of them and say that one is a person, like yourself?"

"No. But that don't make this right."

"The one named Stoker did not believe it was such a travesty as you make out."

"Then maybe he's wrong."

"Most would argue he would know better than either of us."

"Wouldn't be the first time that most were wrong, Quill."

"Do you know what I think of most people?"

"Very little," Nel said. She watched as some silk and perfumed fop led away a half dozen Draugr. It was the smallest sale she'd seen so far; a minimum number was required. This buyer kept his distance, directing others to manage the goods. She could only imagine what distasteful services they'd soon be performing. Something beneath their new owner, no doubt. Silent, uncomplaining labour. The new symbol of wealth and prestige.

"That most people prefer not to think. Few have given much thought to Draugr since they have become known. Certainly none have bothered to think of their well-being or mind their distress. They perform the duties most consider beneath them and those they would rather not consider."

The fop's silks were getting dusty, much to his own dismay. The cloud was kicked up by the Draugr's marching.

Saw a world that drowned in dust. Can't stand it since. Guess us two have that in common. Now there's an unwelcome thought.

"If I knew where they come from I'd be more inclined towards them," Nel said. "Not knowing doesn't sit well with me."

"Did you ever wonder that before?"

"No."

"And now that you see them as potentially people, as individual persons even, you wonder. You care."

Nel glared at him.

"Curious. How an experience can make you question how you view others. Would you be happier knowing that Stoker was right? That all Draugr across the lanes are unthinking, unfeeling automatons, no different from a steam powered construct other than form and function? Would that make you feel less guilty?"

"You think I feel guilty?" Nel growled.

"I think you feel many things. But yes, guilty is one of them."

"Then keep the rest of those thoughts to yourself."

"Where do Kitsune come from?"

"What? The hells does that have to do with this?"

"You wonder where Draugr come from. You wonder because suddenly it is relevant and important to you. Where do Kitsune come from?"

"How is that . . . " Nel sighed but gave it up as lost before she even began. "From their homeworld, I guess."

"Which is where?" Quill pressed.

Nel frowned.

"We have travelled far, you and I. Together and alone. And yet between us neither of us can say where the girl is from."

"What does Violet have to do with anything?" Nel was starting to get angry. Starting, hells, she was ready to throw down.

"Name anyone else on the ship and I could name the world they call home. Point out to me anyone between here and the ship and I could plot us a course to theirs. Yet for the Kitsune . . . I could not even give you a direction."

"So?"

"This bothers me."

"Why?"

"At first, because when she first came aboard it seemed to me the simplest way to rid myself of the girl. In a way that would be acceptable to both you and the captain. If not sooner then later we would find ourselves near her world, a slight detour and we would be rid of her. Home to whatever kindred might favour her. Imagine my consternation when I could not discover such a fact."

Clever, Quill, might even have worked. Must rub you raw.

"And in the time since I have yet to uncover an answer."

"Kitsune might be a touch recluse, Quill, but they're not lost or mythical. Seen whole towns of them, enclaves in cities. Even a ship or two."

"But no world. The ships, these do not surprise me. If one wishes to keep a world secret then one must jealously guard the means of travelling to that world."

"Fine, so the Kitsune world is a precious family secret. And?"

Quill gestured to the pens. "You wonder where Draugr come from. I wonder such about the Kitsune. Perhaps the two are linked. Perhaps they are not. But they are of a kind."

Nel snorted her derision at the idea. "Quill, you took the longest route to the most ridiculously tenuous answer. If anything, the Kitsune world is probably remote, maybe in the Far Lanes. Maybe they keep it secret, maybe you just haven't found anyone who knows. And Draugr must come from some alchemical factory somewhere. Some old timer whose eyes have gone white from quicksilver fumes. As close as anyone will ever get to the transmutation of lead. If they're lucky they're not too senile to enjoy what it brought them."

"And we will be partaking in this transmutation of that which is base into that which is gold?" Quill asked pointedly. "By accepting this run?"

"The hells we will, Quill," Nel shook her head.

"As I said before," Quill said. "You are not nearly so unfeeling nor as unflinching as you would have the crew believe."

"Keep that one to yourself."

"As you wish."

"And buy me a drink before we head back."

"No."

"Why the hells not?"

"Because you have just turned down a significant amount of coin. We cannot afford your indulgences."

"Rather be indulgent than a teetotaller like you, Quill."

"If not for the fact that you perform your duties better when under stress I would indeed recommend you partake in such a lifestyle. It has that happy middle ground you seem unable to balance, forever climbing the mountain and falling down the other side."

"No wonder your own people hate you."

"They do not hate me. They disagree with me."

"The difference being?"

"Hate does not require reason. A difference of opinion requires some appreciable thought into one's motivations."

"You sound like Piper."

Quill glared at her.

"Still can't go home, can you, Quill?" Nel reminded him.

"And who amongst us can?"

Damned Kelpie.

"Ah, and speaking of those who are far from home," the

disagreeable Kelpie said. "I saw more of your former brethren in their pretty uniforms."

"There's plenty of Kelpies in the Allied Worlds too, Quill," Nel told him stiffly.

"Yet they are no kin of mine. How many of your family still make their way wearing such gaudy apparel?"

"Most of them," Nel conceded. "None who'd be pleased to see me."

"I would say the same of those down there. Tell me, do they appear . . ."

"What?" Nel asked.

"They appear to be looking for someone."

Quill was right. There was a handful of Alliance sailors down in the Draugr pens. Except they weren't merely sailors. From the way they moved and the weapons they carried, they were marines. And they were assuredly looking for someone.

"Us, maybe?" Nel muttered.

"Should we be concerned?" Quill didn't sound concerned. Somewhere between annoyed and irritated. "Who would think to look for us? Who would think to look here?"

Nel squinted at one of the marines below. They were definitely on a mission to find someone, or something. It was a blessing that few people ever chose to raise their eyes and look above themselves. A strange truth but a truth nonetheless. She'd seen something on one of the marines—a bared arm, and a familiar tattoo.

Something that nagged at her.

"Let's go," she said. "No sense in us tarrying here."

And she wanted a word with someone back at the *Tantamount*.

"Do you trust me?"

It had seemed an odd question to Violet. Did she trust Hounds? She liked the woman, she knew that much. She hadn't expected to forge much of a connection with any of the new crew, so she was surprised at herself. Hounds' team, for the most part, had embraced life aboard the *Tantamount*, never shy to join in or include the other sailors. Hounds herself reminded Violet greatly of the skipper, from the time before their run out of Cauldron. More fun, less sombre.

She liked Hounds. Did she trust her advice when it came to a new tattoo? That was a different question entirely.

Her face must have said all this.

"A fox?" she repeated, trying not to sound insulted.

"Why not a fox?" Hounds asked. Her face was straight set but the light dancing out of her eyes suggested hijinks.

"Be like you getting one of your lot tattooed on yourself," Violet pointed out, something that seemed blindingly obvious. Hounds apparently didn't see it the same.

"Happens all the time," she shrugged. "Denzel, show her the dancing lady."

Denzel grinned and propped his foot up on the stool next to Violet, reaching for the hem of his pant leg. She held up a hand to stop him from bringing out the dancing lady. It jiggled in a way that made her face grow hot.

"I've seen it," she said quickly. "Knew someone who used to have one like it. Didn't know what it was back then."

"Well, if not a fox, maybe a sea horse?" Hounds suggested. "They have everything here. You can't come to Vice and not leave with some new ink, not at your age. An octopus or a squid maybe? Now what's with the face, lass?"

"A squid? With tentacles?"

"You don't like tentacles?"

"Delicious," Denzel told her, not even cracking a smile as he covered up. "Crumbed with peppercorns and salt back home, then fried up in oil."

Violet thought she might gag. *Battered squid tentacles?*

"Not a fan of the tentacles then," Hounds surmised.

"No," Violet said firmly. "And no water horses neither. Don't need the reminder."

Hounds chuckled and exchanged a knowing wink with Denzel.

"What's this one?" Violet pointed to a symbol, a collection of circles and oblique lines.

"Stay away from symbology and runes," Hounds advised her. "Pretty patterns like that are best left to secret groups like thieves and guilds. Or thieves' guilds. Ones that have their own secret handshake and carve obscene messages to one another underneath bridges that no one but they can understand."

"But I like it," Violet protested, staring at the design. Something about it made her fingers itch.

"How about a compass rose?" Denzel suggested. "Every able seaman needs bearing once in a while."

"Might be useful when you come to find your way home in the big dark black, too," Hounds added.

"How do you mean?" Violet asked suspiciously, turning away from the symbology. *Black, why is it always black?*

"We all have to go home sometime, lass." Hounds winked at her. "Even lost little fox girls."

"Ain't lost."

"I know you ain't, lass."

Violet took a closer look at the compass designs sketched out roughly on parchment. They were short on detail but not crude; more like stencils to give one an idea and the artist something to work from.

"Where does it go?"

"That one? Forearm, often." Denzel held out his own arm, showing an eight-pointed star.

"Or back here," Hounds said from behind her, hands piling Violet's hair atop her head and tapping the nape of her neck. "Won't be able to see it so good but it'll always be there, that sense at the back of your mind."

Bandit chose that moment to remind them of his presence. He had been circling Violet's feet, his fur standing on end. Something had him agitated—the loompa had been skittish for a while now. He made a screeching sound, snapping at a passing customer. The parlour tattooist, a heavily inked Korrigan, looked over in annoyance. Violet reached down to gather Bandit up but he dodged away from her, baring his teeth aggressively.

"Must be in heat or something," Hounds suggested.

"Could be hungry," Denzel said. "I get scary like that when I'm hungry."

"Two foot of hungry fur is scarier than you when you're angry," Hounds said. "You just whinge."

"Found your fancy?" the tattooist asked them. "Got other customers if you're not of a mind."

"We're of a mind." Hounds clapped Violet on the back. "And this is the lady of the hour. Picked one out yet, lass?"

"I don't have the money for this," Violet managed to get the words out, her fingers tracing the layout of an intricate compass in the ledger she was holding.

"My shout, lass," Hounds told her. "In memory of our first run together. Ships and sailors rot in harbour and that's what we were doing afore you came along. This is a small recompense."

"If the boss is paying, best get the works," Denzel suggested. "Maybe an actual rose in there, even an anchor. Or an owl, don't see many owls. They . . ."

Hounds made to cuff her friend. "Don't be listening to this jackass," she told Violet. "Keep it simple and small for now, can always add to it later."

"All right," the tattooist grumbled at them, dragging a stool over and setting his tray of tools nearby. "Where do you fancy?"

"Back of the neck," Hounds answered before Violet could.

"Best place for it," the Korrigan grunted in what might have been approval. "Lean forward, girl, arms on the table, head on your arms. That's the way, now stay like that when I start working, don't want to cut you wrong. Chirugeon charges for stiches, makes my work look sloppy too. Don't like that."

Violet nodded, the very slightest of nods, suddenly afraid to move her head. She heard the tattooist shuffling around beside her, then felt Hounds pulling her hair into a bunch and tying it back. She presumed it was Hounds, from the somewhat gentle touch as her hair was parted out of the way. That and the shade the woman's presence provided from the noon day sun. The shop was little more than a canopied front with sunlight streaming in through the gap. No wonder they'd managed to do so well out of this run to Vice. Not that Violet had been privy to the final numbers since they'd finished the run, but the captain had been happy and even the skipper had cracked a smile when no one was looking.

"Hold still," the tattooist repeated again, setting the edge of the needle-tipped tool against the nape of her neck. Violet let her breath out slowly so she wouldn't scream—she'd figured that out her first time—and braced herself.

It started off as a stinging sensation, almost an itch. As if a gnat or some other biting insect were trying to burrow its way into her skin. She squeezed both hands around her own wrists. It was all she had to hold onto.

The needle tapping continued, moving out from the initial point, like glass being dragged across her skin now. Broken glass and a touch of burning, an unpleasant warmth that spread across the back of her neck, spreading as far down as the top of her shoulder blades. Places she knew the needle hadn't even reached. She shifted uncomfortably, trying not to let her muscles tense up.

"Hold still," the tattooist told her again. Violet made a sound in response, it didn't matter what, just some acknowledgement.

She tried shutting her eyes but that only made her more aware of the physical sensation. Instead Violet let her sight drift out of focus, making everything a blur, almost dreamlike. She could hear raised voices around her, the sounds of the bazaar. People bargaining and hawking their wares. It was too bad she hadn't more time to look around, more so that she hadn't any real money to spend, though she had no particular desire to accumulate possessions. Maybe some of the exotic foods or spices though. She could take them back to Gabby and see what could be made with them.

She could make out specific voices though, Hounds for certain. The woman was arguing with someone, heatedly.

The sound of tent flaps being swept aside, a change in the room as air from outside pushed in, accompanied by someone. The pressure on her neck stopped momentarily and a cloth was applied. Wiping the blood away; she tried not to think about that.

"Violet." Hounds crouched down on the other side of the table, opposite her. "Got some trouble, lass," she said. "You run into any trouble with a group of Kelpies before?"

Violet sat up, feeling the pit of her stomach drop away.

Kelpies, like them who boarded us near Rim. The skipper's old captain, what was her name? Heathen. Like her.

"That'd be a yes then." Hounds observed her closely. Violet nodded, not trusting herself to speak as yet. "Got them outside, been looking for us."

"Outside?" Violet squeaked. She spun around in her chair, earning a sharp rebuke from the tattooist. She saw them: Kelpies, two or more, you couldn't tell with the crowds. Denzel was between them and the shop, arms folded and feet planted. Nobody looked happy about it.

"Easy, girl," Hounds tried to calm her. "Nobody coming through. They just want to talk, matter of a missed cargo, or missing out as it seems."

Missed cargo?

"The *Tantamount* meant to have made a run here before this

one? Maybe in the last few months, mayhap. Something go wrong for you?"

Violet nodded. "Yes, hells, yes. We did. We had to set in to Cauldron for repairs, had to leave our cargo, the Vice run I mean, behind."

"You left cargo on Cauldron?" Hounds looked as surprised as she sounded.

"Had to," Violet said, wondering suddenly how much she ought to say. *Trust Hounds, aye, but the skipper might not like me to talk so much.*

"Had to," she repeated. "Folk got all nasty about cost of repairs and the captain had a bad run at the tables. Says he got shaken down there. Had to buy our way out if it all."

"Right," Hounds nodded. "It's Cauldron, what'd the man expect. Your cargo, you trade it to make off then?"

"No!" Violet insisted, shocked that Hounds would suggest such. "We did a run in exchange, couldn't find the room. Cargo was gone by the time we got back. Not a trace of it."

"Your captain didn't see that coming? Vaughn would have, surely. Never mind, between the devil and the black, you were." Hounds grinned suddenly. "And you were, weren't you, lass? Right, never mind. Get your ink finished, I'll sort the scaly landsmen."

Violet opened her mouth to protest. Hounds couldn't speak for the ship, only the skipper and captain could. And she hadn't even been aboard during the episode at Cauldron. But then she remembered what the skipper had said when first learning how Violet had arranged the run to Vice. Best to say nothing. Hounds was an officer and seemed confident.

"Stay with her," Hounds was saying to Denzel, who seemed to be swallowing his own objections. That was the last thing Violet glimpsed before her head was pushed back to the table and the ritualised blooding of her protesting flesh began anew. She'd almost forgotten the pain. She did have one more thought as her eyes drifted out of focus again. Where had Bandit gotten to?

Chapter 14

Violet had one hand clasped to the back of her neck, holding a wet rag over her newest memento. The ink stung if she moved her neck too much. Standing watch was going to hurt for the next week, but the worst was how her hair stuck to the still-raw skin if she didn't keep it covered. Hurt like blazes before she'd figured that out.

"You and Kelpies don't get along at all, do you, lass?" Denzel said as they backtracked through the market.

"Don't know many Kelpies," Violet said. "Mostly just Quill."

"And that one is mostly enough," Denzel agreed. "Tattoo bothering you much?"

"It's fine," Violet lied. "Where are we going?"

"The Crooked House, least that's what folk call it now. Used to be the Chained Game, but it's all crooked now."

Easy to see why, Violet concluded as the building came into sight. An old brick and mortar building, one side significantly lower than its partner. The outside façade was crumbling but the tavern was swollen to capacity with patrons spilling out onto the streets. Most were cheering, hooting, and hollering as they followed some spectacle Violet couldn't see.

"Hounds is in there?"

"Where she said she'd be," Denzel nodded. "Her and your scaly friends too. The one with the beard recommended it to settle accounts."

"What accounts? What settling?" Violet asked as Denzel ushered her inside. They passed under the gently swaying house sign; it showed a bear manacled by one leg. There were what might have been other smaller bears surrounding it, cubs maybe, but the paint was faded and flaking away. Looking up at it pained her neck so Violet only had a brief glimpse of it.

Inside, Violet discovered the outside of the building wasn't the only thing that leaned. The floor was canted half a turn, like the *Tantamount* when the crew had played with the ballast. Tables and benches were mostly absent, almost all the patrons carried their drinks in hand, but she could make out the servers' bar and saw unattended vessels begin to slowly slide towards the sunken end. That was where most of the patrons were gathered too.

"Some fool built it on marshy ground," Denzel said, searching for Hounds in the crowd. "The name stuck and it would have been too costly to fix anyhow. Folks try to drink til they can walk out and see the house standing straight. Never seen it myself, always the one who gets leaned on for the walk back to dock. There's Hounds."

He pointed and Violet spotted the dark skin and broad shoulders of the new mate, back to the both of them. She stood next to a Kelpie, bearded, like Denzel had said. Like the one from the docks . . .

Violet realised what Denzel had meant by settling accounts. She broke away from him and pushed her way through the crowd of patrons, skidding to a stop right into the back of Hounds and the bearded Kelpie. She'd forgotten the floor sloped and almost fell past them. Hounds reached out and caught her, saving her from falling face-first into a lowered pit, the rim of which was lined by the patrons.

Bandit and the yiqi, the birdlike animal from the docks, were in the middle of the pit. More than a man's height below them in a hole with unclimbable sides, both were tied with strong cord to opposite sides. It didn't stop them fighting but it would stop them escaping. The pit was too big and too deep to be intended for such small animals. Violet knew then what the sign had referenced. Game fighting. Not cubs surrounding the chained bear, but dogs.

"What did you do?" She turned on Hounds, the older woman still holding her tight by the shoulder.

"Had a thing to settle, lass, that's all," Hounds said over the screams of the two creatures below.

"What thing?" Violet demanded.

"Reputation, only thing that counts around here, lass," Hounds said. "*Tantamount's* took a hit missing that run, got other folks crowding runs, runs we want. Like what you walked in on with the captain before. There's work going but we got first call on it, only we don't want it. Kilt here had the idea, easier to settle it out of the meeting hall, negotiate as such."

"You took him," Violet glared at her, clenching her fists. "You left me there so I wouldn't stop you. I would have stopped you!"

A muscle tensed in Hounds face, a touch of guilt maybe. "Trust me," she said. "You said you trusted me, so . . ."

"How could you?" Violet lashed out at her furiously. Hounds caught her by the wrists, easily restraining her. "Get him out of there!"

"It'll be over soon," Hounds said. "Soon as one of them comes out on top we settle up. You saw them at the docks. Bandit's going to be fine."

The Kelpie, Kilt, chuckled, echoing the feeling in Violet's gut. She turned her eyes to the fight below, not believing the assurance. This was a blood sport. The crowd weren't going to be happy until they saw some.

As he had back in the docks, Bandit was choosing to attack with great leaping bounds. The yiqi couldn't fly properly without an updraft, let alone being leashed. Bandit dove at it repeatedly from below and even climbed the walls, only to abruptly turn halfway up and launch himself back down, tackling his feathered prey. They rolled about in the pit with Bandit coming out on top and attempting to bite the yiqi. The loompa couldn't seem to find a purchase as the bird beat leathery wings in his face and tried to rake him with its feet.

Bandit gave a shriek of alarm, or maybe it was Violet, she couldn't be sure, but she saw red. Red on the sandy bottom of the pit and the red suddenly spraying from Bandit. He broke away from the yiqi, twisting and coiling, eyes wide now with fear and pain. Now Violet did cry out and felt Hounds restrain her again.

The yiqi had wire wrapped around its spurs, cut short and rusty. It seemed as surprised as Bandit about the sudden turn of fortunes but now it pressed the attack. Bandit became the hunted, tugging his leash to the limit as he tried to find a way out of the pit. The yiqi harried him, driving him to one side to the hoots and hollers of the crowd. They started to throw things, husks of bread, empty tankards, and plates, mostly aimed at Bandit to encourage him to get back into the scrap.

"This wasn't what we said." Hound pushed the bearded Kelpie in the chest, stepping up to him.

Too little, too late, Violet thought.

"House rules," Kilt chuckled to her.

"Make it stop," Hounds said. "Bet's off."

Another laugh. Hounds swore and pushed the Kelpie again, almost into the pit this time. His fellow patrons caught him and shoved him back with a cheer. A brawl was close to breaking out above as well as down below. Violet saw her chance—a knife tucked into Hounds' belt, easily swiped. And the drop into the pit wasn't that far . . .

Violet ignored the roar as the crowd realised her intention. For that reason, she didn't see the yiqi when it attacked, ripping at her face with wire-wrapped talons. She managed to get an arm up and felt the wire rip through the bandages on her forearm, felt the sensation but not the pain. She lashed out with her other arm, the one holding her knife. She wasn't sure if she meant to hurt the yiqi but her concern would have been wasted—all she succeeded in doing was slicing through the tether keeping it grounded. The bird-thing was smart enough to realise its second turn of good fortune and flapped awkwardly for the ceiling, vanishing into the rafters.

"Hold still," Violet tried to comfort a cowering Bandit. Liquid black eyes followed her hand as she sawed through the rope. She half expected Bandit to run but he was frozen to the ground in shock. Violet gathered him up in one arm, tucking the knife awkwardly through her belt, feeling his small body trembling and limp against her. And something else, a hot sticky wetness against her skin. Blood.

She faced an angry crowd now. Worse, they were all looking down on her from the spectating stands. Bar room missiles were still raining down, though not to the same extent now the yiqi had fled. Violet raised her free arm and turned her shoulder to shield Bandit better. He seemed oblivious to it all, barely holding on.

Hounds crouched at the edge of the pit, hand extended. Violet wanted to throw something at the woman. It was because of her Bandit was bleeding all over her.

"Come on, lass," Hounds said. "We're good to go, don't be wasting time."

Her face said she could see what Violet was thinking.

Good.

But there was no other way of climbing out of the pit. She started to reach for Hounds' outstretched hand when the woman was pulled up by the bearded Kelpie. Violet would almost have cheered for Kilt if she didn't blame him too.

She didn't see who, but someone pushed Kilt. The Kelpie landed in an impossible pile of limbs in front of her and didn't get up. She used him as a stepping stone and grabbed Hounds' arm, locking gazes with the woman. Violet wasn't the one to look away.

"I'm sorry," Hounds said, quietly.

Violet didn't give her a reply, turning her back and beginning the long walk back to the ship.

NEL KNEW HAZE could hear her approaching but the leathery old buzzard didn't give her any sign of it. Engrossed in his work, fingers and bone fid working on a long splice, chapped lips whistling a shanty tune. Every inch the sailor, or the appearance of one.

Haze's hearing was sharp as any and his eyes were probably not as bad as he let everyone believe, but it kept his duties light and sedentary and cut back on his time in the rigging. An easier ride at the end of a hard-lived life. Nel didn't begrudge him his small deceptions; she rather admired him for it. He pulled his weight and earned his keep so he was right with her and the captain. And he was going to be able to shed light on what Nel suspected she'd seen.

Nel crouched in front of Haze, hands clasped over her knees, rocking back on her heels.

"Want something, Skipper?" Haze asked without stopping his splicing.

"A cold drink, a good turn at the tables, and a fat pay-out at the end of my run."

"You don't gamble."

"Not when I might lose."

"Naw. You like your odds, you just don't have a face for cards."

"You can see my face?"

"On a good day, Skipper. On a good day."

She nodded.

"Your girl is watching," Haze inclined his head over Nel's shoulder. She sighed, knowing she'd see Violet if she turned around.

Moody too, right one since she got back.

"Yeah, she does that. Probably watching you though, learn her ropes proper."

Haze leaned over further, partially obscuring his hands, mouth set in a grim line.

"Don't care to be watched."

Nel chuckled. "Your inks. Need to see one."

"Need or want?" Haze grumbled.

"Need."

"Which one?"

"The shellback, sailor."

"Ah, that one. Forget where it is. Left buttock maybe."

"Try right shoulder."

"Could be the shoulder."

"It is the shoulder, old man," Nel said. "Just show me."

Haze grunted in response but put down his rope-work, reaching up to pull his shirt over his head, exposing his upper body and all its adornments. Haze made a fuss of it, groaning and shuffling awkwardly to put his back to Nel.

"Old joints," he wheezed.

"As you say." Nel frowned at the shoulder in question. The skin was wrinkled and saggy, covered in old scars and burns besides. She reached out and smoothed the old skin with the palm of one hand so she could see the faded design better.

"Touching is extra, Skipper," Haze laughed.

"Shut up, Haze." She could feel him chuckle through her hand. "Hold still."

It was a shellback, a turtle. In Haze's case, it was made up of a number of unconnected single shapes and designs that made up the head, flippers, and body; when viewed as a whole they made up the larger animal. More intricate than most, but not dissimilar to what she'd seen at the Draugr pits.

She pulled her hand away. "You've had this a long while."

"Longer than some, not as long as others," Haze allowed.

"Spent so long pulling ropes my own got worn away." He held up his palm to show the truth of his words. His braided tattoo, the one all sailors inevitably asked for, was little more than a smudged black string.

"Needs a splice," Nel said.

"You're funny, Skipper."

"Aye, it's my curse. Where'd you get the turtle?"

"Military service."

Service. If you wanted to live in the High Lanes you had to be a citizen. And if you were born outside of them you had to serve.

Remember a time when I still wanted to live in the High.

"You serve long?"

"Fifteen years." Haze put his shirt back on and reached for his ropes. He set to work again as he talked. "From the ways of the High and Free to the Edge."

The Edge, Nel thought. Beyond all the Lanes—even the Far Lanes. The Alliance used to send ships there, searching for a way through. Never found one and lost good ships trying.

"Couldn't wait to be quit of the limeys by the end of it. Been in the Free Lanes ever since. When I first signed on with Horatio, I figured that would be my last ship."

"Before the *Tantamount*?"

"Aye," Haze winked. "Before our lady *Tantamount*."

"Looks different to others I've seen."

"Most folk like to add their blemish to a piece."

"Flourish, you mean."

"Naw, know what I mean."

Nel sighed and ran a hand through her hair. "Saw one just like this, Haze, right here in Vice. So tell me now, afore I get angry, who was it put the slant on yours?"

"Was a group of us," Haze grunted, eyes living up to his namesake as he recollected. "Twenty years back, maybe. All got stamped together, rite of passage and such. We was young, once. Younger, anyway, suppose I wasn't. Were to keep us close, or so we thought."

"Did it work?"

"No," Haze scowled. "Most of them are dead, so I heard, across the years. Some as not, least not yet. One in particular. Never did like that one, stayed in the Alliance and made a name for herself. Had ideas about how things ought to be done, didn't care to hear otherwise. Damned boot licker too. Heard another did well though, lucky run, retired to some island. Could be true."

"Fellow I saw wasn't old enough to have been born when you got that piece, Haze. Guess your scratcher is still stamping them out on any sailors who come through. Must be getting old. I hear old folks' hands get shaky, can't hold their drink no more."

"Least we're still allowed a drink, Skipper," Haze grinned, showing missing teeth. Still had quite a few for his age—surprising someone hadn't punched more of them out. "And we didn't get no back-alley scratcher to carve this little beauty. Was young Wicker who done it. Fancied himself a bit of a natural at it. Bloody amateur really. Buggered the first one a right mess."

Nel snorted. "And you still all went ahead and got them?"

"Had to, had agreed to, all gentlemanlike. And Rews insisted after he saw his, else he threatened to do them himself with a spike and a barrel of tar." Haze held up the marlinspike and made a stabbing motion. "We did the honourable thing in the end. Went third myself so it weren't as bad, once Wicker did his thing. Then we let Rews do his. Seemed fair at the time. Lad screamed like a lass. Rews didn't have a clue what he was about. Boy had to get it redone at the next port just to cover up the scars."

Nel frowned, thinking her way through the story. "Your man Wicker, what happened to him?"

"Dead, a dozen years now. Caught an infection of the blood, I think. Bad way to go." Haze shook his head, then shrugged.

"So why am I spotting marines with your family crest running around Vice?" Nel said, almost talking to herself. She pushed herself up, prepared to dismiss the whole conversation as a dead end.

Haze grabbed her arm. "Marines? You never mentioned no marines." Nel stared, surprised at his reaction.

"You getting us mixed up in Alliance crossfires again, lass?" Haze demanded.

"Let go, sailor," Nel warned, not moving her arm. She locked eyes with the old man until he did as she said.

"What's this?" she said, once he calmed.

Haze stared up at her sullenly, chewing on his own tongue before he answered. "One I mentioned, one I said stayed on in the fleet."

"The boot licker, lass with ideas."

Haze actually blanched at her words. "Be best if we both forget I said such."

"Why?" Nel growled, trepidation starting to set in.

Haze's face was pale. He missed a tuck on one of his ropes, staring at it in surprise, then swearing.

"Haze," Nel insisted, "who was she?"

"Scariest woman I ever met," Haze mumbled, hands shaking now. His jaw was set stubbornly, teeth gritted as he made a conscious effort to steady himself. "Scarier than you, Skipper. We all hated her. Was afraid of her. Knew she'd go far, get themselves a command, didn't want to be around when they did."

"The name, Haze." Nel resisted the urge to shake him. "What was her name?"

"Forgot it," Haze shook his head miserably. "Forgot her name but could never forget her. None of us could. Got the damned scars too . . ."

He took a deep, shuddering breath, eyes up to face Nel now. "Crew started calling her the Gunner's Daughter. You know what that means, Skipper."

Nel stared into the old sailor's frightened eyes. Old sailors were hard sailors. Tough. Weather beaten. They didn't scare easy. Haze was damned scared.

He was right, she did know who he meant.

And she knew the name.

The Gunner's Daughter . . .

Hells . . .

"You don't look so good, Skipper," Violet risked saying as the woman walked past her. All pale she was, shock of red hair all the more shocking for it. She'd cut it shorter recently, so that it hung raggedly off her shoulders. The skipper wasn't known for her skill with a pair of scissors. In fact she'd probably done it with a knife, maybe in a bout of frustration. Certainly looked like she'd cut it off angry. Violet didn't have that problem. Her hair just curled, took forever to grow down. Unless it got wet. She hated when it got wet.

"I'm fine, Vi," the skipper said, all grim and moody. She stopped, almost mid-pace. "I ever tell you not to listen in on my conversations?"

"No."

"Then I'm telling you now. Don't be listening in on my conversations."

Can't keep secrets from a cabin girl. The captain's words. Made sense.

"Shouldn't talk so loud," Violet said back, wondering at her own cheek.

The skipper made a face that said she was thinking the same.

"What'd you hear, lass?" she asked curtly, folding her arms. Meant she weren't leaving till she got an answer. And not just any answer. Had to be the answer she wanted to hear too.

"Bits and stuff about shellbacks and the Edge," Violet shrugged.

"That it?"

Violet shrugged again. That really was most of what she'd heard. The conversation had got real quiet after that. Like the skipper really hadn't wanted no one listening to what she and Haze were saying.

"Fine," the skipper sighed, running a hand through her hair. "Fine, don't matter none anyway. Seen the captain?"

Violet shook her head.

The skipper scowled at her. "You're sombre and quiet, lass. What'd you do?"

"Nothing," Violet said.

"You sure."

Violet nodded, which only made the skipper's face contort more.

"You got nothing to say?" the woman asked. "Nothing?"

"What's a shellback?" Violet blurted out, unable to hold back the question anymore. "And the Edge, is that a place? Where is it? What is it? Is a shellback a fish? Or is it a clam? Maybe an oyster or some kind of cockle? Am I right?"

The skipper groaned. "Hells, I had to ask, didn't I?"

"Am I right?"

"Hells, girl, you're not even close. A shellback is not an oyster or a clam or any other shellfish."

"So what is it? Is it a—"

"It's a turtle," the skipper cut her off, levelling a finger of warning at her. "The kind with flippers and not feet, before you ask me that too. Sailors who've been to the Edge get them. Mostly . . ." The skipper shrugged. "Mostly fools and madmen.

Ain't no reason to go to the Edge, not if you've a lick of sense between your ears."

Violet nodded. That made sense. It sounded obscure, this shellback tattoo that she'd never heard of before, but then there were probably dozens, maybe hundreds of tattoos she hadn't even imagined out there. Half of the tattoos sailors wore, carried on them like a second language, referenced places or events. Which brought them back to her other question.

"What's the Edge, Skipper?"

"The Edge is the Edge," was the reply. Nonsensical, not helpful at all. The woman was either distracted or was sandbagging her.

"The edge of what though?"

"Of everything." The skipper waved an expansively dismissive hand. "Of this, of all of it, the black, the miasma. Everything."

She turned to face Violet. "The Edge is as far as you can go through the black. It's where the mist ends, where it grows so thin a ship that ventures any further will fall through it. And keep falling. Forever."

"To where?" Violet felt her heart beat faster.

Fall forever? How was that even possible?

"Nobody knows. You can't cross the Edge, can't go around it, or over it, or under it. People have been trying to find a way since it was discovered, but no one ever has. And no one, not one ship, not a single castaway or marooned sailor has ever been found to tell what happens to those who push their luck too far. Not a one, Violet."

"But where is it?"

"Everywhere," the skipped said. "All around us. They say it's like a giant fishbowl, with all of everything inside."

Violet objected to the idea. It was ludicrous. "That doesn't make any sense. I've never even heard of it."

"Neither have most people. Hells, most people have never heard of Hail or Storm. Nobody has heard of Walker and some think Vice is just a bad hobby."

"But . . ."

"You could sail for a year, Violet," the skipper said. "A whole year. If you set out from Vice, right here, right now, in any direction it would take you more than a year to reach the Edge. More, depending on how unlucky your choice was. But at least a year. That's how far away it is. The Edge of the black. The last stop before it all ends."

The skipper straightened up, one hand on her hip, thumb tucked into the top of her breeches. The other hand rubbed at her arm, the one covered in tattoos.

"Shellbacks are sailors who've been to the Edge, Violet. Those few who've made the journey and returned to speak of it. And not many will. Speak of it, that is. Though there's always some who don't return at that. A shellback is someone worth respecting, a sailor who's earned the right to be called such. It's the folk behind such a journey who'd worry me. Them that'd send a crew out on a trip like that, knowing they might not come back and knowing there's no good as has ever come of the Edge."

"Skipper?" Violet asked.

"Yeah?"

"Why are we talking about this?"

The skipper didn't answer. Not directly. "Just old hand's tales, lass. Just that. Need a word with the captain now. Make yourself useful. Go get Haze to teach you his ropes, maybe."

Chapter 15

FOR THE FIRST time Nel could recall, her new mate was in a mood. In the time she'd been aboard there had always been a wry amusement to Hounds, a sense of world-weary mocking at the world's expense, like the woman knew something nobody else did. Only now she looked as though she'd played a bad beat at the tables, a sure winner that somehow got trumped by an even better hand. Nel had seen the same look on the captain's face more times than she could count. With him it was resignation but Hounds made it look angry.

"Hounds, need the captain, you seen him?"

That got no response. Nel found she had to repeat herself, louder.

"Went chasing a vendor." Hounds made a vague motion with her hand. "Sweetcakes, from down the pier. Should be back in a minute."

"Fine, I can wait a minute."

Hounds didn't answer, just left her chin resting against her chest. Anyone could see she was deep inside herself, wrestling with some moral quandary.

Hells, probably should ask her about it.

Should.

"What?" Hounds half turned her head. "What're you looking at me like that for, Vaughn?"

"No reason," Nel said, keeping her tone even. She deliberately looked towards Vice but there was no sign of the captain. Could be lost in the crowd though, hard to pick such a small man out of the rabble.

"Did Violet say something?"

"Violet?"

"Did she?"

"No," Nel said, facing the woman now. "She didn't, but maybe I should go ask her. Something I should know?"

Hounds clammed up again, her teeth clenched and jaws bunching.

"What did you do?" Nel asked again, on the verge of angry.

"Screwed up," Hounds said, to her surprise. "Don't think Vi's going to be talking to me for a while."

Hounds had her arms wrapped around herself, rubbing at her bare arms. It was a habit Nel recognised in herself, a nervous tic, fingers tracing old scars and tattoos. There was one on the inside of Hounds' upper arm the woman was digging her thumb into, almost to the point of breaking skin and drawing blood. And Nel felt a catch in her throat when her eyes seized on that one design.

"I'll talk to her," Hounds said, mostly to herself. "Explain things. Make it right."

"Yeah, you—" Nel stopped mid-sentence. She'd just seen the captain making his way up the gangway. "No, don't talk to her, hells, don't do anything. Give the girl space, Hounds. I need to talk to the captain. But you and I are going to have words later."

"Vaughn," Hounds said before she could go. Quietlike.

"What?" Nel hesitated.

"Like a word with the captain, after. If you could pass that on."

Nel frowned. "Be sure to."

"Nel, look, look what I found," the captain beamed at her, holding out a bowl. It was full of candied treats, the sort that would rot your teeth and send children into maddening high-pitched fits.

"Don't be sharing that with Violet," Nel said. She immediately regretted the words as the captain's eyes gleamed at the idea. She sighed.

Really must learn to keep my mouth shut.

"A word before you drown us in squealing, at least, Captain." Nel steered the captain towards the bridge. She could see Quill there. It wasn't his watch but then where else would he be?

Quill watched them approach. In fact he was watching everyone, cold lizard eyes scanning back and forth from his vantage.

"You have been keeping busy, the two of you," he commented. He eyed the captain's latest find with distaste, as different as could be found from his own palate. The captain for his part didn't seem to notice, lost in his own world again.

Nel looked around. They were alone and no one else was in earshot. Nobody in the galley either—she knew Gabbi and Jack were doing a stocktake below, a laborious process given that the non-perishable supplies were stashed all over the ship wherever nooks and crannies could be found. There was a sea breeze, wind rushing off the cooling land out towards the curtain falls of the edge of the world. Sheer miles away, but every time Nel looked that direction, she imagined she could hear the crash of falling water. It was as private a conversation as they were likely to find on the *Tantamount*.

"We have a problem," she said.

"No, it's a pastry," the captain said proudly.

"Captain, please," Nel said through gritted teeth. Quill glared at her, as though she were responsible.

"No, you're right, Nel." Horatio raised the cheesecloth covering, peeking under. "It's a fruit. Perhaps tart would be the better word, but still a treat of the most succulent order."

"I know who's been following us," Nel said, speaking more to Quill now. If the captain wasn't right then she needed the navigator to be aware. "And I know how they've been doing it."

"How is not the question," Quill said. "How has never been the question, we are all aware of how. Tell us who."

Nel took a breath. She didn't want to say it, the name. Once the words passed her lips it would be real.

"They call her the Gunner's Daughter."

Quill stared. Cold, unblinking reptile eyes.

"Who?"

"Godsdamnit, Quill."

"I have never heard of this daughter," Quill told her. "Is it even a person? What a ridiculous name. Did they choose it themselves or was it forced upon them?"

"The Gunner's Daughter, Quill! The woman's a hells-damned

fleet nightmare. Bosuns used to scare new hands with talk about her . . .”

But Quill would not stop. “I am not and never have been part of your absurd fleet. Are they another pink and squidgy human such as yourself? Or a foul-smelling Korrigan perhaps?”

“No, they’re . . . it doesn’t matter, Quill. The point is . . .”

“Who is it, Nel?” the captain asked. Nel and Quill both stopped to find the captain facing them, looking tired and weary. He’d set aside his bowl of baked goods and had drawn his tattered old coat close around his shoulders. “Who do you think the spy is?

“Don’t give me that look, either of you.” Horatio sounded tired when nobody answered him.

“Hounds,” Nel said. “It’s Hounds, Captain.”

Horatio sighed. “You are sure? What is it that makes you suspect her?”

“Not just her,” Quill put in. “We must consider all those who came aboard with her.”

“Perhaps, Mister Quill,” Horatio held up a hand in appeal, “but I would still hear the evidence first.”

“Shellbacks,” Nel said.

“Sea turtles,” Quill repeated.

“Yes.”

“Your cipher to unlocking the conspiracy surrounding us is a sea turtle,” Quill’s enthusiasm was dropping with every word. “That is . . . unsettling.”

“Hounds has a shellback tattoo,” Nel said. “A very unusual design.”

“Not that unusual,” Horatio said. “Anyone who’s been to the Edge has one.”

“How many sailors travel to the Edge, Captain?” Nel asked.

“I did, once,” Horatio said.

Even Quill started at that.

“I was younger,” their captain said. “Much younger. It doesn’t seem so very grand now but then . . . well, it was a feat to be admired, told in taverns. I even had the tattoo, the shellback. Small though, didn’t care for pain.”

“I’ve never seen it,” Nel said.

“Nor are you likely to.” Horatio’s smile was bittersweet. “It was covered over, you know what by, both of you. The pain was a welcome distraction at the time, I found.”

Awkward silence. Quill even coughed.

Nel still had more to say. "Hounds' shellback, I saw a marine with the same when Quill and I were inspecting the Draugr. The exact same."

"Yes," Horatio said. "And I presume there is more for you to be so certain. This woman you mentioned, this . . . gunner . . ."

"Gunner's Daughter," Nel said. "On account of . . . a reputation of discipline. The design is hers, from her . . . her own younger days, Captain. The ship we kept glimpsing. And it wasn't just here at Vice."

She hesitated. "I saw someone at Port Border, just before Violet brought us this run."

"Ah," Horatio nodded. "This person, someone you knew, we may presume? A person from your past?"

"Yes."

"Inconceivable," Quill muttered.

"Enough, Mister Quill," the captain warned him sharply. "Quite enough. Nel, if I may presume, would this person be a known associate of this woman? That is the connection?"

"Yes."

"And you are certain?"

"We're being followed, Captain," Nel said. "Hunted. Since Port Border, maybe even before. Could be because of Grange and Rim, most likely is, or it could be nothing."

"It does not matter why," Quill said.

"No, it don't," Nel said. "But Hounds is the key. She's what links all of that to us. Whether it was chance she came aboard or not, she's the tie."

"Perhaps," the captain said.

"No perhaps about it, Captain." Nel shook her head. "I wouldn't be saying if I weren't certain. I like Hounds, hells, I did like her. But best thing for us is to drop ropes and leave her and hers dockside."

Quill nodded at this but didn't say anything. Nel was surprised. Said as much.

"It is the logical course," he said simply. "We can recriminate over it later."

Recriminate. Big smart-sounding words.

"Half the crew are ashore," Horatio told her. "So there is no point in making any rash decisions, or rasher actions. We have some time to dwell. And in any case," he shrugged, "I am not convinced."

"Captain," Nel said quickly, "this isn't something we can ignore. The Gunner's Daughter . . ."

"Oh, of them I am quite aware, Nel, I know her reputation. And a filthy one it is." Horatio's voice turned a little dark. He was angry, Nel realised. "It is her reason for pursuing us I question. As I said, I am not convinced."

"Reasons do not matter," Quill argued.

"But they do. Very much so," Horatio said simply. "Nor do I believe Hounds is the spy."

"She was part of the Gunner's crew."

"Oh, yes, quite. Told me so herself," the captain agreed. "We were playing cards one night, a long watch it was. Passed the time. Her and Denzel, both. Not Mantid though, they fell in later. Her story did nothing to improve my opinion of the woman. An officer with no regard for the sanctity of her own crew. Despicable. Truly despicable. It is no wonder they never made captain."

"And you did not mention this?" Quill hissed. He spun away, almost taking the both of them out with his tail. "Unbelievable, the both of you."

"I do know my own crew." The captain shrugged. "And until now it was just one of many things that were . . . better off unsaid."

Nel folded her arms, looking very hard at her captain. He was, and had been this whole time, looking anywhere but at her. And he had been treating this entire revelation oddly. As if he were humouring her, like he might a small child who had some fantastical explanation for the very mundane.

"Captain," she said yet again, "what else has been left unsaid?"

"Ah, Nel," the captain sighed, looking every bit the tired old man. "Quill, my dear friends. It isn't Hounds. I wish it were, in some way, but it never was." He sat down awkwardly against the railing, his back facing out to sea. Reaching into his coat pocket, he produced his journal. It fell open, revealing the Guild letter. The seal was broken.

"You said you weren't going to open that," Nel said unnecessarily.

"I did," the captain nodded, looking down between the pages

of his journal. The ink on the leaves was smudged, creating a faintly smeared mirror on the outside of the letter where it had been wedged in between. It almost resembled the seal, the same jumble of lines. Written in haste, or closed before the ink was dry.

Either that or the captain was trying to copy the seal. Can't put it back once you break it though.

"We agreed," Nel said.

"I was hoping for answers," Horatio sounded resigned. "Yes, perhaps I should have known better. All I found were more questions. Questions about questions, none of it making any sense."

"You're not making any sense, Captain."

"How is the Guild involved in this?" Quill asked.

"They are not," the captain said. "Well, no more than they already are. Were. The letter . . . the letter holds nothing helpful, my friends. Such a quiet ending, it is merely a courtesy from one Ebon Masaius. Mundane details, no more. Nothing about . . ."

"About what?" Nel asked at the same time Quill demanded to know "Who?"

The captain closed his journal on the Guild letter with a snap, begging the question of why he'd brought it out in the first place.

"Captain," Nel tried one last time. "What do you know? What aren't you telling us?"

But he said nothing, only looking down at the journal, a sad smile on his face. Nel spun away from him, biting back an almost-scream of frustration.

"Once the crew are all back aboard," he finally did say, "we will take our leave of Vice. With or without a job."

"The crew are scattered to the wind," Quill told him, matter-of-factly. "Many will not be back for hours, if not days."

"We can wait," the captain said.

"Leaving at once would be safer," Quill said.

"Perhaps it would, but I do not believe the risk an unreasonable one. As yet we have not been . . . threatened."

"I'm not waiting," Nel said, talking out towards the edge. "I can't do it, sit here . . . do nothing."

"Nel," the captain said. "I would ask you, no, I would beg you, not to do anything rash."

She shook her head, shoulders squared, facing away from him. "Don't like being hunted, Captain," she said stubbornly.

"Marines, Captain. Tough and mean but not too bright. Now that I know who . . . what to look for . . ."

"You are going to do something stupid," Quill finished for her.

"Only stupid if I die doing it, Loveland."

"You sound like somebody I used to know," Horatio sighed.

"I'm going," Nel pointed ashore. "Keep everyone here until I get back. And Quill . . ."

"Yes?"

"If you have to . . . you go."

She expected a reaction, from both of them. She didn't get it.

"We will see you when you return," was all Quill said.

VIOLET DID NOT go to old Haze like she'd been asked. Nor did she make a particular effort to make herself useful. Truth was there wasn't much to do other than mend and make ropes until they set sail again. And Haze had that well in hand without Violet being underfoot.

The captain found her, naturally. Or maybe it was Bandit. Seemed he was always bringing folk to her. Couldn't get a moment to herself, not that anyone could aboard the ship. Except maybe the captain with his cabin, the only one still with a door.

She held the captain's present, the water globe, between two cupped hands. It was stormy again, the black mist spinning around inside the glass. As the storm rolled the ship, Violet traced a pattern on the outside of the glass with her thumb. Bandit crouched in front of her, teeth bared and growling. Fur standing on end. His growl made her ears ache, something painful about it. The loompa watched the glassed ship intently, little black eyes following every move. Violet put it down on the deck between her feet, letting it roll towards him. The storm calmed with every rotation, stopping completely when Bandit scratched at the globe, unable to get a grip on the smooth glass.

"It was the most remarkable thing," the captain said, settling down beside her. He carried a wooden bowl covered in cheesecloth, displayed and balanced on the tips of his fingers. "I was coming back to the ship and I passed the most remarkable stall. The smell, Violet, it was like being back in my mother's kitchen. Or perhaps it was my wife, I often forget, but one of them used to make this dish, this very dish. The other one would try but the result was . . . not so good. But this . . . this I have high hopes for!"

The captain whisked the gauzy cheesecloth covering away with a flourish. "Pear," he announced gleefully. "Baked pear and candied almonds. Have you ever seen the like? You must try it with me."

The captain looked at Bandit, standing on his hind legs and sniffing at the plate, somewhere between curious and cautious. "And you too, my dear friend, you as well."

The captain cut off the end of the treat, offering it to Bandit with grave dignity. Violet had to smile when the loompa returned the courtesy, holding the tidbit in both hands and nibbling delicately.

"And for you, my dear child." The captain sliced the pear down the middle, spearing half for himself and offering her the plate. "Savour it, chew it slowly—this is an experience, one must not waste it."

He wasn't wrong. The taste was exquisite. The fruit was still warm and dissolved in her mouth, the centre hollowed and dusted with cinnamon and sugar, stuffed with fresh roasted nuts. Violet had a moment of guilt at what Gabbi might say. It felt treacherous, but it was a far cry beyond anything that came out of the ship's galley. The captain's wink said he was thinking the same.

"What did I tell you, Violet, an experience not to be missed. Nor to be repeated too often, else we both grow fat and our teeth fall out. I have enough left that I should care to hold on to them for as long as I might. One never knows when one might need teeth, yes?"

Bandit gave him a silent look, in between sucking the sugary syrups from his paws.

"I'm having nightmares."

"Yes," the captain sighed. "Yes, you are."

Violet pulled her knees up tight, arms wrapped around. Curled up into a little ball. That would be safe. She wanted to feel safe. "How?"

"Because you sleep, Violet. Badly, perhaps, but you still sleep."

"Captain?"

"Sometimes I wake up, Violet, and I think I'm in my bed. I remember being in my cabin. But I find myself . . . elsewhere. Wandering the ship. Below the decks, on the bridge. Once I even found myself in the nest at the top of the mast. Did I ever tell you how much heights gall me? Took me an age to work my way down. I believe Piper carried me much of the way that time."

"I used to get dizzy in the nest," Violet admitted. "Sick and dizzy, like the world was underwater and I'm swimming with my mouth hung open."

"Do you still, Violet?"

She shook her head.

"Ah," the captain sighed. "But now you have nightmares. I see that, see you having them."

"How?"

He smiled, patting her on the shoulder. "Sometimes my nightly sojourns take me to the lower deck. There is something comforting for the sleepless about seeing that other people can still sleep soundly. But you don't. I see you twisting in your hammock, Violet. I went to wake you once but . . ."

"But what?"

"But I didn't. I think it would be bad."

"I don't understand."

The captain smiled, wrapping one thin arm around her. She rested her head on his shoulder. It was comfortable, until she became aware of something digging into her leg. That thing she found in the nest.

"I found this," she said, holding the tinted lens in front of her. "I don't know what it means."

The captain reached out and took it from her, but his eyes were focused on her. "Where did you find it, my dear girl?"

"In the nest."

"Have you shown it to anybody?"

"To Hounds. She said it was junk, didn't seem to care. Then she took me into town and . . ." Violet's voice hardened as she spoke, the memory of what had almost happened to Bandit too recent and raw. Words couldn't explain it properly.

"Yes, I have already had words with Miss Hounds," the captain's voice was firm. Unlike hers. Barely a quaver. The way it always was when he talked about crew. He pocketed the lens inside his coat. "But that is another matter. You haven't shown it to Nel? Or perhaps to Quill or Gabbi?"

"No. No, sir, I haven't."

"Please do not."

"Sir?" Violet nodded her head but couldn't help from wondering.

"Did you know, Violet," the captain held up one finger close to his nose, his eyes sparkling with mischief, "that sometimes people, people on this ship, they come and they confess things to me. They pick their moments, mostly, they think I won't remember. They tell me secrets, their guilty burdens. When they think I won't remember. Because we all need to tell someone, Violet. It's secrets that are what kills us. Secrets that gnaw away at us.

"But I do remember, I always remember. Other people. The ones I care about, this ship. Or near enough. It's only myself that I forget, that I sometimes can't hold on to."

There were going to be tears. She could feel them. Hot and wet, salty like water should be. Threatening to flood down her cheeks. Violet screwed up her face angrily.

Not going to happen. Not in front of the captain.

"Do you know," the captain said quietly, so very quietly, "why I am the way I am? The way I am now?"

"You're the captain," Violet said, feeling miserable. "I've never known you to be anything else. Other than the captain of the *Tantamount*. My captain."

"Ah, but Violet, once, long ago, or not so long ago, I was. Or maybe the ship was, does it matter? Perhaps not, it seems close enough. Perhaps it doesn't matter, Nel would say as much. But it was a different name then, this was different. The whole world was different. They call it Misery now, I believe. But back then it was Vintage. Back in the day . . ."

He laughed. It wasn't a bitter laugh. There was laughter in it, happier times.

"I had a wife there, a daughter. No, two daughters, Nel always reminds me of that, I ask her why not three, or even more. They were very much alike, my girls. In my head . . . they become muddled, Violet. I'm never sure if I'm thinking of the younger one or if I'm remembering her older sister when she was younger. And I can't remember their names. Only the looks on their faces. But that is the way it should be. I wouldn't want it the other way.

"It was the fog, you see," Horatio said. "Like the mist, only . . . only very wrong. It's supposed to be out there, in the black. Far, so very far away. Not down on the ground. It does funny things to a person. They didn't know that's what it was, of course. Vintage was inside the High Lanes, part of the Allied Worlds. People started . . . started . . . they were . . . "

"Captain?"

"Yes."

"What?"

"Like me, Violet. A whole world gone rather mad. Forgetful. Lost. In just a few weeks. Nobody understood that, of course. The Alliance was frightened. A plague, a weapon, some new malady. They couldn't explain it. Of course they couldn't. How could you when everyone afflicted couldn't understand what was happening to them? They cordoned my world off, a ring of wooden ships and iron men. Nobody was allowed through. They were worried it might spread. A very reasonable, sensible fear when you're dealing with the unknown. Perhaps even the right thing to do.

"That was what I came home to. A blockade of ships around my home. Alliance colours between me . . . between me and my family. I was often away from home, of course I was, it was the life I lived, the life I had chosen. But to come home to that . . . well, it was not an easy thing to accept. And many of us could not. As people returned home, the dissent grew. They wouldn't allow us to land, wouldn't allow us through. And no help was coming. Nothing was being done. So we decided we would do something.

"We ran the blockade, a handful of us. There were ships, mine and others, we would go in, find our families, and escape before the Alliance was any the wiser. Before they could stop us. And then we'd find a way to help them."

"Captain," Violet asked. "Where was the skipper, during all of this? Where was . . . "

"Nel? She was where she was meant to be, of course. A good soldier, holding the line, serving under her captain."

"With you?"

"No, Violet, not with me."

Violet nodded mutely. On the blockade then. She hadn't wanted to think that, to think that of the skipper. But it was real, it had happened. Even without her thinking it.

"So her captain, her captain was . . . "

"Heathen, yes," Horatio confirmed her suspicions. "The same one we met outside at Rim. At another blockade, come to think of it. That never occurred to me before. The black is a curious place, really, so vast yet rather small in a way. Or perhaps we are rather small, afraid to step outside of our routines."

"What happened?" Violet asked. "Your family?"

"I never saw them again." The captain clasped his hands together, resting his chin on them. "I returned home and they weren't there. The house was empty. Others had more fortunate reunions. Only those with families on Vintage agreed to make the run, it was the only fair way. We couldn't ask otherwise. We spent a day and a night searching. But we were pressed, for time and for hands. We had to leave. I remember the run back, looking back at Vintage. I remember seeing it happen."

"Seeing what?"

"Seeing it die."

The simplicity of the captain's words was the most brutal part. Violet couldn't even ask. Her mouth was open but no words came out.

"Dust, Violet, so much dust. It swallowed the whole planet, like a blanket being drawn across it. The planet turned into one giant cloud. Grey or muddy brown, never settling. And then it died. Heathen's work, of course. Naturally, it was why she was there. An option of last resort. But it was because of us. It was our fault."

Violet tried to shake her head. *No. No.*

No.

"They were terrified it would spread. Spread from Vintage, spreading misery across the Lanes. They still didn't understand what it was, where it came from. And there was us, our little band of ships and captains, defying them at every turn. They did what they thought they had to.

"And they caught us, naturally. Threw us in irons, quarantined us aboard our own ships. Or so I'm told. We all started to exhibit the effects of the fog soon after. The time after, the days, the weeks, the months, all rather a blur. But I was told there was disquiet amongst the ranks, on the Alliance ships. The blockade. The death of a world does not sit well. And despite what some would have you believe, there are those with morals amongst the Alliance colours. Sadly."

He sighed. "I say sadly, Violet, and I mean it. Many people were broken that day."

"The skipper?"

The captain smiled. "I lost much that day, Violet. At the time all I had left to me was my ship, this ship. Would it surprise you to know how much I truly value the one thing I did gain that day? A dear friend, the oldest I can remember.

"I like to think," the captain said, "that is I like to ask myself, if there is anything I wouldn't do for the people I care about. Violet, would you like to know a secret?"

Biting down on her lower lip, she could only nod. There was nothing the captain could have asked her at that point, that she could have refused him.

He whispered it to her. "Mantids only sleep in high places. But never in hammocks. If the males aren't careful about where they nap, the women folk might eat them.

"A secret," the captain went on to say, "is only a secret if you choose to keep it that way. And people keep secrets for all manner of reasons, don't you think?" He retrieved the globe from between Violet's feet. Bandit watched intently as it was handed over. "Have you figured out this particular secret yet, my dear? I'm very pleased to see you still have it."

Violet's fingers closed around the water globe. Bandit's low growl dropped away to a confused chirp, his head tilted to the side. The mist was calm inside the globe. The captain patted her on the shoulder.

"I don't understand," Violet said, facing the captain. Bandit climbed up her leg and made his way onto her shoulder, nuzzling against her, paws gripping her hair.

Moody little rat, make up your mind.

"And I hope that it stays that way, my dear," Horatio smiled. "Best to leave some mystery in the black, yes? I must be going now, so many things to do. A few of them I may even remember to do. If I don't write them down, they tend to slip away, very important to write things down. If not, well, I find if I can put something off until the morrow then Nel will usually have done it."

"Captain?" Violet started to stand up. The captain shooed her back down.

"Take a moment to yourself, my dear girl. A moment, just to be yourself. No one will know and such moments . . ." He smiled, a sad, wistful smile. "Well, they are to be treasured."

He leaned down, speaking very gravely to Bandit, his face next to both of theirs. "And you take care of her, master Bandit. We all have our roles and that is yours."

Again the loompa looked puzzled. Or perhaps that was his answer.

Violet shook her head as the captain left her. She loved the man, but by the black was he strange.

Violet managed almost an hour, a whole hour, to herself before Jack found her. And then it was back to duties, another supply run. Gabbi had been keeping their stocks sparse but frequent. Eking out the coins, she said, meant more trips but fresher foods. Violet didn't mind though she kept quiet about the candied pear. Jack complained about her preference for weeds, as he put it, over real food, but he was a vocal minority, the other hands approving a shift in diet.

"You stay," Violet told Bandit, when the loompa tried to climb up on her shoulder. He responded by jumping down and immediately trying to mount Jack's shoulder. Jack batted him with the side of his head to get him off. Bandit grabbed Jack's matted braids and hissed.

"Get down." Violet pointed to the deck firmly. "Down, no arguing!"

The loompa eventually got down, turning and flicking his tail at them both.

"You two not getting along?" Jack asked, handing her the list. Jack could read, after a fashion. He just preferred not to.

"Don't want him," Violet said, feeling miserable about it. "Almost lost him last time. Can't risk it."

"Luck explaining that one," Jack grunted. "What do you want, Kelpie?"

Quill, with a face uglier than Bandit's behind. "Where are you two going?" he snapped. He snatched the list out of Violet's hand. "Supplies? Again?"

"Take it up with the cook," Jack told him. "If you've the nerve."

Quill ignored Jack, handing the list back to Violet. One of his claws had caught, shredding a hole through one corner. "The skipper has gone ashore. She was of a mind that no one else go ashore until she returned."

"You want to eat tonight?" Violet waved the list at him. "Don't know if you do but the rest of the crew will. Gonna stand up and say it was cause you wouldn't let us ashore?"

Folded arms and lashing tail, the Kelpie was right agitated. She could even hear his toes tapping, scraping against the woodwork.

"I will come with you," he decided. "That should be acceptable."

"Not to me it ain't!" Jack objected. "If you're going I ain't."

"We are both going," Quill told him, to both Jack and Violet's surprise. He pointed. "To make sure she returns. And for once," he fixed Violet with a fierce look, "you may stay out of trouble. For once."

Violet staunched up, folding her arms and lifting her chin. "Where's the skipper gone? What's she after?"

"Where that woman always goes, girl. In search of trouble."

And that just explained it all.

Chapter 16

THE CAPTAIN HADN'T liked her idea. Neither had Quill. Gabbi would have disapproved had she been given the chance. Violet . . . well Violet hadn't been told. She would have wanted to come along.

Would have told her no, girl would have snuck out and followed me.

The thought made Nel turn and peer back the way she had come suspiciously. Even linger by the corner to see if anyone familiar came down the street she'd just walked. But no, she was alone.

Alone in a crowd anyway.

It didn't take much for Nel to concede this really wasn't her best idea. Wandering around Vice alone looking for trouble. She had a wand hung low on her belt and a knife tucked into one boot but neither would help much if she ran into serious harm. Alliance marines for example.

Alliance marines. On Vice.

Tell it to the marines, the sailors won't believe you.

Poor marines, if they were here they'd best leave soon before the locals finished swindling them out of all their coin. They didn't train them to be smart in the High Lanes.

But they do train them mean.

Nor could she rely on them being all that stupid, despite the tale she'd spun for the captain.

Piper would have told it better, she thought with a sigh. A tale of wooden ships and iron men. Of sons and daughters of the black.

Just as well, captain wouldn't have any of it. Hells, old man probably knew it all anyway. *He's either forgotten or he's humouring me.*

The thought occurred to her of where exactly she should look. The taverns possibly, but if they were here for Nel and her ship, as she feared, they'd be staying well away from liquor. Regretfully.

Naw, be rougher entertainment, if any. Won't be shore leave, just something for the crew to let off some steam.

She'd found some of her own crew, sent them back to the ship with a boot to the backside. Safer there. No marines as yet.

Except I ain't looking for no marines. Damnit, lad, where am I like to find you? Not carding nor drinking, unless there's been even more years gone by than I can admit to. What does that leave?

Nel shook her head, chuckling to herself. Vice. Tattooed shellback sailors. You didn't visit Vice, one of the most exotic ports in the black, and leave without something to show for it. And if you were a sailor who took pride in your ink, there was only one street. Old Ironsides.

A former hundred-gun ship turned market, the bazaar reminded Nel of the last she had been to, on Rim. The one no one would ever set foot on again, come to think of it, which made the thought all the more powerful. Built around the ribs of a famous ship of the line it now boasted a garish array of stalls and hawkers. Prominent among which were the tattooists.

There were no scratchers here, only artists. Vice's reputation for extravagance and display meant that those who adorned themselves in skinwork wanted only the best. Brilliant colours, full body works, those were common here. Nel had heard of people spending long days totalling weeks in this street, having their bodies transformed to resemble animals; lizards or exotic birds, and mythical creatures. Often for those who were already inked those works would be expanded upon, worked into a larger tapestry that would spread out and cover the wearer's skin.

It wasn't Nel's first visit to Vice. She rubbed at her right arm with her left hand. The skin itched as she passed stalls. She had to admit, some of the work she was seeing was breathtaking.

Tattoos were painful, that went without saying. But pain could be a good thing. It let you know you were still alive. It let you know you could still . . . feel.

But the bazaar didn't limit itself to simple flesh etchings. Nel also passed stalls where customers were pierced and fitted with adornments. And then there was the cutting.

A woman leaned over the back of a chair, her back exposed, while an artist made what seemed like deep cuts into her skin. Nel could feel her gorge start to rise at the sight of the artist literally carving his art into the woman. The pattern involved flames but more than that she didn't care to know.

"Curious customs," a voice beside her said. "Pain for the sake of art, a search for a way to express something."

"Some of us just like pretty pictures," Nel shrugged. She turned after she spoke. The man beside her was Luscan. It was the skin that gave it away, the greyish, leathery skin, and the yellow eyes. This Luscan was of a height with Nel and smiled at her, though oddly without showing teeth. Which was fine with Nel—she didn't need to see anyone's mouthful of eellike teeth. The ritualised scars running the lengths of both cheeks were enough.

Luscans were naturally unsettling, whether they intended to be or not. The important thing, Nel reminded herself, was not to judge by appearance. She put more stock in actions. Such as how this one had his hands resting on the pair of wands in ornate, quick-draw holsters.

That made her cautious, but not enough to reach for her own weapon. Not yet.

"Very telling, how people choose to adorn themselves," the Luscan continued, nodding his smooth head at Nel's right arm, her sleeved one.

"If you say so." Nel took a step back and away, not taking her eyes off him.

"Mors," the woman whose back was being worked on called out. "Bring her here."

"My friend would like a word with you," the newly christened Mors conveyed, extending an arm to the tent.

Mors, Nel thought. *Mors Coldstream. As in the duellist. Hells, as in the company of . . .*

Aw, hells.

Wanted to look for trouble. Captain would laugh before he cried. Quill too. Maybe not Quill. Two choices then, make a scene now . . . or make a scene later.

Later, Nel decided, stepping inside the tent. She brushed past the artist who was doing his best to ignore her and went to stand in front of the woman.

Cold eyes this one, all flinty. Don't like her at all.

"That stays open or we're going to have a problem," Nel warned as Mors stepped inside, reaching for the cord to drop the tent flap. Now she did let her hand fall.

Wasn't no accident I stood so as I could see you both, Luscan.

"As you like." Mors did show his teeth now. Rows of daggerlike, needle-sharp teeth. Like a mouthful of icicles.

"All right." Nel squared her shoulders, pushing on the guard of her wand with her thumb, making sure it was loose. Doubtful it was going unnoticed but that wasn't important no more. "You want to talk, let's talk. You go first. What do you want?"

Quill's skin tingled. No, more of an itch, akin to the feeling of moulting when it was time to shed old scales. He raked ragged claws across his upper arms in agitation but it did no good. In fact the tingling sensation only spread to his hands. Quill stared at one hand in irritation, noting the rough, broken claws, blackened from tar, chipped from life aboard. The short webbing between his fingers was dry and cracking. The climate here did not agree with him anymore than the ice run had. Tell-tale bolts, threadbare and incandescent, played across his palm. The source of the itch in his scales. Nerves.

The sooner we are quit of this place the better, Quill thought. The captain would see the sense of it, he need only convince Vaughn. Or if need be, drag the fool woman kicking and screaming back to the ship.

He wished she would kick and scream. She had been different since the painted one's death. The mad one. Quill rather missed Piper. He had seen less of the feral rat when the bald man had been alive.

At least the rodent was back aboard the ship, Quill conceded, casting a wistful look back towards the dock. That way was filled with people, the mindless hordes that filled this planet. If not for

Vaughn and the girl, he would have gladly have stayed aboard the ship. To say nothing of the Korrigan accompanying them.

"What?" Jack belched at him, a noxious cloud emerging from the sailor's mouth. At least Quill resolutely chose to believe the stench was from that orifice. The alternative was even less palatable.

"We are close, yes?" Quill said, watching the girl scurrying ahead of them. She moved swiftly through the crowd, a leaf in the wind, with as much sense of direction. Could she not keep still? How was he supposed to watch her when she didn't know herself what she was doing?

Quill sighed. Jack plodded ahead of him, upwind, sadly. The Korrigan seemed to have a destination in mind and the crowds did part for him. If not, he parted them anyway. It was a redeeming feature, if a slight one. With luck both Korrigan and Kitsune would arrive at the same destination. The former was much easier to track.

Quill turned his attention to the crowd. It was a considerable task. Quill would not have wasted many supplications on it, but there was yet a chance they would encounter Vaughn on their brief journey. There would be a brief scene, outrage on her part, then they could all return to the ship together. An efficient ending. Quill was an admirer of efficiency.

"What?" Jack repeated again, this time with genuine annoyance in his tone. Quill ignored him, having stopped in the middle of the street. The cow-eyed traffic continued to move around him. Some pulled away in alarm at the charged air around him, others reacted with more open hostility.

He took a step towards what he'd seen, towards a side street. Dimly he heard Jack make a sound of disgust and move away. He paid the Korrigan no heed. Was he right? Had he seen what he'd seen?

There were few Kelpies in this arm of the Lanes. It was far from home and the weather was interminable. Scale rot from damp quarters could take those who knew no better. Not many would choose the life Quill had taken upon himself. But then there were few like him left, those unable to return home. The old ways were not looked upon kindly.

It was something he had in common with the girl, an inability to go home. An unpleasant thought, one Quill pushed out of his mind. The new ways, a sycophantic cult that had taken root in recent generations, was to blame for his exile. His and those like him, though it had been an age since Quill could remember crossing paths with another who shared his views. No matter though. Crossing paths with one who did not share his view could be just as gratifying.

He was sure of it now as he trailed the other Kelpie. The one he had glimpsed was familiar to him. It was not just the infuriating swagger, the ritual beads that spoke of investiture in the heretical new gods. Quill remembered this one stepping aboard the *Tantamount*.

It was difficult for Quill to tell most individuals from one another, a concession he was willing to admit that the *Tantamount's* irregular roster aided him in. A Kitsune, a Korrigan, a scarecrow for a captain, a fat one for a cook. And a bug. The tattoos and markings most of the crew were partial to made it simpler, as good as brandings on livestock. But with one of own his people Quill had no such difficulty, much. Scutes or bony plates, the patterning of scales, such obvious differences. Quill shook his head at the minute discrepancies many humanoid races used to tell one another apart. Madness.

He recalled this one coming aboard, a boarding in fact. Accompanied by others of their kind and Quill's own ill-advised confrontation with them. He regretted it now, needless and stupid. However justifiable one's cause, there was little sense in begetting a losing battle.

This time will be different though, he told himself as he trailed the heretic Kelpie. There was none other that he could see, this one was alone. How very foolish. But perhaps there was little choice in the matter. After all, the Kelpie crew who had boarded the *Tantamount* had sailed the *Killing Loneliness*, a privateer in service to the Alliance at the time. Most of whom had likely perished with their ship, a memory that brought a smile to Quill's maw. Never before had he witnessed such total destruction of another vessel. Had it been any other crew he would even have pitied them.

He continued to follow the other Kelpie through the twisting alleyways of Vice's trade quarter, keeping well back in the milling crowds. With a clear focus they no longer recoiled from Quill as he kept the outward effects of his thaumatics tightly controlled.

Quill was unsure of his own intentions as yet, only that the one he was following was important. Too coincidental, the discovery of the signaller aboard the *Tantamount* and the sightings the girl had reported. And now a survivor from their own misfortunate entanglement with the Alliance. But perhaps he could put an end to that.

Their trek took them south of the trade quarter to the Rises, where the ground began to slope upward into rolling hills. Not the vast mountains found underneath the flat world but a more forgiving gradient, the kind wealthy factions and families liked to build upon to survey their vista. Only on Vice, the Rises served a different purpose, a way-station.

Not a destination or even a point, more a ferry terminal. The tightly packed alleys and corridors that made up most of urban Vice gave way to a more open expanse, and if one looked up, the reason was obvious.

Sky moorings, piers, buoys, and even small docks filled the skyline. Vice was an unnatural world, flat and almost disc-shaped, but that world had been pushed further beyond the natural boundaries by the mining of ether. Tethered to the earth by massive chains and cables at the edge of the planet's own envelope, the floating marina provided a secondary port for all manner of vessels. For those that did not require the facilities of an actual port, who had no need to shift large amounts of cargo to or from their ships, the sky loft was a cost-saving measure. For some ships, whose sheer size or design prevented them entering into the waterborne areas, it was a necessity.

"Damn them all to the black," Quill uttered when he saw it. He knew now where the other Kelpie was going. Even at the great height it was docked at, the *Mangonel Falling* stood out against all the other ships. Massive and garish with its Alliance colours, pennons, and brightwork, a blunt statement of authority.

Seeing it answered several questions. He should have guessed, sooner, before the answer beat him over the head like this. The Alliance survivors from Rim were here. Almost certainly for them. To believe otherwise was to stretch the possibility of coincidence.

Inconceivable.

Quill cast a last, regretful look at his almost-target, then froze. His quarry had continued their journey to one of the ferry craft, one manned by Alliance sailors in crisp white uniforms. Uniforms that were as yet unaware of him.

Quill began to curse, then abandoned the effort as wasteful. Not as clever nor as subtle as he had thought himself. He turned to go and found his way blocked. But not by white-clad sailors. By three more of his own kind, the middle one he most certainly did recognise.

"How predictable." Vaughn's former captain shook her head with a sigh.

"You," Quill's eyes narrowed at her.

"Me," Heathen said. She gestured to her two subordinates. "Restrain him."

QUILL HAD NO intention of being restrained. As the two lackeys reached for him, he relaxed his own restraint, letting the power he normally used to propel the *Tantamount* bleed through his being. The moment one reached out to touch him that power rushed into them. The Kelpie jerked their hand back in pain, cursing. The other was wearing leather gloves, gloves that Quill then felt as his head was snapped back. He fell to the ground hard.

More blows fell, with tails thrown in. Quill curled into a ball, shielding his head. And lashed out with his own tail, taking one of his assailants down. He grabbed for the other's legs and pulled hard, bringing them down on top of himself. Then it was a mess of limbs and teeth as they both fought to climb back to their feet. Only Quill did so, panting but grinning at the twitching body kicking up dust. There were good reasons not to pick fights with thaumatics. One did not wrestle lightning.

"Amusing," a voice interrupted his gloating.

Quill wiped at his mouth with the back of one hand. It came away with a smear of blood. He could both smell and taste it in his mouth too, overpowering both senses. Heathen appeared unmoved by the failed attempt at capture but neither did she make any move to approach him. The scuffle had gone unremarked upon by anyone else, the Vice community sense of deliberate disinterest hard at work.

"You don't have much time," Heathen said. "Neither are you helping yourself."

"I need no advice from the likes of you," Quill retorted. He gestured and a nearby barrel flew through the air towards Heathen. She barely lifted her hand and that same barrel disintegrated into a storm of splinters. The cloud ended abruptly against an invisible wall, turning back on itself before settling to the ground.

Damn her.

Heathen had no need to fear his abilities, he realised. She was by far the more powerful thaumatic, likely capable of collapsing any of the nearby buildings onto him if she was of a mind. Her powers outstripped his by a measure not worth thinking about, he'd seen so first-hand.

"Be still, fool." She advanced a step now, angry. "You are wasting your efforts."

We will see, Quill thought. He reached out, casting his net wider and grabbing whatever he could see. Carts, barrels. Doors ripped off their hinges, windowed shutters and large rocks, any inanimate object he could grasp within two dozen feet he took and hurled at her. The suddenness and the complexity of the effort staggered and dropped him to his knees; the shockwave that shook the square knocked him onto his back.

When he lifted his head, he saw Heathen bearing down on him. The air around her was alive with electricity, bolts thicker than his wrist wreathed her body in blue. He saw them fade away, a massive effort he could read on her face as that maelstrom was quickly tempered.

Powerful and controlled. He was beyond outmatched.

He heard groans from nearby. Her two underlings thrown about as he was. Sitting up revealed wisps of smoke drifting upwards, scorch marks blackening the ground in the radius around Heathen. A crack in a wall, falling timbers. If not for that control she might have levelled the area.

"They are done waiting," she said to him, standing just a few feet away. "They are coming for Vaughn, for your ship, for the girl."

"What girl?" Quill growled at her, forcing himself back to his feet. The ground underneath felt unsteady, shifting and swaying. The whole world was moving in fact.

"The girl was the last thing she saw. The Guild does not forget, outcast. That much you should understand. And the Guild does not forgive."

Quill frowned. *The Guild?*

Scarlett?

Now he took a step towards Heathen, causing the woman to actually halt her own advance on him. He raised a hand towards her, was almost surprised to see it crackle blue and white.

"Stand down, outcast," Heathen warned.

"No." Quill took another step towards her. He could feel the air starting to thicken around them as she raised her own power, partially relaxing that iron control. He forged onward, one hand thrust ahead of himself, cutting through the knotted currents she was raising.

"This is not about you, you misguided idiot," Heathen raised her voice. "Do not test me!"

"You will not have them," Quill said, hearing his own voice climb higher and higher. "You will not have my ship," he took another step forward. "You will not have my skipper."

Only a few feet from Heathen now. Another step and she would be close enough. There was something in her eyes. *Anger? Disbelief?*

He reached out for her. "And you will never come near the girl!"

Inches to go, what would have been the end of it, a dark hand reached out and closed around his arm. He couldn't move, didn't understand. Then he was hoisted off his feet, held dangling in the air by something immeasurably strong and unyielding. All that energy, all the righteous anger, boiled away, absorbed into the cold hand holding him.

Quill found himself face to face with eyes that burned red, set into a black canvas.

No . . .

"You fool," Heathen whispered in a tone he didn't understand.

The obsidian golem hurled Quill away like a child. He barely felt the impact, too stunned by its appearance. When his body came to a stop he was staring skyward.

Up at sky moorings. Where the *Mangonel Falling* and others floated above them.

Quill managed to raise his head. He could see the golem striding towards him on legs the size of tree trunks. Its shadow was already touching him. Quill dropped his head against the ground, staring back at the sky.

You will not have them.

Quill reached for them, distant as they were, pulling, pulling them down towards them. It was further than he had ever tried to draw something from. But he could feel the ether in the hulls and keels of those ships, that which floated the moorings. It was a delicate balance that kept them between tethered and falling. He seized on one of the chains, the nearest to him, tethered to a merchantman's buoy. He pulled, drawing it down towards himself. Towards all of them.

"What are you doing?" Heathen demanded, alarm filling her voice for the first time. That sound spurred him on. A few moments more and there would be no stopping it. The ship would fall. On all of them. If he did this, he would not survive it. The thought hurt, not at the thought of dying, but of the pain from laughing. He could feel the tremor in the ground as the golem took another step towards him. Not much time now.

The memory of a dying crew mate came to him. A life given for the ship and all the souls aboard her. A promise asked. A promise given.

I promised.

A promise was sacred.

Then someone took a hold of his power, directly grabbing the currents he had latched to the tether chain. He had never felt the like before. He saw Heathen almost incandescent with her own power as she grappled with the invisible forces, forces that he had thrown everything into, built up beyond anything he had a right to expect and now had nowhere to go. Heathen found a new direction for them, straight into the ground between the two of them.

The golem was between Heathen and the shockwave that resulted. Quill had no such shield and was thrown again. He retained enough of his wits and some faint reserves to soften an impact that would otherwise have shattered his spine. He found himself in the alleyway leading to the ferry station. Above him, the tethered ship tilted on the brink. It might yet come down upon the Rises. He could feel the stirrings again, Heathen acting to prevent just that. Somehow he found his feet.

They were coming.

THE WOMAN ROLLED her shoulders, letting out a shallow breath as the scalping artist applied damp strips of seaweed to her back. A little something to help close the wounds but the salt present in the plant would also make them scar. Nel could see patterns up and down the woman's forearms, shiny pink and white raised scar tissue. Not her first time. From the expression on her face she might even enjoy it.

"Do you recognise me, Vaughn?" she asked, waving the man off, leaving them alone, the three of them. "Do you know who I am?"

Nel shrugged. "Can't say as I do. Memory like a guppy, never was good with faces."

"Chanel Vaughn," the woman spoke her name. "I remember your name, remember it well. How does it feel to have such a prestigious name, sailor? Does it bear down on you? Do your shoulders tremble under the weight?"

"It's the Free Lanes. Nobody gives a damn what you call yourself."

A smile, like it was the right thing to say. "My name," the mouth behind the smile said, "is Aristeia Quinn."

"Funny. Heard you earned yourself another name. Right scary one, at that."

The smile vanished. "As first mate aboard the *Fata Morgana*, I sail under Arlin Raines, Guildsman, the Seven-Tailed Fox. Do you recognise *that name*?"

Nel ground her teeth together, could feel her heel digging into the dirt beneath her. Too many names, too much information, too many pieces falling into place. And that damned grinning Luscan.

Never going to complain about Kelpies again. Something tells me I've a new crux.

"Let me be blunt here, Chanel," Aristeia Quinn said. "Skipper to skipper. You bore me. Your pathetic ship and your insipid crew bore me. People have an interest in you; we followed you, we watched you. You might be the death of us all. Why you chose a life on the coattails of civilisation, in these backwater Lanes . . ."

"How long?" Nel asked, looking from one to the other. The mocking smiles of predators. How in the hells had she walked right into this?

"Port Border," Mors answered her. "Someone brought you to our attention. Been helping us ever since. And you never noticed."

Damned Luscans . . . who? Who is the damned traitor on my ship? By the end of the day a neck is going to be wrung, black help me.

Assuming she lived through the next few minutes.

"For all the good that did us." Aristeia pulled her shirt up over her shoulders, a light cotton affair, one already damp with salt and blood. "Follow you, was our orders. Watch, observe, wait. For nothing. If we hadn't learned you were bound for Vice, the crew might have mutinied. An ice run. I can't think of anything more boring or mundane but at least you gave us a port worth stepping ashore in."

"What do you want, Quinn?" Nel asked her. *Quinn, does the void have a sense of humour here? Bane of my life. Damn, what I wouldn't give to have the Kelpie here though. Never thought I'd say that.*

"Are you really that dense? What do I want? How many meaningful moments have there even been in your pedestrian life since you quit the corps, Chanel? How many do you think the people outside of that creaking pile of timbers are even aware of?"

The woman stood up, revealing a wand slung in a holster over her thigh. The hilt on it was a match to one Nel had once owned, lost into the black months ago now.

"You bore me, sailor," Aristeia said again, wearily, taunting. "I cannot tell you how much. Nobody cares that you and your captain sail under an assumed name. Nobody weeps for Misery. Honestly no one even cared for what happened at Marching. If there hadn't been survivors no one would have cared at all. But there was. And so we watched you, for weeks, to see if you'd lead us to them, to those . . . poor lost souls. But no, you carried on with your meaningless, dreary lives. And now . . . now I'm tired of watching."

Mors laughed, a chilling sound echoed in Aristeia's smile. "See how the little mouse trembles?" he said of Nel.

"The Fox . . . my *captain* would watch and wait, he has more patience than either of us," Aristeia admitted. "But you're here, I'm here, Mors is here. In fact there's only one person missing and we could resolve this entire interminable situation."

Aristeia dropped her hand, resting it loosely over the pommel of her wand. "Scarlett sends her regards."

Nel drew on her before Aristeia had finished speaking. The woman ducked as Nel's arm came around, drawing her own weapon. In the background, Nel could see Mors drawing too. Gods below he was fast, he could have cut her down any time since she'd entered the tent. Except they'd wanted to toy with her, had even allowed her to make the first move, knowing she wouldn't get a second. At best, with a year's worth of good luck, she might have taken out Aristeia, temporarily. After that it was over for her.

Except she hadn't been aiming for the woman, tempting as that opening was. Nel went for the tent pole holding up the awning. She heard an undignified squawk of surprise from Mors as he was enveloped in the heavy canvas while she dropped to the ground herself, disappearing from sight as the ceiling hit Aristeia next. Nel dove for the back of the tent, ripping up the peg holding the enclosure to the ground and rolling out into the bazaar. Behind her the shop front was a writhing, outraged mess as Aristeia and Mors fought to extricate themselves.

Nel turned and ran, shouldering aside those who were too slow to get out of her way. Running as fast as she could, one thought filling her mind: get back to the ship first.

"JACK?" VIOLET SAID, realising he was no longer beside her.

Jack had dropped behind, the barrow of supplies forgotten in the middle of the street.

"Jack, what is it?" Violet called. Jack didn't answer. He lifted his nose and sniffed the air. Then bared his teeth in a snarl.

"Kelpies," he growled.

"What?" Violet saw them then, half a dozen, emerging from the side streets and shadowed alcoves. All converging on the two of them.

"Who are you people?" She backed up towards Jack, twisting her neck and trying to see them all at once. She heard the rasp of metal on leather as Jack pulled a wicked-looking knife from his belt.

"She is the one," one to her left pronounced. Their voice was heavily accented, nothing like Quill's, nor could she tell if the speaker was male or female. Except that it was bearded, the spiked Kelpie. The one that had fallen into the pit. Come to make good on the debt, no doubt.

"Bind her and take her back to the ship."

No doubt at all.

"What of the Korrigan?" another asked, sounding identical to the first.

A shrug. "Nothing was said of any Korrigan. Kill him and be done with it. We can't have . . ."

The leader never finished their sentence. Jack gave an incoherent bellow and charged them, raising his knife high. Green blood sprayed the air as Kelpie and Korrigan went down in a pile, Jack rising out of the mob with his knife held high. Violet gave a small cry as the other Kelpies rushed in to swarm Jack, except the one who grabbed her from behind, spinning her roughly around.

She froze, staring into reptile eyes. A face dark with blood and dust. A face she did know.

"Quill!"

Her skin burned where he touched her. He removed his hands quickly enough and she saw the blue lightning arc around his body. The forgotten barrow and its supplies, so precious an hour ago, became wayward missiles to him, pummelling his kindred mercilessly. Jack roared in triumph as he regained his feet, shaking the last attacker off, his knife sheathed in gore. His eyes found Quill and took a moment to recognise him. Then the maniacal laughter.

"The ship!" Quill ordered both of them. "Run for the *Tantamount* and do not stop!"

"Scared of a few Kelpies, Kelpie?" Jack said.

"They are not alone, you mindless oaf." Quill shoved Violet down the street, his touch still shocking where it brushed bare skin. "They are with her. With Heathen! The *Mangonel Falling* is here on Vice!"

"The *Mangonel*?" Violet gasped. No, that wasn't right. This was because of Hounds and the yiqi. About reputation.

"Why? What do they want?"

Quill's eyes bored into hers as they ran. "Us."

"Run faster!" Jack growled at them both. It was hard to tell if any of the gore and bile layered on him was his own—the Korrigan looked to have been wading through a swamp.

Quill was still pushing her along, hand on her shoulder near the back of her neck, where her new ink was. The pain was noticeable enough that she cried out when he shoved her forward, throwing her to the ground. She twisted as she fell, enough to see the black shadow that swept Quill off his feet, passing through the space where she would have been. Quill was thrown a dozen feet, curling up into a ball around his middle.

"Jack!" Violet called out desperately, scrabbling backwards. Jack grabbed her by the arm, jerking her onto her feet.

The golem now stood between them and Quill. It had followed her all the way from the black to Port Border to Vice. How?

How? Her mind screamed. But there was no time. Quill was still moving behind it, behind Onyx. Writhing, almost dead to the world.

"Leave him," Jack said, trying to pull her away.

"No!" Violet pulled her arm free, standing steadfast in the path of the golem. Her breath came fast and sharp, if she'd had more time she might have been scared.

"Not dying for the damned Kelpie, girl," she heard Jack say. But it didn't matter what he said. Onyx took a step towards her, reaching with one hand.

"We can't leave him," she said. "Need him to fly the ship. That thing will follow us, Jack. Back to the ship. To the captain, to Gabbi . . ."

She stepped back from the golem's swipe. Not nearly as fast as she remembered, just not right without its master. She'd seen the grab coming almost before it happened, barely had to think about it.

Something it blames me for. Those red eyes, damn those eyes, they . . .

"Jack! The eyes, go for the eyes!" She wasn't even sure if he was still there or if he'd run back to the ship. She cast about for something, anything she could throw at those bloody red eyes.

Violet flinched at the clang of steel on stone and so did Onyx. The golem reached up to its face with one ungainly hand. Jack's knife, buried in the eye socket. The golem staggered, not in pain but momentarily disorientated.

Violet rushed forward, ducking under the other waving arm. Quill, still groggy, barely aware of her. She hooked his arm over her shoulder, pushing them both up. *One foot in front of the other, you damned Kelpie. One foot, two foot, left foot, right foot . . .*

Golem.

Onyx held out the remains of Jack's knife, crushed beyond recognition, and dropped it to the ground. It reached for Violet. She couldn't dodge this time, not with Quill on her back. All she could do was strike out at the limb with her own hand, try and push it away, just enough for them to get around.

It was like when Quill had touched her before, only a hundred times worse. She felt her entire body spasm as she made contact with the black glass monster, pain shooting down her arm. There a flash, an image, of her touching the golem before, on Port Border. The same pain. Her heart might explode, her head burst, her eyes boil in their sockets.

And the golem was thrown away from them as if all that pain were suddenly directed at it.

Violet could only stare, Jack too, wide-eyed stupid at the golem struggling in the rubble of the wall it had collided with. Jack turned to her, slack jawed. Violet stared at her own hand, bandaged and scarred.

Did I just . . .

A panting wheeze from beside her. Quill, she'd somehow forgotten. The Kelpie clutched at his chest, the faintest flickers of blue light around his clawed fingers.

"I told you," he said, voice faint and laboured. "I told you."

CHAPTER 17

"SHOW A LEG and turn out, people. I want to see sails down and sailors stand from under! And standby to weigh that damned anchor!"

Nel and the captain's shouted orders blurred into one long oratory as they whipped the *Tantamount's* crew into action. Sailors climbed high into the rigging to unfurl sails, ropes were winched or loosed as required, hatches battened, supplies secured and all chests downed. Gabbi caught Nel's eye from the galley door. Their situation was grim and both knew it.

The captain stood tall atop the bridge, flanked by their new navigator. The first time the *Tantamount* had boasted two in years and they might already be back to one. Nel had barely arrived only to find Quill missing, traipsed off to town on some whim. And not just Quill. Violet and Jack hadn't returned either.

Nel cast furtive glances at the dock. They were only a few agonising minutes from being able to cast off. Half the lines were already gone and two sailors were standing by to remove the gangway. For the first time, Nel started to give serious consideration to what might have to happen. If her wayward crew didn't return in the next few heartbeats, they might be left stranded at Vice. It was Cauldron all over again. The *Tantamount* had no choice but to set sail. Stuck in their berth they were an easy mark for boarding parties or the trained gunners of the

Alliance ship.

No, they couldn't wait. The whole ship, every soul aboard, was at risk.

"Captain," Nel said through gritted teeth as she bounded to the top of the stairs, reaching the bridge. "Captain, we can't . . ."

"There they are, Nel." Horatio nodded towards the docks. Nel leaned out over the rail, searching for what her captain had seen. A heavy weight lifted from her chest as her eyes found the last three stragglers. Quill was leaning on Violet; he seemed to be struggling. Jack brought up the rear, one of his arms dark and stained to the elbow. But whatever their condition, the three scampered up the boarding plank and onto the deck. The crew cast off the last of the remaining lines, and at the captain's command the sails started to fill as their new navigator pushed them away from the docks.

"Go see to them, Nel," the captain bade her. "Make for the falls," he said to Mantid. "Full sail, as short a course as you can plot."

Nel descended to the main deck with an eye towards the trio.

"What happened?" she demanded.

"They jumped us, Skipper," Violet said. "Me and Jack. Then all of us on the way back."

"Alliance?" Nel held her voice steady.

"Kelpies," Jack spat.

"Heathen," Quill grimaced. He pushed Violet away, grabbing a rope for support.

"You saw her?" Nel demanded of him.

"I recognised her kind, her ship. And worse."

Nel let that go. Now was not the time. Mangonel's *here too. Never rains but it pours and damn if it isn't all coming down on us.*

"You hurt badly, then?"

Quill drew himself up haughtily. "Not bad enough that I can't fly the ship better than that . . . bug." He eyed the bridge disdainfully.

"Get to the captain then. Catch your breath for now, let the Mantid do the easy lifting. I want you ready if things get nasty later on. We aren't out of this yet so save your strength for when we need you."

Quill snorted but accepted her words. Hopefully she'd

plumped his ego enough that he wouldn't try and wrestle the helm away from his backup. He was limping as he made his way to the bridge, holding one hand to his ribs.

"Jack," Nel continued, "up in the rigging. I want every scrap of sail we've got patched and up on our masts. See it gets done."

"Aye, Skipper," Jack grunted. He looked the way Quill had gone, shaking his head in disgust. "Forgot about the damned bug. How'd she make me forget about him?" He went for the mainmast, still grousing. Nel ignored that too.

"What about me, Skipper?" Violet asked.

"You hurt?" Nel asked. "Don't lie to me here."

"No, ma'am, was just Quill who got knocked around some by Onyx. They never got near me."

"Onyx?" Nel seized on the name. *Hells, all our sins are coming back to us. Is there anyone on this rock not out to get us?*

"Aye, Skipper," Violet hesitated. "I should have said . . . I . . ."

"Later. Right now your place is up in the nest, lass, I need your eyes. The *Mangonel's* coming for us and we're dead if she sees us first. You see her or any other ship you sing out and don't be shy about it."

"Aye, Skipper." Violet nodded fiercely, to Nel's mild surprise. Normally the girl did not fare well in the crow's nest but she turned and darted up the ratlines like she was born for it. A small dark blur shot after her: Bandit, racing her to the top.

"We're in deep, aren't we, Nel?"

Nel faced her friend. Gabbi's face was creased with worry lines but she seemed a small spot of calm in the whirlwind of frantic activity that gripped the *Tantamount*. The deck heaved and swayed under their feet, riding the swell of the waves, so unlike the smooth passage through stars. Yet that wasn't what had caused the greyish tinge to Gabbi's face.

"We've been in worse," Nel heard herself say.

"No." Gabbi shook her head stubbornly. "We haven't. We've been in debt, in danger, and in ruin. We've never been on the run from the law like this. Skirted the edges maybe, but never a price or a warrant on our heads. Nothing like this."

"Them out there," Nel gestured vaguely. "They ain't the law."

"They've the name, the uniform, the officialdom. All they need to hunt us down. Might as make no difference."

"We're getting out of here, Gabbi." Nel placed a hand on her friend's shoulder. "I'll get us clear of this. Back to the Free Lanes where none of it matters. Thing's will be just like they were, like they ought."

Gabbi squeezed her hand. "I trust you, Skipper. Always have."

Nel accepted the praise silently. What could one say to it, in any case? She made her way to the bridge, joining Horatio, Quill, and Mantid.

Their new navigator didn't have Quill's finesse when it came to managing the *Tantamount*, though Nel was prepared to put that down to their hasty exit and inexperience with the ship. But he might be stronger. The *Tantamount* was steering a straight line for the edge of the world at an impressive clip. Quill was doing his best to ignore this, fussing over his charts, head coming up to mark the distance to the horizon.

Nel gave the captain a rueful look. It did Quill some good to have competition for his duties aboard the ship, but the expression her captain returned was a grave one. Silently, he handed her his brass-chased telescope.

"Violet sighted her, Nel. We're in for a run to the falls."

Tension coiling in the pit of her stomach, Nel trained the spyglass on the clouds over Vice. Violet had done well to spot the incoming ship. It was still distant but there was no mistaking the expansive silhouette.

"Well, Skipper," Horatio said quietly, "as a former Alliance officer, what would you expect them to do in this situation?"

"They may not be following Alliance guidelines, Captain," Nel cautioned. "This isn't a textbook situation for either of us."

"Heathen was trained in the Alliance, the same as you," Horatio reminded her. "The same as most of those crewing that ship. I doubt they'll become too creative. The simplest plans are often the best. My question stands."

"Aye, Captain," Nel considered. "Boarding craft, either from the *Mangonel* or from Vice. That ship might be faster up there than us while we're still waterborne but if we launch free we can outrun her. They'll try and cut us off at some point, maybe take out our sails or some such. They won't be content to just chase us."

"You think they'll fire on us?"

"Not yet, not here. Too close to the settlement. Official or not, they won't risk that, too many questions, might even provoke a response. When we get to the edge . . ."

"That would be when you come in, Mister Quill." Horatio faced his long-time navigator.

Quill nodded eagerly, though he still held a hand to his side, over his ribs. "I have an idea. The falls . . ."

"Keep us in one piece, navigator," Nel warned.

"Yes, yes," Quill dismissed her concerns. His attention was split between the fast-approaching horizon and the behemoth overhead.

"They're really coming for us," Horatio said, almost musing. He was looking up towards Violet in the nest, and beyond that to the ship in the sky above. "I hoped they might forget about us, I truly did. I should have told you, Nel. I'm so sorry . . ."

Told me what? Nel pushed that thought aside. Too late which meant it was not something to waste thought on. She was more concerned with how their newly inducted crew members might be reacting to being chased by a ship-of-the-line after their first run aboard the *Tantamount*. Questions, too many questions and no time to address them. Her hand came up to touch the key on a cord around her neck, the one remaining to her. Nel briefly considered breaking open the arms locker, but only briefly. If they were boarded it was all over.

Better to be taken prisoner than die fighting hardened marines.

"Warning shots," Quill observed, snapping Nel's attention back to the moment. Cannon fire was coming their way, at the outer limit of the *Mangonel's* range, far outside of what the *Tantamount's* token battery could manage. The first round sent a geyser of water shooting skyward off the starboard bow. Second and tertiary shots marched steadily closer to the ship, each volley causing another column of water.

Underneath Nel's feet, the ship rocked, listing too far to one side. She grabbed hold, waiting for the *Tantamount* to right itself. She saw Quill take a tumble, leaning dangerously far out over the railing towards the tilt of the ship. The ship that wasn't coming back to the plane. A hard glance at Mantid showed a confused navigator, forelimbs flailing in a frustrated dance.

"What happened?" Nel demanded. "They didn't hit us. Feels like half the ballast came loose!"

"Because it did!" Quill pulled his head back from the side. "The ship is breached, taking on water. The garboard!"

Hells. Hells, hells, hells! Nel cursed herself silently with every blue tongued invective she could think of. The damned hole in the hull, the one she hadn't made time to fix. Because of what had almost happened to Violet.

For want of a girl, a ship was lost . . .

No time to think about that.

Another shot struck the water nearby, a column of foam and spray shooting skyward, dousing them all.

"We need to turn!" She had to yell to make herself heard. "Turn hard. Hard as she can, lift the seam out until we're riding the plane."

"Quill, take over," the captain ordered. "Don't let them get that sort of bearing on us."

A smile spreading over his face, Quill resumed his usual post at the helm. The ship gybed immediately as Quill's efforts started to bring them around, the sailors in the rigging moving quickly to respond and rejig the sails. Nel grabbed for a handhold, silently willing Quill not to submerge the ship. It was easy to forget they were restricted to a mere two dimensions here, their movements as flat as the world they were trying to escape.

More shots rained down from above. Falling between them and where they needed to be. Quill pulled the ship higher into the wind, forced off his course.

"We need a diversion, Nel," the captain advised her. "Perhaps the guns?"

Nel stared for a moment, before catching the guise of the captain's thoughts. Another cannon shot smashed into the waves nearby. Nel was already running for the guns.

ATOP THE MAST, huddled and clinging to the inside of the crow's nest, Violet had been one of the first to realise Quill had retaken control of the *Tantamount*. The mad Kelpie had pitched the ship at such an angle the crew on the starboard deck could have reached over and dipped their hand in the rushing waters. It was even worse than a few moments ago, when the ship had listed the other way, crashing drunken and flailing against the waves. Violet clung to the tapered part of the mast, refusing to let herself think about falling. Bandit rode her back, arms wrapped in a death grip around her neck. Whatever happened next they'd have to face it together.

Violet followed the skipper's mad run across the deck, bent low and almost spiderlike, clambering over ropes and winches, the ether in the plane barely strong enough to keep the woman's feet planted against the pull of the flat world.

The skipper made for one of the thaumatic cannons mounted on the sides of the ship. The weapons seemed insignificant compared to what the *Mangonel Falling* could throw at them. Violet had watched the warship manoeuvre into position above them, twisting on its axis to bring its lateral batteries to bear. She'd been counting them. At least three gun decks, with maybe fifty different cannons making up the broadside. Over a hundred in total when the other broadside was taken into account. A full broadside, even at this range, might take them out entirely, yet the *Mangonel* seemed content to toy with them for now.

Violet tried to figure out the skipper's plan, sure there was some method to her madness. She wasn't fool enough to try and outshoot the dreadnought—the best gunners in the Lanes wouldn't take those odds. So what then?

The skipper took charge of one of the guns. Hounds, apparently acting under orders Violet couldn't make out, took another on the opposite side of the ship, the high side. Both pointed the cannons directly at the water and let loose as fast as their weapons could fire. The resulting barrage kicked up fountains of water and spray. The skipper and Hounds kept at it until both their cannons ceased firing, spent. Violet watched the skipper spin her battery around, whacking at the casing repeatedly with her hand until it discharged a burnt-out canister; a practically luminescent crystal the skipper pitched far away from the ship into the water, skimming the surface like a stone on a pond. Super-heated and already volatile, the crystalline ammunition exploded when it finally broke the water's surface with a cracking boom that made Violet duck down inside the nest. A second boom followed: Hounds. Spray rained down on Violet even at that height. When she peeked, she saw a curtain of water still falling.

Both Hounds and the skipper moved to the secondary guns alongside and began again. By then the sea around the *Tantamount* was a blue and white haze of mist and steam, the air so badly obscured Violet couldn't make out the Alliance ship anymore. She signalled as much to the crew below and got a wave in return from the skipper. It wasn't much, their watery camouflage, but enough to stop any sharp-eyed gunners lining up their killing shot.

The skipper's stop-gap smokescreen had bought them the time to reach the falls. And that Violet could see. The falls, where the water tumbled off the end of the world, just like the *Tantamount* was about to. And if they were lucky they'd vanish just as mysteriously into space as that same water. Days before Violet had pestered the skipper about where the water went to. Now she would find out first-hand.

Coming up to the edge, the water frothed and boiled, bubbling over into the black abyss that was space. Quill held the *Tantamount* steady at its precarious and impossible angle, just as Violet clung tight to the mast, one foot planted on the rim of her nest. Bandit clung fiercely to her, still refusing to let go. She considered making a run for the relative safety of the deck but the mast was swaying too violently for that to happen. One wrong step and she would plummet into the water and be swept over the edge. Most of the rest of the crew had descended out of the rigging, leaving her alone up high. It wasn't a comforting thought as the *Tantamount* cleared the falls and . . .

Violet had expected the *Tantamount* to keep sailing, using the momentum of the falls and Quill's thaumatic powers to push out into the void, clearing the world's grasp. Instead . . . Quill held back. The *Tantamount* crested the falls, riding the current for a few brief moments before violently pitching forwards, diving straight down with the rest of the crashing water.

Without the ether hammered into the lining of the hull, the ship and all its crew would have been thrown asunder, following the plight of cascading water or tossed like rag dolls into the black. But up in the nest at the edge of the envelope the ether's grasp was weakest, the air thinnest. Violet and Bandit were thrown against the curtain of the nest, Violet almost rolling over the rim as she clutched with one hand, the other wrapping around the terrified and screeching loompa. Small clawed hands tore at her, desperately. She barely felt the scratches as the ship plunged down, was nearly thrown from the nest again when the ship twisted through a half roll, driving directly through the curtain of the world's waterfall, the sails and timbers of the ship groaning in protest as tons of water crashed down on them. Then the *Tantamount* broke through, emerging into the dark underbelly of the flat world, inside the aquatic curtain.

Quill pulled the *Tantamount* up, levelling their path off relative to the world above them, sailing parallel to the world. Violet stared in awe at that world. It was like a vast, giant cave, blocking out most of the light and shrouding the heavens in something even darker than the black. But from that dark stabbed giant mountains, the craggy roots of the flat world that the *Tantamount* now wove through. The spaces between them were vast but it wasn't long before the ship felt lost in the stone forest. Violet cast around but was unable to see anything beyond the dark in the menhir-like maze. She threw a leg over the nest, ready to make her way back down to rejoin the crew.

And paused, halfway through the motion, Bandit perched on her shoulder. She could see the curtain again through a gap in the massive stalactites, a chance opening that let her see their back trail. Just long enough to spot the dark shadow on the other side of the curtain. Before it broke through.

NEL PICKED HERSELF up from the deck. The entire crew had become one sodden mess. She wiped still-dripping hair out of her face before screams from the crow's nest wrenched her attention up. Nel saw Violet gesturing frantically, signalling be damned. Genuine panic set in for a moment—had the *Mangonel Falling* already followed them through the falls? She'd been convinced Quill's gambit would buy them the lead they so desperately needed. It was madness for a ship the size of the *Mangonel* to try and follow them here.

Above them, dust and debris blossomed from one of the massive inverted mountains. Where above the explosions had been limited to water, here the *Tantamount* was showered with rock and stone. Nel raised a hand to shield her face, running for the bridge. She joined the stunned Captain and navigators, all facing the stern of the ship.

Behind them a bright spot gleamed. Wand fire: ship mounted, pinpoint in the darkness. The stream of turbulent light shot overhead, causing another explosion of rock ahead of them where it hit.

"Quill!" Nel grabbed the navigator by the shoulder, forgetting herself, and snatched her suddenly numb hand back.

Quill took charge again, the *Tantamount* rising in tune with his hands, climbing to dubious refuge amongst the roots of the world. Nel strained her eyes trying to catch a glimpse of the ship behind them, but all she could make out was the discharges of their weapons. Every shot, and they were shockingly few in their frequency, narrowed the gap, striking closer to the *Tantamount*. They were being stalked, hunted, by someone who wasn't just firing blindly anymore.

"Captain," Nel twisted away from the stern to face the captain, "we need to . . ."

Her words were lost as another brilliant bolt lanced out of the darkness, striking true, direct to the main mast, just above the top platform. The mast swayed as the light from the impact faded, cracking, a sound shockingly loud inside the envelope, and began to topple backwards, the top third falling towards the bridge.

It crushed the stern. Nel tried to sit up, not even aware of how she'd been knocked down, trying to wave the air in front of her face clear. The captain lay across her body, looking down at her, eyes bright and shockingly aware. His face was lit up in flashes, the ship shuddering as more thaumatic bolts struck them. The soaking timbers started to steam, then smoulder, then smoke.

"Get up, Skipper," Horatio ordered.

Nel couldn't recall seeing the man so focused. He pulled Nel to her feet.

A wordless cry from Quill. Echoing the pain of the ship. Her poor ship. But that wasn't what had struck at Quill. She saw then.

Violet, still clinging to the nest atop the mast. A nest on the verge of separating from that mast. And in front of Nel's eyes it did. She saw the look on Violet's face as she started to float free of the *Tantamount's* envelope, a certain death in a cold void.

And the nest stopped, hovering, shaking.

Quill. It could only be him. Nel hadn't missed the still and broken form of their other navigator, crushed beneath the mast. She saw Quill then, at the head of the stairs leading to the main deck, framed by a damaged and flaming ship. The successive shots had struck the sails, tearing flaming holes through them. One threatened to rip itself free and blanket the deck. The *Tantamount* was burning. And Quill was ignoring it all, one hand outstretched, almost imploringly, trying to drag Violet in by sheer force of will.

Because he'd promised.

Nel faced her protégé, only a dozen feet away. Violet's eyes found hers, wide, frightened, terrified. And Nel had to look away, her body feeling heavy and sluggish as she turned towards Quill. Each step felt like lead as she closed the distance between them. And then it was Quill's eyes that found hers, filled first with surprise, then with horror, as she crashed into him, carrying them both over the stairs and down hard to the deck below.

Breaking his concentration.

QUILL GRIPPED THE front of her shirt, threatening to rip Nel off her feet. He grabbed her with both hands, pulling her right to his snarling maw. His hands didn't burn like they should, too far gone to even channel his own power. The navigator shook her, wouldn't stop shaking her, incoherent. Rage. Grief? She couldn't tell. Didn't care.

She struck him. It felt like breaking her hand in the process. Quill went down to the deck and lay still, for what felt like a forever moment, before he raised his head to face her again.

"Save the ship, Quill. Save the gods damned ship."

Nel turned her back on him, found herself facing the galley. The galley was exploding, a billowing fireball that threatened to engulf what was left of the ship. Jack was thrown clear, taking Nel down with him. He got up, bellowing. Calling Gabbi's name. But the captain got there first, striding into the inferno, arm raised in front of his face as he forced his way through the smoke. Gabbi was there on the floor, trapped under fallen timbers. Alive or dead, Nel couldn't tell. She shouldered Jack aside, trying to run to her friend's side. The captain heaved aside burning debris, smoke rising from him as well now. His great coat, trailing around his knees, had caught alight. Irritably, almost casually, Horatio threw the burning garment aside, far into the inferno. He stooped, and to Nel's amazement, the captain pulled Gabbi free, turning to face her.

Horatio, Gabbi cradled in his thin arms, took a step towards Nel. And the rear of the ship erupted in flames, smoke and fire swallowing them both.

There was a scream. Was it her? The captain? Gabbi or Jack? It didn't matter. Right then nothing else mattered.

Crushing, stabbing pain on her shoulder. Quill spun her around, away from the carnage. The deck shifted under her feet, and the bow of the *Tantamount* dropped out of sight. Nel stared in disbelief as half the ship broke away, ripped asunder. Ether spilled out into the void between the severed portions, painting the macabre cross section of the gutted ship with a silver sheen. She saw crew above and below decks alike tumbling away.

"The ship's dead!" Someone grabbed her by the shoulders, made her face them. Hounds. "We need to go. We need to go now!"

Nel pushed the woman away, trying to locate what it was that was tearing her ship apart. All around her the timbers screamed in their death throes. Splinters, jibbing, ropes, everything was falling away, disintegrating before her eyes.

A flash of light blotted out the expanse. A heavy battery of wand fire. It ripped up the deck, threw her back. She saw stars. Then only black.

She grabbed at the hands lifting her up. Quill's. He hesitated.

"I told you to save the ship, Kelpie," Nel heard herself say.

Quill's eyes narrowed. "You *are* the *Tantamount*." He threw her and rough hands caught her. Felt like Jack. Smelt like him too. Quill climbed in after her. They were inside a bubble, the hatch closing behind them.

"Let me up." Nel shook off the hands. It wasn't hard, she was already floating. Jack let her go. It was just the three of them inside, already drifting away from the ship. Her head was spinning. Or was that the bubble? It was both. The bubble was spinning, rolling, rotating. One of them. She glimpsed severed cables, their tether and hose. No going back.

The *Tantamount* was burning. In pieces. Like a giant, petulant child had ripped her ship apart in a tantrum.

There was another bubble alongside them. Nel had just registered this when the world lit up. Incandescent streams arcing through the black. They struck unerringly, all seeming to find the other glass sphere.

Then it grew larger. The sphere was stressed, fractured. Behind the patterned cracks Nel saw faces, people she knew. Saw their expressions grow wider before they got closer.

Nel put her hand against the glass as the two spheres collided.

THE SHIP WAS burning, what was left of it. Timbers scattered, bodies of her crew floating. A sail fluttered, some trick of the thaumatics casting it around outside the fractured envelope. None of it seemed quite real, viewed through the glass of the ship's porthole. The small circular window was frosting over, the wash of water from driving through the fall was frozen on the outer hull.

"Is it over?" Gravel asked as Kaspar turned away from the scene.

"It never started." Kaspar shook his head in disgust. "Ship like that . . . never had a chance."

"Captain had some brass monkeys," Gravel marvelled. "Crew must be half mad to follow a man like that. Diving off the edge like that? Through the falls? Never seen the like."

"We went through the falls."

"*We* are in a flying suit of armour," Gravel argued. "Not nearly the same. Was that ship even armed?"

"Of course, it was, you saw what happened above."

"When that dreadnought was chasing it? Bloody ridiculous, Niko. If not for us they would have been free, home and free. That thing never could have chased them down. Never." Gravel laughed bitterly. "And now they're dead. Because of us."

"Not our fault," Kaspar said stubbornly, "we were following orders."

"Orders were to blow them all to hells?" Gravel asked sceptically. "You trying to tell me Mors' gunners couldn't have stopped after they took down the mast?"

There was no answer to that.

"What was . . ." Gravel never got any further, interrupted by the sound of booted feet crashing down the corridor. Hard and heavy, unmistakably marines, but it wasn't them who turned the corner first. It was the prisoner, arms still manacled in the front, tattered and dishevelled, unkempt hair whipping around his face as he dropped his shoulder and charged into Gravel.

Kaspar twisted to avoid being caught up as Gravel went down, reaching out and wrapping his arm around the prisoner's neck and shoulder. The man was scarcely slowed, jerking Kaspar off his feet and along for the mad rush. Then a sudden stop and a pivot. Kaspar felt himself flung around the man's torso and into the hull of the ship. The whole hallway shook with the reverberation of struck metal. He couldn't hear himself groan as the breath was knocked out of him, but he hung on, bracing himself for a second hit.

None came. Kaspar forced open his eyes, found himself staring out into the black again. Through the porthole, over the prisoner's shoulder.

That's what you wanted? I looked. I already looked. There's nothing out there. Nothing!

The man just stood there, staring out into the debris that had once been another ship. Kaspar felt a shudder go through the prisoner, an almost wilting, and then an unexpected impact took them both to the floor. Gravel, tackling low. A moment later the marines piled on, Kaspar ending up on the bottom.

The prisoner was hauled off him, forced onto his knees. The marines lay into him, striking him across the back and shoulders, but if the man felt it he gave no sign. Numb from the repeated beatings, perhaps. Or in shock.

"All right?" Gravel held out his hand.

"Fine," Kaspar winced, letting himself be pulled up. There were more footsteps, officers. Aristeia Quinn, scarred face smouldering like a thundercloud, and worse . . . Raines.

"You caught him," Arlin Raines observed, giving the prisoner the most cursory of glances, pausing to admire the same view. He rubbed at the porthole with the cuff of his shirt.

"A waste. Not what I wanted at all. So much for . . . ah, no matter." When he turned away from the scene, all seven of his tails splayed out behind him like a fan, framed by the stark metal of the ship and ghostly miasma outside. "Did we enjoy our little jaunt about the ship?"

The prisoner didn't answer, still held on his knees by the marines, head bowed and face obscured by lank, unwashed hair. The marines holding him were big, hardened fighters. Both were breathing deeply, taut veins bulging out of their necks and the backs of their hands. One sported a blackened eye, already swelling shut. The other favoured a leg and had blood dribbling down their chin from split lips. Hardened, but clearly second best.

"Exceptional work, you two," Raines addressed Kaspar and Gravel, with barely a withering look for the marines. "Better than those who let him get away in the first place. I'm not even done with him and he's been most uncooperative so far. You have my thanks."

"No need, sir," Kaspar said, standing at attention. Behind Raines he could see Aristeia's mocking smile in his peripheral. But to acknowledge that would be dangerous.

"As you like," Raines shrugged. "Marines, take the prisoner back to his cell. Securely this time. I'll be along soon, Castor."

"There's someone out there," the prisoner, Castor Sharpe, said. His voice was coarse, rough. It was the first time Kaspar had heard him speak since he'd been handed over.

"Out where?" Raines asked, appearing interested for the first time.

"Outside. I saw a survivor. You have to help them."

Kaspar looked through the porthole. All he could see was black.

Out there?

End

To Be Concluded in Fata Morgana

Acknowledgements

The author acknowledges various friends and family, too numerous to mention, including but not limited to the Croquona Country Club, for various anecdotes, repeated encouragement and incessant 'is it finished yet' enquiries, and other footnotes that may have filtered through into this manuscript. The crew at Tyche for keeping the door open. Sarah, Chris, Kelly and Mary for the actual feedback and test reading. And all you others. You know who you are. Oh, and Krista, because I borrowed a heap from your books.

About the Author

Thomas J. Radford is a New Zealand author and frequently introduced at social gatherings as 'our friend the author' in exchange for social currency. His personal circumstances have no probable bearing on the likelihood of happy endings and character deaths, despite any rumours to the contrary.